A GODDESS OF SPRING AND SHADOWS

HADES X PERSEPHONE
BOOK ONE

LENA J. CASTLE

A Goddess of Spring and Shadows

First Edition 2024

Second Edition 2025

ISBN: 979-8-9916825-0-3 (Ebook)

ISBN: 979-8-9916825-1-0 (Paperback)

Cover Design by Jaylene Combs Design

Editing (First Edition) by Lunar Rose Editing Services & Lawrence Editing

Editing (Second Edition) by Sparks Editorial & Dee's Notes Editing Services

To those who keep getting back up, no matter how hard life knocks you down.

AUTHOR'S NOTE

This book contains subject matter that may be difficult for some readers, including violence, murder, explicit intimate scenes (including one scene with survival-driven coercive power dynamics in a captivity scenario involving a character other than the MMC; not romantic in nature), drowning, and depictions of past abuse (shown in flashbacks).

PERSEPHONE

Oh, gods. When is this going to end? The air hung heavy, like it always did when Basile took what he wanted. My muscles recoiled, but I stayed trapped, pinned against the cool marble countertop. The chill seeped into my bones, raising goose bumps across my body. Basile's fingers sank into the flushed skin on my waist, deep enough to leave marks.

My face twisted into one that might make him believe I enjoyed this. He grunted and plunged his length deeper into my center. A low moan escaped my lips, a practiced response. When we first started doing this, I pretended to enjoy it more. Now, I hardly had the energy to keep up the act. So I lay like a corpse as he continued to ram into me.

The sour odor emanating off Basile scarcely bothered me. I'd grown used to the stench. Basile's normally light, wavy hair turned a darker shade of brown as it clung to the sweat on his forehead. He dipped low, bringing his face far too close to mine. The coarse stubble covering his jaw grazed my cheek, provoking a shudder. Basile murmured into my ear. I couldn't make out the words over our skin slapping, his grunts, the buzzing ceiling fan across the room, and the thoughts swirling too loudly inside my head.

Maybe once, a long time ago, I found him attractive. Maybe I'd just needed to feel wanted. His smile used to stir something in me, not love but reckless hope that I could make this feel less like survival. That version of me was gone, buried.

He needed to finish soon. Each slow minute made me want to crawl out of my body more. His face lifted again, and I turned my head, not wanting to meet his brown-eyed stare.

With my cheek pressed against the stone countertop, my eyes pleaded with the rest of the kitchen for solace.

A wall covered in cabinets, a bowl full of fruits at peak ripeness, a stack of gold-rimmed white porcelain plates.

Anything but *him*.

My breasts bounced as he fucked me with an unpleasant rhythm. *He is a means to getting what I want*, I reminded myself. Basile was the easiest to seduce of all my guards. He was my ticket to the Olympian Library, the key to the information I needed to escape this prison. A slow breath left my lips.

"Look at me, Persephone. Take my cock." His deep voice nearly turned the last word into a growl. Not one of a true predator, but the pitiful snarl of a man who thought himself one.

I pried my face from the stone with a low groan. "Ugh."

He tightened his hold on me. It likely sounded like pleasure to him. A bead of sweat fell down the contour of his face and dropped between the valley on my chest.

"Harder, Basile." I forced the words out, sugarcoated lies he loved. "Just like that."

A low grunt rumbled from his throat. "Yeah, you like that,

don't you? Knew you couldn't resist my cock," he panted against my ear, his breath hot. His fingers dug tighter into my hips. "Always so eager for me."

My nails bit into the countertop. *Breathe. Just breathe.*

"Say my name," he said, voice ragged.

I almost choked on the syllables. "Basile," I moaned, soft and breathy, just the way he liked it.

"That's it, baby."

Baby. The word scraped down my spine. My jaw tightened, teeth digging into my lip.

I trained my gaze on the gaudy light fixture hanging from the ceiling behind his head, a large, glittering-gold piece with glass domes over the lights. Everything in this house was pretty. *A pretty prison is still a prison.* Smoke and mirrors. Mother didn't care what I thought, though. To the morals and realms she served, she was the Goddess of Harvest, all warmth and abundance. Behind these walls, she was anything but.

Six months.

Six long months I'd endured the mediocre fucks, but I needed to do it. A moan drummed out of Basile's mouth, drawing my attention away from the light and back to his face. "Your pussy feels so good, Persephone. So tight for me," he said between another few thrusts.

"I'm close. Basile, please," I lied, and exhaled through my teeth. I'd never been a good liar, but it came easy at times like this. "Basile, you're so big," I moaned. "Basile," I repeated his name. I knew the script by heart, knew exactly what to say to pull him over the edge. A few soft moans and the whisper of his name worked every time.

He thrust faster, his hardness twitched inside me. "I'm going to come."

Finally. I moaned loudly and forced all my muscles to

clench, faking my climax. Not that he ever cared about my pleasure. *Took him long enough.* He pumped a few more times, groaning and savoring the feeling before pulling himself out of me.

The soft, wet sound of my skin peeling off the counter broke the stillness as I shifted upright. A shiver trailed across my spine. My bare legs dangled over the edge, heels brushing the cabinet below. A slow smile tugged at my lips. The jingle of his belt drew my eyes.

Basile scooped his red shirt off the tile, studying me with his tired eyes and lazy smile as he fixed one taupe button at a time.

His smile widened when he caught me watching, probably because he thought my rare smile resulted from his prowess. I wanted to scoff. This would be the last time his filthy cock would be inside me. I averted my gaze.

Basile reached into his pocket. He pulled out *the* key, a little gold piece that caught the light tied on a silver string. Harmless to anyone else.

My breath hitched.

He fit it in the lock of the cabinet closest to him. The metal scraped, a soft resistance before the inevitable turn.

Click.

A cursed sound.

My stomach clenched, wringing itself like a rag. I tightened my grip on the counter, knuckles turning white, forcing stillness into my body while tremors gathered beneath my skin. The bottles rattled as he rifled through the drawer. My beating heart thundered in my ears, not like a drum but a fist hammering for release, bruising me from the inside. I bit the soft meat of my cheek, reopening an almost-healed tear. *One more time, Persephone. Just one more time.*

He pulled out the bottle I'd grown to resent so much over

the years, holding the little white pill between his index finger and thumb. "Here. Time for your medicine, sweet Persephone."

I recoiled at the nickname but said nothing. I pushed myself off the counter, my feet landing with a soft thud on the cold floor. *I'm not sweet*, I wanted to say. But my teeth ground together, and I stuck my sweaty palm out. "I'll take it in my room after I clean up." I gestured to his warm release oozing in streams down my leg, and his lips curled into a smirk.

Basile always refused to wear a rubber. I didn't have to worry about pregnancy—conception worked differently among the Divine. Creation of life was a deliberate act. The feeling of his release inside of me was vile, but it was a sacrifice I had to make.

He placed the pill in the center of my palm and ran his fingers along my jaw and up my cheek, making my back straighten. "You know I'm supposed to watch you take them."

I sighed and cleared my throat, knowing better than to argue. I caught my blurred reflection in the glass cabinets. The girl staring back at me was distorted, softened at the edges. Her eyes were dull pits, her mouth just a pink smear. I blinked, but she didn't vanish. *This will be over soon*, I told myself. *Just a little longer.*

"Fine." The pill clung to my palm, fused to the sweat pooling in the creases of my skin, tingling where it touched. I closed my eyes, unsure of where to look. Not at him. Not at my reflection. Not at the bowl of fruit.

I slipped the pill past my lips. With my tongue, I forced the damned little thing into the top corner of my mouth and swallowed hard.

I wiped the faint chalky smear left behind on my palm against my thigh.

Basile hummed the same off-tune melody he always did and moved closer. "Open."

Jaw slack, I stuck out my tongue with an "Ah."

"Can I go now?" I tried to hide the annoyance leaking into my voice.

"Yes." He paused, his smirk growing more irritating. "Unless you want to go another round." Basile placed his hand on my bare shoulder. I fought myself from jerking away. Instead, I took a careful step back, putting more distance between us.

"No… You did an…" I paused, scouring my mind for the right word. "Excellent job."

He beamed at me, misplaced pride plastered on his smug face, like a child showing off a broken toy, mistaking wreckage for triumph. Basile was insufferable.

I turned on my heel. With determined strides, I made my way to my room before he changed his mind and insisted on another round. Thank the gods the guards Mother hired were oblivious fools. Men like them never saw rebellion when it looked like compliance and a side of sex. For once, I was grateful for my mother's arrogance. I'd once overheard her say she didn't need to waste resources on her *obedient* daughter. I'd hated that I could hear the smile in her voice.

The door clicked shut behind me. I hurried to the washroom connected to my room, spitting the pill into the sink. The medicine left a ghost of acid on my tongue and something uglier in my chest—the bitterness of being owned. I cupped water in my palm, raised it to my lips, and swished it around to remove any lingering residue. A light fuzziness filled my head, but I knew within an hour clarity would return.

The sensation stirred memories of withdrawal symptoms I'd concealed for weeks. The nausea. The fatigue. The shocks had been the worst—sudden electric snaps that fired through my nerves.

The water ran steadily as the last fragments of the pill dissolved into nothing and slipped down the drain.

Avoiding the medicine was second nature now. For months, I had practiced with small candies in front of the mirror, ensuring I could conceal them in my mouth without raising suspicion before I dared to try it. Basile used to be more thorough in his checks. Years of my good behavior and becoming an object for his pleasure made him less strict.

It all started with a yellow bird perched on the ledge outside my window six months ago. The sight should have been insignificant, something I wouldn't think twice about. But as I watched the bird launch into the sky and fly away, something stirred inside me. That tiny creature had something I'd never known—freedom.

Already bare, I stepped into the shower and turned the water on. My muscles surrendered to relaxation under the cascade of water. I lathered a bar of Olympian lavender soap until the bubbles made it almost slippery enough to drop. I scrubbed myself, imagining the water could rinse off more than sweat. Scour away Basile's invisible handprints. Erase the bones that had broken and healed. Wipe clean the bruises that had faded from skin but not from memory.

I wrapped myself in a plush towel. I put on a silk set, a black long-sleeved top with matching bottoms, and slipped on my shoes.

I opened my door, peering down the dimly lit corridor. The muffled laughs and low chatter flowing from the dining room gave me a sense of relief. Right on schedule. The guards were immersed in their game of cards, wagering herbs and an assortment of odd items, as they did every evening. Soon, at nightfall, only Basile would be in the house. The others would pretend at their rounds of the estate's perimeter, which they never did. They simply walked far enough to maintain the illusion of diligence and smoked herbs until they ran out while Basile drank and diluted Mother's liquor to cover his theft.

The guards were my mother's puppets, their loyalty bought with gold and promises. To them, I was just another piece in her twisted game. I shut the door with a grin on my face. The beige carpet melted around my knees as I sank to the floor in front of my bed. I pulled out the black bag I'd had packed for weeks. Inside was a small packet of herbs for energy, a detailed map I'd drawn on some scrap paper, a deep, almost black, purple cloak, enough food for a few days, a few pieces of clothing, and a dagger I'd stolen from Basile.

I hated that I could take nothing that mattered to me. There were no photographs of cherished memories or keepsakes to pack, nothing to prove I'd ever been loved. My life had left behind no relics, no evidence I had mattered at all. The only thing I longed to bring could not accompany me. Worse still, I would never return to see the greenhouse again. That was the only place that ever felt like mine.

Freedom was worth the ache.

I paced the room, rubbing my hands together in a nervous rhythm. *This is happening.* Conflicting emotions surged within me. Tears of joy were at odds with the desire to expel my dinner.

I clasped one of the curtain panels. Usually drawn, the heavy folds were a barrier between me and the outside world. It was easier that way—to slip into the comforts of my imagination instead of facing the cruel realities of my life. The weight of the fabric resisted my pull, groaning on its hooks. A stream of tawny-golden light pierced through the small gap I created.

It's almost time. I forced myself to sit on my bench. I needed to reserve my energy. Gods knew I'd need it. My hands raked over the velvet material. Each movement sent ripples through the plush fabric, shifting the emerald green to a deeper hue. My journey was imminent. The sun, with the last of its soft beams, heralded the beginning of my escape from this gilded cage.

The world outside was waiting, and I was going to meet it.

2

PERSEPHONE

The sky had transformed into a labyrinth woven of darkness, stars, and the hazy glow of the moon. I'd never left Olympus. I dreamed for years of a life beyond these walls, where I could see the moons of all the realms I had read about.

The chatter among the guards died. They finished their card game, just like I'd expected. I pulled my cloak out of my bag and draped the velvety folds around me. My weight shifted as I swung my bag over my shoulder. I flicked off the light and took one last scan around my room.

Despite the darkness, my vision remained clear. The magic-suppressing medication no longer bound me. In my mind's eye, I played memories of moments over the years. I grew and changed while the room remained frozen, a silent witness to the passage of time and to everything I had survived. A small bed with a light-green quilt, a white desk pressed against the wall, and a bench in front of the lone window in the room. Though simple, it was mine—a haven I should never have needed.

I inhaled deeply. The jasmine and citrus flowed through

my nostrils, a beautiful but unsettling combination. The scent permeated every inch of this place. I silently wished to never encounter it again.

"I'm ready," I whispered to myself, a quiet contradiction to my feelings.

I'd waited years for this moment, and still, my body betrayed me. My heart stuttered, palms slick, knees threatening to give. If I faltered now, if I let all my plans unravel at the whisper of cowardice, the grip of inevitability would tighten. My fate would be sealed within the confines of a life I'd never chosen. My shoulders tensed, and I hugged myself. I went over the steps. *Create a distraction. Run. Don't get caught.* There was only so much planning I could do. A knot grew in my throat, but I swallowed it down.

Now or never.

The door closed behind me with a soft click—sealing off this chapter of my life. My footsteps were quiet and controlled down the corridor. The kitchen emitted a soft glow, illuminating the corner. I stayed within the shadows, pressed against the wall. I drew in a deep breath, steadying myself before rounding the bend.

There he was, Basile. Alone. Just like I'd planned.

The room was quiet. Basile remained oblivious to my presence, likely lost to the effects of the liquor I could smell in the air.

I glided through the living room, each footfall a whisper against the dense, woven rug. I yanked a blouse from my bag, thrusting it into the ever-burning fireplace. The scarlet fabric smoldered, turning a deep burgundy as fire caught. I chewed on the inside of my lip as the heat licked at my fingers. The skin prickled, aching as though the fire meant to claim me too, but I remained still until flames danced on the cloth.

I pulled it back, draping it over a cushioned chair nearby. As I retreated to the doorway I entered, the flames devoured the cushion. The sharp, bitter scent of smoke quickly filled the room, curling into my nostrils. I resisted the urge to cough but couldn't stop my eyes from watering.

Two doors connected the kitchen to the living room. As Basile's curses tore through the air, growing louder and moving toward the living room, I seized the moment and slipped through one of the doors. I pulled my dagger free and sprinted with silent steps. *Move.* I repeated the mantra.

"What are you doing, Persephone?" Basile slurred, directly behind me. The fire crackled in the living room, but he wasn't putting it out like I'd expected.

He was following *me*.

I hurried my pace, heart hammering. Almost there.

His hand closed around the back of my cloak, yanking hard. The hood wrenched back, snapping against my neck. My body pitched sideways, shoes sliding on the polished stone floor. I stumbled, breath stolen from my lungs, the world tilting. My dormant magic bubbled inside me, pressing against the walls of my skin.

Too risky.

I crushed it down, clenched my teeth, and twisted hard in his grip. My fingers fumbled around the hilt of the dagger. Without thinking, without aiming, I thrust his dagger toward him with force and hope.

The blade sank into his side.

A raw, gut-wrenching cry ripped from his throat. My fingers clenched tighter around the hilt as he jerked back, eyes blown wide with pain and confusion.

Even injured, even drunk, Basile moved fast. Faster than I'd expected. His arm shot up, knocking mine aside as I lunged again, steel glinting between us. The dagger felt too heavy, too big, slipping against the sweat on my palm.

My chest heaved, but I swung again. He caught my wrist mid-arc, his grip crushing, a sneer twisting his face.

All those hours in practicing in front of the mirror had done nothing to help me. Spinning the dagger, twirling it, slashing it through the air. A little fantasy I'd convinced myself was readiness.

I hesitated, and that was all Basile needed. His hand clamped around my throat, lifting me off the ground. My feet kicked uselessly. "Let me go." I kept my voice low so as not to alert the other guards outside.

Basile's glassy eyes, clouded with the effects of the liquor, bore into mine. "You know I can't do that," he grunted, his breath hot against my cheek.

The dagger slipped from my hand, clattering loudly on the tile. I wrestled against his grasp.

He let out a long chuckle. "You really thought you'd get away from me?" he sneered. "After everything I've done for you?" His grip tightened. "Six months of fucking you and sneaking you to the library. This is your thank you?"

I thrashed, throat burning. "You don't own me," I gasped.

His expression shifted from amusement to malice. "Oh, but I do, sweet Persephone. You've been mine since the first time you begged me to slip between those pretty thighs. If you were so bored, you didn't have to stab me." Basile grinned. "You could've asked me to fuck you again. Maybe that's what you need now. You need me to teach you a lesson."

My hands clawed at the fingers that encircled my throat like iron bands.

His lips curled into a cruel, crooked grin as he squeezed. "You made a big mistake."

My only mistake was not trying to leave sooner. The words echoed in my head, but I didn't have enough air to get them out. The room swirled in a disorienting haze. A hollow ache throbbed through my chest. The edges of my vision frayed.

I thrashed and kicked his midsection despite my vulnerable position. A surge of erratic magic flickered within me. The surrounding air cracked, and a buzz made its way through my body.

It pounded.

Begged—*demanded*—to be released. It was risky, but I didn't have a choice.

I let it out. Heat flared beneath my skin. Basile yelped as magical vines wrapped around his torso and spiraled up his arms, forcing his body to straighten. They made their way to his throat.

"Perseph—" The vine tightened, and he couldn't finish my name. A vein protruded from his forehead, throbbing with pressure. His grip loosened around my throat, and I sucked a lungful of air. My body warmed, overcome by the magic.

He released me, and I fell to the floor. The small amount of breath I had was knocked clean from my lungs. Pain shot through me, the impact radiating from my knee and shoulder. I placed both of my palms flat on the cold tile as I dragged in a rattling inhale.

A wet, choked sound pulled my head up—Basile.

My vines made Basile's large form appear small as they corded around him like serpents birthed from a nightmare. A violent ache racked its way through me, magic cracking under my skin.

Too much. Too fast.

My fingers clawed at my temples as the pulse of it moved through me.

"I won't stay here," I said through my gritted teeth. I pushed through the fatigue.

My dagger glimmered with reflections of the chandelier's lights, catching my attention in my peripheral vision. I crawled to it. Each movement sent twinges of pain through my battered form. With every inch gained, it intensified. Basile was a demi-god, not an immortal. *I can do this.*

I stretched my fingers until I could grip the handle of the dagger. I didn't exactly know how to wield my magic, but the surge of adrenaline coursing through my veins banished any hesitation. My eyes closed. I reached deep within, calling my power back with a fervent plea. The dark-green vines untangled themselves and dissipated into nothing. Basile fell to the floor with a loud thud.

The return of the magic dulled my pain. I pulled myself up and crawled to Basile's body.

"You're a fool," he muttered.

"Maybe I am. But I refuse to stay here." For a few heartbeats, all I focused on was the sound of my heaving breath, the rush in my ears, and the way his chest hitched beneath my palm.

I drove the dagger down with all the strength that I could muster.

The blade met resistance, then gave, and his body jolted beneath mine. My arm ached, muscles screaming, sweat stinging my eyes as I forced the dagger in again.

And again.

And again.

And again, until his chest stilled.

I collapsed back, gasping, wiping trembling hands on my cloak. Even though the crimson stains on the dark fabric weren't visible, I could feel them.

The stickiness.

The heat.

I could smell them. The sharp tang of blood mixed with the harsh heaviness of the liquor clinging to the air.

His blood pooled out, a dark halo on the ivory titles, spreading wider and wider until it touched the tips of my shoes.

My head tilted as the life left his body. His eyes glazed

over. Dark-purple and black bruises formed around his throat, decorating his skin.

A laugh bubbled from my throat. My hands trembled, streaked with red, and for a heartbeat, I just watched them. I should've felt hollow. Regret. But all I felt was air filling my lungs, like I was breathing for the first time.

I had never killed anyone before but had always dreamed about it. Not the blood or the mess, but a way to get out. A way to take my power back.

Warmth radiated throughout my entire body. I couldn't suppress the satisfaction of finally releasing a fraction of the anger that had been kindling within me for years. I stood over him, looking down at his lifeless body. I kicked him as hard as I could. It did nothing to move his dead weight. "Not so big now," I muttered.

I crouched and ran my hand over his face, letting my fingers linger on his chapped lips, flakes peeling at the edges. The touch lacked empathy. He had shown me none. He had stood by—*helped*. The moments I thought there was a heart in his chest were only because he wanted to find a temporary home between my legs. The rent had come due for Basile, and I collected it. Mother always told me the Fates had cursed me. Another bitter laugh scraped the back of my throat. Maybe, just maybe, her twisted narrative of fate was right. Let her see what she had made.

"I'll show you exactly how cursed I am."

3

———

PERSEPHONE

I drew the hood of my cloak over my head. My tired muscles tensed, attuned to the rhythm of my racing heart. A cool breeze from the west kissed the exposed skin on my face as I stepped beyond the threshold of the front door. I tugged the cloak's hood down farther. I glanced both left and right.

No one was watching. The guards were too occupied arguing over who could take the next puff of the twisted roll of the herbs to notice me. Thane held the glowing twist between his fingers as Kayde and Nik leaned in, greedy for their turns. They were doing exactly what I needed them to.

I moved.

The grass muffled my hurried steps to the greenery lining the front of the estate. Fresh air filled my lungs. A knot twisted in my stomach. I couldn't tear my eyes away from the structure that had once been a home. Now, I saw it as nothing more than mere architecture—a structure built on lies, filled with pain, and maintained on the weight of secrets.

I wondered if the walls would miss me. I hoped they'd crumble without me.

I stood hidden within the deep green and umber. The brush and shrubs quivered with life in sync with my concealed form. The ground pulsated beneath my feet. Tendrils of ivy and a plush carpet of moss created a pathway through the plants, guiding me away from the estate. Though I didn't use any magic, the plants mirrored my intentions. I took one last look at the structure.

The building was anything but simple. Mother didn't do simple things. It was grand and rectangular, with long white pillars along the front and a set of dark-brown double doors. The large windows spanned from floor to ceiling on the left and right sides. A few of the many chandeliers were visible from where I stood. The windows always let in lots of sunlight. They were one of the best features of the structure —if there had to be something besides the greenhouse.

It was the one thing I would miss about this place. I would let one last mental picture linger in my mind as motivation. I never wanted to be here again. My lips pressed into a thin line, and I turned.

I followed the path until it ended before the iron fence. A narcissus flower sprouted—my favorite. The flower could lure anyone with its beauty. I crouched down, my fingers caressing the glittering ivory petals. The flower leaned into my touch. "I'm sorry. I have to go," I murmured. The surrounding bushes embraced me, offering a semblance of comfort. "I have to."

I winced as I grasped the cold iron, and I hoisted myself over the fence. The ground welcomed me on the other side, but a momentary numbness crept through my feet upon impact. Moonlight cast its silvery glow through the foliage, creating a dance of shadows on the path lined with wildflowers ahead. Each step outside the estate was liberation.

I left my map tucked away, its lines etched into my memory. I had drawn it on one of my trips to the Olympian

Library. Despite my limited outings, the library remained one of my favorite escapes. It held a millennium of history, filled with thousands of books from every realm.

Basile had taken me there from time to time. He enjoyed being able to relax and leave me to entertain myself for hours. I huffed a laugh. The visits were always followed with muttered words about my indebtedness to him as he used my body for pleasure. But a sacrifice was a sacrifice, and Basile was dead.

The estate was on the outskirts of Athens. Although Olympus had many cities, I had only ever seen parts of this one. My brisk pace transitioned into a light jog as the dense greenery thinned, giving way to an open expanse. The lights in the distance flickered.

I cautiously entered the sea of light-colored buildings and cobblestone. Most of Athens' inhabitants were already home for the night, preferring the daylight, but I couldn't afford to be caught.

The cobblestone path beneath my feet made a faint murmur, barely audible amid the roar of cascading water from the fountain at the center square blocks away. I navigated through narrow alleys and empty streets. I encountered only a nymph and a demi-god, and they paid little attention to me. Their heads hung low as they stumbled, likely drunk. A silent understanding passed between us—don't bother me, and I won't bother you.

Lanterns cast a warm glow on the carved facades of the quaint shops. Mother had always kept me sheltered, even before she changed. When I was younger, she would bring me out, though it was rare. Most of the shops were different, some the same. I briefly squeezed my eyes shut and forced myself to keep moving. I couldn't let myself get caught up. It was a habit of mine—looking, indulging in the ideas that allowed me the fantasy of living the life I should have been. It was a comforting escape, even if just for a moment.

Every distant noise and flickering shadow made me jump as I walked through the streets.

There was no one in the center square. *Thank the Fates.* It was different from the last time I'd been here, years ago. I'd only ever seen it during the daylight, when it was alive with color and bustling with people.

In the heart of the square stood the massive fountain. Water burst upward in an effervescent display. The fountain's pool shimmered with a mosaic of light-blue and white petal-shaped tiles. In the center were marble statues of each member of the Divine on the Olympian Court.

Though I was a Divine, a goddess, I didn't have a statue. I wasn't on the court. I didn't mind—I'd never felt like one of them anyway.

The gentle play of moonlight softened their marble faces. But I wouldn't be fooled. The Divine were anything but soft and never to be trusted. My gaze drifted from one statue to the next. Ares, God of War, raising a blade. Zeus, God of the Sky and leader of the Olympian Court, holding a bolt of lightning. Poseidon, God of the Seas and ruler of Atlantis, holding his trident. Then my eyes landed on him.

Hades, God of the Underworld.

He stood with his hands at his sides. It was the simplest pose of them all, and somehow, the most unsettling. While the others held weapons or props or were posed in exaggerated ways, his statue did nothing to perform. It just existed. His face was carved with an expression that was neither cruel nor kind, just… unreadable. I stared longer than I meant to. I pulled my cloak tighter.

Mother's statue came next. Her head was tilted, her lips parted in an eternal half smile, arms holding a cornucopia overflowing with fruits and vegetables. It made her look gracious. *Kind.* My stomach twisted, reminding me of my purpose here, of what I needed to leave behind. I didn't linger on the rest of the statues.

I bit the inside of my cheek and strode across the square to Divine Hall. It loomed over everything, arrogant in its beauty, a monument of Olympian opulence. A long white staircase led to its entrance, each step wide and gleaming under the moonlight. I paused at its base, tilting my head back to take in its full height. The massive doors stood closed.

To the right was a slab of carved stone. This was what I was here for, what I'd read about. The Realm Gateway.

A portal to every realm.

I walked closer to it. Scenes stretched across the stone—gods, rivers spilling from cupped hands, winged creatures. At the center was a carving of what looked like a crystal. Jagged lines radiated from it like sunbeams, carved deeply to accentuate the impression of brightness. My fingers hovered above the stone, trembling. Not from the cool air, but from what this meant. Once I touched it, there was no going back.

Not to the estate.

Not to the version of myself who stayed drugged and silent.

Not to her.

I pressed my palm on the carved surface. Magic pulsed beneath it like a second, slow heartbeat. The vibration surged through my fingers and up my arm. The stone shimmered, then slowly, soundlessly, it gradually opened.

I stepped inside.

The door shut behind me with an echo that I felt in my bones. The air in the corridor was warm, dense, humming with a faint-pulsing energy I'd never experienced before.

The hall stretched before me. Sconces lined the walls. They bathed the corridor in a soft, shifting light that played tricks on my eyes and created an illusion of endless depth. There were so many openings, each framed by identical gold borders, but each holding a different portal within. I walked until I reached the last one.

"I found you. Goodbye, Olympus realm," I whispered.

Without hesitation, I stepped through the black shimmer.

4

PERSEPHONE

The realm of the dead.

I gazed at the iron gates of the Underworld, intricate metal coils against the muted-gray sky and the tan expanse of the ground. Even from a considerable distance, they were large, dominating. They stretched endlessly to the left and right. I could see nothing beyond them.

A long procession of people moved steadily toward the gate. The line continued until I couldn't make out their bodies anymore. The number of people waiting didn't surprise me. People died every day, every minute. Death was a constant, unending stream of arrivals. However, witnessing the vast queue neatly arranged and waiting was chilling. Each person maintained an unwavering stare ahead. No chatter, no breathing, no fidgeting—just an eerie stillness. Only their feet moved forward, in unison, scuffing the dusty ground with a rhythmic drag as the line moved.

"Hello?" I asked the woman closest to me. I angled myself in front of her. Her sapphire eyes remained glazed over and her expression unchanged. Loose waves framed her face, and a simple emerald-green blouse complemented the faint amber tones in her hair.

She held a large round gold coin. The pattern embossed into the coin looked familiar. My brows furrowed, and I surveyed the gates. They had a similar pattern. I scanned the others nearby, each holding identical gold coins. I'd read about payment to the Underworld, but it hadn't mentioned a coin.

Details about the Underworld beyond the gates, or even about Hades himself, were scarce. Mother might consider me useless, but I had ears. I knew of her distaste for this realm. I understood that once you passed through the gates of the Underworld, you became a soul. Here, she shouldn't have been able to track me. *I think.* As for my plan to get through the gates? I wasn't entirely sure.

I quickened my pace to keep up with the moving line. I placed my hand on the woman's shoulder and shook. "Hello?" I asked again.

No response.

I moved to the person behind her, a man with the same vacant stare and another coin in his hand. My chest tightened when my words and shaking didn't work. I gave up trying to communicate after the fifth person.

What if I—

I attempted to pry the coin out of the fifth person's hand. A strong yank didn't budge it. With a sigh, I turned and walked. The gates grew larger and more imposing as I approached. There was a small gap between them where the line funneled through.

The air was stale, like a house that hadn't had its windows opened for years. The closer I got to the gates, the deeper my breaths became. I sucked in a lungful of air, but the fog in my mind only thickened. A persistent little whisper urged me to turn around. I willed my legs forward.

The longer I remained in the land of the dead, the more my head throbbed. *Just keep walking, Persephone.* I shook my head, trying to dispel the dizziness. Time stretched. It felt like I had made no progress to the gate, but I'd been walking for... I didn't know how long.

I peeked down at my feet. Why was I running? My head whipped around. I blinked three times—slowly, or what I thought was slowly. Everything felt slow.

My vision wavered, distorted, as if I were looking through a veil of tears. Hot crystalline streaks traced down my cheeks, leaving a trail of cuts. I lifted my hand up to my face, but it was dry. Through my hazy vision, I could still make out the gates. *I'm close. So close.* The gap between them was wide enough for me to sneak through.

I angled myself and held my breath as I slipped between the metal and the people entering. *I'm doing it. I'm doing it!*

I collided with something hard. My ears rang. A harrowing ache reverberated through my body. I sprawled on the ground, and a cloud of dust enveloped me, creating an all-pervading storm. My skin turned clammy, the dust clinging to it and my cloak. Spots danced in my vision as my heart raced. I inhaled deeply, attempting to soothe the terror coursing through my system, and sucked in a significant amount of dust. The breath I took for relief only induced more coughing.

"The land of the dead is for the dead." The low voice accentuated the word *dead*. "And, goddess, you look alive to me."

I rubbed my eyes and peered through my dust-covered eyelashes. All I could make out was a curly mass of red hair and the lower body of a horse. A centaur. I'd only ever read about them. With them native to Olympus, I hadn't expected to find one in the Underworld. The dust around me settled, and I wiped my eyes again before opening them wide.

My vision cleared, the details of the centaur coming into focus. His green eyes watched me with suspicion. His muscular torso merged seamlessly into the body of a chestnut horse, every muscle rippling under his sleek coat. The dust hung in the air, creating the illusion of a glow around him. He shifted his weight, his hooves scraping against the dry, cracked ground.

"I—" I coughed, getting any last dust out of my system. "I need to get through."

He barked a laugh. "Do you have a coin? Or an invitation from Hades?"

"No, but—"

He didn't let me finish.

"No coin. No invitation. No entry." He turned away and glared over his shoulder. "Return to your mother, goddess."

His words twisted into me like sharp knives. I stood up, no longer letting any force impact me. I looked him up and down. "I am a goddess. I rank far above you. You will let me in."

"Okay, baby goddess. I will let you in."

I was ready to put up a fight at his rude tone, but his words sank in. My mouth dropped open, and I quickly readjusted my surprised expression when it registered. How dare he talk to me like that? But I ignored his comment because he was letting me in.

"Have fun getting past Charon and the Styx River." He focused on his fingernails and picked at the dirt underneath them. "It's been a little while since we had some real entertainment here."

I didn't feed into his power trip, holding my head up high as I walked past him and through the gates. Surely, Charon wouldn't have any problem letting me in. He was only a ferryman, after all.

As I stepped beyond the gates of the Underworld, the

barren landscape transformed into a lush and hauntingly beautiful realm. The ground beneath my feet, once dry and lifeless, cradled me with soft, dark moss and a riot of colorful flowers emitting a gentle, pulsing bioluminescent glow as if they were breathing. Some unfurled petals shaped like little crescent moons. Others spiraled up and outward in impossible geometries, shifting between blue and purple. They filled the air with a strange sweetness, ripeness, almost overripe.

I didn't recognize a single bloom. None of them were mentioned in the few books on the Underworld in the Olympian Library.

Above, the light-gray sky had turned into an obsidian one scattered with stars.

The Styx River lay before me, a dark ribbon stretching endlessly both left and right. I remembered reading about it briefly in the same book that mentioned Charon. This was the river that souls needed to cross. The silvery reflection of the twin moons above danced on the surface of the Styx. A low, continuous murmur came from the water as it lapped against the moss-covered river's edge. I strained to see beyond the river, but a thick fog veiled the far bank and stretched into the distance, obscuring everything from view.

I stood still, entranced by the landscape. "I didn't expect this," I whispered, drinking in the sight. My eyes darted everywhere, trying to catalog everything. I couldn't look away. Every book had described this realm as desolate, a punishment of a place. This was the complete opposite, lush and mesmerizing.

It shouldn't have surprised me that the books didn't describe it truthfully. Not if it belonged to *him*.

Maybe Mother and the other Divine hadn't bothered to see it for themselves. Or maybe they had, and they'd lied. Mother always spoke of Hades like a beast best forgotten, and complained she didn't have access to this realm like the others.

The line of people who passed through the gate transformed, now translucent. Their bodies could still be made out, complete with features and clothes. *Souls*. The procession moved, making its way to a black dock. Charon, the ferryman, plucked the coins from the souls' hands with his skeletal fingers before they boarded. He stood tall, cloaked in black robes. I'd read about him, but all the information was vague. The common thread in all accounts emphasized he never took a break—ever.

I looked down at my dusty cloak and pants. I pushed up one of my sleeves, almost worried I had become translucent too. *It can't hurt to check*, I reasoned, examining my skin.

Nope. I was still me.

Thank the gods.

I made my way to the loading dock. Here, the view of the river was better. The fog was less opaque. I held on to the railing and leaned forward to get a closer look when I noticed movement beneath the surface.

Black shapes swirled and twisted within the water. My lips parted, and a quick breath escaped me. The water taunted me, its song beckoning.

Why am I here again?

The melody weaved around me, drawing me closer. I gave the river a toothy smile. I extended my finger, letting the tip sink below the surface. I succumbed to the warm water, running my hand through it, relishing the buzz it left on my skin. My eyes widened.

I saw a young version of myself—five, maybe six years old. Pink flowers adorned the umber waves of my hair. I wore a lazy grin, my cheeks flushed with a deep-scarlet hue —a time when I remained untouched by the shadows of Olympus. My face carried an innocence only childhood could provide. My head grew lighter. Blackness crept into the corners of my vision, but the warm sensation in my chest made me ignore it.

A hand seized my arm. I made no move to resist, the haze keeping me still. I shook myself back to awareness and tried to pull away. Adrenaline surged through my veins. My magic responded, conjuring forth vines sprouting from my palms without a conscious thought. The thorny vines battled with the persistent grip of the hand, but it didn't budge. They coiled and twisted in a desperate dance to prevent me from being dragged into the water.

I cast a glance behind me. The souls, lost in their vacant states, paid me no attention and shuffled onto the ferry. "Help me!" I shouted. My entwined vines gripped the railing, but they proved futile against the unyielding force. The grip tightened. "Hel—" A mouthful of the dark water silenced my plea, forcing its way down my throat.

What had been warm water turned icy, shocking my system into a panic. I coughed, but it was no use. I was underwater. My vines disappeared. Shadows in the water crept closer at the edges of my peripheral vision, like preda-tors circling.

My arms thrashed, flailing in a desperate parody of swimming. I clawed at the water, begging it to let me rise. Magic sputtered in my veins, then died. My body would not obey me. *I need to breathe.*

Nothing worked.

The shadows moved closer, slick tendrils coiling at my throat. My head jerked to the side, my hair drifting around me like drowned weeds, tangling with the darkness until I couldn't tell where they ended and it began. I tore at my neck with frantic fingers, but water slithered through them. My nails carved lines into my own skin, cold burning along the gouges. *I need to breathe!*

My lungs screamed for air, but only water filled them. My chest constricted, aching iron bands crushing my ribs. Cold leeched through me until my limbs numbed. I clawed at the shadows, struck at nothing. I convulsed once, twice, then grew heavy.

A hand made of darkness seized me by the throat, dragging me down. The light above shrank, receding until only black water pressed in from all sides.

Just before the waters could shroud me in complete darkness, a large dark form emerged from the depths. A whale. I'd never seen one in the Olympus realm, but I knew we had them. A dark sheen coated it. As it drew nearer, the shadows tormenting me relinquished their hold. Numb and exhausted, I struggled to swim toward the surface. Its massive tail created a powerful current, lifting me upward. The whale positioned itself beneath me, helping me breach the surface with a gentle but firm nudge.

I gasped for air. The whale emitted a sharp whistle. I crawled off the massive animal and onto solid ground. Over my shoulder, I glanced at the creature. Its luminescent gaze lingered for a few moments before vanishing back into the water.

Emptiness replaced the water flowing out of my ears. My whimper turned into a cough. One cough cascaded into an endless series, my lungs still burning. Water flowed from my mouth, and my stomach convulsed in a marathon of heaves.

I lay on a mosaic of velvety moss cradling my tired body. Giant willowlike trees stretched their branches overhead, their leaves emitting a soft glow against the dark sky. Each breath I took still stabbed at me. My eyes fluttered closed.

5

PERSEPHONE

Heat flushed my face. I opened my eyes, and they immediately turned to a squint. Twin suns hung high overhead. The warm, bright light filtered through the leaves and branches of the tree above, casting intricate patterns around me. I blinked away the rest of the drowsiness.

The once-dark sky had transformed into a light-gray canvas. The soft, diffused light seemed almost inadequate against the rich greens of the forest and the glowing blooms surrounding me. My eyes darted from flower to flower. Deep purples, blues, and greens. I'd never seen anything like this before. Everywhere I looked, life thrived. A morning mist filled the air, its moisture clinging to everything.

I could no longer see the gates I'd once passed through. I propped myself up on my elbows and let out a long exhale. I licked my dry lips and sat up all the way. I was only a few feet away from the Styx. I'd been too drained from it to crawl farther. My stomach churned at the mere reminder of the dangerous waters. *At least I'm on the other side.* I was far from the loading dock. It was a small speck in the distance, but I wasn't familiar enough with the Underworld to know for sure where I was now.

Exhaustion clung to my limbs as I mustered the strength to get up. Hunger gnawed at my stomach, a reminder of my backpack filled with supplies I no longer had.

I'd gone hungry before.

Sometimes, Mother deemed food a luxury, one I didn't deserve if I disobeyed. The hunger wouldn't kill me. Not as one of the Divine. Immortality came with a price—endurance, not immunity.

We didn't die from hunger. But we felt every second of it, hollowing us out, and shells were easier to manipulate. My stomach cramped, and I pressed a hand against it. "I can do this." My words were weak, but I moved anyway.

My cloak clung to me. With a sigh, I reached for the clasp at my throat, my fingers trembling and stiff. The suns had warmed the metal. It took several attempts, my fingers awkward and fumbling, before the clasp finally gave way. The heavy cloak dropped from my shoulders, landing with a thump.

My first few steps were laborious and clumsy as my legs adjusted to the blood flow restored in them. Each step sent a tingle through my leg. I moved away from the river's edge and ventured into the dense woods. Amid the thick foliage, I found a welcomed break from the relentless suns. I kept my gaze fixed on the ground, careful not to trip over any roots in the underbrush.

I spent the day crafting stories in my mind, weaving intricate narratives of what I would do with my newfound freedom. Each scenario unfolded, alive with possibilities I was still struggling to comprehend. I had planted the first seed; I'd left Olympus. In the quiet moments between my stories, I found myself grinning so much my cheeks hurt.

I pressed on through the thinning trees as the suns

dipped lower in the sky. The incessant roar of my stomach had subsided, a dull emptiness that I had grown used to replacing it. An ache accompanied each step. I had glimpsed a few Underworld animals, translucent creatures, but they paid me no attention. My energy waned, but my determination to keep moving remained.

Fog coiled around my feet, slowly churning thicker and higher. I took small slow steps to avoid tripping. I could make out a cluster of houses in the distance. "Only a little farther," I murmured to myself.

Rustling carried through the trees. It was too heavy to be the wind.

In my peripheral vision, I spotted movement—a sleek, translucent shape darting through the brush. A wolf. I surged into a sprint, my muscles burning. Another shape joined the first, this time to my right, weaving between the thick trunks of towering trees. The leaves rustled, branches snapping beneath their large feet as they ran.

I pushed myself to run faster, doing my best to avoid falling. Branches whipped past my face, leaving thin scratches on my skin. I dared a glance behind me. My heart raced as I caught sight of a third wolf.

The wolves were close enough that their low, measured breathing reached my ears. But they didn't growl. They didn't snarl.

My foot snagged on an exposed tree root. My balance wavered, and the world tilted. I flung my arms out in a desperate attempt to regain my equilibrium. It was too late. I fell to the foggy ground with a thud, knocking all the air out of my lungs. Pain bloomed across my knees, knuckles, and palms. I took a deep breath. My cheek pressed against the damp dirt, tasting the musty scent.

Paws appeared in front of my face. The trio of wolves gathered around me, breathing fogging into the mist. But as the seconds stretched into minutes, they made no move to attack.

Maybe it was the hunger gnawing at my stomach or the exhaustion clouding my mind, but a smile tugged at my lips. The absurdity of running with wolves. Of being in this realm. Of killing Basile. Of leaving my mother.

"This is insane." If I stopped to think too long, maybe I'd shatter. So I laughed until the muscles in my abdomen stung.

Perhaps the sound unsettled them. The wolves left me alone. I pushed myself onto my hands and knees, then forced my body upright. The last light of day bled away through the canopy. Night was coming fast. I needed shelter.

The dense fog and tangled underbrush receded. The trees became less frequent, and I came closer to the cluster of homes. Small black moths shimmered in the fading light, their wings catching the last sunrays. They moved slowly, less like insects and more like drifting embers. I crouched behind the last tree before the clearing. I observed all the homes for a few minutes, looking for any signs of movement.

Nothing.

I approached the house closest to me and farthest away from the others.

The house was dark gray, with black shutters and a matching roof. It was simple, which was exactly what I needed. I grasped the gold door handle, only to find it locked.

Circling the perimeter, I found a weathered wooden bench. It was heavier than expected, and my tired muscles ached in protest as I dragged it beneath the window. I climbed onto it, turned my back to the glass, shifted my weight, and drove my elbow hard behind me. The pane shattered with a brittle shriek. I winced at the sound, jaw tightening. Covering my fists with my sleeves, I punched away the jagged shards clinging to the frame until the opening was clear.

With the last sparks of energy within me, I hoisted myself up and propelled through the empty window, landing on the glass-covered hardwood floor. Pain flared hot through my body at the impact. I lay on the unforgiving floor for a few moments with my eyes closed, trying to get through the discomfort of the abrupt landing.

"Meow."

My eyes shot open. A cat hovered above me, white and translucent. Its gaze was steady, as if it wasn't just watching but studying. It took a few steps back as I pulled myself off the floor, careful not to touch the glitter of broken glass. I moved across the empty room, away from the cat. It meowed again and crossed the distance, rubbing its silken body against my leg. I bent down to its level, moving slowly.

"Who are you?" I whispered as I ran the back of my fingers over its head. Its blue eyes closed, and it emitted a purr, the subtle vibrations resonating through my fingertips.

I gave the cat one last pat before continuing through the house. The cat lingered in its spot for a moment, tail flicking, then padded softly in the opposite direction, slipping out of sight. The house must've been empty—only the cat had stirred at the sound of the broken glass—but I still walked with soft footsteps through the sparse rooms. I meandered through a small sitting room and into the kitchen, hurrying over to the sage-green cabinet and yanking it open.

Every single one was empty. "What's the point of a kitchen with no food? Do souls even eat?" I grumbled, and decided it was time to get ready to sleep.

I shut the door to the room I'd broken into and pushed a dresser in front of it, determined to establish a semblance of security. I repurposed the limited furniture from all over the house to use as a makeshift barricade for both the front and back doors. The cat followed me around, quietly purring and observing me.

I found a single furnished bedroom upstairs, with a washroom off the bedroom. It had the bare necessities, and that was all I cared about. I indulged in a lengthy shower. The warm water relaxed my tired muscles. When I finished, I put on clothing I found in the armoire, a deep-green long-sleeved top and black pants. The fabric engulfed me, its excess pooling around my ankles and wrists.

I stared at myself in the mirror. Deep, dark circles marred the skin under my eyes. Hopefully, my Divine healing would kick in soon. My hair was a matted mess. With each pass of the brush, I winced as it caught on knots, pulling at my scalp. I brushed until I couldn't take the pain anymore. Mostly detangled, only a few small, stubborn tangles remained. I braided it, deciding I could handle the rest tomorrow, along with finding food.

I pushed the armoire in front of the door and crawled into the unfamiliar bed, then adjusted the pillows and made myself comfortable. It didn't take long for sleep to claim me.

6

PERSEPHONE

I jolted out of my deep sleep. My eyes pried open, and I sat up, scooting to the head of the bed. A chill ran through me. I glanced down at myself. My shirt was drenched, sticking to me like a second skin. I dragged my sweaty palms along the fabric and groaned.

I'm definitely not going to be able to sleep any more tonight.

My heart still thrummed loudly in my chest from the dream—no, nightmare—I woke from. Images of the Styx River replayed in my mind, hauntingly vivid. I pressed my clammy hands to my cheeks and moved them to my throat. *I can still breathe.* My chin dropped to my chest. *I'm alive,* I tried to tell myself. The mantra played in my mind, attempting to dispel the unease.

Deep, slow breaths. I inhaled in and exhaled out until my breathing settled. I cleared the tightness out of my throat and closed my eyes. I searched for the cocktail of fear, shame, and regret inside me. Finding it was uncomfortably easy. I shoved the mixture into an imaginary little box deep within myself, hidden behind an ice-coated wall.

A short, hollow sound pierced the stillness of the night. I

clutched the blanket closer to me in a way that felt childish and reminded me once again that I was on my own. Its black folds were a feeble shield against the chill dancing across my skin. My head swiveled, looking for the source of the noise. Everything appeared unchanged, yet my paranoia lingered.

The space settled back into a hushed quiet, an indescribable weight pressing down on me.

Another chill swept over me, and this time, a heightened awareness of my surroundings directed my attention to its source. I pushed away the blanket and dragged myself from the comfort of the bed. My toes scrunched together, and my muscles tensed as my feet met the cool wood floor. I crossed my arms, attempting to preserve my warmth, and walked to the sole window in the room.

The window greeted me with a veil of frost. I hadn't experienced this level of cold before or after the Styx. There was a lot left for me to learn about this realm. To my surprise, the window wasn't open. I ran my palms along its seams, feeling a draft seeping through a subtle gap between the glass and the wooden frame. I rummaged through a nearby drawer, shoving aside a few random items until I found a few thick wool socks. They were scratchy against my skin, but they'd do the job. "Gods, that's cold." I shoved the fabric into the space, sealing out the unwelcome draft.

I shook off the eerie feeling clinging to me and returned to bed. My tired eyes fixated on the off-white ceiling. The slow ticking of the clock across the room became my lullaby, and I listened until I succumbed to the weight of exhaustion.

Potent energy passed over me. I jerked up, pulling myself out of my almost-sleep and back into a state of crystalline awareness. I inspected my hands. *I'm not using any magic.*

Footsteps.

Light, feathery footsteps. So light, my brain came up with ways to tell myself I was only imagining them.

Silence.

"Who's there?" I prayed to the Fates I was only speaking to myself. Adrenaline rushed through my veins, webbing me into a cage of panic. My gaze darted around the room, but there was nothing. No visible presence.

Goose bumps erupted on the back of my neck. My body betrayed me, hyperaware of every nerve, every beat. Cold seeped through me, impossible cold, though the draft in the window had long been sealed.

Something shifted in the room, a feeling I had grown to learn over the years.

Eyes.

I pressed my back as far as I could into the wall and scanned the room around me.

"Little Goddess of Spring. Did you think you could sneak into my realm without me knowing?" A gruff, low voice rumbled from the shadows.

It was too close to me. I kicked off the tangled blanket and swung my legs over the side of the bed. My feet hit the cold floor with a thud.

Before I could make it halfway across the room, the voice spoke again. "Tsk tsk. As if you could trick the God of the Underworld."

Hades.

I whirled around, and my head grew fuzzy. His guttural voice sank dread into me. I turned again. A shadow twisted around my form and pulled me to the center of the room.

My magic unleashed in a torrent of thick, untamed vines erupting from my palms. But they did nothing against the shadows holding me. I couldn't stop them. I cursed at myself, my mother, and the Fates for my lack of control. I kept the expression on my face impassive as panic bubbled inside of me. *Don't look weak.* My neck craned. I looked desperately for Hades. Vines coiled around me with Hades' shadows, enveloping me in darkness.

His magic surged, forcing my vines to wither and vanish as if they had never been. The air clung to me, thick and suffocating. My knees buckled, and I fell to the floor. The old wood groaned underneath me. My fingers trembled with the aftermath of expended magic. Sweat covered my face, my cheek sticking to the floor.

A low chuckle rippled across the room. Hades sat perched on the unmade bed, looming large against the small frame. His stillness made me nervous. I summoned the little strength left in me, pushing myself upright and locking my knees. My attention fixed on the most imminent threat—the dangerous god across the room.

Hades rose, maintaining a calculated distance. Dressed in a cloak of the deepest black with its hood drawn, he was the embodiment of shadows. A muted stream of gray light filtered through the window, casting his front in darkness. Only the lower portion of his face was visible to me; the sharp contours of his jawline, the faint stubble adorning it, and the curve of his lips. His gloved fingers tapped in a steady cadence against his crossed arms.

He pushed his hood down. I tracked every one of his deliberate movements as he exposed his face to me. The darkness around him dissipated. Hades' eyes glowed a pale gray, lacking any expressiveness. It only drew me into him more. Hades stared at me, trying to crack me with the weight of his gaze. I squared my shoulders and refused to submit.

His cheekbones were defined, chiseled and cut. I'd never seen him in person, only his statue in Athens Square. It had failed to prepare me for the living embodiment of the god before me. He was something no lifeless sculpture could capture.

Hades broke the silence. "You need to leave before your

mother tries to come into my realm and collect you." With only a few strides, he bridged the distance until he loomed just a foot before me. "I don't need Demeter trying to cause more problems for me and my realm—"

"Can I stay?" I chipped out, cutting him off.

"Do you know what the Underworld is like?" he taunted me, drawing closer and closer. Hades' voice was like velvet. I hated myself for wanting to hear more. Power radiated from him. I raised my chin, meeting his tilted head that studied my face.

I didn't answer his question. I stared at him, and a smirk crawled onto his face.

"The Goddess of Spring does not belong in the land of the dead," he said with a chuckle.

My face flamed. A dangerous numbness crawled over me. My lips curled into a snarl. Hades remained unmoved, his stare ice cold, devoid of any hint of warmth.

"I need you to let me stay," I said. My voice held stern, though a subtle tremor in my hands betrayed me.

Hades laughed, sharp and low. The sound of his amusement peeled back my veneer of confidence. I steeled myself, determined not to show any sign of weakness in the face of this god. *I am a goddess*, I reminded myself. I ignored the chill pricking at my back.

He took a single step forward. I didn't run. This was his realm. Anywhere I went, he would find me.

A twitch played across Hades' face. "You have come into my realm—without invitation—and chosen to disrespect me." The weight of his gaze bore down on me, his words too loud in the quiet space. "Others have done far less and died for it."

"I'm Divine, just like you. You can't kill me."

His gloved hand extended, and a tendril of shadowy magic whirled me around. He pressed me against his chest.

The suddenness of the motion stole the breath from my lungs. Every movement was too calculated, too precise. He wrapped my braid around his gloved hand, ensnaring it like a leash. His chest vibrated as he growled at me. My scalp stung as he tugged on my hair. I tried to wrench away from him, but I couldn't move. "Oh, little goddess, I can do things far worse to you than death." His breath tickled the back of my neck, but I felt none of the warmth that should've come with it.

Just ice.

His promises of cruelty made my stomach twist. "Let me stay."

He said nothing. I hated the silence more than I hated his threats.

"Please," I added in a low voice. I looked up at him through my eyelashes, the top of my head leaned back against him. He wore a stony look that made me want to crawl out of my skin and hide.

"And how should I know you aren't here on orders of your mother?" He tugged tighter on my braid, making me cringe and whimper from the pain. It was a display of how much power he had over me. "Why shouldn't I send you back?"

"I ran from her," I breathed out.

"I don't believe you."

What can I say to convince him? "It's true," I screamed as he pulled more. Pain built on the back of my neck.

"Bind yourself to me. Prove your loyalty."

"No," I hissed. A cruel irony dawned on me—I'd just escaped from the clutches of one captor, only to be faced with the prospect of binding myself to another. My hands clenched into fists.

"All right, back to your mother you go—"

"Fine," I snarled. The thought of returning to Olympus

felt like a fate far worse than binding myself.

"Say it."

Tears slid down my face. "What do you need me to say?"

"Stop playing stupid. Say the words. I, Persephone, Goddess of Spring, willingly bind myself to Hades, God of the Underworld."

Moments passed. I probed my mind, looking for a solution. Hades tugged again. I screamed, and the words spilled. "I, Persephone, Goddess of Spring, willingly bind myself to Hades, God of the Underworld."

A crackle of dark magic washed over me as the oath left my mouth. The words tasted like ash on my tongue. I wanted to claw them back, to tear the syllables from the air, but it was too late.

Something inside me shifted. Like a thread had pulled taut beneath my ribs and tied itself off without my consent. I felt it there, foreign and cold, but not painful.

Hades released me. I stumbled, backing as far from him as I could. My scalp throbbed. I raised my shaking hands to my lips. "I..." My shoulders hitched, and a sob racked through me. "I take it back." There was no use, but I said it anyway. *I take it back.* The words repeated on a loop.

He shook his head. "I must admit, I never expected you to play into my hands so readily." He smiled like he wasn't sure what to make of me. "It was too easy. I thought you'd have a little more rebellion in you." Hades took a few steps closer to me. His smile vanished, and a cruel glint flashed across his eyes that were not merely watching; they were claiming, marking me like a possession.

For every step he took, I took a step back until I hit the wall. He was too close to me. "Don't touch me," I said in between heavy breaths.

Hades smirked. "I suppose you haven't learned how to whisk." He was right, but I refused to concede it. I held my tongue. Mother never whisked with me, even before she became the shadow of herself. Not that I ever ventured far. Her fear of what might happen to me meant my world was limited to only what she allowed. He reached out, and a chill covered my skin.

Our surroundings shifted. We were in a small room, devoid of any color. The walls were painted in a soft-matte gray. The absence of furniture left the room feeling spacious despite the small size. There were no windows to offer a glimpse of the outside world.

"Minthe," Hades yelled. A woman with blonde hair and black clothing hurried in through the door. "Show Perse-phone"—Hades placed a hand on the small of my back and nudged me forward; I shivered—"to a room."

7

HADES

I slammed my hand down. The wood answered with a heavy thud, the reverberation biting through my palm and up into my arm. She was everywhere. Her eyes, all too captivating, mimicked the rich mahogany wood of my desk.

I shook my head. Her presence in the Underworld had been palpable long before she made it past the gates. Granted, I didn't anticipate her to make it that far. She should've turned around, gone home. She didn't belong in my realm.

I hadn't decided what to do with the goddess until I saw her. Then it became simple. My decision was sealed; I would keep her, against every piece of better judgment I had left. My fingers curled into a fist. "Persephone," I whispered. I didn't like the way her name rolled off my tongue.

I picked up my darts.

Focus.

One.

Two.

Three.

All the darts hit the red center of the target, like they always did.

Light crept into the sky. I didn't get a minute of sleep that night. I turned and gazed out the window, the scene of thick waves of fog rolling through the air greeting me, blocking my view of the courtyard. The damp, cool tendrils of mist brushed against the glass, leaving a subtle trace of moisture.

I hadn't expected her to be so... beautiful. I groaned, haunted by the way her brown braided hair had wrapped around my fist. And the mark she'd undoubtedly find on the back of her neck from binding herself to me.

I exhaled, and my nose twitched. I couldn't distance myself from her stubborn, lingering scent. Persephone smelled of life. Blooming flowers and earthy undertones. I shook my head and paced the length of my study, forcing my attention outward, to the shifting play of dim light and shadow the fog cast outside.

I pulled the darts out of the board and stood back in front of my desk with a sliver of hope they would make me focus on something other than her plump pink lips. I wasn't made for romance. The Fates had made that abundantly clear.

One.

Two.

Three.

Sated for now, I took a seat at my desk. I read over some of the ridiculous paperwork from the court. *Why do we need another building?* Too many of the other Divine were more focused on material items than they were on doing their jobs. But they'd never admit to such shortcomings—willingly.

8

PERSEPHONE

I pulled myself out of bed and yawned. Despite my attempts to rub away the remnants of sleep from my eyes, they clung stubbornly. Sleep hadn't come easy that night—another nightmare and grappling with the fact I'd tied myself to one of *them*.

The worst part? I had *chosen* it. I escaped one cage and ran headfirst into another.

I'd done a brief survey of the room when Minthe brought me, but it was only now, bathed in light, that I could truly take it in. I hadn't anticipated Hades giving me such a nice room. I wasn't sure what I expected, but it wasn't *this*. This bedroom dwarfed the one I grew up in—perhaps double, if not triple its size. An intricate embossed pattern covered the ivory walls, a flourish that only added to how carefully put together the space was. Everything about it was refined.

Thick fog veiled the view outside. Through the haze, I could just make out the outlines of the distant mountains. Twisted trees broke through the mist, their branches reaching out like skeletal fingers. Every now and then, a hint of vibrant, glowing color pierced the gray—flashes of green, red, blue, and purple.

The first task of the day was to make my new bed. I was tempted to leave it disheveled and abandon the routine… but I couldn't. In Athens, routine was all I had. Each morning, I would rise at the same time. I'd wait for a guard to bring me breakfast. Then I'd spend the day reading, tending to my plants, and crafting stories in my head. Evenings were similar. Dinner, reading, Basile using my body, my medication, and lights out at ten.

Routine was survival. Predictable pain was easier to endure than unpredictable cruelty. If I could measure the hours, I could measure when I had to disappear into myself to make it through them.

I pulled the burgundy duvet up to make the bed until it covered the matching pillows. I arranged the decorative ones on top by size. Using the palms of my hands, I smoothed out every wrinkle. "There, that's better."

The attached washroom had ivory walls, black stone floors continuing in from the bedroom. A large gold claw-foot tub was the centerpiece of the room, with a floor-to-ceiling, mosaic stained-glass window behind it. It reminded me of the greenhouse ceiling at home. I shut my eyes and shook my head. *That's not my life anymore.* I splashed cool water on my face, patted it dry with a towel, and peeled off my sweat-soiled clothing.

The closet brimmed with clothes, all impeccably tailored to my size. Even though I'd grown up in a world of magic and knew this was a result of Hades' abilities, I was still surprised. I picked an emerald-green long-sleeved dress that reached an inch above my ankles. The simplicity appealed to me. I lacked the energy to fuss over coordinating a matching top and bottom.

I unraveled my hair from its braid and finger-combed out

the knots. A knock broke the quiet. "Please don't be Hades," I whispered under my breath as I moved through the room and eased the door open.

Minthe. I couldn't decide if she was better than Hades. Minthe had an unsettling aura I didn't like. I stalled for a moment, but then I reminded myself—anyone was better than Hades. The nymph smiled at me, but it didn't reach her green eyes. "Hades would like to invite you to breakfast," Minthe said through gritted teeth.

The thought of seeing Hades again made my heart pound. I gripped the door handle until my knuckles paled. My stomach grumbled as I stayed silent, so I nodded. "Okay."

She gestured to follow her.

"I need a moment," I blurted out, then hurried over to the perfectly made bed and launched my body onto it. The duvet crumpled beneath me and the pillows scattered, a few falling onto the floor. I got off the bed and smoothed out my dress. My fingers twitched at my sides, yearning to fix the mess I had created. I needed to leave it. Olympus wasn't my life anymore. I needed to escape the routine that bound me for so long.

Straightening my dress one last time, I walked back to Minthe. She gave me a strange look but turned and started walking. I swallowed. I focused on the way her blonde, almost-white hair swayed as she moved. We traveled through several long halls and down flights of stairs. My fingers fumbled with the end of my sleeves. I should've been paying attention to where we were going, but I was too busy mentally preparing myself. *Never trust the Divine.*

Chatter grew louder with each step we took. I managed to stir up enough courage to pull my attention away from the back of Minthe's head. The corridor widened into a grand room. Ribbons of light filtered through the clear glass panels embedded in the high ceiling. At the heart of the room stood a long wood table surrounded with tall-backed chairs. The rich, dark color matched the intricate wood detailing on the walls.

I swallowed hard as I met Hades' eyes, then looked away quickly, but I found no solace. His face was clear in my mind, etched with an intensity I didn't like.

Persephone! I scolded myself. I couldn't think that way.

I thought of the magic I'd foolishly invoked, binding myself to him. I clutched my hands to steady the tremors threatening to break through my body. I made a mistake, and now I had to navigate the consequences.

Hecate, Hermes, and Thanatos also sat at the table. My every muscle went taut. I'd read about these Divine. Hecate, the Titan Goddess of Witchcraft, who'd sided with the Divine during the Titan War. Hermes, God of Trade and Messenger among the Divine. Thanatos, God of Death and Reaper for Hades.

I stumbled over myself, but I continued to follow Minthe. The nymph pulled out a chair for me next to Hecate. I forced a smile and sat. My hands instinctively tightened around the edge of the chair. "Hello," I said with more confidence than I felt.

Hecate acknowledged me with a nod, her violet hair shifting. Her eyes were the same color, sparkling as a warm smile spread across her thin face. Thanatos paid me little attention. His dark, nearly black eyes narrowed and skimmed over me with a cold, assessing gaze. The muscles in his face twitched.

"How are you, Persephone?" Hermes asked, a laugh bubbling out of him. His hazel eyes scanned the visible half of my body. Hermes propped his head on his hand and leaned on the table, his dark curly hair falling onto his forehead.

"I'm fine." I forced another smile.

"Interesting little thing you are."

My face burned. I chuckled to fill in the awkward gap in conversation. Hades shot Hermes a glare.

"You know, your mother believes you were abducted," Hermes said. He removed himself from his propped position and took a sip of the water.

The blood drained from my face. My foot tapped lightly under the table. "Well, Mother has always excelled at entertaining delusions," I replied, and took a sip of my own water.

Hermes raised an eyebrow. "Ah, family dynamics. Always a delight."

My fingers drummed on my leg. "Regardless of what Mother believes, I am here of my own accord." I emphasized the word *own*. A male soul entered the room, carrying a large platter adorned with neatly cut pieces of bread, an assortment of fruits, nuts, and jams. He positioned the platter at the center of the table.

Hermes leaned back with a smirk, unfazed. "Well, however you got here, it's caused a stir in the Divine circles. Missing goddesses tend to do that."

Minthe chimed in as she set a stack of plates next to the platter. "Looks like you're the talk of Olympus, Persephone. Quite the scandal."

I scowled, and my voice dropped. "I'm not interested in being a topic for gossip." I smoothed out the imaginary wrinkles on the bottom half of my dress under the table. To have all the years I suffered reduced to a mere scandal felt like a cruel joke. Each night spent in fear, each moment of pain—all dismissed as though they were nothing more than fodder for gossip. They knew *nothing* of what I'd gone through.

Minthe turned around and left the room. I followed the lead of the other Divine at the table and picked up a plate. I arranged a few pieces of bread and an assortment of fruits and nuts. I couldn't be bothered to ask about the flavors of the jams, so I settled on the reddish one closest to me.

I should've been hungry. The growl of my stomach said otherwise, but my appetite had vanished. I picked at the food as if moving it around might spark some interest. I had to eat —I hadn't eaten since coming to the Underworld—but it was a chore. I listened to the conversation among the Divine and forced a small chuckle when appropriate.

I cast a subtle glance at Hades, observing him as he consumed his meal. The small trail of the jam escaping onto his gloved finger didn't go unnoticed. He met my gaze, sucking the jam from his finger in a gesture that felt like a challenge.

"Why don't you take your gloves off to eat?" My question cast a temporary hush over the table.

His jaw tightened. "How I dress and eat is none of your concern, little goddess." The back of my neck burned. I rubbed the irritated area, but the sensation continued for a few seconds. A bead of sweat trickled down the back of my neck, making my hair stick to it.

"What does everyone think of these jams? They are absolutely amazing," Hecate interjected. The other Divine, excluding Hades, easily brushed off the tension and resumed their discussions. I was a mere observer, contributing nothing more than the occasional side comment.

Hades, however, radiated an intensity I couldn't shake. A new platter arrived with an array of meats and cheeses, and I reached for a cube of cheese. Hades stood up and walked out of the room without a word. I looked around at the other Divine. "What's wrong with him?"

"He's being Hades," Hecate responded with a light sigh and a wave.

I took a few minutes to muster the courage, my eyes fixed

on Hermes as I wrestled with my nerves. "Would you be able to spread a rumor for me?" I finally asked, my voice steady.

He smiled mischievously. "That's my favorite thing to do. I knew I liked you."

"Can you spread a rumor that I ran away? Maybe that I'm hiding somewhere in the mortal realm? Maybe Faerie? You can make up more as you see fit," I continued, laying out the details of my scheme.

He nodded as his eyes lit up.

"What will it cost me?"

"Nothing," he said, finishing the last of his water.

I shook my head slightly. "Favors from the gods always cost something." I wasn't experienced, but I knew enough. I had made far too many mistakes, the biggest last night. I couldn't afford any more.

"You're lucky. Seeing your mother humiliated is worth the effort." He sat back in his chair.

I questioned his motives, his sincerity. Could I trust him? Could I afford not to? He waited for a response.

I nodded and clasped my hands together. I needed this favor. "Thank you."

He smiled.

I finished my food, keeping to myself and ignoring the occasional probing looks from Thanatos. I stood up, feeling like the conversation had been exhausted. The chair scraped softly against the floor. "I don't mean to be rude, but I'm going to head back to my room."

"Of course, do not worry. We get together every so often. We'll see you soon," Hecate assured, and she returned to her conversation with Thanatos.

I wasn't going to worry, but I didn't tell her that. I nodded my farewell and left. Hopefully, I'd be able to get back to my room without relying on Minthe's assistance.

9

———

PERSEPHONE

I spent the rest of my first full day in the
Underworld confined to my room, my mind
going wild. The hours bled together, marked only by the
quiet arrival of meals—breakfast, lunch, and dinner—delivered by a silent soul. The weight of what I had done had fully
sunk in. *I left home—successfully. I killed Basile. I bound myself to
the God of the Underworld.*

I'd already spent most of today cloistered in my room.
Over the years, I had mastered the art of losing myself, adept
at slipping away into the depths of my mind and letting the
time pass. I wasn't stuck in my pretty prison at home, but a
self-inflicted prison was no better. I needed to get out.

I walked through the halls of gold and stone. I created a
mental map of each turn and staircase. I didn't have any
paper to note it.

Paintings covered the corridor walls, their colors
breathing in the half light. I drank them in, pulled toward the
intricate details. They stirred a familiar sensation, the same
pulse that drove the stories I crafted in the sanctuary of my
mind. My stories were not mere daydreams; they were vivid

scenes unfolding that I could *feel*, for the moments they lasted.

I attempted to open every door I encountered. Almost all were locked, but my persistence paid off. I found a library, its towering shelves crammed with books. In the heart of the palace, there was a courtyard with a lush, secluded garden. I couldn't afford to linger. I needed to keep my mind busy. If I lingered, my thoughts would start to wander, and I wasn't ready to face more of them.

Not yet.

I pressed on, descending a massive, sweeping staircase, eventually reaching the foyer on the first floor. I craned my neck, studying the painting covering the vaulted ceiling. It depicted a battle. The artist had frozen the moment of chaos, capturing its intensity.

A lone round table accentuated the room's emptiness. A gold and white vase on top held amethyst-colored flowers. My fingertips brushed against the petals, leaving a trace of silvery purple dust. "Beautiful," I murmured.

I pushed one of the heavy double doors open and stepped outside. The temperature was perfect—not too warm, not too cold. I'd have to ask someone about that. What was with the unpredictable weather? Thankfully, today it was in my favor.

A breeze played with tendrils of my hair as I gazed upward. Never before had I seen a more beautiful structure. Hades' palace stood impossibly tall, commanding attention. Balconies and pillars adorned its sides, and windows crafted from stained glass added a touch of color to the black palace. My cheeks ached from smiling. *Liberation.* It was a strange word, and an even stranger feeling. I reveled in it. While I had bound myself to the God of the Underworld… this was a freedom I'd never experienced.

There was an expanse of flowers outside the palace,

releasing a heady perfume into the air. I walked along a cobblestone path lined with neatly trimmed shrubbery toward what appeared to be a village. Beyond it, the land-scape rose into the foothills of dark mountains. It would be good for me to explore the Underworld. Necessary, even. I didn't have any plans to leave soon, even if Hades let me. My head moved on a swivel as I walked. I needed to stay aware.

As I approached the homes, laughter and music wove their way into my ears. It was a recognizable combination but not entirely familiar. Small homes similar to the one I'd broken into littered the village in front of me. They were scattered with no distinct pattern. Between the houses lay a patchwork of open cobblestone, moss, and small booths carrying a variety of handmade trinkets, from crystals to books.

A pair of young-looking souls raced past me. A smile played on my lips. I weaved through the bustling community, and eyes tracked my every step. When our gazes met, the onlookers would offer silent nods before casting their eyes downward.

"Lady Persephone?" A gentle voice interrupted my thoughts from behind. Though the tone carried no menace, my muscles tensed. I spun on my heels to find a soul. The woman was petite, with short black hair framing her round face. "My name is Iris." She bowed. "I am a guide here in the Underworld."

"A guide?"

"I guide souls once they leave purgatory," Iris explained, motioning for me to join her. "Walk with me?"

I followed her instruction, and my steps fell in sync with hers.

"You are very much alive, but you are here in the Under-world. King Hades instructed me to show you how things work around here. The Underworld can be a dangerous place."

King Hades? Gods, he is arrogant. I let her keep talking, allowing the conversation to remain one-sided as we strolled through the community.

"When someone dies, from any realm, they come to the Underworld. They automatically get a coin that allows them to cross the Styx River, guided by Charon's ferry." Iris looked over at me, and I nodded. I didn't let her see how uncomfortable the mention of that godsforsaken river made me.

"When the souls get off the boat, they are forced to confront the worst things they've done."

My head jerked. I'd read what little the Olympian Library offered about the Underworld, but the scraps were vague. A veil of secrecy surrounded the realm and Hades himself, but I knew the most important thing. Mother did not have access to this realm like she did the others, and she made sure to complain about it often. Even though I couldn't use my magic, she often forgot I had ears. I absorbed every word of her conversations, and I'd never heard of *purgatory*.

"Except those who die by suicide. Special treatment and help are given to those souls. All others go through the purgatory stage."

"Purgatory." I half mumbled the word.

"Yes, they learn their lessons. When they finish, a guide like me greets them and helps them find a place to stay."

"Where are those in…" I paused. "Purgatory?"

"Well, there are many levels of the Underworld. The deeper the level, the longer the purgatory stage. They reflect and reckon with their pasts."

"Are there people who never end that stage?"

"Some," she responded.

Where was Basile?

"Up on this level, you are mostly safe, but do not wander

too far, and stay away from any rivers. There are many communities on this level."

I wouldn't be touching another river for a long, long time.

"Stay where the souls are. Otherwise, you may find yourself wandering too far. This land is ever-changing."

I nodded, my lips forming a tight line. "This realm seems to stretch on forever." I glanced out into the distance.

"The Underworld has no end." Iris looked flustered for a moment, rushing over her words. "I must go. My duties call."

"Wait." I stepped forward. "I have a question."

She turned. "Yes, Lady Persephone?"

My mind flashed back to the cat in the house I first stayed in and the empty cabinets. "Do souls eat?"

Her eyes crinkled at the corners. "Unfortunately, no." Her gaze drifted for a moment. "I do miss food. Is that all?"

"I saw a cat when I first came here. It was alone."

She nodded. "In a home?"

"Yes."

Her expression softened. "It's waiting on its owner. They may be in purgatory or still living. Love doesn't end just because life does. If they loved that cat in life, they'll love it here too."

I swallowed hard. My fingers toyed with the hem of my sleeve. Even in a realm built from endings, some bonds continued despite them. It was reassuring to know it wasn't abandoned. "Thank you."

Iris disappeared.

I wandered around the community. I lost track of the hours, mentally cataloging every new plant or animal I encountered. This was a realm like I'd never imagined. I found a small black bench and observed the souls from a distance. They were a mix—mortals, faeries, vampires, and beings whose origins remained uncertain to me. The dynamics of their coexistence were fascinating. I scarcely noticed the passage of time until the suns painted the horizon with strokes of amber and rose.

Small orbs created a dance of floating lights in the air. I leaned forward. They emitted a low, steady hum that resonated deep within me. Their purple hue shifted between a deep violet and a softer lavender. My eyes darted back and forth between them. I couldn't look away.

A tingle crept up my spine, raising the tiny hairs on the back of my neck. "Enjoying yourself?"

I jumped in my seat. That voice—smooth, low, and impossible to forget—could only belong to one person.

Hades.

A rush of emotions surged through me as I looked over my shoulder.

He stood behind me, a smirk curving his mouth. I refused to give him any satisfaction, so I said nothing. Silence was my only defense.

He sat on the bench. His large frame made it too small for both of us—suffocating. The dark wooden slats beneath us creaked under his weight. The warmth of his body encroached on mine, even as I inched over, my thigh teetering on the edge of the bench.

Still too close.

We sat for a few minutes, silence between us. I tried to ignore his presence and fix my gaze on the small, glowing orbs drifting before us, but a subtle shift—a small movement of his leg—made him the center of my attention. I couldn't resist. I watched him from the corner of my eye.

There was nothing soft about the way he looked at the purple orbs, as if they had wronged him.

It made me shiver.

He must've felt my eyes. Slowly, he turned his head.

Our eyes locked, his gray ones holding my mine like a hook. Something inside me stuttered. A tug at the deepest part of me. I turned away too fast, my breath hitching. I hoped he hadn't noticed.

Hades cleared his throat. "Spectral wisps," he said. "They change color based on who they are near." His voice smoothed back into neutral control.

I forced my voice to work. "What does purple mean?"

He hesitated, his gaze remaining forward, fixed on the orbs. His gloved fingers flexed once, twice. "Something truly awful." His lips thinned, and he placed his hands in his lap.

Still, he didn't look at me. I didn't dare ask what he meant.

Silence stretched between us. Then like a gust of shadow, he was gone, whisking away without a sound or warning.

The bench creaked with the absence of his weight. The wisps remained, drifting lazily before me. One moved closer, pulsing brighter than the rest. I reached out, but it floated away beyond my grasp.

HADES

*P*urple. I'd never hated the color so much. *Royalty.* I didn't need the wisps to confirm something I already knew—something that could never be.

For days, I'd watched Persephone. Maybe it was curiosity. Or just necessity, as I told myself. The Underworld was dangerous. She was inexperienced. I needed to ensure she didn't destroy anything. That was the excuse I clung to.

I didn't watch her constantly, but enough. Enough to learn the shape of her habits. She wasn't the pampered daughter of Demeter I'd expected.

In the short time, she went from rigid to not completely relaxed—but mostly. She was curious but cautious. She played with the animals and talked to a few souls. Through watching, I learned about her. It was a forbidden taste I shouldn't have indulged in, but I did anyway. She didn't know I was watching her. I made sure of it.

Persephone sat perched on an elongated stone bench in the courtyard. Steady gray light touched her skin. A spiraling mosaic of stones with clusters of flowers surrounded the bench. Despite the colors around her, she was the only thing that stood out to me. The blood-red, orange, purple, ivory, and green were no match to her.

She sat with her legs crossed and a white plate sitting in her lap. Seeing her dressed from head to toe in clothes I had selected for her stirred something dangerous inside of me. I knew every piece of clothing in her closet, down to the lingerie, and I regretted that.

Persephone wore a loose black blouse with two thin straps. I created a cool breeze in the courtyard. She shivered and bit her lip, rubbing her palms over her exposed skin.

The breeze passed, and she carried on savoring the yellow and orange pieces of fruit on her plate. Her eyelids fluttered closed for a fleeting moment, and I could only imagine the moan she'd likely let out. I never thought I'd learn so much by watching her. Persephone pushed her hair to the side and exposed one side of her neck. It was messy and still far-too alluring. My eyes paved a deliberate path from her face and down her neck.

I groaned. She was intoxicating. It was impossible to focus on anything but Persephone. She filled my every thought. I tried to pull away from her. It couldn't happen. I was only torturing myself by giving into my pull toward her. I wanted to touch her…

Whenever I tried to tug away from her, it only made me hungrier. *Maybe I should just fuck her until I'm sated.* I shook my head. I couldn't. Persephone wouldn't die. She was immortal, but I'd hurt her. It was safer to keep my distance.

I had never been one to choose safety over danger.

Since the Fates had given me the touch of death, I hadn't experienced intimacy. But with her presence in my realm, I realized I'd been merely waiting—for Persephone. Despite the revelation, I still couldn't have her.

My head fell back, and I sucked in a breath. I turned from the window. With one slow step in front of the other, I pushed myself to sit at my desk. My muscles coiled tight with tension; each step hurt.

I read the words on the paperwork in front of me, but they all blurred together. I blew out a breath, and my eyes darted to the window. The only thing I could focus on was the goddess sitting outside. It was like she knew my study was here. Like she *wanted* to taunt me out of my den to attack her. My thumb traced circles on the paper while the rest of my fingers tapped and twisted the edges of the sheets. I cleared my throat, placed my palms on my desk, and pushed myself up. The court could wait on their paperwork.

I walked back over to the window. Hermes stood in front of her. I muttered curses under my breath. She gazed up at him through her eyelashes, a small smile playing on her lips. That fucking god. Always drawn to things that had no business interesting him. A burning sensation filled my chest. I created another gust of wind—this one strong enough for Hermes to know it was a message from me.

He stilled as my magic moved over him. Persephone shivered. He took off his navy-blue jacket and placed it around her shoulders. Persephone held up her hands and shook her head. The way she protested put a smile on my face. *Good goddess.*

Hermes persisted, like he always did. Another gust swept through. Persephone rose from her seat as if she was making plans to come inside. Hermes glanced at my window, flashing a placid smile before putting an arm around Persephone and guiding her inside.

I picked up my darts and hurled them at the board.

One.

Two.

Three.

A forceful knock echoed through my study, and I knew it was Hermes. I could hardly believe his audacity to show up after that display. Through gritted teeth, I mumbled, "Come in."

My back remained turned. The door clicked loudly as it shut. Swinging around, I unleashed a knife made of shadow, hurtling it toward the god. It grazed his face, embedding itself in the wooden door behind him. His eyes widened, and Hermes raised his hands in surrender. "Relax," he urged.

I couldn't, and that was the issue. "Stay away from her with your filthy cock." In Olympus, Hermes was a notorious player. Even before the Titan War, back when I still lived there, it was a well-known fact. His free time was filled with the company of new women, one after another. He wouldn't be good for the goddess. Nor would I, but the thought of him with her made me want to find ways to end his immortal life.

"My cock isn't filthy because I use it a lot. Maybe if you got laid, you wouldn't be such a prick." Hermes smirked.

His words instigated another knife thrown at him, this time grazing the other side of his face.

"Stop, Hades. Don't damage this thing." He patted his face, still using that joking tone that irritated every piece of me. "I'm not interested in the goddess."

My chest heaved shallow breaths as I stared at the god.

Hermes waved a hand. "I like messing with you."

"It would be wise not to mess too far." My words were slow and steady.

His smirk fell. Hermes took my threat seriously. I saw it in his face, but he brushed it off like it meant nothing. He shrugged. "I'm just being friendly with her, that's all."

I began to tell him how friendly I could be too, but he cut me off.

"I came to tell you Demeter has threatened to shut off the food supply to the mortal realm if her daughter doesn't return to her."

"She's bluffing," I responded. Demeter was power hungry

and twisted, but she was more calculated than that. Shutting the food supply would be a rash decision. The mortal realm was important. It was the neutral ground among all the realms, essential for maintaining the cosmic balance. Any disruption to the it would lead to not only the suffering of mortals but escalate conflicts between the Divine and beings from other realms.

"I don't know, Mr. Doom and Death." Hermes tried to lighten the mood, but all it did was irritate me. "She seems serious. I don't know why she wants Persephone so much when she treated her daughter badly enough to make her run to the land of the dead. Most other realms will be fine without Demeter's help, but the mortals are in danger."

As much as I wanted to defend my realm, I didn't argue. I knew the Goddess of Spring did not belong here, but self-ishly, I liked her in my realm.

"I will think about it," I responded. "Thank you."

I sat back at my desk.

"Hades."

I glanced up.

"You can have the goddess. I didn't think it would be a big deal to ruffle your feathers."

I shook my head. "It could never be. Thank you for bringing me the information." I wanted him out of my hair. At the end of the day, Hermes was loyal to only himself. That was why he made a fine messenger between the Divine, but that also meant I needed to watch my back.

11

PERSEPHONE

I'd been in the Underworld for a week now. Seven whole days. Hades had been absent since our encounter with the wisps in the village. There was no explanation, no brooding or giving me that unreadable stare. Just… silence.

I'd tried to distract myself from him and from my own magic, burying myself in books, wandering the stone halls until my legs ached, lingering in the courtyard.

It didn't work.

The time had come. I couldn't delay learning my magic any longer.

Mother never sent me to school. I'd had a private tutor for as long as I could remember, but magic lessons were never part of the strict curriculum. I longed for the chance to have learned, to have prepared. But wishing wouldn't change my present reality. I'd have to teach myself.

I made sure not to stray too far from the small community of souls near the palace but ventured far enough to find my own space. I stood on a patch of moss in a clearing between some trees. The wind picked up loose tendrils of my hair. I cleared my mind. Images of the last time I'd wielded magic flooded my thoughts—the tingling energy surging through my veins, the subtle vibration beneath my skin. I tried to call on it.

Nothing.

My eyelids clamped together, producing flickering tiny white dots from the pressure. They parted, and the surge of brightness made me squint.

I let out a long breath. "This is ridiculous." I kept walking. Stepping out of the clearing, I ventured deeper into the dense thicket. I followed a narrow, earthy path only wide enough for one foot in front of the other. Sticks crunched under my boots and mingled with the sound of the gentle breeze rustling the leaves on the trees.

The wind picked up. Opaque fog blanketed the ground and gathered at my feet. I turned around, retracing my steps. Growing thicker with each passing moment, the fog ascended until I could no longer see. I slowed my steps, using the toe of my boot to probe the path, careful not to trip.

Something pulled at me.

All my visibility disappeared. I looked down, and I couldn't see my feet or my arms—or anything. The fog, which had been white and then gray, darkened further to black. I battled the instinct to shut down and kept walking.

An uncomfortable, painful buzz crawled across my skin. I thrashed, but there wasn't anything holding me. My breaths turned heavy, attempting to compensate for my shallow ones. An unseen force yanked my body, and a guttural scream escaped my lips. Not gently. Not gradually.

A thick haze settled over my mind—like the one I'd felt when I first arrived in the Underworld, whispering *you don't belong here.*

As I stood rooted in place, my head grew dizzier with each passing minute. I pressed my thumbs into my temples and groaned. My head swarmed, but I took a step forward anyway.

Every part of me itched, and my skin prickled like I'd walked through thick cobwebs. I rubbed my palms against my arms. I shuddered, unable to shake off the discomfort.

My eyes slowly adjusted to the darkness. Faintly glowing bioluminescent plants covered the uneven ground and clung to the twisted trunks of trees, providing a hint of light.

Though some of the details remained obscured, I could make out the silhouette of a towering gate resembling the one at the entrance of the Underworld. I drew closer. My arm lifted involuntarily, and I couldn't put it down.

"Do you feel it, child? You're made of it." The voice laughed. "Energy so pure."

Despite my desire to stop walking, the force dragged me closer and closer. There was a series of wailed moans. My head whipped around. They continued, coming from behind the gate. "The Goddess of Spring in the Underworld? My, my, my, Hades has gotten himself into some trouble," a different voice said with a low chuckle.

"Goddess of Spring, have you ever met a Titan?" another voice asked.

My spine stiffened. I fought against the pull with all my strength, but the invisible force persisted. I knew about the Titans. I'd read about them in the library.

Invisible hands guided my every movement. "Release us from this prison, goddess. We've been in Tartarus for far too long," another voice whispered.

"Enough!" I yelled, but they continued. My fingers stretched forward. A large white stone with jagged edges—a shard of a much larger piece—was embedded where the two gates met. It was iridescent with shades of blue and gray, shimmering despite the low light. My fingers grazed the stone. It was cool to the touch but pulsated with a strange warmth. A shiver rippled through me. The edges pressed into my skin.

The stone glowed, responding to my touch. At first, the warmth radiating from the stone comforted me. But as moments passed, the warmth grew hotter and painful. Every instinct told me to pull away, to sever the connection. But it also felt like something else—*home*. It was a feeling I hadn't felt in a long time…

The energy swirled around me. I gritted my teeth. I used every ounce of force I could muster to pull away, but my hand stayed glued to the stone. The gates released a loud groan as the metal began to move.

"Persephone!" Hades' voice was sharp, cracking like a whip. "What do you think you're doing?" He yanked me away from the gate. I stumbled back with his gloved hand clasped around my arm. My gaze flickered between the visible anger on Hades' face and the gate. His brows knitted together in a deep scowl, all the harsh lines on his face sharpened.

I raised the hand that had touched the stone, a tingling sensation still lingering. My chest heaved, but I managed to get out a few words. "I don't know."

Hades gripped my arm tighter. We whisked, our surroundings shifting. A blink later, we stood in my room. I tried to take a step back from him, but his grip held me in place. I angled my head. "Let me go."

Hades' fingers flexed against me, and he pulled me closer. His gray eyes narrowed. "You dare try to command me?"

"Yes." My lip trembled. I closed my eyes and took a deep breath, but it proved to be a mistake. The smoky scent of leather intertwined with warm notes of amber, wrapping me like a cocoon. His smell was intoxicating. It stirred something deep within me.

"You don't get it, do you?" Hades didn't give me a chance

to answer before he continued. "You know nothing of what's at stake. Opening that gate could have been catastrophic."

I swallowed hard, struggling to find my voice. "I didn't know what I was doing. Something pulled me."

Hades ran his free hand through his tousled hair. He released me, and I fell backward onto my bed. A tingling sensation spread through my arm as circulation returned. He took a step closer. My fingers tightened on my duvet. "You are reckless. Do you have any idea what kind of power you were meddling with?"

I shook my head, a sinking feeling gripping me. "I couldn't resist it."

Curiosity kindled in his eyes, but it was gone quickly. Hades let out a breathy chuckle. "Of all people, I thought you would know of the pieces of the stone." He crossed his arms. "Considering your mother's fascination with them."

I sat up, hands still clenching my duvet. "The stone?" Was he talking about the stone I'd just touched?

His eyes narrowed. "The only thing I need you to focus on is learning how to use your magic. You are a liability, goddess."

"That's what I was trying to do today. How did I get there? I was in a thicket, then I wasn't." My words were breathier than I'd intended them to be.

Hades shook his head. "The Underworld is ever-changing, as Iris should've told you. I will have a word with her about—"

"She told me." The words burst out sharper than I'd intended.

"And you chose to ignore her?" His voice was a low growl.

"I didn't wander far. I wanted to learn my magic."

"You traveled between layers of the Underworld to Tartarus."

"I'm trying my best, Hades." I pushed myself up from the

bed, chin lifting. "You may think these things are obvious, but they are not."

His lips thinned, his expression a mask of cold disapproval. "Try harder."

I flinched, heat crawling up my neck, all the way to my cheeks, burning with the kind of shame that made me wish I could just disappear. "You're horrible." It came out quiet. Pathetic, even.

He huffed a humorless laugh. "I've been called far worse." Hades scowled at me and whisked out of the room.

I stood in silence, my heart hammering. But my body didn't care. It didn't care that he scolded me. That he called me a liability. That I hated the way his voice made me feel small and seen all at once.

I'm not attracted to him. I'm not attracted to him. I'm not attracted to him. Though the words repeated on a loop, they felt no less like a lie. "I'm insane," I whispered. My head lowered, shoulders tense.

This wasn't normal. It *couldn't* be.

The heat pulsing low in my belly had no permission, no invitation. It was wrong. Hades was cruel, cold, infuriating. And yet, images of him pushed their way into my mind. The scent of him clung to my clothes. I stared at the wrinkled, rumpled folds of the duvet on the bed, the way the creases formed a spiderweb of lines. Some were shallow, others deep. The longer I stared, the more it looked like a map.

I needed the lines to distract me. Because the second I stopped focusing on them, he'd come back into my mind.

And he did.

I sprawled back on the bed, staring at the ceiling as if it might deliver mercy. My hands betrayed me, traitorous things, gliding over the places his gloved fingers had once been. I let them wander, slow, reverent, pretending they were his. Each phantom touch set fire beneath my skin.

For a few moments, it was sweet. It felt *good*.

But the high faded fast, and all that was left in its place was shame. Cold. Heavy.

What is wrong with me? I sat up, nausea curling low in my stomach. My fingers trembled as I dragged them through my hair, trying to make sense of myself. I slapped my forehead once. Then again, harder, as if the action alone could exorcise him out of my system. "Get out," I hissed through clenched teeth. "Get out of my head."

12

PERSEPHONE

The door of Hades' study was ajar. I pushed it open, my body protesting the early hour. A yawn crept out of my mouth. Hades glanced up from the papers scattered across his desk, his gray eyes meeting mine with an emotion I couldn't decipher. Maybe curiosity, maybe annoyance. He gathered them into a neat stack. "Persephone."

Seeing Hades was strange. I had fought so hard to stop thinking about him. I'd chastised myself for most of the night. It was foolish. "What do you want? I don't appreciate being woken up so early." Glancing over my shoulder, I met Minthe's smug gaze in the doorway, her presence a reminder of the unwelcome interruption to my sleep.

Hades stood and strolled to the window, his footsteps silent. The first rays of dawn kissed the horizon. The amber glow reached him, caressing his form in a halo of light. It gave him a warmth I wasn't accustomed to.

Hades glared at me. "You're always so pleasant to be around," he said dryly.

My back straightened under the weight of his gaze, and I fought to rub the lingering traces of sleep from my eyes. I hadn't slept well. A sharp twinge ran through my back. My muscles were stiff from the hours of tossing and turning. Despite my curiosity about why Hades had called for me, I was too tired to summon the energy to truly care. "Can I go back to bed?"

Hades didn't answer my question but turned. "Minthe, you're dismissed."

"Yes, my king." She flashed a nauseating smile before leaving.

Hades closed the distance between us. He stared at me, unwavering, as if he were searching for some hidden truth within me. "Persephone," he began, his voice low, "I don't think you're fully grasping the arrangement we have here." He took another step closer to me.

I swallowed hard. My sluggish mind snapped to attention.

Hades hooked a finger under my chin and forced my eyes to his. "You do what *I* say. You don't ask me *why*. You are bound to me." His voice came out like a purr. Each syllable was a deliberate taunt, a reminder of the power he wielded over me. The words dripped with arrogance. I wanted to lash out, but I froze under his scrutiny. I hated the way he could reduce me to this state with just a few well-chosen words. "With that mark on the back of your neck to prove it," he finished.

My hand flew to the back of my neck. I rubbed the skin, and a tingling sensation bloomed under my touch. My eyes narrowed. "What mark?" I demanded.

Hades smiled. It was the first time I'd seen it reach his eyes. He let go of my chin and stepped back. With a wave of his hand, his magic wove an intricate pattern that mirrored the design etched into the Underworld's golden coins.

The symbol twisted and writhed in the air. Power pulsed from it, and I could not look away. Then his hand fell, and the vision unraveled into nothing. Gone—yet branded into me, scorched behind my eyes. "You belong to me."

I trembled against my mind's own wishes. "I belong to no one."

"Except me," he added. "You would do well to remember your place in my realm. You may be a goddess, but I am the ruler of the Underworld." I stayed quiet, unsure of what to say. He cleared his throat. "I have asked Hecate to help you with your magic. There's something amiss with it."

The sudden shift in conversation was jarring, but I was glad to have moved on from his display of power. "What's wrong with it?" I asked.

"I can sense a block on your magic." He ran a hand through his hair. "Hecate specializes in these kinds of things. My realm is far too dangerous to have you here without control."

He was right, but I wouldn't tell him that. Hades grabbed my arm and whisked us to the courtyard.

The twin suns were higher in the sky but were far from fully ascended. Hecate sat on the bench in the center of the courtyard, and she rose with a smile. "Ah, good, you're finally here." She hurried over to me, her hand reaching out to grasp mine. I pulled back, not allowing her to touch me. She paused and gestured for me to follow her. We walked to a section of the courtyard with a circular patch of moss nestled off the stony ground. "Sit."

I did as she said, sitting with my legs crossed and my hands in my lap. I glanced behind me. Hades still stood across the courtyard—watching. I turned to Hecate and tried to ignore the feeling of his eyes boring into the back of my skull. *Focus on the moss, Persephone.*

I ran my fingers through the moss, rubbing a small piece between my thumb and index finger, savoring the feeling of the velvety fibers. It was moist with the remnants of morning dew, but offered enough dryness to provide a comfortable seat.

"Persephone." Hecate's voice broke through my thoughts.

I looked up at her. "Huh? S-sorry," I stammered, and dropped the small piece.

She raised a brow and puckered her lips. "Are you all right? You seem a little distracted."

I forced a smile. "I'm okay."

"If you say so." Hecate's features softened, the tension in her brow easing. Her lips curved into a small hesitant smile. She made herself comfortable, mirroring my own position. With a gentle sigh, she reached out, her hand resting lightly on mine. I tensed, my instincts screaming at me to recoil. "Persephone, you know you can confide in me," she said softly.

I met her gaze but looked away quickly. "Can I?" The words slipped out before I could stop them. "Can I really trust any Divine?" I bit the inside of my cheek. I couldn't let myself forget. I didn't know much about Hecate, but knowing she was a court member was enough.

"I understand your doubts." Her eyes softened more. *Pity.* "I want to help you."

I tugged at my sleeve and pulled it over my hand. I glanced over my shoulder at Hades and back at Hecate.

"Hades," Hecate yelled.

Hades made his way across the courtyard to us. I didn't need to look at him. I could feel his presence behind me. "Yes," he said, his voice a low rumble that made every muscle in my body light up.

I closed my eyes. He was too much.

"I think we'd like some privacy. I'll make sure Persephone goes back inside when we're done." Hecate pointed to the door.

"If you insist," Hades said. In an instant, the energy shifted around me, the telltale sign of his departure.

I let out a long breath, and my shoulders sagged. Hades was gone, and I could finally breathe again.

"Are you all right?" she asked.

"I'll be fine." I chewed on the inside of my lip. "Can we get on with this?"

Hecate nodded. "You don't have to face this alone, Persephone." She clasped her hands together.

My stomach tightened, but I nodded. I'd faced everything alone. That would not change.

"I know you don't trust me. I can sense it, and that's fine." Hecate paused. "You don't have to trust me, but please do your best to cooperate so you can learn how to use your magic." She pushed a piece of hair away from her face. "For you, Persephone. Learn for you."

"I'll try." I straightened my posture. "Mother never taught me anything." The word *mother* felt wrong to use. As a Divine, your powers didn't emerge until your early teens. I'd had access to it for a week before she changed, and the pills started. I was twenty-three now with no control over my magic.

"I see," she murmured. "Hades told me you've used your magic."

"A few times. When I needed it."

"So your emotions triggered it. Let's see if you can call it without that."

"I'll do my best."

Hecate smiled. "That's all I ask." She closed her eyes. "Now, let's get started."

A strange tingling gnawed at the edges of my consciousness. I grew lightheaded as her purple magic prodded. I closed my eyes, seeking solace from the uncomfortable feeling. A sense of peace washed over me, and I relaxed. I opened my eyes, and her magic disappeared.

"Your body is trying to protect you by keeping your walls thick."

"Is there anything you can do for that?" My fingers tapped against my leg.

"You need to meditate."

I scoffed at the suggestion. "You seriously think meditation will solve all my problems?" I asked with a chuckle.

Hecate didn't laugh. "You don't trust others, but you also don't trust yourself. Meditation will help you learn how to trust and exist in a life that is solely your own."

"All right," I murmured. "How do I do it?"

"Okay." Hecate's smile returned. "Close your eyes and focus on your breathing."

I followed her instructions, even though it was difficult. With each breath, my mind grew more chaotic, racing from one thought to the next. "How do I stop my mind from wandering?" I peeked through my eyelashes.

"You don't. Redirect your thoughts back to your breath."

I watched the rise and fall of Hecate's chest before closing my eyes again.

After a few minutes, Hecate spoke. "Now I want you to visualize a pool of energy at the center of your being. This is your magic, waiting to be unleashed."

I conjured an image of shimmering light in my mind's eye. With each breath, the pool of energy grew brighter and more vibrant.

"Now," Hecate continued, "I want you to reach out to that energy, to connect with it on a deeper level. Feel its warmth and strength flowing through you like a river of light."

As I delved deeper into the visualization, reaching out to the pool of energy within me, I expected to feel a surge of power, a spark of magic igniting within my core.

Nothing.

No warmth, no strength, just an empty void inside me.

I kept trying. I pinched my lips together and sighed.

Hecate's voice broke through the silence. "Keep trying, Persephone," she urged. "You're closer than you think. You've used this magic before when in danger. Tell your body you are safe."

You are safe. I repeated the affirmation for minutes, but I still didn't believe it.

Nothing still.

My jaw ached from clenching. I opened my eyes and found Hecate's still closed. "I'm sorry," I whispered. "I just can't seem to feel anything."

She sighed. "It's all right, Persephone. It takes practice. Practice this every day." Hecate stood up and offered me a hand. "Hopefully, next session we'll have you using your magic."

Hecate pulled me to my feet and drew me into a quick hug. The scent of gardenia clung to her like a heady veil. "Thank you," I said steadily, though I couldn't disguise the tension running through me.

"Come. Let me walk you back inside."

13

―――――

PERSEPHONE

I sat in the greenhouse. Lush plants surrounded me and brought me joy like they always had. Light trickled in through the stained-glass ceiling, producing a colored glow on the plants. I'd helped Mother pick each color. They worked together to create an image of different flowers.

"My lily." Mother's words took me out of my daze. Her soft touch on my hair made me relax. "I will be out for a few hours. Don't stay in here too long. The plants can live without you long enough for you to eat."

"But I love it in here." I looked up at her.

Her blonde hair twinkled underneath the colored light. A delicate smile graced her lips. Her brown eyes melted into pools of warmth. "I know you do."

I stood up, and she pulled me into an embrace. I breathed deeply, burrowing my head into her. Her lily scent comforted me. Don't leave! I wanted to say, but I kept my mouth shut. I knew she had to fulfill her duties as the Goddess of Harvest.

"Bye, Mother."

"Bye, my lily. Remember what I said."

I nodded, and she smiled at me. She chuckled as she left, knowing I probably wouldn't listen to her.

I sat in the greenhouse for another hour, tending to my plants. The white narcissus flower glistened when the droplets of water trickled on the petals. It was my favorite flower. It was ethereal in a way that didn't compare to the others. I stroked the petal, and it leaned into my touch. I looked over all my plants, making sure none needed anything else, when my stomach rumbled. Maybe I would listen to Mother, just this once.

When I finished eating, the sky was dark, and it couldn't be much longer until Mother returned. I walked over to the living room. My palms brushed the fabric of my clothes, making sure I didn't have anything on me before sinking into the couch. Mother had already scolded me for that before.

I was tired, but I still wanted to wait for Mother.

A door slammed. Who could that be? Mother did not slam doors.

Heavy footsteps became louder as they got closer. Mother stood in the doorframe, her usual cheery expression gone like it was never there. A swollen, crimson hue ringed her eyes.

"Mother, I waited up for you!" Joy bubbled in my voice, slowly dying at her troubled energy.

She pinched her nose and groaned.

"Mother, what's wrong?" My heart picked up in my chest. I walked over to her and placed my hand on her arm.

"Persephone, just shut up," she yelled. Mother shook her arm, and my hand fell. "Please." She rubbed the skin as if my touch hurt her.

"Did I do something wrong?"

She gave me a look that sent terror running through my body. My heart shrank in my chest, and my stomach clenched and turned. Mother struck my cheek, hard. It burned.

My face twisted and tears welled. One fell down my cheek eerily slow over my burning skin. I ran my hand across the painful skin. Her touch left my skin rough and bubbling. She used magic on me.

No. Mother wasn't like that. "Moth—" I tried to reason with her. My voice trembled.

"Do not speak to me unless you are asked to, Persephone."

My heart sank in my chest. She never called me Persephone. Only her lily. My knees were forced to the ground—not by my own will. I could feel the press of her magic on me again.

"Open your mouth," she commanded. Mother held a little orange bottle with a black lid that came off with a click when she twisted it. She pulled out a little pill, pressed it between my lips, and pushed it into my mouth. "Swallow." Tears fell down my face, but I did as told. "That's for being cursed," she said.

She paced back and forth. Her head shook, her hands pressed into her temples. I looked down when her gaze met mine. A sudden tug at my hair seared my scalp. Mother forced my eyes to meet hers. She looked down at me, her lips curling in disgust. Her eyes were cold, lacking all the life and love they once held. "You do as I say, or you will end up with the dead."

❧

HADES

The moonlight spilled through the windows, casting a soft glow over Persephone's sleeping form. She tossed and turned, her movements agitated. Persephone's brow furrowed in the grip of another nightmare. She'd had them every night since her session with Hecate a week ago.

I told myself the nightmares were good. Better to be broken open than sealed tight against her magic. This way, at least, something spilled out. So I watched from the shadows.

She screamed in her sleep as she thrashed against the

sheets. With a heavy sigh, I stepped closer to her bedside. Persephone's distressed whispers—fragments of words and memories—spilled from her lips in a disjointed stream of consciousness. I pushed back the strands of hair clinging to her sweaty forehead, then wiped the tear glimmering on her cheek with my gloved thumb. Lifting it, I studied the drop as the light of the moons caught on its trembling surface. I hated the salty little thing. I brushed it away on my pant leg. "Quiet, little goddess. You're safe, Persephone. I won't let anything harm you."

Her rushed, heavy breathing gradually evened out into a steady rhythm.

"Good." I rubbed her shoulder and pulled the duvet over her. A strange and uncharted feeling tightened in my chest. Even through the Titan War and the challenges of being assigned to this realm, I had never felt anything like this before. This bond ran deeper than she knew. For years, I had shut off my feelings, but now they surged to the surface. I closed my eyes and took a deep breath, forcing them back. The breaking open that would set her free was never meant for me.

14

PERSEPHONE

I felt it yesterday—a faint pulsating energy coursing through my veins. It took two weeks of practice before feeling anything at all. I swallowed my pride and confided in Hades since I didn't have a choice. I didn't know how to contact Hecate myself. I needed answers, even if it meant placing some trust in the hands of the Divine.

I followed Minthe to the courtyard. I tried to ignore her, but it proved difficult. The fabric of her dress rustled with each step, a constant reminder of her presence. Her steps were purposeful. She held her chin high and her shoulders back. I kept my breaths shallow, unwilling to let her woody fragrance seep into my lungs.

I balled my hands into fists. I didn't need to see my palms to know my fingernails had created crescent indentations. "Breathe," I murmured to myself. I wouldn't let Minthe bother me at such an early hour. She was not worth the energy.

The cold morning air swept across my face as we stepped outside to the courtyard. Hecate wasn't here yet, but she'd come soon. Minthe's previously perfect hair whipped around. She sneered at the breeze. Her manicured fingers attempted to tame her unruly locks in quick, agitated gestures. The breeze continued to toy with her hair. I chewed on my lip to stifle my laugh. Minthe looked me up and down, her lip curling, before turning on her heel and stalking away without a word.

"Persephone." Hecate's voice cut through the quiet of the courtyard.

I turned, a small smile tugging at the corners of my lips as I met her gaze. "You're here." My voice came out just above a whisper, tainted by morning. I cleared my throat. "Thank you for coming."

Hecate offered me a warm smile in return, the edges of her eyes crinkling. "Of course. It's my pleasure." Hecate guided me back to the familiar spot on the moss we'd used last time. "I must say, I was excited to hear from Hades that you'd made progress."

We settled into a comfortable position on the ground. Hecate guided me through the familiar motions of meditation, her voice soft and soothing. With each breath, I sank deeper into a state of calm. In my practicing, I had improved at meditation, my mind more adept at quieting the constant chatter and distractions.

I searched for the pulsing energy I'd felt the previous day, delving deeper until I found it. "It's there," I whispered. "I can feel it."

"Good. Allow it to flow through your body. Let the feeling grow," Hecate said.

I focused on the pulsating magic coursing through me. A wave of fatigue washed over me, but I kept pushing. The magic surged.

"Excellent, Persephone. Keep focusing on that. How do you feel?"

"I'm not sure. I feel my magic, but the more I focus, the more tired I am."

"Let's try something different," Hecate said.

I let go of the feeling.

"Your stamina with magic will grow over time," she assured me, extending her hand. I hesitated for a moment before accepting her offer, allowing her to pull me upright with ease. "Let's try to use your magic."

My mouth dried. "Are you sure I'm ready for that?" I fumbled with the sleeves of my dress.

Hecate's gaze softened. "I wouldn't suggest it if you weren't." Her voice was firm but comforting. "Let's start with something simple. I want you to try to grow a plant. It should be one of the easiest tasks for someone with your abilities." She smiled. "I'll walk you through it."

A rush of dizziness washed over me, and my vision blurred at the edges. Hecate said something, but I couldn't hear over my pulse in my ears. I shook my head and took a deep breath. "I'm sorry. Can you start again?"

Hecate brushed a hair out of her face and nodded. "Close your eyes. At some point, you won't need to, but it will make things easier for now. I want you to find that energy inside you, like when we meditated, and envision a plant."

I swallowed and did as she said.

"Envision the way its roots spread into the ground, the way its leaves look."

The familiar surge of magic came easier this time. With each heartbeat, I focused on the task at hand, envisioning a small seedling taking root in the patch of soil among the stones of the courtyard. I peeked out of one of my eyes. Nothing.

"Try again," Hecate urged.

I continued to try again, over and over. With each

attempt, my movements grew slower, my muscles heavier. A deep weariness settled into my bones, the sinking feeling in my chest mirroring it. My shoulders drooped, but I gritted my teeth and tried once more.

Something shifted this time. I opened my eyes. A flicker of green appeared amid the patch of soil, a tiny sprout emerging. "I did it!" I turned to Hecate with a wide grin. My heart leaped as the seedling grew, energy jolting to my tired limbs.

"I'm proud of you, Persephone."

I looked at my small plant. It stood for a few seconds. But just as quickly as it had appeared, the leaves curled. The vibrant green faded to a dull brown. The stem sagged. All its vitality drained away, leaving nothing but a small pile of its withered remains. "What happened?" I asked. "Did I do something wrong?"

Hecate placed a gentle hand on my arm. I didn't flinch away from her. "No, not at all." Hecate guided me over to a nearby bench. "Sit."

I laced my fingers together in my lap.

"You must understand, the magic of the Underworld is unlike anything you have encountered before. This is the realm of the *dead*. Life does not flourish here," she said. I gestured to the plants around us. Before I could get any words out, Hecate spoke. "All of this greenery around us, it's a figment of Hades' and the realm's magic."

I nodded, studying all the lush foliage surrounding us. I ran a leaf between my index finger and thumb. My fingertips trailed over a nearby flower. I'd learned about it in the Underworld's library—nebula orchids, native to this realm. The library here contained information the Olympian Library didn't. A single dewdrop balanced on the edge of the shimmering purple petal, magnifying the veins threading through the plant. "Amazing." I had spent my entire life around plants, the one luxury Mother afforded me. How had I not noticed these were Hades' magic?

"For now, let's focus on being able to consistently use your magic, then I will teach you some tricks to keep your plants alive."

I continued gazing at all the foliage. "This is incredible. To think that all of this—"

"—is but a mere illusion. But an illusion doesn't mean it isn't real," Hecate finished. I tried to process her words. How could an illusion be real? She sighed, her gaze drifting toward the sky where the twin suns had risen. "As much as I'd like to stay longer, I must go."

"Thank you." I nodded, standing up to meet her.

"Call for me should you need anything," Hecate said. She whisked away.

As I wandered through the courtyard, I observed everything around me with keen interest. The vibrant colors, the delicate petals, the golden dust of pollen scattered at each flower's heart—it was all so breathtaking. It was meticulously crafted, from the clusters of dew-covered pink blooms to the small thorns running along strings of vines. And to think, it was all a product of Hades' magic.

"Admiring my handiwork?" Hades said from behind me.

I turned, fighting a smile. "I'm just marveling at how you manage to create something halfway decent."

Hades smirked. "So you admit it's decent."

The tease caught me off guard. This wasn't typical of him, and I was unsure how to respond. I hated that I noticed the way his eyes sparkled with amusement. I scoffed and crossed my arms. "Let's not get ahead of ourselves," I muttered, trying to smother the warmth leaking into my voice.

"So stubborn," he mused, stepping closer. His gaze lasered on me in a way that made my pulse quicken, like he was reading every microexpression, every stutter of my breath. It wasn't flirtatious. Just… focused.

I didn't retreat, but every inch of my body went still. He was standing close enough now that I could see the shift of light across his face, the pull of tension in his jaw.

"Weren't you taught it's rude to stare?" I asked.

"It depends on the intent."

I hummed. "And what's yours?"

"Still figuring that out," he said.

Hades lifted a gloved hand slowly. A tendril of shadowy magic spiraled in his palm, folding in on itself until a single narcissus flower appeared.

He held it out to me.

"What's this for?" I bit the inside of my lip. His sudden softness unbalanced me, but I told myself not to read into it. Not to read into anything that had to do with him. Still, something fluttered unwelcomely in my chest.

Hades stayed silent for a few moments. "Consider it a gesture of… goodwill."

I stared at the flower for too long before I reached for it. My fingers brushed his glove as I took it, and my stomach flipped in a way I resented immediately. "Goodwill?" I twirled it between my fingers, then brought it to my nose. Despite it being a product of his magic, it still smelled and felt like a true narcissus flower. "Do you give unsolicited flowers to all your palace guests?"

"Only the particularly irritating ones."

And still, his eyes never left me.

"I don't need your gifts." I shook my head and thrust the flower back toward him.

Hades rolled his shoulders. The flower I held in my hand disappeared into black shadowy magic. "You wound me, little goddess." His words were a low, dangerous murmur.

I forced myself to meet his eyes, even though my heart rattled against my ribs. "Good."

For a few heartbeats, we just stood there, neither moving. Then, without another word, he disappeared.

15

HADES

As I approached, I took in every detail of Persephone. The way her brow furrowed in concentration, the way her fingers trembled ever so slightly as she attempted to channel her magic—it was both maddening and mesmerizing.

I watched her in the courtyard from the window of my study for hours every day. Despite having arranged another session with Hecate, I couldn't bear to watch her kill the plants any longer. The frustration etched into her delicate features every time the plant died was unbearable.

"Put more power behind your magic," I said. Persephone met my gaze with those familiar brown eyes that appeared in my mind when I closed my own. Just as quickly, she looked away.

"What are you doing here?" she asked sharply.

"This is my realm. I can go wherever I wish," I replied with a smile.

"You know what I mean." Persephone fidgeted with the hem of her dress.

I took a step closer, unable to resist the pull toward her.

"Do I?" I shouldn't have come down here. I told myself it was just about the plants, and that had been a lie.

"Don't you have something else to do besides bother me?" She brushed her hair out of her face with a soft sigh. "I'm busy, Hades."

Persephone attempted to walk away, but I blocked her path. "Busy killing all those plants you keep growing."

Her cheeks warmed slightly under my intense scrutiny. She shifted uncomfortably. "Your realm is killing them." There was a small tremor in her voice as she spoke.

I chuckled and resisted the urge to reach out to her. Persephone was determined, I'd give her that. But determination alone wouldn't be enough. She needed a little push in the right direction.

She conjured another plant. The leaves curled and browned. Within moments, the dark color followed through the rest of the plant until it dissipated into nothing. "Use your power to create a shield around it," I instructed. "Visualize your shield covering the part of the plant you can see and all the roots."

Persephone said nothing. She nodded, her gaze flickering between me and the wilted plant before us. With a deep breath, she closed her eyes, concentrating once more.

She grew another plant, this one with a faint shimmer of energy enveloping it. It stayed for a moment or two but then faltered, and the plant died. "I thought I had it," Persephone murmured.

"Try again."

Persephone rubbed the mark on the back of her neck before attempting. She tried three more times. "You're not concentrating enough," I said as she struggled once more. "You need to focus, Persephone. You can't let your mind wander." My words came out harsher than I'd intended, less instruction and more frustration.

I hated how she flinched.

"And how am I supposed to focus with you here?" Persephone's cheeks flushed a deeper shade of red, the rosy hue spreading from her cheeks to the curve of her neck. "I mean—"

"Am I *that* distracting?" I meant the question as a joke. Mostly. But the heat in her cheeks made something twist inside me.

Her eyes widened slightly. "You're *that* irritating."

I almost smiled.

She shook her head, her expression pained. "I'm trying. It's not as easy as you make it sound." Persephone's hand went to her forehead as she squeezed her eyes shut, swaying where she stood.

Instinct overrode thought—I reached out and gripped her shoulder, steadying her before I could think better of it. "What's wrong?"

"I get tired when I do magic. That's all." But her eyes revealed an uncertainty she couldn't hide from me.

"You're done for the day." I guided her away from the courtyard. Usually, she'd stiffen at my touch or shoot a snarky remark at me, but this time she stayed silent. That alone unsettled me. It was clear she needed rest. Pushing her any further would only do more harm than good.

I whisked her to her room, and she climbed into bed, her movements sluggish and labored. Her eyelids drooped, and she made no attempt to resist sleep. Her chest rose and fell, her breathing soft.

My jaw clenched as I tried to push aside the uneasiness settled in my gut. This level of fatigue wasn't normal, even for someone inexperienced with magic like Persephone. There was something more at play here.

16

———

PERSEPHONE

My footsteps were soft against the stone floors. My stomach grumbled. Fatigue had taken a toll on me, and I'd slept for most of the day. "Quiet, we're going to eat soon," I said to myself. Laughter drifted out of the dining room as I grew closer. I recognized the timbre of Hades' voice mingling with obnoxious, high-pitched laughter.

Minthe.

I stepped into the room. Hades sat alone at the table with a stack of papers. Minthe set a drink in a short glass before him, lingering in her bent position to give him a good look at her low neckline. "You work too hard, my king," she purred with artificial honey.

I tried to ignore the burning in my chest and forced myself to look away. I couldn't stomach the sight of them together. Candles flickered, casting soft shadows onto the wood walls. They didn't help distract me like I'd wanted.

Hades cleared his throat. He turned away from her, sipping on his drink.

Minthe straightened and walked out of the room with a scowl on her face.

The sight of Minthe flirting shamelessly with Hades made my stomach churn, and the thought of food grew unappealing. I turned on my heel, but before I could take a single step, shadowy magic wrapped around my waist, pulling me back into the room against my will. "Hades," I yelled. "Let me go."

Hades' magic pulled me until I reached the chair across from him. "Sit," he said. Before I could protest or resist, his magic pulled the chair back and guided me into it. The force of the shadows left me with no choice but to comply. Hades regarded me with an amused smirk. "I was hoping you'd be up around now. You must eat."

"Bossy," I said through gritted teeth. Several souls entered the room with two plates of food, glasses, and a basket of bread and fruit. A medley of aromas wafted through the air— roasted meats, savory potatoes, and freshly baked bread.

Hades shoved his stack of papers aside and drained the last of his drink. A soul took the used glass while another set down full plates and empty, stemmed glasses. A third soul cradled a bottle of faerie wine in his hands. He tilted Hades' glass and filled it halfway before moving to pour into mine.

"Absolutely not. Persephone is not to have faerie wine."

The soul recoiled. "Apologies, my king."

"She is to have water," Hades said.

I managed a tight smile and placed my palms on the table, my eyes narrowing on the drink. "And what if I want faerie wine?"

"It's too strong for you," Hades said as he took a sip of his.

"Is this part of binding myself to you? You control what I drink now too?"

Hades smirked. "You seem to keep forgetting who rules this realm."

"You're arrogant." My voice wavered slightly. I lifted my chin, meeting his gaze with as much defiance as I could muster.

Hades raised an eyebrow, a smirk playing at the corner of his lips. Amusement flickered across his eyes, only fueling my irritation.

I bit the inside of my cheek. "Is something funny?"

He leaned back in his chair, utterly relaxed. "Only you, Persephone. You're entertaining."

I groaned. "You're rude. Add that to the list."

"And handsome?" Hades' fingers traced the rim of his glass.

If I'd said no, I would've been lying. "Don't be so sure of yourself."

He chuckled. "Oh, little goddess. I'm sure of very few things in this universe. But of you and me? I have never been more certain." His words hung between us, thick with meaning that begged to be unraveled. Hades' eyes bore into mine, silently inviting me to ask what he meant. But I held my ground, refusing to give him the satisfaction.

"Don't tell me you're tired of talking now." The challenge was clear in his voice.

I stayed silent, meeting his smirk with my own forced smile. Hades cleared his throat. "It's not a good idea to drink while you are experiencing symptoms of fatigue." A soul filled my glass with water. The clear liquid shimmered with the reflection of candlelight. I didn't bother protesting. It was no use, and Hades had a point, as much as I didn't want to admit it.

My movements were stiff and awkward as I ate. Every bite was a struggle. It was like an invisible thread connected us. All I could focus on was his presence and the intensity of his gray eyes. We sat in silence, other than the occasional soul asking if we needed anything, the clinking of silverware, and the soft rustle of fabric as I shifted in my chair. *Why do I feel like this?* I gripped my fork so tightly, my knuckles turned white.

"You're quiet," Hades mused.

I didn't look up from my plate. "I'm hungry."

"You're a terrible liar."

I took another bite of my food, examining it as if it could solve all my problems. His gaze was too strong. "I don't feel like talking."

He leaned forward. "Are you afraid of what you might say?"

"No."

All Hades did was chuckle. He was correct. I was a terrible liar. I picked at my food until my plate was empty. I glanced up at the glass ceiling. The twin moons were high overhead with a sky full of twinkling stars behind them. Even the beautiful display did little to distract me.

I made a mistake.

I looked at Hades.

The soft candlelight accentuated the sharp angles of his face. I bit the inside of my cheek until a coppery tinge filled my mouth. "Is something wrong?" he asked, lifting his glass. He drank slowly, and my gaze betrayed me, fastening on his lips.

"No," I said too quickly.

The souls came in and removed everything from the table. "I hardly believe that," Hades said.

"Why do you make them do this?" I gestured to the souls cleaning up our mess. "When you could so easily take care of it with your magic?"

"Sometimes, it's better to let others handle the little things. It keeps them occupied, gives them purpose. You should not completely rely on your magic for everything. Everyone needs breaks."

I scoffed. Hades whisked and disappeared from his chair. Before I could react, his gloved fingers slipped through my hair. Gently. My back arched at the surprising touch. He grazed the mark on my neck. I shut my eyes and tried to release the breath stuck in my throat.

"Oh, little goddess," Hades whispered. My traitorous body leaned helplessly into his hand. His nearness was suffocating. "You ask so many questions… So curious."

As his fingers traced the curve of my neck, a wave of heat washed over me. My every nerve screamed for his touch. "Hades, I—"

"Shh." His voice was low. His fingers trailed from my neck to my lips. He placed a finger on my bottom lip. "Persephone." He spoke my name with a gravity that made the air itself feel weighted, each syllable drawn out in a strange inflection, unfamiliar, consuming. His touch smothered my senses until there was nothing left but him.

If it had been cold, I wouldn't have known.

If the palace had been on fire, I wouldn't have known.

All I knew was *him*.

A soft sigh left my lips. But just as the moment seemed poised to tip over the edge into something more, Hades pulled away, leaving me breathless. I twisted in the chair, glancing behind me. I was alone.

Just like that. Like none of it had happened. "I'm losing it," I whispered to myself.

I couldn't want him. But my body hadn't gotten the message. It had leaned in. Betrayed me.

Heat and confusion and pressure built beneath my skin. And it didn't stop. Not even after he had left the room.

17

HADES

I closed my eyes. *I need to get out of here.* I couldn't be in the same realm as Persephone. Adrenaline coursed through my tense body as I whisked to the mortal realm. The world blurred around me, twisting and distorting before snapping back into focus in a new location.

Joseph Macarter.

He would be first today.

I stood in Joseph's office, or "Joe," as his friends called him. It was likely larger than any other in this building, overlooking the city with floor-to-ceiling windows. Everything was too flashy. A large gold plaque sat at the head of his desk with *Dr. Macarter* engraved in a fancy script. Beside it was a gaudy, matching framed picture of his family. I picked it up and studied the group of four.

A wife and two girls, all blonde, the daughters resembling their mother. Joseph had his arm wrapped around his wife with a smile plastered on his face, like he wasn't a monster. On the outside, they looked like a perfect family, standing in front of a large perfect house on a neatly trimmed lawn.

What a shame. His wife was attractive by mortal standards, but not even comparable to my goddess.

I shook my head. I couldn't. *She cannot be my goddess.*

I didn't have to wait long—about four minutes. I could've gone and found him... but it was always better to have them come right to me.

The door handle jingled before it opened, and the disgrace of a man came in. What kind of man had a wife and children and a career as a doctor, and spent his days assaulting his patients and threatening them into silence?

A dead man walking.

As he stepped in, a waft of his cologne hit me. As I inhaled, the sandalwood invaded my senses so forcefully, it coated my tongue. Strange, for a doctor in a place meant to be scentless. Concealed in the shadow of a towering cabinet, I studied him as he settled his belongings on the desk. I whisked behind him, threw up a sound barrier, and yanked his arm.

I would make this quick. I had a list to get through. This was what that fucking goddess did to me. She made me crazy. This usually relaxed me—I enjoyed removing scum from the mortal realm—but all my mind could focus on was Persephone.

He screamed, like I had expected. My magic bound his limbs and gagged him. Joseph looked at me with glassy, wide eyes.

Control. I always had control.

Except around her.

Joseph tried to scream, but the gag prevented him from making more than a muffled sound. I ungagged him—I needed to hear him. I needed to feel something. Persephone's name was a relentless haunt in my mind. His screams were electrifying—exciting. I formed a knife made of shadow.

A vein in Joseph's neck and forehead protruded as he

screamed for help. His cries grew louder and more desperate when he noticed the knife. "I'll give you money," he panted. "Anything you want. Just let me go. I won't tell anyone this happened."

I pressed the knife to his neck. Satisfaction budded within me as his skin creased and the crimson fell from the fresh cut. "I'm not a petty criminal who wants money," I scoffed, and pressed the knife deeper.

"Just tell me what you want," he pleaded. Tears and snot streamed down his face.

"I'll be frank with you." My eyes stayed on the knife, tracing its edge as Joseph's presence thinned into background noise. "The only thing you could give me is your death, and even then, it wouldn't be enough."

He shook his head, forcing the knife pressed into his neck deeper. "Why?" The end of his question trailed off as fear laced his words.

"Joseph, did you truly believe you would escape the consequences of assaulting women? At their most vulnerable too. You were the person they were supposed to trust. But you sit in your fancy office, far too comfortable, collecting too much money."

"I didn't do anything." His voice trembled. They always tried to deny it.

I removed the knife. "I believe you."

His eyes widened, and his shoulders sagged in relief.

"Just kidding," I said with a chuckle. "All right, I don't have much time for this. See you in my realm, *Joey*."

I brought the knife across his throat and cut deep. Joseph's head slumped to the side, and a gurgling sound came out of him as he choked on his own blood. He wasn't dead yet, but he would be soon.

I released the bindings of my magic and pushed him. He fell to the floor with a loud thump. The blood from his throat didn't take long to soak into the tan industrial carpet. He would have an agonizing, slow death—that, I would make sure of.

On to the next.

Chandler Stockton, serial killer.

I whisked into his home and waited for him to return from his day job before he took more lives. This one rubbed under my skin a little more than normal. I wasn't sure if it was his actions that bothered me despite having grown numb to most things over the years, or if it was the goddess still lingering in my mind.

Chandler killed with what seemed like no motive. It baffled mortal police. They didn't understand him. He was an unpredictable attention seeker. I couldn't comprehend how they hadn't caught him yet. Chandler was sloppy. With that unpredictability came mistakes. I expected little from them, anyway. I was glad I'd be the one to deliver justice.

I tapped my fingers against my leg as I listened to his car door shutting and the gravel crunching under his feet through the pathetically thin windows. Perfect timing. I shifted on the gray love seat in his living room. It was lumpy and uncomfortable. The man had poor taste. The room appeared as if someone had selected its contents through a poorly executed game of chance. A love seat, a small tan sofa, and small trinkets littered on the coffee table around a lamp.

The door creaked as Chandler entered. He muttered some words about how badly his day had gone. I waited patiently. It was always more fun to surprise them.

His footsteps made their way through the kitchen on the tile. The clunky pitter-patter died when his feet touched the worn, shaggy brown carpet. I smiled at him and waited for his eyes to meet mine.

When they reached me, I wasn't disappointed. The hunter finally was hunted. Funny how that worked.

He turned to run, but he would never match the speed of a god. I whisked to him before he could even propel himself into a sprint, towering over him by two heads.

I prowled around him, my magic wrapping his body in a thick black rope. He choked on his screams and tried to fight my control. My prey's nostrils flared, and sweat beaded on his forehead, making his brown wavy hair stick to his face. Chandler's face contorted as my magic burned through him from the inside out.

I sensed Thanatos before I saw him. "Hades, don't play with him too long," he said, though he knew I wouldn't listen to him.

Thanatos wasn't always fond of my methods of torture, but he understood why I did this. Darkness spread quickly. I had to keep it contained, lest it consume me.

As my reaper, Thanatos held a unique connection to the Fates, guiding him to those whose lifelines were nearing their end. He eased their release and ushered death to those whose threads were naturally concluding, such as the sick or elderly.

It was more merciful for Thanatos to take them early, to press his hand over their eyes and hush them into silence, rather than leave them to time's cruelty. His magic was a dark lullaby.

I took a more direct approach, severing threads of the mortal scum and quickening their expiration. To cross uninvited into other realms and cut threads before their time would bring recourse, so for now, this realm would do.

I shot him a lazy smile. Blue and black marks appeared on Chandler's neck. Lack of oxygen had drained all the color from his face. I loosened my magic. I didn't want to end him too quickly. He had spent weeks murdering innocent people by suffocation, and his turn had come.

"How's Persephone?" Thanatos asked over Chandler's low whimpers, sitting on the lumpy love seat.

My magic didn't falter around the mortal, but my eye twitched. "She's all right." I kept my words short. I didn't want to think about the goddess, though the stubborn woman hadn't left my mind.

"She's all right," he mocked.

My eyes narrowed. "If this is what you came here about, you may leave." My magic returned to choking the man at full strength, making his eyes bug out of his head. "You don't even seem to like her. Why do you care?"

"I'm worried about you."

I scoffed. "There's nothing to worry about."

He raised his brow at me. "You aren't worried? Demeter has already started her rampage, and the goddess has you wrapped around her fing—"

"No one has me wrapped around their finger."

"Then why is she still in the Underworld? Get rid of her. It's not worth starting problems with Demeter."

I let my magic die, and Chandler collapsed to his knees and curled into a ball on the floor. A pile of weak man. I kicked him toward Thanatos. "Deal with him." I turned to leave.

"Hades."

I stilled.

"Just sit."

I listened to him, not because I had to, but out of respect. I'd known Thanatos since we were boys, our bond made stronger through the Titan War. When Zeus assumed leadership of the court and assigned responsibilities to each member, Thanatos volunteered to stand by my side in the Underworld. He helped me navigate the realm I now ruled. Thanatos understood the burdens I carried. Throughout my life, he'd been the only Divine I could trust.

Thanatos toyed with the man in the center of the living room as I sat on the tan couch, this one no more comfortable than the love seat. Thanatos rarely engaged in torture, but he took part today—just to prevent me leaving.

"I've seen the way you look at her," Thanatos said.

I folded my arms. "You've seen me look at her once."

"Once was all I needed." Chandler fell to the floor, dead.

"What's your point, Thanatos?"

His eyes narrowed. "My point is, having her in the Underworld poses a risk. You know that."

I sighed, rubbing my temples. Thanatos was right, of course. Persephone's presence in the Underworld was a delicate matter. "She's not leaving the Underworld." Each word was measured.

Thanatos shook his head. "Hades, you know the risks. She's not one of us."

I couldn't deny the truth. "Her presence is necessary."

"How could it be necessary? This will only cause us more issues."

"She's my mate." The admission hung heavy in the air as I uttered the words for the first time. Saying it out loud made it real.

Persephone. My *mate*.

The bond between us was undeniable. It was clear from the moment I had first laid eyes on her, even before she bound herself to me. I resisted the urge to probe the binding between us. It was a one-sided connection, a safeguard to ensure her mother hadn't orchestrated her arrival. Initially, I allowed my power to reach out just enough to confirm that she had escaped.

Nothing more than that. I couldn't allow myself to go further. The temptation to delve deeper—to feel her emotions, uncover her history, and know her thoughts—was overwhelming. It would give me a glimpse of what it would be like to share a completed mate bond with her... and that was something that could never happen.

Thanatos stayed silent, grappling with the new information like I had for weeks. "The court won't take this lightly."

"She will stay. No matter the cost."

Thanatos approached me, settling into the love seat. "Whatever decision you make, you know I'll stand by you," he said with a soft smile.

I swallowed. "I know."

18

PERSEPHONE

"*You deserve this and everything coming to you,*" *Mother said. She continued to talk as she dunked my head into the cold water because I refused to take my medicine. Water flowed into my ears, muffling her words.*

My lungs screamed, begging for mercy. "Mothe—" Tiny stabs crested on my scalp as she pulled me back again before shoving me down. An intensity of cold water cut off my words. I coughed when she pulled me back up, but before my lungs could get the genuine air they needed, I was back in the water. I thrashed until my limbs went limp, and I gave up.

~

Three days had passed since the dinner with Hades. He kept his distance from me, and I hated the way it made me feel. Every day, the ache in my chest grew stronger. In a desperate bid for a distraction, I immersed myself in practicing my magic out in the courtyard and reading in the library. At my last session with Hecate, she'd told me to keep practicing. The plants were showing some improvement, lasting slightly longer than before. While it was a small victory, it was one step in a long journey ahead.

"Persephone." Hades' voice came from behind me.

"You've emerged from hiding? Maybe you should've stayed," I snapped.

He smiled back at me and moved to stand at my side. "What the delightful little goddess you are today," he said wryly.

"I'm always delightful." I crossed my arms and fought the flush rising to my face.

He snickered, and I rolled my eyes. "How is your progress?"

"It's coming along," I said.

"Are you still getting fatigued?"

I just nodded.

His lack of a response surprised me. He stood several feet away, putting a significant distance between us. I wasn't fond of it, but I knew it was for the best. I called my magic and repeated the monotonous cycle—growing the plant, creating a barrier around it, and watching the poor thing wither into nothingness. Pain throbbed in the back of my skull. I cringed but ignored it.

Hades remained silent as I carried out the repetitive routine. He was cold… distant. His gaze suggested I was failing in some way. He was *different* now, and I didn't like it. I cursed at myself, shoving away the piece of me craving his approval.

Hades whisked away without a word. I sucked in a deep breath.

19

PERSEPHONE

"How's life in the Underworld treating you?" Hermes' words snapped me out of my quiet observance of the room. The flickering candle lights danced across the walls, painting swaying shadows.

I shifted in my seat, wiping the sweat off my hands and smoothing the soft fabric of my dark-blue dress. I angled my body to address Hermes. "I'm adjusting." I sent him a tender smile, my gaze briefly flitting to each of the gathered Divine before settling back on Hermes. "Life here is… different, to say the least."

My heart raced as I sat among the Divine again. I'd grown fond of Hecate, but the rest… *I just need to survive this dinner.*

"I'm glad you're adjusting." Hecate, sitting to my right, clasped my shoulder warmly. Across from her sat Hermes, with Thanatos beside him. Both Thanatos and I were next to Hades, who claimed the head of the table.

Several souls entered the room balancing plates of hot food. I glanced up at the soul who set a plate in front of me. "Thank you." She bowed her head with a smile.

The souls filled up the stemmed glasses with faerie wine,

omitting mine. I chose not to engage in a losing battle. Picking my fights wisely was crucial, and squabbling over wine wasn't worth the effort. Minor conversation flowed between the Divine at the table. Their conversations passed over me, leaving me untouched and unseen—disconnected. I was an outsider peering in through a fogged window, able to see but never truly be one of them.

It was strange how, even in a room with four other people, I could still feel utterly alone. I busied myself with my meal, my focus split between half-heartedly moving my vegetables around my plate and half listening to their words.

Thanatos' eyes had been locked on me from the moment I set foot in the dining room. I'd tried to ignore it, but the strange awareness grew too strong. "What do you want?" I finally said, looking up at him.

He glanced between me and Hades. "Nothing, I apologize." Thanatos returned to eating his meal and conversing with the Divine like nothing happened.

Odd. I went back to picking at my food, pushing around the vegetables. My thoughts inevitably wandered to Hades. I squeezed my eyes shut and shifted my mind in another direction. I took a sip of water to soothe the dryness in my throat.

My head snapped up at the mention of my mother's name.

Just her name put a nervous flutter in my chest. I'd suffered for years at her hand, the memories still haunting the corridors of my mind. The distance I put between us was supposed to be enough. But it wasn't. The past never really disappeared. It followed me.

I tried to ease the burning threatening to spill from my eyes and watched the shadows—until I saw her face among them. I flinched, turning my gaze away, but the familiar pain already swelled, washing over me.

I was angry again.

Angry at her. Angry at the years she stole from me. Angry that no matter how far I ran, she still had this power over me. It boiled in my chest.

I forced myself to tune into the conversation, Hermes' urgent tone drawing my focus. "Eventually, you must take action." Hermes set his fork down and leaned closer to the table.

Hades waved him off. "She does not worry me," he replied steadily. But Hades glanced at Thanatos for a moment with a look that contradicted his words. Had I not been watching, I would've missed it.

"What about my mother?" I spoke up. "Has something happened?"

"It's not of your concern."

My stomach churned. "How can you say that?" My palm struck the table harder than I intended, rattling the plates and cutlery.

"She deserves to know," Hermes added.

My lip curled as I turned to face him. "Then you tell me." My voice cracked. I was used to things being kept from me, but this stung. My nails bit into my palms. I had allowed myself to get too comfortable in the presence of the Divine.

A few silent moments passed. I shook my head, though it did little to ease the pain radiating through my jaw from clenching. I pushed back my chair and stood up, the scrape of wood loud against the stone floor. Hermes stumbled over his words. "I—"

"Persephone. It is not of your concern." Hades' words held an air of finality.

I stormed out of the room. Hecate and Hermes called out after me, but I didn't stop to listen. My thoughts swirled. I needed to be alone.

I was halfway to my room when a force collided with my body, stealing the breath from my lungs.

Hades.

I didn't need to see him. I could *feel* it was him. I staggered, and all my muscles tensed. I thrashed against the hold of his magic. It wrapped around me, constricting like a serpent coiling around its prey. "Let. Me. Go," I hissed, a surge of energy pouring from me and punctuating each syllable.

My magic attempted to free me from his hold, but it did nothing. Blackness crept into the edges of my vision.

"Stop. You're draining yourself," Hades said.

My magic continued to push harder despite my attempts to stop it. My teeth hammered together. "I can't."

A wash of Hades' magic swept over me, snuffing mine out. The power that had swirled around me disappeared. My heart didn't slow, but I stopped convulsing. A dizzy feeling still floated around in my skull like a ship at sea, with no hope of returning to shore. My vision blurred as I fought to stay upright. The muscles in my body, once tight with resistance, were unresponsive. My knees buckled, and I collapsed toward the ground.

I prepared for the harsh impact of the stone floor.

But it never came.

Hades' arms caught me, an embrace devoid of warmth. My cheek sagged against the fabric of his black buttoned shirt, too drained to lift my head. We remained like that for a few moments—motionless, suspended in uneasy stillness.

Through the black cloth, I caught the faint thrum of his heart. The rhythm soothed me in spite of myself, easing the fatigue that dragged at my bones. I drew in a deep breath saturated with the rich scent of leather from his gloves.

I shifted, and the hard nub of a button pressed cruelly into my cheek. The pain startled me, a reminder of where I was, of who held me. I tried to pull myself away from him despite my body's desire to stay.

"No, little goddess." He pulled me closer. Hades scooped me into his arms and carried me through the nearest door—into the library.

I ran my thumb along his shirt, trying to distract myself. But with him so close, it was hard to focus on anything else. I shifted, pulling slightly away from his chest.

Towering shelves filled with ancient books stretched toward the vaulted ceiling. The scent of aged paper filled the air. This had become one of my favorite rooms in the palace, often reading through the frustration practicing my magic had produced.

Hades lowered me onto one of the couches nestled in the center of the library. My senses dulled as I settled into the cushions. I shut my eyes, seeking the comfort of Hades' embrace within the confines of the couch.

It didn't come.

"This isn't normal." Hades' voice cut through the silence.

I pried my heavy eyes open. "What do you mean?"

Hades sat on the other end of the couch, putting more distance than I wanted between us. "Your magic." He ran a gloved hand through his hair. "It shouldn't drain you to this extent. Something is wrong."

My stomach twisted. "Is it a side effect of the pills? I thought I'd gotten rid of the withdrawals."

"Pills?" His voice lowered with an edge I hadn't heard before.

A humorless laugh slipped from my lips. "My mother," I said with a sigh. "She started giving me pills once a day, shortly after the first sign of my magic. They suppressed it." I stopped there, omitting the details of that day that I wasn't ready to give voice to.

Hades' jaw ticked. "Demeter gave you pills?"

I didn't answer his question.

He shook his head as if trying to convince himself of what he'd just said aloud. "The stone has done damage to her." I began to ask what he was talking about, but he cut me off. "It is not a withdrawal symptom. I can assure you of that. You've been here too long without them." His fingers tapped on his thigh.

I sank into the couch a little farther. The mention of Mother brought a tide of feelings I wanted no part in.

"Persephone, you are a goddess," he said, his voice softening with concern. "Your magic is a part of you, but it should never leave you feeling so depleted."

"Hecate said it would go away."

He shifted closer, fingers still restless. His head tipped, and he let out a long breath. "I will take over your training from now on." Hades rose to his feet.

I stood up too quickly after him, and my head spun. "Wait."

His hand closed around my forearm, steadying me. "You should rest. I'll whisk you to your room."

I should've been furious. He still kept the information about the stone from me. I should've known what was happening, especially when it came to my own mother. But I couldn't. I was too conscious of his hand on me. "No, wait."

Silence stretched between us, long enough to feel endless though only moments had passed.

"Little goddess, I'm listening." Hades took a step closer. "What is it you're so determined to tell me?" He placed his other leather-covered hand on my cheek. I couldn't help but lean into his touch.

"I-I don't know what I wanted to say," I stammered, frozen in place.

Hades let out a light chuckle. "Flustered, are we?"

His nearness wrapped around me, making it impossible to focus on anything else. The way the world seemed to narrow to just him—his scent, the power radiating off him, the pull that made my body betray every logical thought. I should've been angry with him. He wouldn't tell me what was happening. I swallowed hard, my heart pounding in my chest as I struggled to find the right words. *I shouldn't want him to stay.*

"Don't go." They were the only words that managed to spill from my mouth.

His eyes darkened. "I must."

A shiver ran through me despite the leather barrier between our skin. The ticking of the clock across the room aligned with the rhythm of my heartbeat. An overwhelming urge coursed through me.

My hand moved of its own accord, fingers outstretched as if an invisible force drew them. But as I was about to make contact with his skin, Hades grabbed my arm.

"Persephone," he murmured, his voice thick with emotion. "No."

My fingertips hovered mere inches from his skin. Hades guided my hand back to my side. His gaze bore into me as if each moment he continued to look at me caused him physical pain.

I chewed on the inside of my cheek. "Why can't I touch you?"

"I will hurt you."

My face went slack. "No—"

"My touch kills, Persephone. Mortals die at my touch."

I followed the bob of his throat, trying to wrap my head around his confession. I'd never read that in any of the books in the Olympian Library.

"Though you are immortal, the agony it would bring you…" He shook his head. "I could never bear to subject you to such pain." His warm breath caressed my cheek, a cruel contrast to the chill of his words.

I fought the urge to flinch.

"Do you know why I get so angry all the time?" Hades' voice was a rough whisper.

I shook my head, fighting back the tears threatening to spill.

"Because every minute of the day, I want to reach out and touch you, but I can't. I won't hurt you." His eyes mirrored the sinking feeling I knew were in mine.

A chill raced over me. Reckless ideas filled my mind, but I pushed them away. Hades tugged my hand into his gloved palm, the size of it dwarfing mine. He ran his fingers across my skin, as if committing the shape of them to memory. My body swayed, a treacherous reaction I struggled to control. I drew a steadying breath. This moment—this simple touch— felt more intimate than any other between us.

Hades whisked us to my room. He released my hands and disappeared. I was alone, absently tracing the invisible patterns he had left on my skin.

HADES

My gaze homed in on the bull's-eye's center with laser precision. I clenched the dart in between my fingers, index and thumb. The grooves of the metal barrel etched into the leather of my gloves. My tense hand flexed, trying to contain the pressure within me. I launched it at the target and picked up the next.

One. *I.*

Two. *Want.*

Three. *Her.*

Four. *I.*

Five. *Can't.*

Six. *Have.*

Seven. *Her.*

I left the darts embedded in the target's heart. They wouldn't be enough today. The darkness already spilled out of me. My breaths came in short ragged gasps. The Fates were cruel for guiding Persephone to my realm.

Every time she looked at me, it was gut-wrenching.

But it wasn't enough.

The faint crease between her eyebrows that appeared

when she fell deep into concentration. The slight tremor in her hands when she spoke of what she feared. The soft timbre of her voice when she said *my* name.

It was too much.

I needed to leave my realm.

The smell of motor oil, cigars, gunpowder, and bourbon assaulted my senses as I materialized in the mortal realm. Even among the odors clawing at my senses, *her* scent cut through. Harsh fluorescent lights cast long shadows through the smoke veiling and stretching across the room. Men stared at me with wide eyes, their chests rising and falling with panicked gasps. Each of them had a hollowed face. Pallor gripped their features in a ghostly hue—an obvious result of Demeter's actions in the mortal realm. Several of the men held up their guns, fingers trembling on the triggers, poised to unleash a hail of bullets upon me.

Mortals didn't know of the Divine, or any other beings. They wandered through their brief lives, ignorant of the powers that shaped their fates. Some believed in us, others thought of us as mere stories concocted to sell more statues and books. I loved showing them just how real I was. There was a certain thrill in it, a heady rush that surged through my veins as the realization dawned on their faces. I grimaced. *As if a bullet would save them from their fates.*

Gunfire filled the air, a cacophony of noise reverberating off the brick walls. I flicked my wrist, deflecting their pathetic bullets. I forced all the men into binds of my magic. The guns clattered loudly on the floor as they slipped from their hands.

Originally, I had planned on taking them one by one in their homes over the course of a few weeks, letting them fear and wonder who would be next—but things had changed. If I didn't find a way to purge some of this darkness, it would spill over, tainting everything and everyone around me. Especially her.

I couldn't—I wouldn't hurt Persephone. Nor would I release her to Demeter. She was mine, entwined with my very existence.

I walked through the center of the room while I gagged all my targets. Pleasure roiled through me as I injected fear into all of them. I closed my eyes, and Persephone appeared behind my eyelids. She was constant—overwhelming. My eyes snapped open, and the magic poured out of me stronger.

The smell of urine wafted through the air. It wasn't pleasant, but I'd gotten used to it. It came with the nature of what I did.

I controlled my steps as I made my way to the leader of the group, Nico Lorenzikoe. Of all the men, Nico had been the one to wet himself. A dry laugh left my lips. His eyes tracked my every movement, each flicker of my hand, each shift of my body. The man's face turned red from his muffled screams, though the gag stifled any meaningful noise. I whisked behind him.

I knew he could feel me. I made sure he did. "Are you scared yet?" I whispered in his ear. He screamed again, but the sound that emerged was nothing more than a muted gargle. I took off my gloves. *Time to get busy.* I placed my palm on his bald sun-damaged head, and within seconds, his neck slumped to the side.

Dead.

One done, fourteen to go.

I walked to his right-hand man, Danny Forton. His gaze flickered to me, then back to his lifeless boss. Realization danced across his features. He was alone now, stripped of the power and protection he had always relied on. And most importantly, he was next.

I didn't feel bad for these men. They were lucky I used my death touch. It was a quick death, but the fear I incited before made it all worth it. "Oh, Danny. Did you know your wife hates being hit? So do all the other young women you find." His eyes were wide, and his muscles strained as he tried to shake his head. Danny struggled against the binds, but I placed my hand on his neck, and his eyes went blank. His irises were no longer visible as they rolled back into his head.

I went through each of the men, one by one. All of them deserved it.

I scanned the scene of dead men, their lifeless forms strewn across the room. The unmistakable evidence of their terror stained the floor beneath them. The stench in the room had intensified. Killing these men would have usually calmed me—helped me control myself—but the goddess was still clear in my mind.

2 1

———

PERSEPHONE

I closed my eyes, savoring the warmth of sunlight caressing my skin. The light of the twin suns flooded the dining room through the glass ceiling. I picked at the array of fruits and cheeses spread out on the white plate before me.

"Persephone."

I looked up, placing the apple slice in my hand back on the plate. "Hermes, hello."

Hermes wore a crisp white button-up shirt with gold embellishments on the sleeve, the bottom tucked into navy trousers. The small smile on his face did little to soothe the anger I harbored toward him. "I want to show you something," he said.

"Unless you're *finally* going to tell me what my mother has been up to…" I paused. "I don't want to hear it."

Hermes' smile faltered. "That's why I'm here." He plucked a few grapes from my plate and popped them into his mouth. "I feel badly about how it went the last time I saw you. I should've told you."

"You should have."

Hermes winced at my sharp tone. "You have to understand. Hades is just trying to protect you."

I folded my arms across my chest. "How is keeping me in the dark supposed to protect me?" My hands fidgeted in my lap. "It makes me more vulnerable. I deserve to know what's happening, especially when it concerns my own mother."

Hermes nodded. "I can show you."

"How?"

"Give me your hand," he said, extending his palm toward me.

I hesitated. The simple gesture carried the weight of everything I feared *and* everything I wanted. Did I truly want to see? My chest constricted, torn between dread and gnawing hunger for truth.

I lifted my hand and bridged the distance between us. When my skin met his, there was no turning back. "Close your eyes," he urged.

I did as he said, and his magic seized me. It pulled at me, the ground dropping away. My stomach lurched as my vision shifted. We stood on the outskirts of the countryside. It unfolded before us—color and life. Rows upon rows of crops stood before us. Beyond them, rolling hills carpeted in emerald-green grass stretched out as far as the eye could see.

But that vision, so achingly beautiful, was fleeting. It faded and curdled before my eyes, the once-vibrant countryside becoming an expanse of cracked earth and withered vegetation. The palette shifted to muted browns and grays, with patches of sickly yellow and green. Sweat gathered in beads on my skin as the unforgiving sun shone down on us. Heat rose from the ground, radiating in heavy waves, blurring the edges of the horizon.

Hermes tugged my hand, pulling me deeper into the ruin. The ground beneath us was jagged, broken, eager to catch my stumble. My lips trembled shut at the sight of the animals, starved, skeletal. Some staggered aimlessly, their hollow cries cutting into me. Others lay collapsed in silence, their ribcages visible.

The scent of decay—vegetation and life—mingled together into a stench that clawed the back of my throat. I swallowed the bile rising there. "The mortals don't deserve this," I murmured. It was one thing to endure my mother's cruelty myself. To see her reach spill into them was unbearable.

Hermes nodded beside me. "It's always the innocent who suffer the most." His voice was low, stripped of the cheer I'd grown used to.

I swallowed as the scene around us shifted. Here, the streets were narrow and shadowed, the buildings were jagged towers of lights, metal, and stone, windows glinting. My clothes had changed—a thick jacket, heavy pants—yet the cold still needled through me. *We're in a city, I think.* I'd never seen a place like this before, only read stories.

Snow drifted from the gray sky, powdering the ground in uneven patches of white and dark-brown slush. I held out my palm. Each snowflake melted the instant it touched my skin, leaving only a wet trace behind. I had never seen snow before. Hermes' magic made it too real.

The city itself was overwhelming. I had only known Athens, with its cobblestones, marble, and pastels. This place was different. Mortals shuffled past with faces hollowed by hunger, skin dull and chapped. They fought with each other over scraps of food, eyes wide with animal desperation. Children wailed, their cries high and piercing, swallowed quickly by the shrieking wind.

"It's never snowed here before," Hermes said.

I exhaled, a long sigh that left a white plume in the air. The wind funneled like a whip through the street, between the buildings, slapping my exposed face raw. We walked past a line of mortals stretched before us, outside a place marked *Food Bank* in crimson peeling letters.

They huddled together, shoulders touching, trying to steal warmth from one another. Their fingers, raw and red, clutched empty bags. One by one, they reached the door, only to be refused. The look in their eyes as they were sent away was worse than any scream.

A woman inside the food bank lifted a cardboard sign and pressed it against the frost-clouded window that read *Closed. No food.*

Some of the mortals scattered, disappointment etched in every line of their faces. Others refused to move. They stayed in line, waiting for the chance of nothing.

"This isn't right," I said. "I thought the mortal realm was the neutral realm. How is Mother able to do this?"

"It is," Hermes said as he dropped the vision.

We were back in the dining room, dressed as we had been before. My eyes dropped to the plate before me, piled high with fruit and cheese. I looked away. The abundance mocked me. Every fresh, glistening piece was a cruel reminder of the hollow faces I had just seen.

All I could see were the emaciated bodies from the vision. I thought of the ones I hadn't seen too. How many had to suffer because of me?

I was here with my belly full, daring to complain. Mother had always called me selfish. Maybe she was right.

"Demeter has grown more powerful over the years. Most of the members of the court are too scared of her, though they would never admit that." Hermes placed a hand on my shoulder. "At the last court meeting, Demeter made it clear she won't stop until you return to her. There are some whispers that Zeus will order her to stop at the next meeting."

"How do we stop her?" A simple solution filled my mind,

but I couldn't say it out loud. The thought of returning to Olympus made me shudder.

"All the Divine on the court are bound to perform the duties they swore they would. I believe Zeus will challenge her violation." Hermes' gaze darted around the room. "I need to go. Hades will grow more suspicious if I'm here any longer."

"Thank you." Hermes' lips tipped up before he whisked.

I ran through the corridors, the pounding of my footsteps matching my pulse. How long had Hades allowed my mother's actions to go on while I lived in privileged ignorance in his realm?

I neared the door of his study, ready to whip it open, but I slowed. It was ajar, two familiar voices drifting from the room. I pressed my back against the cool stone wall. My hand rested on the wooden doorframe as I leaned closer.

"Are you accusing me of what I think you are?" Hecate asked, her voice shrill, the antithesis of the times she'd talked to me. The shift was jarring.

I couldn't see her, but I didn't need to. I could imagine her clearly, shoulders drawn back stiffly, jaw tight. She was likely standing near the center of Hades' study, planted like a pillar, arms crossed over her chest in a defensive knot. Maybe her fingers drummed against her elbows. She didn't sound angry but cornered.

"Answer the question," Hades demanded. I flinched at the force of his voice and shifted, forcing my bouncing leg to calm. *I can't let them hear me.* My back pressed against the stone wall, and I listened.

"I have done nothing wrong. I have Persephone's best interests in mind," Hecate told him. "I have yours too, Hades. I always have. You know that." Her voice softened.

"Do I?" Hades asked. "Persephone told me you said her fatigue is normal."

"She is inexperienced," Hecate said quickly.

"You and I both know that's not normal." Hades' tone deepened.

"Hades." The way Hecate said his name left a bitter taste in my mouth.

Hades cleared his throat. "I think it's best if you leave."

"I've always been on your side, Hades. Always," Hecate whispered.

Each of those eight words hurt. They held history. My mouth dried. Why did I care so much? *I shouldn't feel like this.* I shook my head and willed the emotion down. And yet, I couldn't unhear the words.

"Persephone, you may come in now," Hades said with a chuckle. The sound caught me off guard after what I'd overheard only moments ago.

I stayed pressed against the wall. *Breathe in. Breathe out.*

The door swung open completely. "It's impolite to eavesdrop," he added.

I peeked at Hades' form through my eyelashes, remaining still as a statue. Hades placed his hand atop mine, which was still resting on the doorframe. My traitorous body relaxed. "I wasn't eavesdropping," I said, struggling to make my words sound convincing.

He arched a brow, the corner of his mouth twitching. "I can feel you anywhere in my realm. Come in."

I stepped into Hades' study. Hecate was gone, but the echo of her voice still lingered in my ears.

Hades studied me as I entered, but his expression gave nothing away. "And what brings you here?"

I opened my mouth, then closed it again. Pressure built behind my eyes, the images of the mortal realm conjured in my mind. "I know what my mother has done."

"Hermes," Hades said his name like a curse as his lips

twitched into a scowl. "Always meddling in things he shouldn't."

I steadied my breathing. "I should've known these things. You kept them from me."

Hades closed the distance between us. He stopped so near, I thought he might touch me. I wasn't sure if I wanted that. I knew I shouldn't. "They would have brought you pain," he said softly.

He crossed the room, each step echoing louder than it should have, and lowered himself into the chair behind his desk. The space between us yawned wide again.

"I'm not a fragile flower. I deserve to know these things." I forced myself to meet his gaze.

"I will not apologize for protecting you." Each word was delivered with infuriating calm.

"I don't need your protection." I raised my voice, like volume would make him *hear* it.

He didn't respond.

Hades disappeared from his seat. I flinched, spinning to scan the room.

I felt him before I saw him—his presence pressed against my back. I stiffened, every nerve going taut. His gloved hand curled around my chin, tilting my face upward with a steady pressure. My breath caught, ragged and sharp, and I let out a strangled sound I couldn't smother fast enough.

"Do not tell me you don't need my protection when you ran to my realm seeking it." A dangerous edge crept into his low voice. His fingers ghosted along the line of my jaw, back to my chin, and down the column of my throat. He didn't squeeze. He didn't have to. The gesture alone made it clear who held the power here.

His nearness stirred a tangle of fear, familiarity, and something dangerously close to comfort. This wasn't the time, not when so much hung in the balance. "I want answers."

"Even if you are not ready to hear such truths?"

"Yes." My eyes flickered to the window, chasing anything that wasn't him. I pushed the question out before I could lose my nerve. "What's wrong with me?"

His gloved hand on my throat moved down across my collarbone and to my shoulder. "I don't know."

It was honest. And terrifying. "Why did you accuse Hecate?" I couldn't hide the frustration in my voice. "I'm tired of not knowing."

"When I know, I will tell you," Hades said. "Hecate sees more than most. Whether it's something she missed with your magic or something she chose not to speak of, I can't tell."

I stiffened, impossibly more than I already had. His touch was grounding, but I didn't lean in.

"All I know is what you are experiencing is not normal," Hades added. His touch lasted for a few more moments than necessary before he let me go.

It almost sounded like he cared about me. The thought caught me off guard. Why should he care so much about what happened to me when he had known Hecate far longer? The question pressed at me, but another forced its way out instead. "And what about my mother?"

"The court will handle it." His voice was steady, dismissive, but I could hear uncertainty peek through.

"And if they don't?" I hated how small my voice sounded, but I needed to know.

"It will be handled." He said the words too quickly, as if he could command the outcome into existence.

"It's all my fault." I looked away at the wall of books lining the shelf behind Hades' desk. I fixated on the spine of a leather-bound volume halfway down the second shelf titled

The Principles of Divine Order, the gold leaf lettering beginning to flake. The book leaned too far left, throwing off the symmetry of the shelf. Focusing on the book was easier than facing him, or the guilt clawing at my insides.

He moved, standing in front of me. "Persephone."

I said nothing.

"Look at me." His voice was low.

I raised my chin slowly until my eyes met his.

"The only one at fault is your mother."

I nodded, just once. I didn't trust myself to speak. My thoughts were a tangled knot. I walked out of his study and to my room. Was this the price of my new life? To be in the dark and to let others suffer because of me?

PERSEPHONE

I jolted awake.

"Persephone, wake up!" Hades' voice crashed over me like thunder as he pounded on the door.

I pushed to my feet, sleep still dragging my limbs, and stumbled toward the sound. My clammy hands fumbled over the knob before I yanked the door open. "What do you want?" I growled.

Hades lowered his raised fist. His head tilted, a faint smile tugging at his lips. "Good. You're up—"

"Of course I am. You're making a racket." I glanced back toward the window, and it was still dark outside. "Whatever cursed hour this is, it's far too early. You could've whisked in and woken me up like a normal person instead of pounding on the door."

His smile deepened. "Do I strike you as normal?"

"Good point," I muttered, crossing my arms. "I'll remember this. One day, I'll pound you awake the same way —" I froze, internally cursing the Fates for letting my mouth move faster than my brain.

Hades' brows lifted.

Heat surged into my cheeks. "That's not—no. I meant pound, knock, on your *door*." My voice cracked, and I winced. "Not… not you. Gods, that sounded wrong. I just meant—" The words tangled in my throat. "You know. A normal knock. A very boring knock." I raised a hand halfway, then dropped it before I could demonstrate the motion. "Forget it. F-fuck you for waking me up so early. I can't even get my words straight." His silence pressed harder than any reply might have, leaving me to stew in the mess I'd made.

His chuckle was low, dangerous, like velvet draped over a blade. "Get dressed and meet me in the sparring room." His gaze dragged over me, pinning me in place. "You look beautiful."

That was unexpected. Hades had never called me beautiful. He'd called me a few things, but *beautiful*, never. My mind struggled to follow the shift in conversation, still tired. I shoved the comment aside. "Sparring room?"

"Two doors to the right of my study."

I nodded and shut the door on him.

His smile loitered in my mind as I peeled off my clothes, putting on fresh ones that allowed for movement. Glancing out the window, I studied the absence of the rising suns and the stars still covering the sky. "Why so early in the morning?" I said through a yawn.

I went into the washroom and faced my reflection. *Beautiful*, he'd called me. The sight before me was anything but flattering. My hair was a tangled mess, piled on top of my head with strands sticking out in every direction, some clinging to my sweaty skin. I cursed under my breath, splashing water on my face and quickly wiping away the dried slobber coating the lower corner of my mouth. Hades was messing with me.

I walked to the sparring room, mentally preparing myself for whatever Hades had planned. The large door opened on silent hinges. No windows broke up the white walls covered in gleaming weapons. It was more weapons than I'd ever seen before—a hundred, maybe more. Overhead lighting cast a sterile brightness on every surface, the sole source of light in the room. A soft, gray mat spanned the entire floor. In the corner stood a small table, a pitcher of water and a few cups sitting on top. Compared to the rest of the room, it seemed like an afterthought. Hades stood to the side, polishing one of the swords with a red cloth.

"You've finally arrived," Hades said, as if I'd left him waiting a long time. He balled up the cloth, and it disappeared from his hand. "I'm assuming no one has ever taught you how to fight?"

"I have fought before, once, but I've never had any formal training."

Hades walked to the center of the room, gesturing for me to follow.

"When I left, I fought my guard, Basile." Perhaps I should have been worried that I felt no remorse. Basile deserved to die. "I killed him—" I swallowed. "With his own dagger."

A smile bigger than I'd ever seen on him filled Hades' face. He stepped closer, his eyes full of genuine amusement. "Vicious. I like it."

I was at a loss for words. Praise from the God of the Underworld was the last thing I'd expected. I shifted my weight, searching for something to say that wouldn't make me sound foolish. I had done enough of that today.

Hades regarded me with a look that felt dangerously close to approval. "We're going to start today with some basic fighting."

My eyes flickered to the weapons.

"Not with those."

"You're boring," I said, surprised by the surge of boldness.

"Perhaps if you survive my *boring* training, we can entertain the thought of weapons soon." His gaze was a silent dare. Hades surged forward, his hands a blur as they moved. Instinct screamed at me to dodge, to retreat, but I was too slow.

His fist connected with my side with a force that stole my breath, sending me staggering backward. A sharp, relentless pain exploded through me. My teeth gritted together, and copper flooded in my mouth. My hands flew outstretched at my sides as I struggled to regain my balance.

Shock rippled through me. I steadied myself and pushed through the pain. I aimed for any opening, any vulnerable spot I could find. But Hades was too skilled. Every blow I threw at him, he blocked.

My fist propelled toward his chest, but before it could land, he caught my wrist. Our eyes locked. I tried to pry myself from his hold, but it didn't work. Every muscle in my body screamed in protest. I let out a frustrated growl and kept trying to get myself away from him. Hades let me go. I stumbled backward from the sudden release and fell onto the floor. My fingers stretched on the cold mat, and I took a deep breath as I propped myself up. "What was that?"

"Do you expect an attacker to announce their intentions before they strike?" I opened my mouth to respond, but he cut me off with a raised hand. "You stay ready," he continued firmly. "You never yield. And you never hesitate. Ever." Hades stretched a gloved hand out for me.

I thought back to the girl I'd been before I left Olympus, pacing my room, staging imaginary battles, convinced my daydreams would harden into skill. Gods, I'd been naive. I had believed my stories could prepare me for the harsh realities of this universe.

I was no longer practicing choreographed movements in the safety of my room. I needed to learn how to survive now. I ignored his hand and picked myself up off the ground.

"You are weak. Inexperienced. This is the only way for you to learn. You can't always rely on magic, and until we figure out what's wrong with yours, you shouldn't use it."

I hated that he was right. I swallowed down any sharp remark threatening to spill from my lips. "All right."

"First lesson, keep your feet shoulder-width apart, knees bent, and weight evenly distributed. And most importantly, keep your eyes on your opponent at all times."

I tried to follow his instructions, but it was difficult to concentrate with him so close.

"Like this," Hades said, stepping closer until our bodies were almost touching. Goose bumps pebbled on my skin as he adjusted my stance, manipulating me into position like putty. He reached for my hips first, fingers curling as he shifted me a fraction to the left. His hands slid down my arms, repositioning my elbows, guiding without hesitation.

He steadied me with his hands on my shoulders. Then he nudged my feet a little farther apart with the toe of his boot and pushed lightly against the back of my knee to make me bend more. The press of his hand at the small of my back coaxed my weight evenly onto both legs. His touch was firm, yet oddly gentle. "Better," he murmured, his voice husky. "But you need to be more grounded, more centered."

Hades moved away from me. Thank the gods.

"Lesson two," he began. "How to hit. It's not just about strength. It's about precision. You need to know where and how to strike." Hades waved a hand, and a training bag appeared, faint traces of his shadowy magic lingering in the air. "Watch," Hades said, stepping forward to demonstrate. "You want to aim for vulnerable spots—like the throat, below the ribs, or the knees. And when you strike, use your body weight to generate power."

He launched into a series of controlled hits, each blow landing with precision and force on the canvas training bag. I cringed at each loud thud reverberating through the room. The force of his blows made the bag sway, the fabric rippling under his touch. His strikes stopped. "Now, you try."

I watched him move, and something uneasy stirred beneath my skin. I tried to ignore the way he pushed his hair away from his sweaty forehead. The long-sleeved shirt he wore clung to his every contour, leaving little to the imagination. I swallowed hard.

I averted my gaze, focusing intently on the reflection of my own strained expression in the polished surface of a nearby dagger on the wall. Blood rushed to my cheeks. *Get a grip*, I told myself. I was here to train, not to notice things that didn't matter.

Hades cleared his throat. "Begin, Persephone."

I launched into the sequence, focusing on my target and channeling every ounce of strength I possessed. My strikes were clumsy and uncoordinated, but I continued. Hades stopped me every so often to correct my form, each adjustment sending a jolt of electricity through me. Every brush of his fingers was a reminder of just how easily he could undo me. I had to fight the urge to lean into his touch in order to complete the sequence of blows.

"Better," he said, reserved pride in his voice. "You still have a long way to go, though."

"Tell me about the stone you mentioned before," I said between breaths. *I need to know.*

"This is not the time to discuss that."

"I don't think I could name a better time."

He hesitated. "The Nexus Stone is made of the energy that created the universe. There are seven pieces scattered across the realms. There's also a spell crafted by that same creation energy that would render the stone powerless." Hades ran a hand through his hair. "The spell is fractured into three pieces. Your mother already has two pieces of the stone and one piece of the spell." Hades placed a hand on my shoulder. "I will not keep talking unless you keep training."

I sighed and continued to strike the canvas.

"The court—Zeus mainly—refuses to acknowledge this, even though we all know she has them. There's no proof."

"Then how do you know?"

The lines of Hades' face hardened, annoyance flashing in his stone-colored eyes. It was as if my simple question had offended him. "What your mother doesn't realize is when the dead come here, their secrets follow. That is how I know."

"What happens if she gets all the pieces?" I asked. "And the spell?"

"The same energy that can create realms can also destroy them. She would be inconceivably powerful. And if she had the spell too"—Hades' face turned graver than I'd ever seen— "she would be unstoppable."

I was silent. I had far too many questions as I tried to grapple with the new information. My mind raced. I sifted through my memories in search of any mention of the stone, but there were none.

My arms burned. My torso burned. My legs burned. But I kept going. The pain made me feel *something*. I needed to be stronger if I wanted to be able to protect myself.

"Stop thinking so much."

"How am I *not* supposed to think? I'm thinking about your hands and where they might strike me next. What my mother is doing. Who she is starving, who she's torturing. What this stone is. And what my role in all of this is."

Hades' throat bobbed. "And now you know why I didn't wish to tell you."

My shoulders squared, and I lifted my chin. "Keeping the truth from me will never make it disappear."

"I believe we've reached our limit for today." He shook his

head. "Your movements are slowing. Pushing yourself too hard won't be beneficial."

But I didn't stop. I wasn't ready to let go. The ache in my arms, the burn in my lungs were a reminder that I was no longer the girl pacing her little bedroom in Olympus, imagining strength she didn't yet possess. I launched one last strike.

With a simple wave of his hand, the training bag vanished. My fist cut through the empty air, momentum carrying me forward. I stumbled, already bracing for the fall—

"Enough." Hades' hand caught my arm, gloved fingers wrapping around my wrist to steady me.

I froze.

His grip wasn't rough, but it was firm. My gaze lifted on instinct, my eyes meeting his. He didn't look away. Neither did I.

My pulse thundered in my ears as something quiet passed between us. Just when I thought he might speak, might do *something*, he vanished, whisking away.

His absence hit harder than it should have. I stood there, arm still half raised. I let my hand fall to my side, flexing my fingers.

PERSEPHONE

 set the stack of weathered books down, their ancient bindings creaking. Every muscle protested as I lowered myself onto the couch—a testament to the training session with Hades earlier. I shifted my weight, attempting to get comfortable. The cushions molded to the contours of my body.

My mind still stirred with the information Hades had shared. The Nexus Stone, the fact my mother possessed two pieces of it, and one piece of the spell that countered it. It had driven me to the library.

I needed answers. Hades had been vague when I tried to press him for more information, dismissing my questions and telling me he had other matters to attend to. I'd found comfort in this library before, lost in the pages of books about the flora of the Underworld and the myths of mortals. Today was different. I pulled the first book off the pile.

"Creation of the Realms."

I'd read this book in the Olympian Library, but there had to be something I missed. There had been no mention of the Nexus Stone. I flipped the book open and glossed over the familiar pages, my finger trailing over each line of the too-small text. The first few pages were the same as I'd read in the Olympian Library. But as I delved deeper into the text, there were differences.

In the beginning, there was a chaos of creation energy. One day, there was a spark. That spark birthed the stone. It was the catalyst that gave birth to Faerie, Olympus, the mortal realm, and countless others beyond. A spell was born along with the stone designed to balance the immense power it held.

The Titans were powerful beings of insatiable ambition. They sought to claim dominion over all the realms and bend them to their will. The Nexus Stone not only created the realms but was also an artifact capable of granting immense power. It made anything possible. The Titans' children, the Divine, waged war against them and used the stone to defeat them. I had trouble imagining the Divine uniting for *good*. They had long strayed from such ideals.

My finger traced over an image of Hades. He'd been the Divine chosen to rule the Underworld. He was given great power, but it came with a price.

His touch of death.

The Divine used one piece of the stone to strengthen Tartarus and keep the Titans imprisoned. The stone had a will of its own. After its purpose was fulfilled, the rest of the pieces dispersed across all the realms again.

My body went cold. The memory of my fingers touching it—of feeling the raw power radiating from it—sent shivers over my skin. *That's why Hades had been so angry.*

I lingered on the image of Hades, put here in these pages long before my time. His gray eyes, like orbs of polished steel, held an intensity that drew me in. The straight lines of his face exuded authority. And despite the passing of centuries, Hades still had the same tousled black hair.

Even through the page, he had an aura of power. A feeling I understood—but didn't want to understand—bloomed in my chest. I shifted on the couch, desperate to feel the ache of my muscles. It did little to shift my focus from Hades. I closed the book with a sigh and picked up the next one on the stack.

I kept reading.

My eyelids grew heavy. A yawn slipped from my lips. The words on the page blurred before my eyes. I blinked, trying to shake off the fog coating my mind. I slumped on the couch as the exhaustion of the day caught up to me.

I had tried to skip the medicine and angered Mother.

I screamed, though I knew no one could hear me. My heart pounded. The wooden walls of the box pressed in around me. Frantic gasps filled the space, each one more desperate than the last. Dried blood caked the walls. I continued to claw at the wood, no longer able to feel my fingers or the pain.

I was alone.

Trapped.

Powerless.

My stomach clenched. With fear or hunger, I didn't know.

Eventually, I stopped crying. I stopped struggling. I stopped. I was numb.

Mother let me out three days later.

~

HADES

*T*he scent of old books and flowers greeted me as I stepped into the library. My gaze swept across the room. Persephone lay sprawled on the leather couch amid a sea of books. A soft whimper escaped her parted lips. Her face was flushed. It was clear to me another nightmare plagued her.

I crossed the room. I ran my knuckles across her warm cheek. She stirred with another whimper. I gathered her into my arms, fitting her perfectly against my chest. "Quiet, little goddess. It's just a dream. You are safe," I whispered.

My pulse boomed in my ears as I cradled her close. Her fingers curled against my chest, seeking my reassurance even in her unconscious state. It felt *too* good to hold her in my arms. The warmth of her body seeped into mine. She felt so fragile—delicate—though she was far from it.

I whisked. Persephone's room took shape around us. I flicked my hand, and my shadowy magic unmade her neat bed. I held her for a few more seconds. *Let her go*, I told myself. I set her down under the duvet and rested her head on the pillows. The twin moons' silvery glow illuminated all of her now-peaceful features. It appeared as if the nightmare had never touched her.

Tucking the covers around her, I lingered for a moment, drinking in the sight of her sleeping form. Some nights I stayed here, watching. The Fates were cruel. The ache to touch her, to feel her soft skin beneath my fingertips, was a constant, throbbing pulse. I'd always been a selfish man. I did what I pleased, consequences be damned. But I couldn't do this. It was a battle of restraint, knowing I could never live with myself if I gave in. I could never see her in pain.

Her chest rose and fell in a steady rhythm, her breaths coming slow and even. It was a comfort to know the nightmare had settled. I stole one last glance at her before I whisked back to my study.

PERSEPHONE

"Next lesson. The key to survival in combat is not just striking your opponent but avoiding their attacks. This applies whether or not you are using magic." Hades gestured to the center of the room. "Today, we'll focus on defensive maneuvers and evasive techniques."

I nodded and prepared my stance—feet shoulder-width apart, with knees bent to lower my center of gravity. My skin prickled with awareness, all my senses heightened. I kept my breaths measured. I didn't take my attention off Hades. I wouldn't let him take me by surprise again. My muscles were tense and ready.

"Read your opponent's movements. Observe their body language. Anticipate their attacks before they happen. Watch." Hades shifted into a series of strikes on the canvas bag, narrating each. My eyes tracked every single move he made. I studied the way his muscles tensed beneath the navy fabric of his shirt. The subtle changes in his stance.

I caught myself hanging on each of his words. Hades looked at me but said nothing. A flush crept up my neck, but I was grateful for his silence.

He continued for ten minutes. "Got it?" Hades snapped me out of my transfixion.

"Yeah." The word wobbled on my tongue, slipping out in a tone far less steady than I intended.

"Good." Hades stared at the floor, his jaw clenched tight. I shifted uneasily.

Hades extended his hand, and tendrils of shadowy magic curled around his fingers, coalescing into a dark figure mirroring his stance. It lunged forward, striking with the same fierce intensity Hades had demonstrated moments before. Hades narrated his defensive moves. His movements were fluid and precise as he dodged and weaved.

His magic disappeared. "Now, you try with me."

"I don't get to go against your magic?"

"Scared of me?" The weight of his question sank into my chest. My stomach tightened, and I swallowed hard, unsure if we were still discussing training.

Yes.

The word bounced around my mind, a confession I dared not speak aloud. Instead, I forced a dry laugh. "Please. Not even a little."

He stepped forward. "Then stop hesitating and show me."

I brushed my reservations away and forced my body into attacking, mimicking his. He dodged every blow. "You're going to have to do better than that, little goddess."

I launched my fist forward, a tingling sensation rushing through me. Before my blow could find its mark, Hades shifted, his movements a blur.

His strike landed with brutal precision, knocking me off balance and sending me hurtling toward the floor. "Is that all you've got? You'll need to be more creative. Using my own moves won't catch me off guard. Of course I'll see them coming."

Hades' body towered over mine as I lay sprawled. His

expression was unreadable. "Go take a water break. You need it."

I sneered at him, pushing myself up. I almost wanted to fight him on it, but he was right. I needed it.

I poured myself water, sipping on it slowly before setting down the glass. The moment I stepped back into the center of the room, he launched at me. Every time, he'd find an opening to knock me down. But with the repetition, I tried new ideas, new maneuvers.

I honed my focus on anticipating Hades' attacks. He came at me harder. Occasionally, he caught me—his years of practice showing. But I moved with an agility I hadn't known I possessed.

"You're a quick learner, Persephone," Hades mused. "Or maybe I'm a fantastic teacher."

I ignored the compliment and shifted my stance. "You think highly of yourself, don't you?"

"I do." He took a step closer. "As should you."

I squared my shoulders. "Careful," I said, forcing my voice to steady. "You're starting to sound like you believe in me."

"I do." Hades flexed the fingers of his right hand. "And one day, you will too."

Before I could react to his words or closeness, his hand shot out. It collided with my shoulder, jolting me with pain. My balance faltered. I reached out and clung to Hades.

Hades staggered backward with me, cursing under his breath, a flicker of surprise washing over his features. The stumble turned into a collapse, pulling us hard to the floor.

We remained silent for a few moments, entangled in a pile of limbs. My cheek brushed against his chest rising and falling beneath me, fast and uneven. Not calm. Not controlled.

A soft chuckle broke free from his throat.

I laughed too—awkward, breathless. "That was… not graceful."

"No," he murmured.

His body didn't move. He didn't loosen his grip on my torso. Why wasn't he pulling back?

Worse, why wasn't *I*?

His arms held me there, one slung across my back, the other anchored low around my waist like he'd forgotten he could let go. The silence swelled. My brain screamed at me to shift, to say something, to break whatever line we were toeing. "You should move," I said quietly.

His mouth twitched at one corner. "You're the one on top of me."

"You broke my fall," I said, though I didn't try to move.

His gray-eyed gaze flicked down to my mouth and back up again. "And yet here you remain."

"You should probably…" I whispered, "let go of me."

He didn't. His hand flexed against the small of my back. "Yeah. Probably."

In one fluid motion, he reversed our positions, his body rolling over mine, pressing me down into the mat. His arms bracketed either side of my head, gloved palms flat against the floor. Not restraining, but close enough. His body caged mine with heat and impossible stillness.

His breath drifted across my cheek. Close. Too close.

I stilled beneath him, barely breathing. My heart crashed against my ribs like it was trying to escape. "Hades," I said.

He didn't answer. His gaze raked over my face. "You're not afraid of me." His voice was hoarse.

I swallowed. "You don't know that."

A flicker of a smile ghosted across his lips. "You wouldn't look at me like that if you were."

"How am I looking at you?"

He let out a long breath, lowering himself, just a fraction.

The solid weight of him blanketed me, and my skin lit up. Still, he didn't touch me beyond the pin of his body against mine, fabric a barrier between us.

"You should move," I whispered again, but I didn't push him away.

"Say the word," he said. "I'll get off you."

My traitorous fingers slid to his cloth-covered forearm. Not to push, but to ground myself. He closed his eyes— maybe enjoying the moment, I didn't know.

My hand moved of its own volition, drawn inexorably to his face. My trembling thumb brushed across his stubbled jaw. I tried to tell myself my fingers were only shaking from the exhaustion of training, but that was a lie.

It was him, his closeness.

His eyes snapped open, locking onto mine.

The heat of his skin was disarming, a contrast to the cold, smooth leather I had grown accustomed to. I braced for agony, for the searing bite I knew his death touch should bring, but it never came.

A jolt passed between us. It wasn't audible. There was no crack of thunder, no glowing light or Divine declaration. But I felt it. Deep. Violent. Like the very marrow in my bones had just realigned.

It ripped through me, scorching and blinding, more than electricity, tearing through my soul and settling into my very being like it had always belonged there. My breath stuttered. My vision blurred around the edges.

The world didn't just fall away; it disintegrated.

No more sparring room. No more ache in my arms and legs. No more air in my lungs.

Just him.

Just us.

His heartbeat thundered above me, but it wasn't separate from mine anymore. It was as if an invisible force had braided our pulses together, rhythm syncing beat for beat until I couldn't tell where mine ended and his began.

Tethered.

Hades shoved himself back, away from me. He scrambled to his feet like I'd burned him, like our skin touching had been a mistake he couldn't undo fast enough. He moved across the room. "Are you okay?" he asked, with a detachment I didn't like.

Like none of *that* had just happened.

I turned my head, gluing my eyes to the mat. I couldn't look at him. "Yes." My voice cracked.

There was a long pause where I swore I could still feel his weight on top of me again. His heart beat against mine. "Are you hurt?" he asked.

Physically?

"No," I whispered.

Emotionally?

Yes.

I curled my fingers against the mat, gripping it like it could ground me. My chest rose and fell too fast. In my peripheral vision, a shadow twisted in the corner of the room.

Hades whisked, reappearing in front of me. His brows were drawn, eyes sharp. He crouched slowly, like any sudden movement might spook me. One gloved hand reached for mine, and I didn't resist. He pulled me upright with an ease that made my legs buckle, but he caught me before I could fall. His arm wrapped around my back like a shield.

He pulled me close. The heat of his body seeped through the layers of fabric. I shifted my stance, balancing my weight. Hades didn't speak. He just held me, cradling my face like I was made of glass.

I blinked up at him, unsure whether I wanted to thank him or shove him away for making me feel this much. His thumb hovered near my jaw, the barest pressure keeping me rooted. His silence wasn't empty. It was full, bursting at the seams with everything neither of us dared say aloud.

I didn't want him to let go.

Not yet.

Hades' eyes scanned every inch of my face like he was memorizing it, searching for pain, for doubt. His fingers tightened fractionally where they rested on my spine, and then he leaned in, slow enough to give me space to pull away.

I didn't.

His warm breath brushed against my lips. I closed the last inch between us, pressing my lips against his.

Hades didn't move for a heartbeat, two… and then he kissed me back. Just barely. A featherlight press.

He pulled back. "You're okay," he whispered, as if he were trying to convince himself this moment was real.

His forehead came to rest against mine, and we stayed like that, breathing the same air. "You don't know," he said, his lips brushing against the corner of my mouth, "how incredible it feels to have your skin against mine."

I exhaled slowly, my hands sliding up his chest until they found the edge of his jaw, the light stubble rough under my fingertips. His eyes fluttered shut, head turning just slightly, the scrape of his cheek against mine sending a shiver down my spine.

"I'm okay," I whispered, my fingers brushing across the sharp planes of his face before sliding to the back of his neck, pulling him closer, needing more—needing him. They didn't stop there. They moved up into his hair, curling. "You're not hurting me."

He didn't move at first.

But his chest rose—once, hard—and then rumbled with a sound so deep, so low it set every nerve in my body on fire.

"Fuck it." The words tore from him like a man breaking a promise to himself.

He crushed his lips to mine like he'd been starving for this. For *me*. There was nothing soft about it now. No hesitation. No holding back. It was heat and chaos and too much and still not enough.

His mouth claimed mine with a desperation that stole my breath, and I let it. Let him. His hands slipped down from my face to my waist, fingers digging into my sides.

"I need you, Hades," I breathed. The words left me before I could think better of them. No romance or poetry, just the truth.

His entire body tensed, and his hands gripped me even tighter, fingers flexing. "Don't say that to me." Hades' eyes contradicted his words, pupils blown wide. They flared with hunger. Lust. Need.

I leaned forward, pressing the lightest kiss to the corner of his mouth. He shuddered, and I felt it. Every inch of his control strained between us. "I want your skin against mine," I whispered, lips brushing his pulse. I shifted in his arms. "I want to feel you… everywhere."

He hissed through his teeth, jaw clenched. "Persephone—"

"Don't pretend." My voice cracked, but I didn't care. "You want me too. Don't pretend you don't."

His head dipped, eyes closing. "You don't know what you're asking for."

"I do."

"You're not ready."

I swallowed hard. "Don't tell me what I'm ready for."

His eyes snapped open. "You don't understand. If I let myself have you, if I take that step, I don't know how to go back to being anything else."

"I'm not asking you to go back," I said.

He breathed sharply. "You undo me."

"And yet you're still holding on."

"You don't want this," he said. "It will change everything."

I shook my head. "You don't get to tell me that."

In a slow, deliberate motion, Hades lifted his hand to his mouth and gripped one of the gloves with his teeth. He tugged it off, each pull too slow. Hades let the glove fall to the floor. He repeated the process with the second glove, each tug feeling less like removing leather and more like stripping away the distance between us.

His bare hands traced a path from my elbows down to my wrists and back up again. The heat of his skin seeped into mine, his touch more than just comforting; it was possessive, claiming, branding. His hands should've hurt me. His death touch should've stolen my breath in the worst way, but it didn't. The question of why coiled inside me, even as his touch urged me closer.

I could feel his restraint beneath every slow movement of his fingers. "This room," he murmured, "isn't where I want to take you."

Hades' fingertips brushed along the curve of my neck, pausing just below my jaw. "I want to explore you. To learn what makes you gasp. What makes you beg." His thumb dragged lightly across my bottom lip. "And I will," he added. "But not here. You deserve more than a sparring mat." He paused, hands sliding down to my waist, holding me like I might vanish if he let go.

"You deserve a throne."

I swallowed hard.

His eyes tracked the movement like a predator sighting the twitch of prey. "And I deserve to worship you." He whisked us, leaving the sparring room behind in a blur of motion.

PERSEPHONE

"Welcome to *our* throne room." His voice was low and rough. I couldn't ignore the emphasis he put on the word *our* or the way it made my body light up. He lifted me bridal style, one arm under my knees and the other braced firmly around my back. I let out a soft, startled sound, but he didn't loosen his hold.

Torches lined the walls leading to the dais, their flames casting long shadows that twisted across the expanse of the room. A wrought iron chandelier hung from the ceiling. A slow gasp slipped past my lips before I could stop it.

At its center, metal arms extended outward, each one cradling a globe of light. Black gemstones dangled from the iron arms, capturing the reflection of the flickering flames and globes.

It was beautiful. And intimidating.

But even that couldn't hold my attention for long, not when I could feel Hades' gaze on me like a physical touch.

I looked back at him.

The light-gray hue of his irises had deepened into a darker shade like churning storm clouds. He watched me like

I was the only thing that existed in the room. A flutter bloomed in my stomach. Another pulse echoed lower, deeper in my center.

I looped my arms around his neck, holding on tighter. Hades kept walking, each step slow and deliberate. I opened my mouth to speak, but the words didn't come. My thoughts were a mess.

His gaze dipped to mine, brief but intense. Every brush of his breath against my temple, every flex of muscle beneath my body as he moved, they all pulled tighter at the coil inside me.

The torches hissed on the walls as we approached the dais. At its peak stood a throne crafted from dark intricately carved stone. Patterns wrapped around the armrests and the back of the chair.

We reached the first step, and Hades climbed the stairs slowly. His body shifted beneath me as he ascended, but he never once loosened his hold.

Hades turned and sank into the throne like he belonged there, which, of course, he did. Every inch of him exuded power. But the moment his body met the stone, his focus returned fully to me.

He adjusted me in his lap until I was straddling him. My thighs pressed into his hips. His heat seeped into me, through me. Every part of me aligned with him—my chest to his, my breath and heartbeat mirroring his.

Hades' hands started at my elbows, gliding up and down my arms. Goose bumps followed in their wake. Each pass sunk beneath my skin. He wasn't just touching me. He was learning me.

When his fingers reached the nape of my neck, they stilled there. I leaned in.

He tugged me forward, just enough for our mouths to

hover inches apart. Our breathing mingled as his lips brushed mine, and then he closed the distance.

The kiss started soft. His mouth moved with infuriating patience, like he had no intention of rushing through this, like he wanted to savor every second.

Hades' tongue swiped across my bottom lip, and I parted them with a sigh. He tasted like home—not the one I'd left behind, but the sanctuary I'd been searching for.

One of Hades' hands slid into my hair, tangling in the strands and angling my head just where he wanted it. The other explored lower, fingers dragging down my spine, tracing the shape of my waist, then gripping my thigh.

The kiss intensified. It turned possessive. Brutal. His teeth grazed my bottom lip with just enough pressure to make me gasp. He swallowed the sound. I rocked forward, unable to stop the movement. My body was desperate for friction, for closeness, for him.

Hades groaned low in his throat, and the sound sent a ripple of heat through me. His hand on my thigh tightened, pulling me down against him, guiding the rhythm between us. His hips shifted, a hard line beneath me.

I flattened a hand on his chest. Hades' bare hand settled over mine, guiding it lower between us and pressing my hand firmly against his length straining through his pants. I let out a slow breath. "You want me?" I asked, breathless, my lips curling into a slow, teasing smile, because I already knew the answer.

"I crave you," he said, "in ways I can't and don't want to end."

We moved. Not with footsteps, not with sound. Just a rush of Hades' magic that curled around us, leaving me sitting on the throne with him on his knees before me between my legs. His broad shoulders fit perfectly between my spread thighs. His hands settled onto my legs. "Don't worry," he murmured, voice dropping to a rasp, "I'll show you just how much I want you." His hungry eyes caressed me, dragging slowly. "I've waited so long for this," he rasped.

His touch trailed upward along my thighs, holding me in place. "Tell me you're okay." His hands brushed along the waistband of my pants. "That this is okay."

I trembled on the throne. His touch, his eyes, his presence. It was all too much. I bit my lip until copper filled my mouth. "I'm okay." I cleared the lump building in my throat. "Better than okay."

Hades didn't move until I finished speaking. I fumbled with the waistband, urging him to move faster. He chuckled. "So eager." With a flick of his magic, my pants disappeared.

His hand slid beneath the hem of my shirt, pushing it up, exposing the bare skin of my stomach to the cool air. His other hand grazed my damp underwear.

A low sound escaped him. His lips curved up into a dark, satisfied smirk. "Look how much you want me too." Hades' fingers moved in slow, deliberate circles, rubbing my clit through the fabric.

My head fell back against the stone, a moan slipping past my lips as electricity danced across my skin. My awareness narrowed to the place where his unrelenting fingers moved.

"Tell me you want me," he said.

"I want you," I gasped, pushing my hips forward, needing more.

"Far too much fabric." His breath warmed the skin on my inner thigh as he placed a kiss just at the edge of my underwear. Then another. And another. His magic coiled around me, the rest of my clothes vanishing.

Despite the inferno of heat coursing through my veins, the sudden chill made goose bumps prickle across my skin. The contradiction of sensations was a tangible reminder of the paradox of our existence. Death and growth.

I stared at the God of the Underworld between my legs.

Hades placed a hand on my abdomen. His palm was warm and firm. "I've thought a lot about how you would taste," he said as his mouth moved to my center. My legs trembled as he hovered above my clit.

My breath caught.

"How you would feel quivering under my touch."

"Please," I whispered.

He glanced up at me. "As you wish."

His tongue stroked my slick core, slow at first. He moved up to my clit, circling it in gentle, rhythmic strokes. Each pass of his tongue made my back arch, a moan slipping from my lips before I could stop it.

"You taste so fucking good," he groaned. "So much better than I imagined."

My fingers tangled in his messy dark hair, twisting in the inky strands as I pulled him closer. I couldn't help it. The heat of his mouth, the sound of his low groans vibrating against my core... it was too much and not enough all at once.

I rocked against his mouth, chasing each stroke. Hades let me, hands firm on my thighs now, holding me open for him and guiding my rhythm. "More, please," I moaned. I wanted his hands—his mouth everywhere.

He obliged without a word. One hand released my thigh and slid up, dragging his fingertips across my stomach, then ribs, until it found my breast. His thumb and forefinger pinched and rolled my nipple, just enough to make my hips jerk beneath him.

My eyes fluttered shut at the onslaught of sensation. Pleasure coursed through me in waves; his tongue, his mouth, his hand, all working together in devastating harmony. My moans spilled into the air, echoing off the walls of the throne room.

"Eyes on me, Persephone," Hades said.

The sound of my name snapped my eyes open. He released my nipple with a parting brush of his thumb. My back arched off the throne instinctively. He gripped both my thighs and pulled me to the edge of the throne with a smooth motion.

His tongue returned to my swollen clit. Two thick fingers slid into me, and my breath stopped. Hades moved slow at first, curling them inside me, then speeding up. "You're so wet, little goddess."

I bucked. "Hades." My breaths were choppy.

"How does that feel?" His lips brushed against me between each word.

All I could manage was a broken whimper. He didn't need to ask. I was sure Hades could feel my fervent heart beating for him. The wetness pooling at my center, the way I trembled beneath him.

"Too good," I finally said. My words held the truth pulsing within my veins. His teeth grazed my clit, and my head grew fuzzy at the pleasure. I couldn't think.

Hades pulled away, his lips glistening with my wetness. "You don't understand how hard I tried not to crave this." His tongue darted across his bottom lip. "Not to crave *you*." He rose, bracing his hands on my thighs. "I don't fail at much, little goddess," he said. "But resisting you was never a fight I had any hope of winning."

He leaned in, lips brushing my inner thigh. "I told myself it could never happen." His mouth pressed higher, closer to my center. Hades glanced up. "But then you looked at me the way you do. You touched me… and you're not hurt."

Silence followed.

"And now you're here, open. Needy. *Mine*." He moved, sweeping me off the throne, one hand splayed against the curve of my back, the other beneath my thighs. Shadowy magic bloomed around his legs and spread outward and upward in quick tendrils as he sat, settling me in his lap.

When his magic cleared, he was bare underneath me.

Hades didn't look like a man. He looked like art. *All* his features were harsh and perfect, like a living, breathing sculpture. My hands found his shoulders, my fingers flexing.

His cock twitched beneath me, pressed exactly where I ached most. His thumb grazed my nipple, drawing a sharp gasp from my lips. My hips rolled, grinding against him. I *craved* him. "I need you."

My head spun, dizzy from the hunger, the heat, the *rightness* of him beneath me.

I had never wanted like this.

With Basile, sex was a foul, empty chore that left me colder each time. This—*this* was something entirely different.

Hades pulled me into a rough kiss. His mouth claimed mine like he needed it to breathe. I gasped against him, my body melting forward. His hand cradled the back of my neck, the other brushing the curve of my jaw.

He pulled back, breathing hard. He gripped my hips with both hands and lifted. The blunt head of his cock pressed against my entrance. A tremor ran through me at the contact.

"I won't rush you," he murmured. "You lead."

I nodded as I wrapped my hands around his neck for balance. Then, slowly, I lowered myself.

The stretch burned—perfectly overwhelming. "Breathe, Persephone," Hades whispered. One hand cupped the base of my spine, the other cradled my hip. "You're doing so well. Let me have you."

I did, inch by inch, until I was nearly seated on him. I let out a soft whimper and closed my eyes.

"Eyes open." His voice cut through the haze. "Look at me."

I blinked through the pressure.

"Good goddess," he whispered. "That's it."

I rested my head on his shoulder. He kissed my temple.

"You were made for me, Persephone." His hips flexed, just enough to make me gasp. "You're perfect."

I started to move, and Hades guided my hips up, then dragged them down again. "Hades—"

"There," he said. "Just like that."

My head fell back as I rolled my hips. He thrust into me hard, burying himself deep. "You're mine." His words rumbled through me, promising something far deeper.

I felt it. Not just between my thighs, but everywhere. My breasts bounced with the movement as I chased every ounce of friction. "I'm yours," I gasped.

My nails bit into his shoulders as the pleasure started to build higher. His skin was fever-hot beneath my fingers, taut and flexing with every thrust. Hades gritted his teeth and brought one of his hands from my hip to the bundle of nerves between my legs. His fingers found my clit, slick with need, and began to circle.

My back arched. My toes curled. "Don't stop," I gasped.

He pressed a kiss to the base of my throat. "I won't," he breathed. "Not until I've learned every sound you make when you come for me."

I gasped, clenching around him.

He thrust again, slow and deep. "Do you even know what you do to me?"

I didn't have a chance to answer before he continued.

"You make me want things I don't let myself want. I've had centuries to master control." Another thrust. "But with you? I'm on fucking edge." His fingers on my clit sped up. My body shook. My thighs clenched around his hips. He knew I was close. He felt it in the way my body responded to him.

He pressed his lips to my temple. "Take what you need."

I moved harder, faster, every roll of my hips sending lightning through my veins. "I'm-I'm close. Oh, gods."

"Say my name," he groaned. "Don't you dare cry out for other gods when you're on my cock. You say *my* name."

I whimpered, the climax building closer. "Hades."

He groaned into my neck, low and wrecked, teeth grazing my skin. "That's it," he breathed. "That's fucking it."

His thrusts turned deeper, messier. His control was gone, his rhythm wild. But still, his fingers on my clit never faltered. "You're so close," he whispered. "I feel it."

"I-I—" My body clenched around him, the tension finally snapping. My climax slammed into me. My mouth parted in a silent cry, and his name slipped from my lips again. "Hades."

My entire body trembled, racked with wave after wave.

With a desperate groan, he drove into me. Four more times. His body tensed beneath my hands. "Persephone," he choked out as his cock throbbed and spilled into me, forehead pressed to mine. His thrusts slowed until they stopped.

For a beat, there was only silence.

Tendrils of black magic spiraled around us, each crackling with dark power. They moved like they were alive. My chest grew hot. A crown materialized atop Hades' head. In that same moment, a weight settled on my head—a crown of my own. I grew dizzy, but Hades held me steady. Despite the disorienting sensation that swept over me, I refused to tear my gaze away from Hades. It was as if an invisible thread wove itself between us, pulling tighter with each beat of our hearts.

An onslaught of raw emotions hit me. For most of my life, I ran from emotions, locked them away in the deepest recesses of my mind. For the first time now, I embraced them. Joy. Desire. Security. Warmth. It was difficult to comprehend. The connection between Hades and me defied simple categorization into singular emotions. I felt them *all*.

Lines appeared on Hades' skin, dancing across his chest

to form a complex design pulsing with energy. A tingling sensation spread across my flesh. I glanced down. Marks appeared on my body, mirroring Hades'. They pulsed a soft-white light for a fleeting moment before fading back to black. I'd read about these marks.

The magic swirling around us stopped, and I slumped against Hades' chest. Only our hard, rhythmic inhales and exhales broke the silence between us. "My beautiful mate," he whispered.

Not just a title. A *truth*.

PERSEPHONE

We whisked to Hades' room, and the sight that greeted me there left me speechless. I thought the room I was given was nice, but this was unlike anything I'd ever seen before. Tall, arched windows lined one wall, offering an unobscured view of the Underworld below. Unlike my previous room, there were no drapes. Despite the darkness outside, the twin moons illuminated the landscape enough to reveal glimpses of the scenery below. Everything was at a height and angle I hadn't experienced before. This must have been the highest room of the palace.

I drew closer to the window, my hand in Hades'. He stood behind me and pulled me close, wrapping his arms around my shoulders. He trailed a gentle finger along the crown, reminding me of its presence atop my head.

My breath caught—not because of the crown, but because of the way he touched it. Like it meant something. Like *I* meant something.

I soaked in the warmth of his embrace as I studied the flickers of violet and white dancing among the stars. They pulsed like tiny heartbeats.

"It knew," Hades said.

"What?"

"The realm. It knew who you were—who you'd become." He ran his hand over the new marking covering my chest. Every nerve in my body lit up like it recognized him all over again. "Did you ever wonder why the realm helped you out of the Styx? Why it guided you to a safe place to rest? Why the wisps drew close to you?"

All the moments lit up in my head, one after the other.

The whale during my near drowning. The glowing violet wisps. The realm nudging me forward to a safe place. None of them had been coincidences. "Did you know I was your mate?" I asked.

"Mm-hmm," he hummed as he brushed away my hair and placed a kiss on my neck. "But I couldn't see how it would work."

The heat of his lips against my skin was both comfort and chaos, like he'd unlocked something caged inside me and set it ablaze. I shivered at the sensation. "And here we are." I tilted my neck and leaned farther into his touch.

"Did you know?"

"No," I sighed, and that was the truth. "I sensed something, but I didn't recognize it as the mate bond. I'd read about it but experiencing it is entirely different." It was louder, wilder than anything I'd ever read.

Hades' arms tightened around me. "It's not something easily understood until it happens." Hades let go of me, and an instant ache filled the space where his touch had been. He took my hand. "Come."

I followed, but part of me struggled to catch up. Not physically, but emotionally, like my body had accepted something my heart hadn't caught up to yet. This new version of Hades—the softness in his voice, the way he touched me like

I was something sacred—was so different from the god I'd known before.

He'd kept himself at a distance, and now he touched me without hesitation. Looked at me like I was his. The shift was jarring, and yet I didn't want to pull away.

Hades led me into the washroom. Candles cast a warm, golden glow over the obsidian tiles and the grand dark stone tub in the center of the room. Hades waved a hand, the muscles in his face tightening. *Uncertainty.* "I hope this is to your liking."

"This looks—" I stumbled over my words. "It's beautiful." I placed a hand on my chest. "Truly." It was more than beautiful. It was thoughtful, intimate.

I walked closer to the tub. Hades reached out, assisting me as I eased myself into the water. Steam rose around me like a veil, smelling of eucalyptus. Hades joined me, settling in behind me.

I sat in between Hades' legs and rested my head back on his chest. His heartbeat was steady. Grounding. Beside us were an array of different soaps, oils, bath salts, a bottle of wine, and two stemmed glasses. The weight of the crown on my head disappeared, and I glanced up at Hades, seeing his was gone too. He smiled at me.

Hades' strong hands glided over my skin as if they'd been doing it for lifetimes. They drew lazy circles on my back.

I closed my eyes and breathed him in. Every pass of his fingertips wrote something on my skin. It was a language I didn't fully understand, but I wanted to.

He reached for the wine bottle, his magic swirling around it, making the cork vanish. As he poured two glasses, the rich aroma of faerie wine wafted through the air. He set the bottle down and handed me a glass.

I hesitated, my eyebrows knitting together. "I thought I was not to have faerie wine."

"We're celebrating." He took his own glass into his hands. "You should be stronger now that we're mated. The mating bond enhances our connection on every level, including magic. I suspect it will help us in figuring out what's wrong with yours."

I lifted the glass to eye level. The soft glow of candlelight cast a warm, white sheen that danced on the surface of the amber liquid. I twisted the stem between my fingers, swirling the wine. Tiny droplets of condensation glistened in the soft light of the room. With a small smile, I brought the glass to my lips.

"Try it," Hades urged. "It's a vintage from Faerie, one of my favorites."

I took a cautious sip. It tasted floral and sweet. "It's fantastic."

We sipped our wine, each sip golden warmth spreading through me. Hades refilled his glass while I opted to stick to just one. I swished my hands through the water, the gentle ripples tickling my skin. The bubbles moved atop the surface, reflecting the soft glow of the candles with a pearlescent sheen.

The silence between us wasn't awkward, but it was new. Like neither of us wanted to speak too soon, afraid the wrong words might shatter whatever this was becoming. I traced the rim of my glass with my finger, a soft hum vibrating under my touch. "This is new," I said.

"Yes." The word was quiet, steady.

I looked down at the water. "It's a lot… to be told I'm someone's mate. That I'm meant for this. For you."

"The bond chose us. But the trust, that has to be earned," Hades said as he swirled his wine in the glass. "And I plan to earn yours."

My eyebrows lifted slightly. "I didn't expect that answer."

"What did you expect me to say?" he asked.

I turned in his arms, facing him. "I don't know. *We're mates now, deal with it?*"

His mouth curved into something that was almost a smirk. "I could've gone that route, but you don't strike me as the kind of woman that would respond well to that. You didn't exactly love initially binding yourself to me when you entered our realm."

I narrowed my eyes. "There you go with the word *our* again."

He gave a slight shrug and took a sip of his wine. "I like the way it sounds."

"Careful, Hades. You're charming me."

"I'm not trying to charm you."

"No?"

He shook his head, droplets clinging to his hair before sliding to his temples and down his jaw. "I'm trying to be honest with you. Even when it would be easier not to be." Hades tilted his head. "If I were charming you, there would be thousands of roses."

I snorted. "Subtle."

"Subtlety has never been my strength."

Heat pooled at my center. Perhaps it was the wine or the mating bond thrumming with life inside of me, but I was filled with need. My thighs clenched, and I wrapped my legs around his torso, pressing closer.

His eyes darkened as my fingers drifted down between us, under the water, skating lightly over the surface of his hardness.

"The frenzy is kicking in," Hades murmured, moving his hand down from my neck. My core throbbed harder every inch he moved lower. I sucked in a deep breath as his finger circled my clit. "Should I stop?"

My core throbbed, clenching around nothing. I shook my head. "No." The word darted off my tongue.

Hades chuckled. "I'll never get enough of you, Persephone."

My name was a caress on his lips. I leaned forward and pressed mouthy kisses along his neck. He tasted like warmth and want. His hands gripped my waist. "You're shaking," he said.

"Doesn't mean I want to stop," I whispered against his skin.

He stilled for a breath, then stood, rising from the water with me still wrapped around him. I clung to him. Water streamed from his body, droplets gliding over muscle and trailing down him in rivulets. Hades stepped out of the bath and carried me out of the washroom. He stopped there, running his fingers in a circle on my back.

The scent hit me.

Floral.

I turned my head, still clinging to him. Thousands of roses filled the room from floor to ceiling. The crimson flowers overwhelmed the space. Some were open, others were still curled tightly, buds that would soon bloom.

He carried me through them. "I thought you weren't trying to charm me," I said.

A smile tugged at the corner of his mouth, but his eyes stayed on mine. "I changed my mind."

He laid me on the bed scattered with petals. They clung to my wet skin, cool and soft. Hades hovered above me, water still dripping from his hair. He ran a thumb along my jaw and up to my lips. "I said there would be thousands of roses," he murmured.

"You're absurd."

"I'm your mate," he said simply. His hand slid from my

mouth to cup my cheek. "And I cannot leave my mate so full of need."

His words echoed in my chest. The bond pulsed between us like a tether pulling tighter. "Then don't," I whispered.

HADES

I'd never seen someone so beautiful. I found myself holding my breath, afraid to disturb the peace enveloping Persephone's sleeping form. Seeing her in my—in our—bed made this all the more real. I couldn't count the number of nights I'd spent awake, thoughts of her consuming me.

For nearly a week, we'd spent most of our time in this room. When we left, our bodies remained full of need. The mating frenzy had taken over, not that I was complaining.

We talked, we laughed, between the touches and between silences. After the week, need still clung to our skin. But it was no longer just hunger, it was connection.

Something real.

Something growing.

"I feel your eyes," she said.

I stroked her loose brown hair. Her eyelids fluttered open, revealing gray eyes that now mirrored my own. I'd never appreciated the shade until they were reflected in Persephone. The first time Persephone noticed her new eye color, I expected her to be disappointed, but instead, she gushed about how much she loved them. "Am I not allowed to appreciate my beautiful mate?" I still wasn't used to the word, but it felt right.

"Flattery will only get you so far," she teased. "But if you're trying to win my favor, you're doing a fine job of it."

"I think you underestimate the lengths I would go to earn and keep your favor." The duvet draped over her, obscuring the mating bond mark. I pushed the fabric aside, revealing the intricate black lines inked on her skin. I traced them with my fingertips, and they responded to my touch, the lines momentarily pulsing a shimmering white. A surge of warmth washed through the bond, and pride swelled within me. If I looked at her much longer, I wouldn't be able to leave. I brushed a light kiss on her temple. "I have to go. I'll be back soon."

"Do you have to?" Her voice was soft. She trailed her fingers along my arm. "Please stay?" She peppered kisses on my jaw.

This feels too fucking good. I wasn't accustomed to touch, but I knew that would change with Persephone. She'd already left her own personal brand on me.

"Stop, goddess. Otherwise, I will never."

She smiled and crawled on top of me, straddling my waist. "So you're saying I should continue?" I groaned as she rolled her hips into my already hard cock.

"Don't make this harder for me."

"You're already hard." She let out an airy laugh.

"Not what I meant, little goddess." It took everything in me to lift her naked body off my lap. Her smile deflated, and it tugged at my heart. *I will make it up to you,* I said through the bond. She jumped slightly, still not used to my voice in her head, but she nodded and smiled. It was weak, not reaching her eyes. Her shoulders dropped, but she straightened them again.

Persephone seemed unaware of the extent to which her emotions were now apparent to me. I shielded her from the worst of my own. Her disappointment was clear through the bond. I placed a kiss on the top of her head and forced myself to look away. I used my magic to dress myself. Before I could change my mind, I whisked out of the room. *I have to do this.*

The hardness in my pants motivated me to make this quick. I wouldn't play with the man today, even though I wanted to. I needed to be in and out so I could return to my realm.

Fraser Morris' office was small and plain—a desk, a metal file cabinet, and a computer, with no personal items anywhere. The door to his office was glazed, the lock engaged. The light sound of slapping skin filled the room. My eyes narrowed on Fraser, stroking his cock with parted lips as he stared at images on his computer screen. I didn't look closely at his computer. I already knew what was there.

I guess I showed up at the perfect time. Fraser hadn't noticed me. I didn't wear my gloves today. I reached out and placed my palm on his neck. Fraser's hand slipped from his cock, and his head lolled to the side. I shoved his body from the chair, and he crumpled into a pile of vile man on the floor.

Dead.

I hummed as I stared at the man. My death touch still worked. There wasn't a book to explain why it didn't work on Persephone, no rule to point to, but I knew the truth in my bones—because she was mine, my mate. I walked over to the door and disengaged the lock. I pounded on the glass. The mortals would find him soon. They probably began rushing over the moment they heard the banging.

Mortal doctors would likely attribute his death to an unexplained heart attack or a similar medical event. His coworkers would feel disgusted and betrayed when they found the pictures still on his screen as he lay dead next to them. They would know who he *really* was.

Fraser's wife would weep upon receiving the news from the authorities. Behind a closed door, she would offer a silent thanks to whatever faith she believed in, knowing he could no longer harm the twins, whom she wished he had not fathered.

I saw what I needed to see. As his coworkers neared the office door, I whisked away. My *mate* was waiting for me in my realm.

HADES

I will never get used to this. Persephone lay bare on my chest, her presence a tether, grounding me to reality. Waking with her like this had become my favorite part of the day. The stillness. The softness.

Before the mating bond, my mornings had always begun in silence. Not peace, but silence. But now, now I woke to the warmth of her body against mine. Every sensation was magnified, as if the world had sharpened into startling clarity. It was all so *real*.

I studied the gentle rhythm of her breathing. My fingers trailed a path along the contours of her spine, mapping out the curves and valleys of her form. I relished the feeling of her smooth skin. I inhaled, letting the floral perfume of her hair fill my senses. The fragrance was intoxicating—the embodiment of spring, of life, in a single breath.

I lay on the bed, lost in the sensation of *her*. I marveled at the sheer improbability of it all. To think *I* had a mate. It was still hard to believe. I pressed her delicate body closer to mine.

I wanted to show her our realm. The idea created a warm

sensation I'd never had before Persephone. Showing her the Underworld was unveiling a part of myself, putting it on a pedestal for her to see. I wanted her to see every single facet of me, the shadows and all.

The mark covering my chest thrummed against hers. I closed my eyes and allowed myself to bask in the moment. Persephone shifted. I could feel her eyes on me. "Good morning, little goddess." I opened my own again, meeting hers.

She wore a lazy smile. "Hi," she whispered. Her breath ghosted against my skin. Persephone ran her fingers on my chest, tracing the mark. Her touch ignited a fire blazing beneath my flesh. Did she know how much she made me feel?

"I was hoping I could show you more of our realm today." I caught the subtle widening of her eyes at the use of the word *our*. It was a brief flicker of surprise before her smile broadened.

Persephone pressed a light kiss to my jaw, and that stirred the desire already burning inside of me. "I'd love for you to show me."

She let out a yelp as I flipped us over. My arms caged her. Trapped.

In my bed.

In my mind.

Forever.

Her soft breaths turned ragged. I pressed my hardness into her. She bit her plump little lip and squirmed. Her nipples were already hard, waiting for my touch. I smirked, bringing my lips to the sensitive spot on her neck. "I think showing you around can wait a little while," I growled against her throat.

~

"There are many layers to the Underworld. You've experienced Tartarus already."

She paled. "Yes, I remember…" I squeezed her hand and guided her forward.

The silence was so complete that only the sparse vegetation beneath our feet disturbed the quiet. Around us, the landscape stretched out in muted browns and oranges. The expanse of land was rough but flat. The air was heavy with an oppressive stillness. To others, this layer might have looked ugly, but to me, it held a strange kind of beauty. "It's so silent here," she said.

She studied the listless movement of souls around us. "There are so many of them." Her head turned as she watched one pass us.

I nodded. "They can't see or hear you."

"They just wander?"

"Yes, until their purgatory stage is over. They move between layers, going up as they get further through the stages. When I sentence the souls, I decide which layer they start in."

"Will you ever show me that?" she asked. "Sentencing the souls?"

I nodded, a surge of warmth flowing through my body as her eyes lit up in genuine interest. Persephone wandered ahead, tugging my hand. She paid attention to each soul that passed her. Persephone stopped and whipped around to face me. "And you control everything?"

"Yes, and someday, you'll control it too."

Her lips parted. Shock pulsed through the bond, but there was a glimmer of something else. Excitement maybe? *Had I said too much? Was it all too much for her to take in?*

"What do you mean?"

"You're my mate. You *will* be the Queen of the Underworld." Even though I'd mentioned the word *queen* before, her eyes darted around. There was a minuscule change in her breathing that only I could notice.

I brushed aside a few stray strands of hair that had fallen across her face, coaxing them into place behind her ear. The gesture calmed her. "Don't worry about trying to wrap your head around it right now. We'll do everything as you are ready."

"So much has changed for me." She stared up at me through her thick lashes. Her chest rose and fell in time with mine. I pulled her into a deep kiss, unable to resist. The bond between us thrummed with need, but I wanted to show her this realm. I needed her to understand that everything I had was ours. "Look, I'll show you a purgatory phase."

She squeezed my hand. "Okay."

"Come." I guided us to the nearest soul and placed my hand on their shoulder as I held on to Persephone. My vision changed, and I was sure hers had too. We both now stood in the landscape of the soul's mind. "We're in her mind."

The soul whose mind we inhabited stood across the room, solid and mortal. A translucent version of her watched with watery eyes as a scene played out in relentless repetition. "These memories are the worst things they have done. They go through all of them."

We observed silently from the periphery of the room. The mortal stared at her husband lying motionless on a hospital bed. The memory unfolded vividly around us—the steady beeping of machines, the antiseptic smell of the hospital.

The mortal tugged strands of her brown hair. A few clumps fell from her head at the force. She clenched her hands in her hair and tears streamed down her face, the harsh fluorescent lights making them glimmer. "I should've done a better job killing you." Every one of her breaths looked like a struggle. Her neck twitched. "Poisoning you wasn't enough. You were always strong," she scoffed, hitching her sagging shoulders up. "Too strong."

Her husband lay clad in a gown, a light blanket draped over him. Wires and tubes snaked from his body, connecting him to machines that hummed and beeped, keeping his fragile system functioning on the brink of shutdown. The mortal rubbed her tears away with her palm and groaned. "I can't take this fucking beeping anymore." Her hands trembled at her sides as she moved away from the bed and unplugged the machine.

She pulled a syringe out of her pocket, managing to steady her grip. With a quick flick of her index finger, she tapped the barrel twice before inserting the needle into his flesh. Deep stress lines etched across the mortal's face as she pressed the plunger, injecting him.

She tossed the syringe onto the floor and then with both hands, ripped every tube and wire hooked to the man. Blood, spit, and fluid made a mess. The mortal twitched again and rubbed her hands on her pants before walking out of the room.

I leaned closer to Persephone, my breath brushing against her ear as I pointed out the translucent version of the soul observing her mortal counterpart. "See her," I murmured. "Notice how she no longer looks sorrowful—how she appears satisfied with what she's done. That's why she remains trapped in purgatory. This memory will repeat until she confronts the truth of her actions."

Persephone nodded slowly. It was evident the vision shook her. "Let's go." I pulled us out of the memory. "Justice is always served here for those who couldn't get it while they lived." I took a few steps. "I want to show you another layer."

"Okay." Persephone seemed to still be processing the extent of my realm, so I didn't push her to say anything else.

"Only Thanatos, Cerberus, and I can travel the layers of

the Underworld freely. You will have that ability when you are tied to the realm."

"How did I get to Tartarus that first time?"

I had hoped she wouldn't ask that question. I didn't know. "I'm not sure."

She swallowed.

~

PERSEPHONE

We materialized in a new layer. My eyes widened as I drank in the sight. Patches of glimmering wildflowers dotted the rolling hills stretched before me like scattered jewels. Souls walked among them. I tilted my head back, staring at the sky. No sun; no clouds to break up the perfect hue of pale blue. "Beautiful," I whispered. It was a relief to be out of the last layer.

Hades' gaze was already trained on me with an intensity that made me suck in a breath. "I agree."

Heat flushed in my cheeks, and my grip tightened on his hand. I turned my attention back to the landscape. Hades continued, "This is where those who have committed suicide go. They have a place here to heal with others who understand them. It gives them a community of support. There are guides dedicated to this layer, and when the souls here are ready, they are introduced to the general population on the main layer."

"Can they see us?"

"Yes, they can also talk."

"Wow." My eyes narrowed at something in the distance. "Is that a—"

"Yes." Hades whisked us closer. The roar of crashing water sent palpable thrums through the air. Mist veiled the waterfall, carrying the scent of wet stone and ancient earth. Rainbows danced in the spray, swirling with color.

The water plunged from a large formation of rocks covered with moss and ivy, striking the waiting pool below. "Do you know how to swim?" Hades' question took me out of my haze.

I shook my head. A tremor rippled through my chest. *Do you know how to swim? Do you know how to swim?* Ghosts of my memory clawed their way to the surface of my mind. I stood several feet away, but it was as if I could already feel the unrelenting water filling my lungs once again.

"Persephone." Hades' voice competed with the roar of the rushing water. My muscles tensed. "Persephone."

I took a deep breath, and the cacophony in my ears calmed. "Yes."

"You're scared." His voice held a certainty that told me he didn't need the mating bond to tell him that.

"Yes." I stared at the white foam the crashing water created. I chewed on the inside of my lip, swallowing hard. Beneath the fear was something I hadn't expected. Longing. I longed to break free of the past, to reclaim the pieces of my mind stolen from me. My hand twitched at my side, the other still in Hades'. The words came out of my mouth before the rational part of my brain could stop them. "I want to go in."

"Would you like me to teach you how to swim?"

I stayed silent, crouching to where the water met land. With trembling hands, my fingers brushed against its warm surface. I studied the contours of my face in the rippled reflection. Hades stood right behind me. "Yes." I needed to take my power back. I placed a hand on my knee and pushed myself up.

Hades shrugged off his jacket. He tugged his shirt over his

head and tossed it to the ground. I glanced back at all the souls who paid us no attention. "In front of them?"

"They're not paying attention to us, but I'll humor you." A shimmering veil appeared between us and the souls. His magic swirled around him, taking the rest of his clothes off. I went hot at the sight of his naked body. He stepped closer, and my mouth went dry. "Just you and me now." Hades ran the fabric of my dress between his fingers. "May I?"

I nodded, too wound up to speak. His magic worked around me, leaving me bare. His hand extended toward me. I took it, his warmth seeping into my skin. A knot tightened in my stomach, but I pushed it away as Hades guided me into the water. "I'll keep you safe."

He didn't banish my fears, but he dulled them, easing the sting even as the wound beneath stayed raw. Hades' grip moved up my arm as we walked deeper into the water. "Are you ready?"

I hesitated for a moment before nodding. Hades pulled me close, and I was weightless. He stood firm while my feet dangled. He adjusted his grip, and I wrapped my legs around his waist, my arms securing around his neck. We moved deeper into the water, his legs now moving and keeping us afloat. He squeezed my ass, and I yelped. A wicked grin curled on his lips. "Sorry, I couldn't help myself."

One of my arms slipped from around his neck. I ran my fingers through the water, my hand cupping to scoop some. I splashed it in his direction, the droplets sparkling on his skin and hair. He chuckled, a deep, warm sound. His black hair turned an even deeper shade, clinging to his forehead. I brushed it back from his face, holding his jaw in one of my hands. "You keep looking at me like that."

His eyes narrowed. "Like what?"

As though he was trying to memorize every feature of my

face. My voice lowered. "Like I'm the only thing that matters."

Hades pulled me closer, the heat of his body pressing against my bare skin as the water lapped around us. "Get used to it, little goddess," he said with a light chuckle. I rested my head on his shoulder as he waded us deeper. The air vibrated with the powerful roar of the water.

I shifted my weight, my legs still wrapped around Hades' torso. I leaned back, letting the upper half of my body float on the water's surface. I twirled my hands through the water, a giggle escaping my lips.

"You're doing great. Let the water support you."

My body relaxed further.

Hades released his hold on me, and I thrashed in the water, my head popping up as I struggled. His arms slid underneath me.

"Calm down," he urged, his voice soothing. "Relax. You're floating, see?"

I stared at him as he held me.

"You're doing so good," he purred.

His praise gave me the confidence I needed. "Let me go for a moment."

He did, and I stayed afloat. I closed my eyes, allowing the water to cradle me. "I'm doing it!"

"You are," he mused. There was a lilt in his voice from his wide smile.

29

PERSEPHONE

"So how does this work? We're in your study. Don't you have a special room for this?"

Hades smirked. "You'll see." He sat in his large leather chair and pulled me into his lap, his arms encircling my waist. "Take a few deep breaths."

I was confused, but I listened. He squeezed my hand, and my vision shifted. We were in the throne room. Everything was the same as it had been before—the high, vaulted ceilings, the crystals hanging off the chandelier, the large stone throne beneath us—but it felt different. Hades glanced down at me with a smile. "You're in my mind."

I looked at him with wide eyes. "*This* is where you sentence souls?"

He chuckled. "Correct. The line doesn't move unless Thanatos or I are sentencing. Time works differently here. One day in my mind is equivalent to about a minute in the Underworld. It has to be that way. Death never stops."

The thought was disorienting. He gave me a quick squeeze. The simple act and the warmth of his chest on my back anchored me in the present.

With a wave of his hand, a long line materialized before us. It stretched out through the doors. Each soul stood silent. "You may begin," Hades said, his voice reverberating through the room.

The first soul fell onto their knees, a man with brown hair. Though I couldn't tell his exact age, he looked young. A raw cry tore from his throat. Tears streamed down his unwrinkled face. His shoulders shook with each sob and ragged gasp he took. "Please—please give me mercy."

The soul bowed their head low, forehead nearly touching the floor. My fingers twitched.

I feel bad for him, I spoke into Hades' mind.

Don't. "I can see his entire life," Hades whispered in my ear. I shivered at the brush of his stubble against my ear. "Do you want to see?"

I nodded. A mosaic of memories hit me, none of them my own.

Everything was dark. His heart thrummed in his mother's womb. The memory shifted, unfolding like a nightmare. A child screamed, the soul. The stench of burning flesh filled my nostrils. The screams echoed in my ears. Heat seared at my skin as the village burned. "Come," the soul's mother shouted, and pulled her child into her arms, tears pouring down her cheek. "We're lucky to be alive."

I was thrust into a dimly lit room. I looked through the soul's blurred, drunken vision as he struck an innocent man. "That's what you get," he howled. The memories continued, each getting progressively darker and more grotesque. I clutched my chest as my vision shifted back to the throne room. "Do you still feel bad for him?" Hades whispered the question.

"No," I choked out.

"My name is—"

Hades cut him off. "Rohan."

"I have done some bad things…" His voice trailed. "But I'm committed to showing you how sorry I am."

Hades pressed a kiss to my cheek as if he were bored of the man. "Do you believe him? I'll let you decide his fate."

"Based on what he has done, no."

The soul broke down. Tears and snot covered his face. "Please."

"Enough." Hades held up a hand. The soul's mouth still moved, but he was silenced, and then he disappeared.

I understood, but I asked anyway. "What happened to him?"

"I sentenced him. He is off in purgatory now."

"What level did you put him in?"

"In level five."

I understood the depths of what Rohan had done, but as I mulled over Hades' words, a chilling realization washed over me. *I* had dictated someone's fate.

"Stop," Hades said. "I feel your turmoil through the bond. Don't feel pity for him. Think of everyone he's hurt."

Faces flickered in my mind. Wounds. Empty chairs at dinner tables. Grief I couldn't unmake. The sorrow curdled, turning to anger. Hades smiled at me. "There she is." He placed a soft kiss on the back of my hand. His mouth lingered, the heat of it sinking into my skin, sending shivers racing up my arm. "What you just witnessed was justice. Every soul here has left a mark on the universe, some of them often causing devastation without a second thought."

We went through the same process repeatedly. I yawned, exhaustion settling in. It was draining to see so many, often horrible, memories. The room shifted around us, and we were back in Hades' study. I let out a long breath.

"That's enough for today."

I turned in Hades' arms. "Does that ever bother you? To hold the burden of seeing so many horrible memories?"

Hades shrugged. "I suppose at first it did, but I got used to it. I learned this is a cruel universe… and the line will always continue."

30

PERSEPHONE

*E*ach strike I landed against the canvas training bag sent vibrations up my arms, reverberating through bone and muscle.

"Harder, Persephone." Hades' voice cut through the air. His eyes bore into me, analyzing each of my movements.

I clenched my fists tighter, ignoring the throb of my knuckles. My skin had split, shallowly, but enough to make each punch hurt more. I shifted my weight, drew from somewhere deeper, and struck again. My muscles screamed. I exhaled hard through my nose.

"I'm trying," I grunted, delivering another punch, less forceful this time. "I'm still so sore."

This wasn't new. My body had lived in pain for years, in different forms. Since coming to the Underworld and training with Hecate, I'd been in pain from the fatigue, but that was more manageable.

Before that, the pain at the hand of my mother had been different. Sharper. Meaner. It had been the kind that didn't fade after rest. The kind of pain I'd learned to live with, to fold it down, tuck it in so she wouldn't see and make it worse.

So yes, I could handle this. I had handled worse.

Since we'd mated, Hades hadn't held back. If anything, he'd pushed me harder with training. He'd given me the frenzy week off, at least, that one week after our bond formed where my body was consumed with want, like nothing else existed except my mate and the aching need that tied us together. It had felt like being submerged in a haze. Everything had been heightened, louder, hotter.

I'd welcomed the blur it came with, numbing the sharp edges of everything I didn't want to deal with. The memories. The grief. The weight of the magic I still didn't understand. For a little while, it had all felt far away.

But now, the haze had cleared.

I stole a glance at him between swings. Concern creased between his dark brows, his lips pressing firmly together into a line.

I hadn't had the bond for long. Just a few short weeks now. I was still figuring out what it meant, how to live with it. Everything had come fast.

Usually, the bond between us was a quiet, steady hum, something I could lean on. It was different now, charged with an emotion I didn't quite know how to hold.

Worry.

It pressed in on me through the bond like a weight behind my ribs. I cringed at the sensation. I still wasn't used to feeling someone else's emotions so closely, especially not Hades'. He kept his feelings locked down, only ever letting them slip through when they were positive, reassuring ones. This wasn't that.

I dropped my arms and tried to catch my breath. *What's wrong?*

Hades' jaw flexed.

There was a slight tightening of his jaw. "I'm concerned your magic isn't healing you as quickly as it should. I've been funneling some of my magic through the bond to you, but it doesn't seem to have helped."

I blinked. That was news to me.

He sighed. "I've already reached out to a few contacts for advice. I feel the block on your magic through the bond, but I'm not sure what it is."

"Hecate?" I ventured, recalling the cryptic conversation I'd overheard between Hades and the goddess I hadn't seen since our last session.

"No."

I couldn't swallow my curiosity. "Did anything ever happen between you two?"

Hades let out a sigh. "We were together for a brief time. A long time ago."

"Together romantically?"

"Yes."

The single word landed heavier than it should have. I looked away, pretending I didn't feel the sharp flare in my chest, hurt and heat tangled up together. I hated the sting of jealousy crawling under my skin, but it was undeniable.

My mind drifted back to the memory of the way Hecate had uttered Hades' name during their conversation. It was a venomous sound at the back of my mind. I placed a palm on my chest, the mating bond pulsing underneath it, as if trying to soothe me.

It didn't help.

"You've slept with her," I said, more to myself than him. Hades was older than me. Of course he had a past. But knowing that didn't make it any easier to swallow.

"No." He rested a hand on my shoulder, and it helped

soothe the insecurity roaring inside me. "You're the only one I've been intimate with since my death touch." Hades sent a wave of reassurance through our bond. "There's no need for jealousy."

"I'm sorry," I murmured.

"Persephone." As he took my hands in his, a sense of further calm washed over me. "There's nothing to apologize for."

I took a slow, easy breath, trying to push the ache to the background. Hades' eyes dropped to my knuckles. He stepped closer and took my hands in his, careful not to apply pressure to the torn skin.

Hades lifted my hands to his lips and pressed a gentle kiss to each bruised knuckle, like the act alone might erase the damage. His lips were warm, soft. "Let me take care of you."

Before I could wrap a lie in pretty words to tell him I was fine, that I didn't need anything, his magic spiraled around me.

It wasn't forceful. It was a pulse of warmth that slid across my skin. The bond between us lit up, magic humming as it poured from him into me, sinking deep into my sore muscles and scraped skin. The pain began to ease quickly, the tightness in my shoulders unraveling thread by thread.

Hades pulled me closer until there was barely space left between us. My breath hitched. His arms wrapped around me, steady, like the world could fall apart and I'd still be safe here.

I still wasn't used to that.

My mother's arms had turned cold after years of being warm. I let myself lean into the terrifying comfort of being *held*.

He leaned down. "Never try to hide your pain from me." His breath tickled my ear. "You don't have to anymore."

I rested my forehead against his collarbone, breathing in his smoky-amber-and-leather scent.

"We can continue training tomorrow," he said. "Right now, you need rest." Hades pulled back from the hug, staying close, and he turned a loose strand of hair from my braid behind my ear. His bare fingers brushed along the curve of my cheek. He leaned in slowly.

Hades' lips finally touched mine. At first it was just a soft brush of mouths, but it deepened quickly. His hand slid to the back of my neck. My fingers curled up into the front of his shirt. I didn't realize how tightly I'd been wound until I felt myself unraveling.

We broke apart, breaths mingling, foreheads nearly touching.

A sudden, sharp ache flared through my body. I jerked, muscles locking as the pain spread like fire across my nerves. A low groan slipped past my lips before I could stop it.

"Persephone," Hades rushed out.

My vision swam, and my body pitched forward, but Hades held me still. I felt his magic surge, then the sensation of movement as he whisked us away.

The next thing I knew, I was on our bed, the cool duvet beneath me barely registering against the waves of pain. Hades hovered above me, funneling his magic to me through the bond.

His throat bobbed as he swallowed hard.

The pain ebbed slowly, leaving a dull, heavy ache in its wake. I forced myself upright, propping up on my elbows even though my muscles protested. "What was that?"

"Something is wrong. Cerberus will watch over you while I find out."

Within seconds, the large black three-headed guardian dog of the Underworld I'd read about in the Underworld's library appeared next to the bed. Muscles rippled beneath its midnight coat.

Hades had mentioned the name too, but I hadn't expected the creature to look like this. "That *thing* is going to *watch* me?" I pushed myself away from the creature. Its glinting eyes fixated on me.

Hades ran a hand over one of its heads, and it leaned into his touch. "Cerberus will protect you." One of the dog's heads dipped and licked my hand.

I looked at my wet hand. The hot drag of its tongue should've sickened me, but instead it was oddly comforting.

"If you need anything, let me know through the bond," Hades said.

My head went fuzzy again for a moment. "Let me come. What's wrong?"

"Someone is here." Hades paused. "Someone that doesn't belong in the Underworld."

My icy mental wall shook. The implications of what he was saying... *It can't be.* "Did you feel me when I entered the Underworld?"

"Yes, but not like this. I must go."

"Let me come," I demanded.

"Not this time, Persephone." His voice was heavy. "There are dangers you are not prepared to face."

Disappointment lanced through me. "I want to be by your side," I protested. "I want to help."

Hades' gaze softened, a ghost of a smile tugging at the corners of his lips. "You will," he told me, "someday."

Someday.

The reminder of my inexperience stung. I'd come so far, and it still wasn't far enough. I crossed my arms and fought the burning in my eyes.

"I care too much to put you in harm's way." Hades leaned down and pressed a quick kiss to my forehead. "I'll be back."

He sent a surge of more healing energy. It flooded my body with its warmth, but even as it enveloped me, it did little to soothe my ragged panic.

My thoughts raced. I racked my brain, searching for who could possibly force Hades out in such a rush. Deep down, there was a whisper of truth, one I dared not speak aloud.

31

HADES

The connections that bound my realm together pulsed beneath my skin, woven through every soul, every structure, every layer, every ancient law.

Lock the gates, I commanded, my voice rippling through the network of threads. *I* was the command. *No one goes in or out of this realm until further notice.*

A ripple of unease surged through the realm, tangible and unsettling. My fingers twitched at my side. The Underworld recoiled at my command. The realm pulsated with its own energy, reacting to the disturbance like the living force it was.

Something was wrong.

Someone was here.

I had no doubt in my mind who it was.

I steeled myself as I whisked to Tartarus level. I focused on each beat of the mating bond thrumming between Persephone and me. It anchored my mind. *She is okay.*

Darkness greeted me, broken only by the faint glimmer of light emanating off the bioluminescent plants. I walked along the rough, uneven ground closer to the gate of Tartarus. It stood tall, still locked by the glowing piece of the Nexus Stone. The cries of my prisoners and the Titans echoed through the depths of this level. Despite the appearance of normalcy, I could feel *her*.

A tingling prickled at the nape of my neck like invisible fingers tracing a chilling path. The weight of her gaze bore down on me. The prisoners and Titans fell silent, attuned to the shift in energy. Slow, deliberate clapping sounded around me. Each clap was a taunt, a mockery of her presence in my realm.

I pivoted to face Demeter. She wouldn't dare attack me directly—not yet. When we took our oath to the court, we vowed not to inflict harm upon each other. It was a pact forged with blood to prevent war among the Divine. The court's magic still bound her. Demeter lacked enough pieces to break through it. I stood firm. I had my goddess and the piece of the Nexus Stone to protect.

She stepped forward, the dim light casting a glow around her willowy form. The shadows danced in harmony with her movements. Her appearance was deceiving—elegant even, with delicate features and graceful movements that belied the darkness inside her. Her lips curved upward in a smile. It was a practiced, calculated expression that didn't reach her eyes. I checked on Persephone through the bond. Still all right.

I resisted the urge to snarl. To recoil at the sight of her.

I maintained my composure. I wouldn't let Demeter shake me. It would bring her far too much joy. "Always a pleasure to see you, Hades," she said with a snicker dripping with false sweetness.

I raised an eyebrow. "What are you doing in my realm?"

"I forgot. You don't do pleasantries." She raised her chin, her gaze locking onto mine. "I've come for my daughter."

I clenched my jaw. "Persephone isn't here." I kept my voice monotone.

"You aren't fooling me, Hades," Demeter sneered. In an instant, her face smoothed into a neutral mask again. The shift was jarring. "Hmm. I think it's hardly fair we talk about her without her here." She spoke too casually, as if she were discussing something unimportant. "Persephone..." she yelled, her voice trailing off.

With a flick of her wrist, Persephone's form materialized before us in a faint shimmer of magic. The mating bond flared to life, full of panic and anxiety. I rushed to her side. Persephone looked around with wide eyes as she stumbled forward. Her movements were unsteady. A strangled gasp escaped her lips as she crumpled toward the ground. I rushed to her side and caught her before she fell. I gathered her trembling form in my arms and tried to send her some energy.

But it didn't work.

"Persephone," I whispered, cradling her close to my chest. Power drained from my body.

It was as though an icy hand had clamped around me, squeezing until I could scarcely draw breath. I tried to steady myself against the onslaught. It was not just physical; it was a psychic assault, a draining of essence, leaving me vulnerable.

A realization illuminated in the dark recesses of my mind with terrible clarity. I tugged at the mating bond, confirming the truth I feared. With all of us here together, it was clear. The bond between Persephone and me pulsed with a shimmering thread of connection, but I sensed another—a thread stretching from Persephone to Demeter.

Demeter was siphoning Persephone's magic.

32

PERSEPHONE

The world around me spun. I tried to make sense of what was happening, but my mother's voice was in my ears. Was I in another nightmare? I knew Hades held me —I knew his touch. "Hades." I tried to move my limbs, but they were unresponsive. Every attempt to gather myself and move drained what little strength remained within me.

Are you all right? Hades spoke into my head. His voice cut through my mother's laughter.

What's going on?

Your mother was all he said.

I took a few deep breaths despite the swelling anxiety. My heartbeat quickened. I blinked, trying to focus my blurry vision. *I am in control,* I told myself. I repeated the phrase until the haze over my vision disappeared.

I saw my mother's face. For years, I'd avoided looking into her eyes. I didn't like them or the look they always held. But I forced myself to meet them now and take in every detail of those cruel brown irises. They were a deep umber with shards of gold throughout. Others likely thought they were beautiful, but all I saw in them was hatred.

Her face was twisted with malice. It was a sight I'd fought so hard to forget. The Underworld had helped me, offering me peace from her. I didn't see her every time I shut my eyes anymore. She only lurked in the twisted landscapes of my nightmares. But now, seeing her again, the old wounds reopened, dredging up a storm of emotions.

The years of her torment flooded back to me. I tried to shut out the overwhelming barrage of feelings assaulting me. My fingers clenched, nails digging into the soft flesh of my palms. I fought to ground myself in the present. The scent of lilies filled the air. I went stiff.

Don't let her see you weak. Hades spoke through the bond.

I forced away the tears threatening to spill. Forced the memories back into the depths of my subconscious, sealing them once more behind the walls I had erected when I came to the Underworld. I glanced up at Hades. He wore an impassive look, his features set in stoic calmness that seemed unnatural.

"I always knew you were a little whore, but I didn't think it would ever help me. All because you couldn't keep your legs closed…" Her words trailed off.

"Leave my realm," Hades commanded.

But my mother responded with a casual flick of her wrist. The air crackled with power, and I watched in horror as Hades' figure stiffened, his face contorting in agony. My lip curled.

"Hades—" My words dried up at the pain reverberating through our bond. I grabbed his hand and squeezed. As Hades struggled, my mother's cold gaze turned toward me. The air grew thicker with every step she took closer.

"It's your fault I'm here." She laughed. "If you hadn't mated with him, I would've never had access to this realm. You've finally done something right, my lily."

Her accusation struck me like a physical blow. My

stomach churned. *Have I led her right here?* I cringed at the pain still radiating through the mating bond. *Hades,* I yelled. I forced myself out of Hades' arms and tried to stand up. My movements were slow, still weighed with fatigue. "Leave," I cried. I needed to fight.

"Oh, my lily, when will you learn?" She took a few steps closer.

I charged at her. I pulled on the ounce of strength inside of me, desperation fueling my every stride. Hades roared, a primal sound that split through me. He grabbed my arm and pulled me behind him. In the chaos, I lost sight of my mother. All I could see was Hades' figure, now standing squarely between us. His black magic surged, a shadowy torrent pouring out of him. The air crackled with dark energy as tendrils of his power snaked through the space between us and my mother.

A tingling spread through me and the bond. *Hope.* The unfamiliar feeling bloomed in my chest. Time slowed to a crawl as the black magic looped back around. It grew closer, headed right for me. Each moment stretched. The hope disappeared. "What are you doing?" I yelled. The ground beneath my feet felt unsteady.

Hades glanced over his shoulder and his expression softened, though the intensity of his gaze remained. *I'm sorry.* Hades pushed the feeling of love along the bond, but it did nothing to soothe the frenzy of emotions inside of me. In the suspended moment, every detail of his face became painfully clear. Hades often didn't let his emotions show, but his features betrayed him. Fear, regret, sadness flashed across his face.

What is he doing? What is he doing? What is he doing?

The tendrils of his dark magic wrapped around my body. My teeth gritted together. The pain came.

Agony.

I gasped for breath. The magic swirled around me. It was a pain unlike anything I'd ever experienced. I crumpled to the ground. Through the haze of magic, my mother's cruel laughter still pierced me like a poisoned dagger.

Hades' magic stopped.

Bones crunched, the sickening sound reverberating through me. *My* bones. My head fell on something sharp. Small stones dug into my cheek. The taste of copper flooded my mouth. Maybe I was covered with blood—maybe not. I didn't know.

My mate hurt me. *Never trust the Divine.*

My eyes cracked open. My mother took a strangled gasp. "What have you done?" she yelled. Her pale-yellow magic rushed at Hades. Despite the agony racking through my body, I couldn't tear my gaze away from the clash of yellow and black.

From the corner of my eye, I watched as the piece of Nexus Stone dislodged itself from in between the gate. The stone pulsated white as it hovered in the air, bathed in the yellow glow of my mother's magic. "No," I tried to scream. My lips parted, but no sound escaped. I pushed away my anger toward Hades—it could wait. *Hades. She's taking the stone.*

The piece of Nexus Stone held the gates of Tartarus shut. If those gates opened, the Titans—monsters that even the Divine feared—would be free. Their power could tear apart the fabric of our universe. Hades looked to his left as his magic clashed with my mother's, but he was too late. Her magic drew the fragment to her, and she wrapped her fingers around it. "Thank you for the stone," she said. Hades lurched forward to stop her. She was too quick and far too powerful.

The gates groaned, their ancient hinges shuddering as a chorus of pained wails echoed around us. Hades' magic surged forward, wrapping around the gates and preventing them from opening. I felt his energy draining through the bond.

How could he? How could he? How could he? I repeated. *How could he hurt me?* But even as my anger threatened to consume me, a bitter truth remained. Releasing the beings imprisoned in Tartarus was not an option. I had led her here. I had brought her to the artifact that could end everything.

And I had been too weak to stop it.

I sent the last few drops of energy within me to Hades through the bond. My vision blurred and darkness took over.

HADES

*P*ersephone lay still, her usually vibrant presence reduced to the faint, rhythmic rise and fall of her chest. I studied her face, looking for any change. Any sign of consciousness. Any twitch of a muscle or flutter of her eyelids. Anything. My actions had led us to this moment. I had chosen to put her through pain. *I had to,* the words sounded in my mind, but they did little to reassure me.

I failed her. *I should've realized the tether to Demeter sooner. I should have found another way.*

The room was full of flowers, at least a thousand of them. I'd lost count. Poppies, irises, roses, narcissus flowers. My magic had shaped each one despite the weight pressing down on every ounce of power I had left. Every petal had cost me. With my magic still holding Tartarus shut, I couldn't afford this kind of indulgence. But I did it anyway.

When she woke, I wanted her to see beauty. She deserved that.

I brushed a stray lock of hair and dabbed a wet cloth on her fevered forehead. "Wake up, little goddess," I whispered. I channeled the little energy I had to Persephone through the bond. The strain was immense. I didn't know how long my magic would hold the gates.

Thanatos' voice snapped me out of the unpleasant thoughts. "It's been three days, Hades. You need to sleep."

"Okay." I couldn't sleep—I wouldn't sleep. Every time I closed my eyes, I saw the pain etched across Persephone's face when my magic struck her.

Thanatos stepped closer. "She is your mate. She will understand. Her body needs time to heal."

"What do you want, Thanatos?" He didn't deserve my harsh words, but the exhaustion weighed on me.

"I wanted to let you know the fae are here. They can wait for you to rest, though."

"Enough. I'll be there after I visit Divine Hall." The decision had been delayed too long already. These matters couldn't wait, no matter how much I wanted to stay by Persephone's side. Thanatos gave me a wary look but didn't argue. He knew better.

"Cerberus, watch Persephone," I commanded. The three-headed hound rose from the corner, surrounded by flowers. One of his heads sniffed at a bloom as he stretched, then moved quickly over to us, soft paws padding across the floor.

One head nuzzled into Persephone's shoulder, another draping protectively across her legs, and the third lifted toward me, waiting.

"No one touches her," I said. I rubbed between his shoulder blades, my fingers curling into his thick fur. "Not until I return."

The dog growled, not in anger, but with understanding. Cerberus climbed onto the bed, careful not to step on Persephone.

I placed a hand on Persephone's and gave the bond between us one last squeeze before forcing myself to go. I whisked to Athens in Olympus.

Wind whipped at my clothes as I climbed up the marble steps leading to Divine Hall. The grandeur of the building enveloped me as I strode through the corridors, my footsteps tapping loudly on the too-polished floors.

I knocked on the oak door of Zeus' study. I only had to wait a few seconds before it opened. A red-headed nymph I'd seen before greeted me. "How may I help you?" she asked, polite but distant.

I ignored her and walked through Zeus' open door. Zeus looked up from the paperwork on his desk in irritation. "Still haven't learned your manners, I see."

I ignored the insult. "I came to report a situation in my realm." I didn't wait for him to respond. "Demeter has stolen the piece of the Nexus Stone keeping the Titans in Tartarus."

His features went blank as he considered my words.

"We cannot afford to delay a plan for action. Demeter must suffer consequences."

Zeus leaned back in his chair, his fingers steepling. "My hands are tied, Hades. You need to report it at the court meeting tomorrow, and we can take a vote."

My jaw clenched. "You cannot be serious. You want the Titans to be released?"

Zeus sighed. "Of course not." His voice was annoyingly calm. "But we must follow protocol. Your realm should be strong enough to keep them contained for now."

He didn't get it. The realm didn't just hold the Titans. When I'd been assigned to the Underworld, the land had become an extension of me. We were one. Our magic was fused. And Zeus sat behind his polished desk talking about protocol and pretending to understand things he never would.

My patience wore thin. "We do not have the luxury of time. If the Titans get out, they won't stay in Tartarus. They'll come for all of us."

He didn't flinch. "Then I suggest you hold the gates." Zeus regarded me with a steady gaze, unmoved by my plea. "When did this happen?"

"Three days ago."

His brows arched. "And you didn't come to me sooner?"

"I had other matters to attend to." *My goddess.* Exhaustion made me sloppy.

"I understand your concerns, Hades, but we must abide by the rules of the court. Tomorrow's meeting will provide an opportunity for discussion and resolution."

I turned on my heel and exited his study. There was no point in arguing with Zeus. The nymph closed the door behind me. I looked left and right. No one was in this corridor.

I braced myself on the wall, sucked in a deep breath, and tried to ignore the ache running throughout my body. It was a constant throb. I closed my eyes. Just for a second. Summoning the last remnants of my strength, I pushed off the wall and continued walking.

I froze.

For the first time in three days, Persephone tugged on the mating bond. The sensation was faint but unmistakable. Not long after, Cerberus tugged at me.

I didn't waste any time. I tore through the halls, running until I made it outside. The second I cleared the threshold, I whisked back to the Underworld.

I materialized in our bedroom. Persephone was already on her feet, examining the flowers. She reached out, brushing her fingers over the edge of a rose I'd conjured. The sight of her standing, moving, knocked the air from my lungs.

She came toward me quickly. I went stiff. Every instinct braced for the worst—anger, confusion. Instead, she threw her arms around me. I didn't move. The shock of her warmth threw me off.

Persephone pulled back just enough to place her hands on my shoulders. Her eyes searched my face, full of concern, not blame. The bond pulsed between us.

"What happened to you? You look terrible."

I felt her try to push energy to me through the bond, curling with warmth through the connection. I caught it before it could reach me, forcing a shield into place. I wouldn't take from her. Not while Tartarus still needed to be sealed. That was my burden to carry.

I stayed silent for a moment, trying to tame my unruly thoughts. "How do you feel?" I managed. I tugged at the bond, probing. There was no sign of Demeter's magic. None of the dark thread I'd torn away. Just ours.

Persephone tilted her head, then placed a hand over her chest. The mating bond mark pulsed softly beneath her palm, glowing white through the thin fabric of her shirt. "I feel great."

My shoulders sagged. It had worked.

I reached for her, arms sliding around her waist, and pulled her against me. She came easily, without hesitation. My eyes closed as I buried my face in her hair. Her heartbeat thudded against my chest. "I'm so sorry, Persephone. I didn't want to hurt you, but it was the only way."

Persephone pulled back and shook her head. "What are you talking about? You didn't hurt me at training." Her bright-gray eyes searched mine for answers. They held confusion and something softer, a deeper affection. Maybe even something like trust.

She didn't remember her mother. Or the stone. Or me tearing out the beast that had lived inside of her for far too long. I had focused all my energy on the connection to Demeter, channeling the full force of my power to drive her out and sever the link. I took a deep breath. "There are things you don't remember. But you're safe now. That's what matters."

She didn't flinch. "I trust you," she said. "Whatever happened, I know you would never hurt me."

The words landed like a blade and a balm at once. I cringed, not visibly, I hoped. Would she hate me when the memories returned? Would she see the necessity of my actions?

34

PERSEPHONE

I stared out the window of our bedroom. The Underworld lay before me, devoid of its usual lush landscape. The rich hues were gone. The light of the twin moons bathed the flat expanse of tan sandy ground.

Behind me, the room was thick, overflowing with flowers. Why were they only in here?

I pressed my trembling fingers against the cold windowpane. Hollowness filled my chest at the sight. I reached for the mating bond, and a comforting warmth spread throughout me. "What happened?" My voice shook.

I continued to study the land, stripped of everything but the Styx and the homes that housed the souls.

"You don't remember?" Hades placed a hand on my shoulder from behind.

I shook my head and shut my eyes. *How could I forget something happening?* I clawed at my mind. Every attempt to seize fragments of my memory felt like grasping at wisps of smoke, slipping through my fingers and leaving me with nothing tangible. The harder I strained, the dizzier I became.

I stayed silent, and Hades took it as an invitation to keep

talking. "My magic is tied to the realm, as yours will be when you perform the Rite…" His voice trailed, something deeper leaking into it. "The magic that creates the landscape of the realm is holding Tartarus closed. I cannot let the Titans out."

I turned from the window. I absorbed his words, but despite their significance, my mind refused to latch onto them fully. I couldn't bring myself to voice questions about the Rite. I didn't care—well, not now. Hades was all I could think about.

I pulled him close, running my thumb across his jaw. Hades' skin was so pale. Deep, violet-tinged semicircles marred his under eyes. He leaned in closer. The touch of his lips on my forehead sent a shudder through me; they were cold. "Hades." My fingers brushed his hand. "Have you been sleeping?"

"I'm fine, little goddess. I'll manage. I always do," he said with a veneer of calm, clearing his throat before I could say anything else. "Let's have something to eat. You must be starving."

My stomach roiled, a reaction that caught me off guard. Hades tugged at my hand. He didn't bother whisking, and that worried me. We walked through the corridors in silence. My lips repeatedly parted, but each time, the words faltered and died on my tongue.

As we entered the dining room, Minthe was the first to greet us. Her usually sharp features were softened. She rushed to pull a chair out for Hades. I didn't stop her. For once, I didn't mind Minthe's behavior. My own thoughts were reflected in her expression.

She stood straight, holding it ready, her eyes darting between Hades and me. Without a word or glance her way, Hades pulled a chair out for me. I settled into my seat and cast Minthe a glance. Her expression shifted—disappointment—but she quickly masked it with a forced smile.

Minthe's hand twitched as Hades finally took the chair she prepared for him.

Within seconds, souls rushed in with practiced ease, setting plates in front of us. It was a simple spread, meat and vegetables, but the scent alone elicited a grumble from my stomach.

I picked at my food, the taste of it lost on me. The flavors blended into the background. Pick up food. Chew. Swallow. I continued the simple routine.

Only a few bites remained. Hades sat before me. Silence stretched, only our muted chewing, the distant noise of the souls lingering in the kitchen, and the clattering of our forks on the porcelain plates filling it.

I raised another bite slowly. Just as it touched my lips, it hit me. I jerked the fork back. "Hades," I whispered. The word was both a plea and a question.

I closed my eyes as all the memories rushed back to me. Each recollection crashed over me like relentless waves. The scene played vividly in my mind's eye. The pain that seared through my body, my mother's face, the moment she stole the stone—and Hades.

My grip on my fork slackened, and it slipped from my fingers, clattering against the plate and tumbling onto the floor with a sharp sound. Emotions surged within me too quickly for me to process any of them.

I pressed a hand to my chest, trying to ground myself, but it was like falling.

"You remember?" Hades' voice cut through the silence.

My throat tightened, words catching in my throat. "I do," I choked out. I stood up, bit the inside of my lip.

Hades stood. "Persephone."

I wish I could just—

I whisked across the table in front of Hades. He looked up

at me with wide eyes, and I glanced back at where I had been standing.

He gave me a weak smile and lifted a brow. "That is certainly a development."

It wasn't funny.

My jaw tensed. The intricacies of my magic were insignificant, the wave of fury casting a shadow over all else, drowning them. I took a step closer to Hades. "You hurt me."

His voice hardened. "I had to."

"You had to, or you chose to?"

"I had to. Listen, Persephone, calm down." His voice was softer, but it did nothing to calm me.

"Calm down?" I scoffed, a bitter laugh escaping my lips as I shook my head. "How am I to calm down when my mate is the one who hurt me? Is this another part of being bound to you? I'm just supposed to let you do as you please with me?"

"Sit." He pulled out the chair next to him at the table. "Please," he added.

Hades sent a wave of comfort through the mating bond. I stood frozen, every instinct screaming at me to fight, to push back, but the bond—the damn bond—pulled at me, threading calm through my anger. It was like being smothered in something warm when all I wanted to do was lash out. Though my pride bristled at yielding, I sat.

Hades didn't waste any time. "I had to cut the bond between you and your mother."

"What?" My voice cracked. I narrowed my eyes and tried to process his words.

"I realized that Demeter had been siphoning your energy. That's why you were always so fatigued. I don't know how she created the tether, but I assume those pills she gave you did not stop your magic. It just made it so you couldn't use it —or retaliate."

Pieces of a puzzle fell into place with devastating clarity.

A heavy weight settled in my chest. My eyes drifted to the floor, unable to meet his gaze. Sweat beaded on my skin. "I —" *How could I not have felt it?*

"I didn't have time to explain it to you in the moment." Hades reached out, settling his hand on the back of my neck over the mark from binding myself to him. The touch wasn't possessive. It was supportive. "It was the only way to free you."

"Free me," I repeated. My breath came in short, shallow bursts as the pieces came together. I could feel the truth of Hades' words deep in my bones, but that didn't make it any easier to accept them. "You took away my choice."

"I had no other option."

"Are you always going to decide for me, just like her?"

"Don't compare me to *her*," he growled, his lip curling.

Silence wrapped around us. Hades didn't move. He just stood there, his gaze locked on me. He was so still, but I could see the tension in his shoulders, the rigid line of his jaw. He was bracing for my anger, my rejection.

And gods, part of me wanted to give it to him.

But the truth was there too. Hades had cut the tether. He *had* freed me.

"I know you're angry," Hades said, his voice soft. He leaned in, closing the distance between us. "And you have every right to be. But I need you to know that I did this for you. Not to control you. To free you." He reached for my cheek, and I didn't pull away.

I closed my eyes, letting his warmth seep into me. I let myself believe him. Despite the anger and the hurt, I couldn't deny what I felt when he held me like this.

My eyes burned, a tear falling before I could stop it. Hades pulled me up from the chair and wiped it away with his thumb. He kissed me, slow and careful, like he wasn't sure if I'd let him.

I kissed him back, and with it, I let the bond carry everything I couldn't say out loud—my gratitude, my fear, the fragile threads of trust I was still piecing together. His hands settled on my back. He pulled away just enough to rest his forehead against mine.

The space between us crackled with something soft and sharp all at once.

Without warning, he lifted me, carrying me out of the room.

"Let me walk," I protested.

Hades shook his head. "Absolutely not."

I pushed myself off his chest, but he wrapped his arms around me tighter. I stopped resisting, unable to move.

"Let me take care of you."

I sighed and nestled against him. Hades walked through the halls to our room. Each one of his steps reminded me of his weakened state. Hades typically whisked everywhere. I tried to push the worry away. *He is okay*, I repeated. *We will be okay.*

We crossed the threshold of our room, and he lowered me down onto the bed, pressing a kiss to my forehead before straightening. "Wait here. I'll call you in a few moments."

I nodded, knowing any protest would be unsuccessful. Hades shut the door behind him. I stood up and walked to the window, drawing my arms around myself. The night sky stretched endlessly above. The stars twinkled, though their lights were dulled. Already, I missed the rich foliage. The Underworld looked drained of its essence.

Lost in my thoughts, I barely registered the passing minutes. Just as I began to wonder if Hades had forgotten about me altogether, his voice pierced the silence. "Persephone."

The sound of my name on his lips sent warmth through me, drawing me back to the present. I hurried to the washroom and pushed open the now-cracked door. Steam curled around me, the scent of rose and lavender suffusing the room. Hades stood next to the bubble-filled tub, smirking at me. "Come here." Hades outstretched a hand.

I placed my hand in his and he tugged me toward him. His fingers brushed the hem of my sweater. His touch was gentle, hesitant. Hades met my gaze—asking without words.

I nodded.

He lifted the fabric slowly, and I raised my arms to let him pull it over my head. His fingers moved again, slower this time, ghosting over the strap of my bra. "Tell me if you want me to stop."

I didn't.

He reached behind me, unclasped it, and slid the straps down my arms.

Next came my pants. He knelt before me, hands steady as he slid the fabric past my hips and down my legs. I stepped out of my pants and underwear one leg at a time.

He stood again. His fingers brushed the mating bond mark sprawled across my chest. I swore my lungs forgot how to work.

"I don't think you realize," he whispered, "how beautiful you are." His fingers continued grazing my skin, tracing the soft, pulsing glow of the mark. Every pass left a trail of heat in its wake.

I closed my eyes at the sensation.

His hands drifted from my chest, up my neck to my chin. I met his gaze.

"I've always prided myself for my control. But this…" He dragged his thumb slowly over the mark again. "Seeing you with this mark undoes me."

A shiver ran down my spine. We stood there, quiet, breathing the same air. He reached for my hand and guided me toward the tub.

I climbed in, goose bumps rising on my exposed skin as the hot water enveloped the rest of my body. I gripped the edge of the tub and turned toward Hades. "Are you coming in?"

"As much as I'd love to"—he squeezed my shoulder—"not now."

The smile playing on my lips fell. Hades dipped my head back and wet my hair. With gentle hands, he guided me to lean back against the edge of the bathtub. Hades poured shampoo into his palm, massaged my scalp, and combed through the tangles in my hair with his fingers.

I closed my eyes, the tension loosening its grip on me. "You know, I don't think I ever said it, but thank you." I leaned farther into his touch, surrendering to the moment. "For everything."

Hades chuckled, the low sound like velvet against my ears. "There's no need for thanks. Taking care of you is my greatest pleasure."

As he reached for the conditioner, I asked the question gnawing at me. "What happens now, with my mother and the stone? And us?"

Hades paused, his fingers stilling in my hair before he resumed his gentle ministrations. "We will deal with it," he said finally. "Together." Before I could ask any follow-up questions, he added, "I saw Zeus earlier. I tried to report what your mother did, but he wouldn't have it. He said I needed to do it at the next court meeting."

My relaxed body went tense. "When is it?"

"Tomorrow."

I straightened. "I'm coming with you." I was tired of hiding in the Underworld, of being on the outside. The Divine needed to see me next to Hades. We needed to do this together.

Hades sighed and guided me back to my relaxed position. "You can't."

I stilled. "Why?"

"Only members of the court are permitted. You will be able to watch. I'll show you later." Hades continued to work his hands through my hair. "I also have a few people to introduce you to."

"Who?"

"My team. Think of them like a court for the Underworld or advisers. Admittedly, I waited too long to call them."

"When do I get to meet them?"

"In a little while," Hades assured me. "But for now, let's focus on the task at hand. There will be plenty of time for introductions later." Water cascaded over me in warm rivulets as Hades rinsed my hair. "You know"—Hades' words were a low murmur, almost lost in the rush of the water—"you have the most beautiful hair I've ever seen."

Warmth spread through me that had nothing to do with the water. "Thank you."

"Stand."

I did as he said. Hades washed my entire body with a cloth, his movements patient. Bubbles lingered on my shoulders and stomach. He rinsed me. My gaze traced the contours of his face as he pushed some of his hair. The strands glistened with droplets of water. He grabbed a towel, handed it to me, and helped me out of the tub.

Hades leaned forward and captured my lips in a tender kiss. He pulled back, hands lingering on me. "Let's get you dressed."

35

PERSEPHONE

Once I was dressed, Hades held my hand as we walked through the corridors of the palace. The coolness of his skin was a sharp contrast to my clammy palms. "Relax, Persephone. There is no need to worry."

I bit my lip, stopping just shy of the door to his study. "What if they don't like me?"

Hades halted. "They will love you."

His words did nothing to calm the anxiety swelling inside of me. Hades opened the door. I glanced around, taking in the familiar surroundings.

The room was shrouded in dim light, the fireplace casting shadows across the space. Hades' study remained unchanged since my last visit. The shelves filled with leather-bound books still lined three of the walls. Bookshelves framed the door to the room while the window, also surrounded by shelves, continued to overlook the courtyard. The desk still stood in the center of the room, covered in documents and books. Hades flicked his wrist, and a door materialized on the one blank wall. Hades grasped the gold doorknob. The mechanism clicked, and with a gentle pull, the door swung open, revealing a stone corridor. Hades gestured. "After you."

I stepped through the doorframe. Torches flickered on the walls. I trailed my fingertips along the rough stone. Hades followed me.

The corridor opened to a large space. Paintings adorned the walls, and a large board covered with notes hung prominently on the center one. Plush furnishings were scattered throughout the room. A wooden table dominated the center, with five individuals gathered around it.

Four strangers and Thanatos. Hades placed a hand on the small of my back. "This is Persephone," he said, gesturing for me to step forward. "She will be joining us today."

I forced a smile, my lips curving in what I hoped was an expression of confidence. I took a seat beside Hades, who stood at the head of the table, next to a woman of ethereal beauty. All her features were delicate. High cheekbones cast gentle shadows on her face in the dim lighting. Her skin was smooth and unblemished, with a faint shimmer. Dark lashes fanned over her pale-blue eyes. Her lips were a light rosy hue, full and curved up into a smile. "Allow me to introduce you," Hades began.

He gestured to the man with deep-brown hair, standing tall beside him. The man's eyes were a vivid red, glowing like embers. "This is Orion, a member of the Autumn Court."

Orion inclined his head, a faint smile playing at the corners of his lips. "A pleasure to meet you, Persephone," he said.

Hades turned his attention to the woman next to me. "Aurelia." Hades pointed to the man seated next to her. "And Cassius Frost." They had the same last name? The woman pushed her hair behind her ear—a pointed ear. *Fae.*

"You are bound?" The words slipped from my lips before

I had a chance to stop them. I'd always been curious about binding ceremonies. I tried reading about them in the Olympian Library, but the requirements were vague. I'd always dreamed of it, the big ceremony and declaration of love.

The ceremony was nothing like the bond I had been compelled to form with Hades when I came to the Underworld.

Aurelia and Cassius both blanched. Their body language mirrored each other as they leaned away from the table. "No, no. We are siblings."

"They are from the Winter Court," Orion added.

My chin dipped. "Understood," I said with a slight tinge of embarrassment.

Hades offered a reassuring nod before turning his attention to the man seated at the opposite end of the table, who had light-brown hair and striking green eyes. His lips were in a thin line, but his eyes crinkled at the corners. "And last but certainly not least, this is Gabriel of the Spring Court."

"I've been excited to meet the mate of Hades," Gabriel said.

Hades turned to Thanatos, who watched the exchange with a quiet intensity. "And you know Thanatos," Hades said, with a hint of amusement. Thanatos inclined his head in acknowledgment, a faint smile gracing his lips—a rare sight to me. With the introductions complete, Hades took a seat.

"Can I ask something?"

"Go ahead," Hades said.

I hesitated. "You are all fae?"

Aurelia laughed. "Yes."

Hades must've sensed my confusion. "I spent much of my early life in Faerie. I trust this group of people the most." Hades glanced at each person for a moment. "All the dead in the universe find their way to the Underworld, and the fae are no exception. They care about this realm as much as I do."

Is that why you like faerie wine so much? I spoke into Hades' head.

It is, indeed.

"What about Hermes and Hecate?" I questioned, hating the way Hecate's name felt on my tongue.

"They are a more recent development. Hermes and Hecate are valuable allies," Hades said.

Thanatos interlaced his hands and rested them on the table. "The politics of the Olympian Court are twisted. Having dependable allies, especially in times of uncertainty like these, can mean the difference between success and failure."

Hades cleared his throat. "Thank you all for coming."

Orion let out a long grunt. "Took you long enough to call us."

Hades shrugged him off. "As you know, there's an important court meeting tomorrow. You all will be able to watch from this room, as we've done before." Hades glanced at me. He waved a hand, and his magic danced in an intricate pattern. A portal of swirling magic materialized. I gasped, seeing myself and the others sitting in the room through the lens of Hades' eyes. I raised my hand, moving in sync with the reflection in the portal. Hades waved, and it disappeared.

"And you already reported to Zeus that Demeter stole the stone?" Orion asked, not fazed by Hades' magic.

Hades groaned. "Yes. He said I was to report it at the meeting."

"I don't know how someone can care so little about potentially releasing the Titans. Especially him," Thanatos added.

"Persephone isn't a member of the court, right? So you can't count on having her vote?" Gabriel asked.

"No," Hades answered before I had a chance to.

Gabriel tapped his fingers on the table. "You should consider having her become a member. It would be helpful to have another reliable vote in the future."

"No," Hades said again.

"What do you mean no?" I shot back. "How do I become a member?"

Hades stayed silent. I looked at Thanatos. He gave Hades an apologetic glance before speaking. "The moment you are born in Olympus, the court takes a portion of your power. This is to preserve hierarchy, ensuring it remains unchallenged." Thanatos leaned back in his chair. "As it stands, you are indeed a goddess, but you only have access to part of your potential power. The rest lies dormant, sealed away in the Olympian Court. To claim your rightful place among the Divine and unlock the full breadth of your abilities, you must prove yourself worthy by completing the trials."

"Trials?" I asked.

"Every member of the Olympian Court has completed them to earn their spot. We have also taken blood vows to the court," Hades explained.

"And that is why we're still members of the damn court," Thanatos scoffed.

Unease crept over me. It was a reminder of just how little I knew about the Divine. "And how do I complete the trials?"

"You don't." Hades shook his head. "You are not participating. It's not worth it. End of discussion, Persephone." Hades sent love through the mating bond, but I sent back my annoyance. *The trials are too dangerous*, Hades spoke.

I crossed my arms. *You think I can't do it.*

That's not what I said.

That's exactly what you said, Hades.

"Can you let us in on your mental conversation?" Cassius barked a laugh.

"It's not necessary," Hades said.

Aurelia leaned closer to me and whispered, "Don't worry, Persephone. Hades is still in the extra possessive phase of the mating bond. Fae bonds work the same way."

I gave her a polite smile, unsure if Hades would ever leave that phase.

"Since Demeter already knows you are here, I am planning to propose your emancipation from her. You are an adult. She shouldn't have any more say over you. And she should not be able to starve the mortals because of that." Hades sent love again through the bond. "By the way, Gabriel, how has bringing food to the mortals been working?"

Cassius snorted a laugh. "I can tell you. Gabriel has supplied food to some but has also spent a lot of time with a mortal woman." Cassius wiggled his white eyebrows.

Orion laughed, sharp and too loud, the kind meant to sound amused, but it rang empty. I'd laughed like that before when I hadn't meant it.

"Enough," Gabriel said with a scoff. "The Spring Court's efforts have been offsetting some of the devastation to the mortals."

"Why do you help?" I paused when I realized how my words sounded. "I mean, yes, the mortals shouldn't starve, but I don't understand why the fae would help?"

Gabriel sighed. "Your mother doesn't do anything without a reward. That's why you think that way. But most others do not. There is a balance between the realms, and we must make sure that continues."

"What do you propose we do about the stone?" Cassius asked.

"We'll see how the court meeting goes, but I am not hopeful," Hades said.

Cassius' face was unreadable. "So we're going to have to find the rest of the pieces of the stone or the spell?"

Hades nodded. "I believe so."

Aurelia rose from her seat and made her way to the board covered in notes. "Demeter has three pieces of the stone now. She doesn't have any pieces of the spell, right?"

"Yes, but she does have one piece of the spell."

Aurelia sighed, brushing away a scattering of notes with her sleeve. Her eyes narrowed as she scribbled down the information we had. "We know there is one piece of the stone hidden in Faerie. The remainder are scattered across the realms," she continued.

My fingers twisted in my lap. How did they know there was a stone in Faerie? Questions built inside me, one after the other, but I kept them at bay. Asking would only slow them down, and I was already struggling to catch up.

"And we have no idea where those are." Cassius let out a sarcastic laugh. "Wonderful."

"Also correct," Hades said.

Orion leaned forward, his gaze sweeping over the board. "What do you propose we do with the first stone piece once we find it?"

"Well, first things first. Tartarus needs to be sealed. I cannot hold it forever."

"Agreed, you look horrible," Orion said.

Hades ignored that comment and looked at me. "Orion and Gabriel will be staying in the Underworld with us, though they will likely spend some time in Faerie. As royal fae, Cassius and Aurelia need to attend to their own court duties. They will come here for meetings."

I nodded.

The discussion continued between the group. I found

myself drawn into the intricacies of the conversation, though I contributed little. There was a sense of awe I couldn't brush aside at the depth of knowledge and experience gathered in the room. Though I was still annoyed with Hades, I spoke through the bond. *Thank you for including me.*

Hades dipped his head, and the corners of his mouth turned up. *I told you we'd do this together.*

I decided I'd have to ask Hades more about the trials later.

36

PERSEPHONE

I had been awake for a few hours, staring at the ceiling with Hades' arms wrapped around me. He was still asleep, but anxiety swelled through the mate bond. Despite the calm mask Hades wore, turmoil simmered beneath the surface. The immense strain of magic sealing Tartarus had stripped Hades' ability to mask his emotions as effectively as he once could.

I shifted in his arms, my fingers trailing over the pattern on his chest and studying the dark hollow skin under his eyes. They looked better today, but still there.

"Good morning, little goddess." Hades' voice was soothing. I rested my chin on his chest and smiled. A rush of warmth spread through me as he ran his hands over my back.

We relished each other's presence for a few more minutes before rising to dress for the day. Silence enveloped us as we got ready; the usual morning chatter absent, the soft rustle of clothes replacing it. The day ahead weighed heavily.

When we got to the meeting room, Orion, Aurelia, Cassius, Gabriel, and Thanatos were already there. The room hummed with expectant energy. Hades' viewing portal swirled to life before us. He pulled me into his arms and pressed a gentle kiss to my lips before he and Thanatos whisked.

～

HADES

I stood next to Thanatos at the edge of the courtroom. Towering marble pillars met the painted ceiling. Intricate carvings of the Divine covered every inch.

"Gods, I cannot wait for this to be over," Thanatos said.

As our eyes met, understanding passed between us. I raised an eyebrow ever so slightly, and the corners of my lips quirked up. "Likewise."

Sirens sang within the confines of the inverted U-shaped bench, with the court seats stretched across its length. The melody enveloped me but failed to soothe the storm inside of me.

I couldn't shake the sinking feeling that this meeting would be far from productive. "Would you like some ambrosia, Lord Hades and Lord Thanatos?" A nymph stood in front of us, her gaze downcast as she held a golden platter covered in matching goblets, each brimming with crimson liquid. The spiced scent mingled with the incense burning throughout the room.

"I'll pass." I waved. Ambrosia was exclusively reserved for the Divine. It flowed in large amounts at every Olympian event and court meeting. I'd never been a fan of it.

Thanatos took a goblet. "Thank you." He took a swig of the drink as the nymph paled and tried to collect herself. She likely wasn't used to any respect or manners coming from a

Divine. Other nymphs walked around the room, some with ambrosia and others with desserts, but each with their faces a blank mask of subservience.

I studied the other Divine. They talked with each other, dressed in robes and garments covered in jewels. Some stayed close to their court seats. Others didn't. Thanatos and I stood in front of ours. I had no interest in wandering around the room to engage in meaningless small talk.

I suppressed the urge to groan as Hecate approached our side, and forced a smile in her direction. "Hades." She nodded. "Thanatos."

"Hecate."

"Listen, Hades, I don't like the way things were left between us. You know I would never wish—" Hecate stopped herself before uttering Persephone's name. "Any harm."

I wanted to believe her, but so much had changed, and nothing was certain now. Hecate had a wealth of experience with magic, and I couldn't shake the feeling her silence about Persephone's magic was more than just an oversight. "I over-reacted." *Lie.* "I apologize," I said with a smile. *Lie.* "I know you'd never have bad intentions with the goddess." *Lie.*

Her tense shoulders relaxed. "I'm glad you understand that now." She looked at Thanatos, and he smiled and waved. "I should get closer to my seat."

"It was nice seeing you," I said. *Lie.*

"You two as well." Hecate turned and walked across the room.

"You're awfully forgiving today," Thanatos said with a chuckle. He knew we had to play nice. We needed every vote we could get.

I forced a smile. "Forgiving is one way to put it."

"We'll get through this."

I hoped he was right.

The sirens stopped singing, and they filed out of the

room, trailing after the nymphs. The meeting would begin soon. The other Divine made their way to their seats. Thanatos and I followed suit.

I could feel the eyes on me. I straightened my shoulders. Many of the Divine viewed me with suspicion and mistrust. Thanatos and I were outsiders who would not be swayed by the petty politics of the court. The fate of the Underworld—the universe, even—hung in the balance, and it was my duty to defend it.

Thanatos and I took our seats. I ran my gloved fingers over the golden plaque with my name carved into it. A rumble of thunder filled the room, and Zeus appeared in his seat at the head of the inverted U. He'd always possessed a flair for theatrics, a quality that had undoubtedly played a role in his ascent to the head of the court.

"Esteemed members of the Olympian Court." Zeus' voice boomed, echoing off the marble walls and silencing the murmurs that had filled the chamber. His gaze swept across the assembly.

"We convene today to address matters of utmost importance," he continued. "Our first matter is about fellow court member Demeter. As we all know, the mortal realm has suffered from food and resource deprivation. The mortal realm is essential to keeping the balance in the universe. But before we proceed, it is imperative we hear from those whose actions have come into question."

Zeus turned his attention to Demeter. She stood. "Demeter, you are accused of neglecting your duties to the court, which you agreed to when you completed your trials. Is there anything you wish to say before we proceed to vote on your punishment?"

Demeter's chin lifted. "Yes. There is something I wish to say."

I fought the urge to scoff.

"I admit I have failed my duties to the court, but you must understand depression has plagued me ever since my daughter, Persephone, was abducted." She paused, brushing a few stray tears away that I knew were fake. She sniffled and continued, her voice trembling with false emotion. "And I have reason to believe the one responsible for her abduction is in this room."

The Divine exchanged glances.

"That is a serious claim," Zeus said.

"You must understand, while I'm a member of the court, I'm also a mother." She stressed the title she was unworthy of. "Hades has my daughter imprisoned in his realm."

A murmur of shock filled the room. I stood up quickly, the legs of my chair protesting as they scraped against the floor. There was no need to hide the truth anymore. "She is not imprisoned. Persephone ran to my realm to escape your abuse."

The Divine broke into chatter. Zeus raised his hand. "Silence." The room hushed. "Hades, you will have an opportunity to speak if you wish, but that is not now. Demeter, we are only addressing your duties at the moment. We have listened to your testimony, and we will take it into consideration as we proceed with the vote."

Demeter's face went hard, fighting the urge to scowl.

"Now, we must vote. Cast for punishment or no punishment."

A parchment appeared in front of me and every other member of the court. I scrawled the word *punishment*, and with a dramatic poof of smoke, it disappeared. When everyone cast their vote, Zeus stood up. "A decision has been made. There will be no punishment for Demeter's actions. However, she is to immediately resume and uphold her duties as Goddess of Harvest." The courtroom erupted with reactions. Some Divine nodded in agreement while others expressed their disapproval.

I tapped my fingers against my leg.

One.

Two.

Three.

Four.

Five.

I took a breath and forced the frustration down. *Are you okay?* Persephone asked through the bond.

I'm fine. Just frustrated. Neglect of duty was a serious offense. I glanced around the chamber. Demeter's emotional plea had resonated with some among the Divine. It was obvious in the subtle nods of sympathy. But I knew there was something else. The Goddess of Harvest had accrued power long before she had any pieces of the stone. Secrets. She used those invisible threads to force others to bend to her will.

With a sigh, I resigned myself. I knew my warnings would be ignored.

The meeting moved to the next order, the construction of new buildings in Athens. I tuned it out. It was a trivial proposal in comparison to the issues facing the universe. With the Titans at risk of being released, how could anyone be concerned with such petty matters?

Zeus addressed the assembly, his words filled with enthusiasm and optimism. The other Divine seemed eager to move forward with the construction project, their minds already turning to the possibilities of the new buildings. I shook my head in disbelief. While the rest of Olympus was content to bask in their own complacency, my realm was left to bear the weight of the possibility of impending doom.

"Are there any matters anyone would like to add?" Zeus said.

Finally, my turn. I stood, along with Artemis, Goddess of Hunt.

"I have one matter to address," Artemis said.

"I have two," I said.

Zeus gestured to Artemis. "You may go first."

I sat and listened to her proposal of more statues of the Divine throughout Olympus.

"Ridiculous," Thanatos murmured, loud enough for me to hear. We cast a vote, which passed.

"Hades, you may have your turn," Zeus said.

I stood. "I come to you with a matter of grave importance." I could feel everyone scrutinizing my every word and gesture.

"Recently, the piece of the Nexus Stone holding the Titans in Tartarus has been stolen," I continued, my tone measured. "Demeter is responsible for this heinous act."

Murmurs rippled through the room, a chorus of disbelief and outrage.

Demeter jumped from her seat. "I beg your pardon. How could you accuse me of such a thing?"

Zeus stood. "Silence, Demeter. And what evidence do you have to support these claims, Hades?"

I met his gaze. "Others, myself included, have witnessed Demeter's involvement." I looked around the room. "If you do not believe me, I invite you to have a look for yourself in my realm." My voice was steady despite the rage brewing within me.

"We must vote. This is a serious allegation. Cast your votes for or against exploring these matters further."

A few of the Divine offered nods of solidarity. Thanatos, Hermes, Hecate, Athena, Goddess of Wisdom, and Poseidon, God of the Seas.

As the votes were tallied, a heavy silence descended upon the chamber, only the sound of parchment rustling and pens scratching breaking it. My heart pounded in my chest like a drumbeat.

"The council has reached a decision," Zeus said. "In a close vote, it has been decided there is not enough evidence Demeter has taken the Nexus Stone piece."

My jaw ticked. "I told you to look for yourselves. Do you know what's at risk? Do you want the Titans to be released?" The mention of the Titans paled many of the Divine's faces. It wasn't a word uttered in the courtroom often.

I didn't know how long I could hold the seal on Tartarus. The strain was relentless, but I refused to draw any power from Persephone. I wouldn't risk draining her. No one could offer me any aid; my magic was uniquely tied to the Underworld.

"Hades, you know the rules. You swore an oath to this court when you completed the trials. We all did. We can recast the votes at our next court meeting. I'm sure many of our dissenting votes would love to see the evidence for themselves."

"What good are rules and procedures if they don't work?"

"Enough, Hades. What is your next matter?"

I swallowed the words full of anger threatening to spill from my mouth. "I wish for Persephone to be released from the custody of Demeter. She is an adult and has the right to choose not to return if she doesn't want to."

Demeter growled. "She signed a document relinquishing those rights." A piece of parchment appeared in her hand. My eyes narrowed, and I clenched my knuckles at the crimson signature at the bottom.

"That is not valid. You forced her to do that." Persephone would never sign a document like that of her own volition. Just as the words flowed out of my mouth, Persephone tugged on the bond.

Hades. I didn't sign anything.

Don't worry, little goddess. I'll never let her have you again.

"Hades, there is no evidence of the abuse you claim. Persephone must be returned to her mother."

"She is my mate. She belongs in my realm." The mark on my chest pulsed under my clothing. Eyes widened, darting from one face to another. Murmurs grew louder.

Zeus folded his hands. "Persephone is not a member of the court. It doesn't matter if she's your mate. We will abide by her signature."

Thanatos rose next to me. "Even if they have a binding ceremony?"

"Persephone is still in the custody of her mother. You would require Demeter's approval and for her to relinquish her rights for a binding ceremony to take place."

I didn't bother arguing. It was no use. We'd find another way.

"You have thirty days to return Persephone to her mother," Zeus said.

The words struck me with force. I stayed silent. Persephone would never return to her mother. Not now. Not *ever*.

"Are there any other matters?"

Silence.

"This meeting is adjourned."

Thanatos struggled to keep up with my brisk pace as we walked the corridors of Divine Hall. Whisking in or out of the building was forbidden; it wasn't even possible.

The Olympian Court started as a noble idea, a way to prevent corruption and war. But it had become something far from its original purpose—a place where power and ambition took focus, rather than facts and order.

37

PERSEPHONE

The raw power of my magic lashed out with a ferocity that left me panting. Vines, suffused with a dark green so deep it bordered on coal, moved around me like serpents of shadow. Seeing my mother's smug face in the viewing portal brought back memories I wished I could forget. Scrub from my mind. Banish to the recesses of Tartarus.

"Breathe, Persephone," Cassius said at my side.

But I couldn't. All I could see was her. And hear her voice. And smell the perfume of lilies she always wore. She was everywhere. My ears rang. *I want to be free.* Her influence on my life was like a stubborn stain, tainting every action.

Spots filled my already hazy vision. My magic grew more out of control. Without being tethered to my mother anymore, my magic had changed. It felt like a never-ending well in comparison. My chest continued to tighten, making it difficult to draw in a full breath. Every word she spoke at the court meeting…

Hades tugged on the bond. I could feel his nearness, but I couldn't see him through the rush of magic flowing from me.

Hades and Thanatos must've returned. Turmoil still raged within me.

There was a touch on my shoulder.

Hades.

His touch sent a surge of warmth through me. His black magic surrounded me, and my onslaught of magic ceased. He pulled me into a hug. *I'm here*, he spoke. My body crumpled slightly, but Hades held me up.

His touch and words anchored me back in the present. I blinked away tears, focusing on the steady rhythm of his breathing. I matched it with my own in an effort to regain my composure. The world gradually sharpened into focus again, my panic dulled. Hades guided me to a seat at the table, sitting next to me. He held my hand, squeezing it every so often. "We have to make it a priority to teach you how to control your magic."

"Agreed." Cassius choked out a laugh without any humor. "Gods, Persephone, you are powerful." I studied everyone sitting at the table and massaged my temples. Each face wore varying degrees of concern—maybe curiosity. Thanatos swallowed and placed his palms flat on the table.

"It's likely because she's never fully experienced her magic. It was siphoned by her mother," Aurelia said.

I cringed at the pity in her voice.

"Imagine if she were ever to become a full goddess," Gabriel mused, gaze drifting to me before shaking his head slowly. The spotlight of their attention was too bright.

"Enough about that," Hades said. "Let's focus on the problems at hand."

I drew a steadying breath. *Thank you*, I said through the bond.

No need to.

Well, I'm doing it anyway.

Hades shot me a small smile. "So obviously, the court

does not believe—or enough of the court does not believe Demeter has a piece of the stone, much less more than one piece," Thanatos said.

"Right." Orion placed his palms on the table. "Which means we're right back to the original plan. Find the rest of the stone or the spell, maybe both, before Demeter does."

"Correct," Gabriel added.

I sat as they discussed, focusing on the lamp across the room. I fixated on the small specks of dust dancing in the light. The longer I stared, the more little white spots filled my vision. It was a welcome distraction from the conversation swirling around me. The Frost siblings had been looking into the stone in Faerie while everyone looked for leads elsewhere. I shouldn't have, but I tuned it out. My fingers traced an invisible pattern underneath the table.

Persephone, Hades spoke into my head. *Are you okay?*

I was sure he could feel the answer, but I responded anyway. *I'll be fine. Seeing and hearing my mother brought up bad memories.*

I'm always here. Remember that.

I will.

"Next problem." Gabriel cleared his throat. "Persephone." Hearing my name drew my attention. "Persephone's custody."

Aurelia's long white hair shifted as she shook her head. "The court needs a new system. This is ridiculous."

"Tell me about it," Thanatos said.

Hades squeezed my hand. "Persephone signed a document."

I bristled. "I don't remember signing anything." I sank into my seat. "To be fair, I was also numb, high out of my mind a lot of the time… so it's possible."

Hades sent more warmth through the bond. "I know you

would've never signed it if you had known what it was or if you were in control."

Thanatos sighed and turned to me. "Even if the signature was done unwillingly, it's signed in blood," he explained. "You are bound by Divine law."

"How can I get out of it? Is there any way?"

"We'll figure it out," Hades said.

"There are a few ways," Thanatos piped. Hades shot him a glare, but he continued. "If we were to find all the pieces of the stone we need, we would be able to overpower the contract. The other way is if you were to complete the trials, you would be a court member, and the contract would no longer apply. But we"—he glanced at Hades—"have determined that's not an option."

Gabriel added, "Because it's a custody contract, and being a court member would make her an adult?"

Hades nodded. "Correct."

"So what happens if I don't oblige?" My voice shook, but I did my best to mask it.

"You are immortal, but there are a few ways for you to die." Hades cringed at the last word. "When you sign something with your Divine blood, you are making a contract with the Fates. If you do not fulfill it, they will cut your thread."

My pulse quickened. "So I'd die," I repeated. I had mulled over the concept countless times before I left Olympus. Death. Dying. All of it. Sometimes, I'd wished for it. I prayed to the Fates to let me be done, but every day I woke up again and faced my cruel reality. Maybe I would've acted on it had immortality not shielded me. But now that I was confronted with it… I wanted to live.

If I died, I'd be here. I tried to grapple with the idea—to find some twisted semblance of comfort that if the worst happened, I would still be okay. The souls seemed happy enough.

Do you really want to be confined to one realm for the rest of your existence? Hades spoke.

No. I never wanted to be confined again.

"It will not come to that." Hades' voice carried a firm edge. "We'll figure something out."

"I'm tired of vague promises and empty reassurances. I want…" I paused. "I need solid answers. Let me do the trials."

Hades went rigid. "No." His tone left no room for argument, but I did it anyway.

"Why do I need your permission? Because I'm still bound to you?" The mark on the back of my neck pulsed at the mention.

"Persephone, you may be bound to me, but you are free. I understand you're upset, but you do not understand what the trials entail—"

"Then tell me," I shouted.

"I can't." Hades squeezed my hand, but I pulled it away. Hurt flashed across his face. "I only want what's best for you."

I narrowed my eyes. "Best for me? Or for you?"

I want the best for you, always.

I shoved back the tears threatening to spill from my eyes. I didn't want them to focus on me anymore. I swallowed the lump forming in my throat. I looked away at a piece of art across the room, to keep the tears from falling.

The painting was dramatic, a vivid depiction of a battle frozen in time. Dark clouds bruised the sky above the battlefield, streaked with bolts of lightning, illuminating the scene in an eerie glow.

Below, the ground was covered in a mess of mud, blood, and bodies. The artist had captured every detail. I focused on the center of the painting where two figures stood. My eyes settled on one particular warrior: the one to the left.

His features were unmistakable—the strong jawline, the intense gaze, the dark hair. It was Hades. Or someone who looked so much like him that my breath caught in my throat. I had to look away. The art offered a temporary refuge, but now it felt like a cruel reminder of the person I was struggling to stay composed in front of.

I turned my mind to the stories in my head. They'd never let me down. I was in a garden, laughing, smiling as the conversation continued around me. We couldn't rely on the court, so we needed to find the pieces of the stone and spell ourselves. Everything hung in the balance. We couldn't afford to let my mother succeed.

I hoped Hades had a plan. Otherwise, in thirty days, I'd be back with my mother.

HADES

I sighed and ran my hand across my tired face, trying to dispel the tension within me. I stared at the paperwork, but I didn't read any of the words. My pen slipped from my fingers, leaving a blot of ink on the paper. I rubbed my temples and tried to ignore the pounding in my head.

My chest tightened with the dull ache that had begun at the first mention of Persephone completing the trials. I couldn't bear the thought of her risking herself in them. I closed my eyes, but the turmoil still churned inside of me.

There was a knock on my study door. "Come in."

Hermes. I'd been expecting him, but he wore a smile that was far too large. "Hermes," I said, more monotone than I'd expected, "to what do I owe the honor of your visit?"

He cringed. "Gods, you look terrible."

A laugh laced with bitterness left me. "Everyone keeps telling me that." I placed my palms flat on the desk. "Flattery is your strong suit."

His lips quirked up slightly. "I'm serious, Hades. You do not look well."

"I'll be fine." If I kept telling myself that, it would become true.

His expression turned unreadable. "I have a message for you from Olympus. A few court members wish to schedule visits to the Underworld and have a look at Tartarus themselves."

I wrung my hands together under the desk. "Which seek entry?"

"Zeus, Apollo, Hera, and Ares."

I pursed my lips. "Very well. Inform them I'm eager to extend them my *hospitality*."

"How is Persephone?"

I sighed and leaned back in my chair. "She is as good as she can be, considering the circumstances. Her mother needs to be punished."

Hermes looked down. "I agree. But alas, the fucking rules of the court bind us."

My posture straightened. I wasn't used to Hermes talking so freely. I supposed I wasn't the only one realizing the court had strayed far from its original purpose.

I gave him the biggest smile I could muster. "Bound by blood."

Hermes swallowed loudly and nodded. "I will say hello to Persephone before I leave."

~

PERSEPHONE

I stood in the empty courtyard. I missed the pulse of magic that used to be here. I closed my eyes and sent Hades love through the bond. I knew he was still struggling, though he brushed my—and everyone else's—concerns aside.

I took a deep breath, the familiar thrum of my power coursing through my veins as I focused my energy on the task at hand. I saw a plant in my mind's eye. My magic swirled within me. Since Hades had broken the tether between me and my mother, every day, my magic appeared to grow stronger. I was determined to master it so I could protect myself, and more importantly, so I could help take the load off Hades.

A small green leafy plant grew. I envisioned the thin shield around it necessary to keep anything alive in this realm. As the magic flowed from me, it didn't feel right. My magic swelled and swirled around me in chaotic spirals that defied my attempts to control them. The small plant grew rapidly into a massive tree. Its gnarled trunk rose from the ground like the twisted spine of an ancient beast.

I clenched my jaw and knuckled my fists into balls as I struggled to rein my unruly magic. I poured all my concentration into it, but with each passing moment, it grew more erratic. Flowers bloomed and withered in rapid succession around me as the tree continued to grow. I staggered backward.

Persephone, I'm coming, Hades spoke through the bond.

A wash of magic made everything pause, freezing my chaotic scene. I turned, my heart racing, to find Hermes standing behind me. Hades materialized before me, surveying the tangle of magic. Hermes flicked a hand, and my magic dissipated. "Thank you," Hades said.

Hermes took a breath. "No problem." His words were steady, though a shift in his expression suggested otherwise.

"Now that everything is under control, I'll give you time to talk." Hades pulled me into a hug, squeezing briefly before releasing me. *Let me know if you need anything.*

Always.

Hades nodded, then walked back into the palace.

"Thank you," I whispered. "As you can see, I'm having trouble controlling my magic."

Hermes chuckled. "Control will come with practice."

"It's good to see you. If you don't mind me asking, what brings you to the Underworld?"

"I had to deliver a message to Hades. Some court members will be visiting to take a look at Tartarus."

"That's a good thing, right?"

Hermes sighed and shook his head. "I wouldn't be so hopeful yet. Even once they see for sure the stone piece is indeed gone, they still may not vote in favor."

"But don't they understand what's at stake?"

"Of course they do. Nobody wants the Titans released—except maybe your mother." Hermes took a step closer. "But the politics of the court are tricky. Some members have too much pride to admit they are wrong. Or they fear what would happen if they do not side with Demeter."

"That's pathetic."

Hermes crossed his arms. "I agree."

"And there's no way to get around the court?"

"As I'm sure Hades already told you, we are bound by blood to the court."

Silence continued between us for a minute or two. "If I ask you something, would you answer honestly?"

He shrugged, a glimmer in his eye. "Depends on what you ask."

"What do the trials entail?"

"I can't tell you."

I tried not to snap at him. "Why?" My voice came out like a sigh.

"Remember when I said we are bound by blood to the court? Certain things are unable to be shared for that reason."

I frowned, toying with a piece of my hair. "Hades doesn't want me to do them."

"I'm afraid I agree." The pity in his eyes stung more than his words.

I straightened. "I'm not a fragile flower." I tried to project the confidence I desperately wanted to feel. Why did everyone doubt me? Was I as weak as they believed?

"If I could do it over again, I wouldn't have completed the trials. I would've never become a member of the court."

"I don't want to join the court…" My gaze dropped. "But it would solve a few problems. Like freedom from my mother, and Hades would have another vote he could count on."

Hermes' face scrunched. "Do you truly think completing the trials would solve your problems?"

"Some of them."

"Oh, Persephone. You have so much to learn. Becoming a court member would create *more* problems."

I gave him a weak smile, the corners of my lips trembling slightly. I hated that everyone seemed to know more than me. It was a dark cloud hanging over my head, a constant reminder of my inadequacy. Again, I was on the outside looking in, an unwelcome observer.

The harsh lines on his face softened. "Don't worry. Everything will work out."

"I won't." My lips pinched together.

I'd have to find the answers myself.

~

The smell of books did little to remove the guilt gnawing at me. I stepped deeper into the library, heading toward the section with books on the Olympian Court. I trailed my fingers along the rows of weathered spines, cracked and worn with age. I scanned the titles, my eyes darting over gilded letters and faded ink, searching for any mention of the trials. I found none. One by one, I plucked books from the shelves. I flipped through the pages, scanning over the passages.

Once I'd given up on each book, I set it on the floor, adding it to the growing stack I had already gone through. In some twisted way, this felt like a betrayal to Hades. He didn't want me to do the trials, but the voice in my head insisted they were the only way. I just wished I could find some information.

With a sigh, I added another book to the pile. I ran a hand through my hair, my fingers getting stuck in the tangled mess. I pulled at it. My jaw tightened, and I clamped my eyes shut, trying to hold in the stinging tears threatening to shed. *Why can't anything go my way?* I straightened my spine and walked out of the library. I'd had enough for today.

39

PERSEPHONE

I gripped the handle of the door to our room. The door swung wide. My breath caught in my throat. I'd been expecting to be alone, and there stood two souls. One of the souls stepped up. She was tall and translucent. She had curly tendrils of hair gathered into a tight hairstyle at the top of her head. The other soul was shorter but had a similar hairstyle.

"Lady Persephone, this is for you."

My eyes narrowed on the folded white card she held in her hands. I took the card and opened it.

Meet me in the foyer at dusk. - Hades

"We are here to help you get ready," the other soul said. She held up a dress on a gold hanger, hooked on her index finger.

It was beautiful. The fitted top transitioned into a flowy skirt from the cinched waistline. Intricate floral embroidery embellished the long lavender dress, becoming denser as it approached the hem. "It's gorgeous," I whispered.

"I know," she gushed, and swirled around, still holding the dress up.

The other soul cleared her throat. The one holding the dress immediately paused and bowed her head. "I'm so sorry, Lady Persephone. I got carried away."

"There's no reason to apologize," I assured her. "What are your names?"

The first soul blushed. "Right." She fumbled with her fingers. "Well, my name is not right. I didn't mean—"

"Her name is Sera." The soul gave Sera a smirk. "I'm Evangeline."

"Nice to meet the two of you."

"The pleasure is ours," Sera said.

Evangeline nodded as they worked together to lay the dress on the bed. Sera pulled out a seat in front of a vanity that had not previously been there. "Please sit, Lady Persephone. I will do your hair, and Sera will do your makeup," Evangeline said.

I took a seat. "By the way, just Persephone is fine."

"Are you sure—"

"She said just *Persephone*, Eva," Sera snickered.

"Sorry about her."

I laughed and shook my head. "You two are friends?"

"Worse. Sisters." Evangeline raised her eyebrows.

The new bit of information prompted me to scrutinize their features more closely. As I observed them side by side, the subtle similarities emerged. Their eyes, though differing in color, shared the same shape, a gentle curve mirroring the arc of a crescent moon. The tilt of their noses bore a striking resemblance too, each with a slight upturn at the tip. And when they smiled, their lips curved in an identical way.

"And you found each other in the Underworld?"

Evangeline nodded as she started on my hair. "We were humans. I died first. A crash," she explained impassively. "I was a hairdresser. I'm not sure how long I was here before Sera joined me."

Sera chewed on her lip. "After I faced my purgatory stage, my guide led me to Eva and the other passed family members."

"Do you like it here?"

Sera leaned in and carefully applied creams and powders to my face, layering each product. "Yes," they said in unison.

"In death, we have found a new kind of existence," Sera continued. "One that transcends the boundaries of mortal life. During my human life, I always lived in fear of death. I thought it would be painful—that my time with my family would be over. I'm glad I was wrong."

"Here, there's a peace that eluded us in life," Evangeline said. The sisters fluttered around me like butterflies as they helped me get ready. All their touches were delicate.

"Do you ever miss the mortal world?" I couldn't help but ask. There was so much for me to learn about the Underworld.

They exchanged glances. "There are moments we remember. Beautiful memories," Sera said, her voice tinged with nostalgia. "But in the end, we have found a sense of purpose here."

"Thank you for sharing with me."

Evangeline's lips curled into a soft smile. "Of course." She weaved small flowers into the elaborate braid she created.

"And one last thing." Sera twisted a tube of lipstick up. "Open," she prompted, and put it on me. The sisters stepped back and studied me before shrieking.

"King Hades is going to lose his mind," Sera said.

"You think so?" I glanced at my reflection in the mirror. I'd never felt so beautiful. I'd never had my hair or makeup done before. Mother thought I shouldn't have so much attention on me. I cringed.

Sera's face fell. "You don't like it."

"N-no. I love it." I sucked on the inside of my cheek. "I've never had my hair or makeup done."

"Well, it's our honor to be the first to do it for you. Let's get you into this dress." Evangeline grabbed the garment and tossed the hanger on the bed. I stepped out of my clothes quickly, uncomfortable with being so exposed, and into the dress. Evangeline laced the back while Sera helped me slip into the matching heels. "And here we are. All done," Evangeline said.

"You are beautiful," Sera whispered.

"You two worked some serious magic on me."

Evangeline scoffed. "We already had a beautiful canvas. Enjoy your evening."

"Do you know what Hades has planned?"

The sisters smirked at each other. "We've been instructed not to tell you that. We look forward to having an opportunity to serve you again." They bowed before I could stop them.

"Thank you."

With smiles lingering on their lips, they left. I stole a few more moments to admire the gown. With a final glance, I turned and made my way to meet Hades.

Hades stood in the center of the palace foyer, just as the note said he would. The mating bond thrummed as I approached him. My hand moved of its own accord, drawn to the mark emblazoned across my chest.

"Persephone." The low rumble of his voice made me shiver. His eyes darkened. "You are the most stunning woman I've ever seen." He reached for my hand, spun me, and the bottom of my dress billowed out. His touch ignited a flame that traveled through every inch of my body.

Heat rose to my already rosy cheeks. "Thank you." I squeezed his hand. Hades wore a suit crafted from the finest fabrics. Its rich-black hue was pronounced against the crisp gray button-up beneath. The fabric hugged his form, every line and seam tailored to perfection. "You look rather handsome yourself."

"You are breathtaking." He paused, eyes still roaming. "Shall we?"

I nodded. "Yes."

We walked, hand in hand, out of the foyer and the palace. My smile faltered when I saw the dusty landscape of the Underworld. It was a constant reminder of the issues at hand. I yelped as he scooped me up into his arms. The sudden movement made my stomach flip. Hades held me close, cradling me in his arms with an effortless strength. "We can't have this beautiful dress getting dirty, can we?"

I clung to him. "I'll let you carry me this time."

His eyes sparkled with amusement. "Only this time?"

"We'll see."

Darkness crept into the sky as Hades carried me. "Where are we going?"

"It wouldn't be a surprise if I told you," he teased.

My eyebrows rose. "Can I have any hints?"

"Absolutely not."

I shifted in his grip and kissed his jaw. "Are you sure?"

"That's not fair."

I continued peppering his neck and jaw with kisses. "It's completely fair."

"Lucky for you, we're here."

I glanced up. I'd been so distracted trying to get answers out of him that I didn't notice we were approaching a large greenhouse. The twin moons cast a gentle glow on the structure. "This is—" Hades stepped through the door and set me down on the plush carpet of moss.

"Incredible," I finished.

A symphony of colors and scents enveloped us. The fragrance of blooming flowers, damp soil, and plants mingled together. Shafts of moonlight filtered through the glass ceiling above, creating moving shadows through the foliage.

Everything in the greenhouse was a kaleidoscope of life and color. Large shrubs reached toward the clusters of orchids hanging from the ceiling. Orbs of shimmering golden light floated through the greenhouse, casting their glow on everything. In the center stood a small table set up with matching plates and an array of candles and flowers. Beside it lay a large blanket spread over a section of moss.

A sense of peace flowed through me that I hadn't felt since my mother broke into the Underworld. My mouth hung open. I turned to Hades. His eyes were alight with warmth. I didn't know what to say, so I pulled him into a hug. "What's all this?" I murmured against his chest.

"I created this for you. A while ago. This is the only foliage left in the Underworld at the moment. It's all I can manage. Now feels like the perfect time to give it to you."

"It's beautiful."

Warmth throbbed through the bond. My head tilted back, taking in every detail. I pulled out of the embrace, and he led me to the table, offering a chair. I leaned in, planting a soft kiss on his lips before sitting. "You shouldn't waste your energy on this."

"It's not a waste if it makes you smile."

I tilted my head back, studying all the details of the space.

"I'm glad you like it," Hades said, pride filling his voice.

"I-I don't know what to say."

"You don't have to say anything at all. Just enjoy."

A soul appeared and filled the stemmed glasses at the table with faerie wine. Another soul set two plates in front of us, and they disappeared with a smile before I had a chance to thank them.

Hades and I reached for our glasses and took a sip. I moaned at the taste. Faerie wine had grown on me. "Thank you."

"There's no need."

"There is. I truly appreciate this."

"I wanted a chance to spend some time with my mate. Recently, we've been occupied with other stressful matters."

Stressful matters put it lightly. I swallowed another sip of wine and tried to ignore all the thoughts creeping in at the edges of my mind. We continued to eat.

When we finished, Hades offered me a hand. I took it, rising as the table vanished. He guided me to the blanket on the moss, and we lay down on it. Hades smiled at me. "Watch this." He flicked his wrist, and all the floating orbs of light disappeared, plunging us into darkness. The stars in the sky became so clear.

Hades interlaced his fingers with mine as the stars flickered. I turned my head, studying him and recalling the days when I had seen him as nothing more than a figure of cruelty. "You're a good man," I said quietly.

He stiffened. "I'm not."

"You are," I insisted.

He exhaled, long and slow, his grip tightening around my hand. "Don't mistake me for something I'm not. I don't want you to be disappointed."

The sharp angles of his face were softened by the faint starlight. I had witnessed so much of his goodness—the way he cared for me and his realm.

"If ensuring your safety meant letting others suffer, I wouldn't hesitate. You're all that matters to me." Hades' thumb traced small circles on the back of my hand.

I remained silent. He didn't see himself as worthy of the

kindness I saw in him. My heart, however, still clung to the truth that Hades was a good man.

We lay there for hours, staring at the stars and talking. I yawned as the first light of dawn crept over the horizon, soft and pale. The stars faded one by one. I didn't want the night to end. There were still responsibilities waiting for us. "Come. Let's get some rest." Hades gripped my hand and whisked us back to our room.

40

HADES

The morning suns bathed the dining room in light, illuminating the table as we savored our breakfast. Persephone and I had indulged in a late start to the day, a result of our late night—or early morning. I watched Persephone closely. It was nice to see her so relaxed. Unfortunately, I wasn't certain if our tranquil day would persist once I told her about the impending visit from the court members.

Persephone placed a few pieces of fruit on her plate. All her movements were unhurried. She glanced up at me with a small smile playing on her lips. "I like these moments to ourselves."

"Me too." I took a few more bites of my pastry before deciding it as time. "There's something I wanted to ask you."

Her eyes met mine. "What is it?"

"A few members of the court will be visiting today to see for themselves that Demeter took the Nexus Stone piece." I paused. "Would you like to accompany me?"

Her eyes lit up, but a thrum of nervous energy pulsed through the bond. She glanced away from me, twirling her fork. "Are you certain you want me to come with you?"

"Of course I do. Only if you would like to join, though," I added.

Persephone paused, her lips pursed as if she were wrestling with the thought. "I would. Thank you for including me."

"They should be here later today."

~

*P*ersephone and I stood side by side at the entrance of the palace in the foyer. I took a long look at her. She looked beautiful in her crown. The jewels glimmered as they caught the light. She was more than just my mate—she would be the queen of my realm one day. We were sending a message with this visit. Her hand brushed against mine. I interlaced our fingers, her touch a comforting anchor.

Thanatos approached us, flanked by Zeus, Apollo, Hera, and Ares. Their gazes trailed upward as they grew closer, inexorably drawn to the crown atop Persephone's head. I hoped the sight would sear into their memories—a reminder of Persephone's place.

I'm nervous, Persephone said through the bond.

I squeezed her hand. *I'll be here the whole time. Don't let them intimidate you.*

Easier said than done.

Thanatos gave Persephone and me a smile.

Zeus stepped up, his white billowing robes kicking some dust up. "Thank you for having us."

I nodded. "I hope I'm able to show you the truth."

Hera stood next to him with her lips curled into a sneer. She wore a long navy gown covered in shimmering crystals. Her piercing blue eyes narrowed, prompting Zeus to clear his throat and shoot her a look. The face of the Goddess of

Marriage turned into a mask of polite indifference. They were bound, but not by love. It was a calculated arrangement of court politics and power.

"We'll see," Ares said. His gaze was sharp and predatory.

Persephone stiffened next to me. I sent some reassurance through the bond. Ares' tangled mane of dark curls framed his face. He wore a jacket and pants dyed the same shade of rich brown. Ares stood as one of the most challenging court members to sway to our cause. The God of War had a thirst for violence and conflict, and that's exactly what the Titans being released would create. I hoped his need for self-preservation would soothe his craving for chaos.

Apollo's wavy shoulder-length auburn locks came alive in the sunlight. His eyes swept over Persephone and me. His lips twisted into a feline smile, the corners of his eyes narrowing slightly. "Always a pleasure to see you, Hades." He pursed his lips. "And what an honor to meet the stolen goddess!"

I wasn't surprised at Apollo's position on Tartarus and the stone. The God of Archery and Knowledge had been tainted over the years. Truth used to guide him, but now he only followed power.

"I was not stolen." Her chin tipped up. "I ran." Persephone's voice was stern and balanced. A swell of pride unfurled in my chest.

I smiled at her. "Persephone is here of her own accord and is to be treated as my equal."

"Equal?" Hera scoffed. Zeus' hand on her shoulder silenced her. She crossed her arms but said nothing else. He was the only one who could ever get her to quiet. Long ago, Hera had been kind. She had championed love and equality. That goddess was a distant memory now.

Thanatos gave me a weary look. "How about we get started? Let's go to the Tartarus level."

"That is an excellent idea. For security purposes, you will have to whisk with us. Thanatos will bring you down." They all touched Thanatos' body as Persephone and I whisked.

I've never been that close to any of them, Persephone confessed. We appeared in front of the gates of Tartarus before Thanatos and the other members of the court.

Don't let them treat you like they're better than you. They are not. My eyes adjusted quickly to the darkness of this level. Previously, the luminescent plants provided some soft light, but they were gone. The ground beneath our feet was slick with moisture. The air was cold and smelled of decay. Persephone didn't say anything, but I sensed her discomfort through the bond.

They arrived.

Hera shrieked. "This is foul."

"I agree," Apollo breathed.

The Divine stepped closer to where Persephone and I stood in front of the gates. Each of their steps produced a squelching noise.

"Don't worry, Zeus," a voice moaned from behind the gates, "we'll meet again."

Zeus tried to look impassive, but he was already paling. I waved at the space between where the two gates met. "As you can see, the stone is gone."

"I see..." Zeus trailed. "How long do you think you can keep them contained?"

"Hades' magic is growing weaker," another voice said with a loud, deranged laugh. "We'll be out soon. And I'm coming for you first."

I didn't answer Zeus' question directly. "We need the piece of the stone back."

"And what do you propose we do?" Hera added. "Demand it back? We know the stone is gone, but how can you prove Demeter took it? She is a good woman."

"She is not a good woman." Persephone's voice came out as a near-growl.

"What do you know, *child?*" Hera stepped closer to my goddess. I stayed silent. Persephone needed to handle this if she ever hoped for any respect from the Divine.

"I know you are a brainwashed puppet. If the Titans are ever released, I hope you extend your gratitude to Demeter."

Ares' eyes danced with amusement. The prisoners behind me laughed and moaned.

Before Hera had the chance to say anything else, Zeus stopped her, his irritation palpable. "Now is not the time, Hera." He clasped his hands together. "So would you like to stay here and continue to observe the stone that isn't here, or would you like to discuss in a more comfortable setting?"

"I don't know about them, but I've seen all I needed to see here. I'm ready to get out of this filthy place," Hera said with a snarl.

"Me too," Ares said.

"All right, we will go. Thanatos will take you again."

I tugged on Persephone's hand and whisked us back to the foyer. My magic materialized seating before us. The court members appeared, visibly glad to be out of Tartarus level. No one sat.

"Now, what do you propose we do?" Apollo said.

"We can call for an investigation on Demeter. If the vote passes, then we can try to find evidence she took it," Zeus said.

"And if she didn't?" Hera glanced at Persephone before returning to Zeus.

"Then we have larger problems. The stone will still be missing, and we won't know who took it," Thanatos said.

Hera rolled her eyes.

"How long will it take to vote on a call for an investigation?" Persephone asked.

Excellent question, I praised. Her cheeks heated just enough for me to notice.

"I will call it at the next meeting."

"And when will that be?" Persephone leaned forward. "As you have seen, time is of the essence."

Zeus scowled. "I have. You are not familiar, but there are rules we must abide by. Despite what you probably think, the court is not a free-for-all."

"It very much is," Thanatos muttered under his breath, loud enough for me to hear. I choked back some laughter.

Zeus angled his body toward the door. "Thank you for having us."

I stood, nodding. "May we solve this in the most efficient way."

"Yes."

"Thanatos will see you out." I waited until they left before speaking. "Well, that went exactly how I thought it would go."

Persephone sighed. "At least no one got hurt."

"Someone would've if it wasn't for the court rules we're bound to." I chuckled darkly.

"So what now? It seems like all of this is going in circles."

"It is." I pulled her close. "We will have to find the stones and spell ourselves."

41

PERSEPHONE

In the dimly lit meeting room, Hades and Thanatos took turns updating the group on how the court visit had gone.

"Hera was very rude," I added after they went over the important details, trying to keep my tone even. Her glares had practically scorched my skin.

Thanatos snickered, his dark eyes glittering with amusement. "That's how she is."

"So, Cassius," Hades said, "you and Aurelia had a lead?"

Cassius leaned forward. "Yes, we believe there may be a piece of the stone in the Spirit Court."

Aurelia nodded. "Our spies have reported unusual energy fluctuations."

Hades laced his fingers together. "That's promising." His head tilted. "We'll need to investigate that further."

"Spirit Court?" I interjected. I'd only ever heard of the four courts—Winter, Summer, Spring, and Autumn.

"Yes, there are six courts. Winter, Spring, Summer, and Autumn are the most widely known to people of other realms. They rarely know about the Spirit and Air courts."

Aurelia stood up and walked to the board on the wall. With quick, assured strokes, she sketched a simplified map. She divided the land into each court with clear lines.

"Spirit Court is dangerous," Gabriel added. "Every fae court has unique magic. Spirit Faeries can enter other fae's minds. They can make you see something that isn't there. They can even destroy your mind from the inside out."

I shivered. "What about people who aren't faeries?"

"They can tap into most minds," he corrected. "The magic from every realm is different, but it's all similar, in a sense. Old, experienced fae can tap into even Divine minds, but only in the Faerie realm. They wouldn't have enough magic once away. Fae are stronger in Faerie."

"They keep to themselves. There is prejudice against them," Orion added.

"We don't know if it's a piece of the stone or the spell. We'll have our spies move closer to the energy. Depending on what we hear, you all can look for it." Aurelia gestured to the rest of the group, aside from her brother.

"You wouldn't come?" I asked.

She shook her head. "We're royals. Being gone for an extended period would draw too much attention."

"And both you and Hades have touched the stone. When you are near it, you'll likely feel it, and that will help alert you to its location," Cassius added.

"Keep us updated," Hades said.

Cassius nodded. "As always."

Hades placed his hand over mine. "Tomorrow, we will train. We need to get your magic stabilized, especially if we end up going to the Spirit Court. You have to learn to control your magic before learning how to shield your mind."

I swallowed and nodded. *Here we go.*

42

PERSEPHONE

I launched myself forward, my fists meeting the bag with a satisfying thud. Each impact sent a shock-wave reverberating through my arms. The energy coursing through me was raw. I came to the sparring room often now, replacing the library.

The library had transformed into a room of anxiety. It reminded me of how much I didn't know or understand. The pursuit of information was a double-edged sword. With every page turned, questions remained unanswered, joined by a flood of new ones. I'd taken a break from the room, knowing at some point I'd need to confront the harsh realities. Today, however, was not that day.

I kept my breathing even, like I'd been practicing. I'd grown stronger since venturing into the Underworld. My muscles, once frail, now thrummed with strength. Each strike released a bit of the tension coiled inside of me. Even through the chaos of my racing thoughts, I found clarity in the precision of my movements.

My actions were fluid. My body knew exactly what to do. All I had to focus on was each blow and the way the bag swayed. Not my mother, the stone, the court, or the fate of the universe. It was just me and the bag.

"Are you ready?" Hades asked as he walked in.

I stepped back, my chest heaving. I nodded, wiping at some of the sweat glistening on my skin. My pulse quickened at the thought of trying to tap into my magic again. "As ready as I'll ever be." My voice shook, though I hadn't intended for it to. Gabriel walked in as the last word left my mouth.

"Gabriel will help us today with your training. Though he's experienced with fae magic, he's powerful."

Gabriel's face contorted into an exaggerated smile. His eyebrows arched. "You flatter me."

Hades' lips twitched, suppressing a smile as he continued, "This way, we can ensure you can practice with nothing going wrong."

I stretched my lips into a smile, feeling the tightness in my cheeks. A nervous flutter ran through me.

With a flick of his wrist, Gabriel summoned a barrier of shimmering energy, encasing the three of us in a dome of pale-yellow light that cast a warm glow over the entire room. "Let's start with calling your magic," Gabriel said. His voice was gentle, but it still held a command.

I closed my eyes.

"Focus," he whispered. "Feel the magic flowing through you, like a river waiting to be guided."

My magic pulsed in response as I called on it. It surged, yearning to be unleashed. Little currents danced across my skin.

"Channel it into your palm," Gabriel said.

I followed the guidance, picturing the magic swirling within me. It coalesced into a radiant ball at my center. I tried to channel it up my core, through my arms, and to my right palm. The warmth moved through me. Everything was calm—until I opened my eyes.

The energy surged forward in my palm, growing too large. It came with a sense of imbalance, a dissonance between my magic and my body. My pulse quickened. "Steady," Hades said.

I closed my eyes and took a deep breath, trying to draw the chaotic energy back into myself, but it surged. A wave of Gabriel's magic washed over me, and the wild energy inside me stilled. *Will I ever be able to do it?* My shoulders sagged under an invisible weight—failure.

"I think I know your problem," Gabriel said.

My eyes snapped open.

"You don't have any problem calling the magic. Your problem is control."

I already knew that, but I said nothing.

"Control is not about suppressing the magic. You are the magic—you and the magic are one. Stop thinking about it like some external thing. It's not. When you call on it, you must guide it, shape it."

"Like a sculptor shaping clay," Hades added.

"Exactly."

Or putty. Like your body in my arms.

I scowled at Hades, but all he did was laugh.

Gabriel looked between us. "Anyway."

My thoughts returned to my magic. I tried to imagine what control would feel like, but doubt still gnawed at the edges of my mind. *How can I control something that feels so wild?*

"Pay attention." The surrounding dome pulsed. Gabriel held his hands open, a sphere of magic shifting from his left hand to his right. "I'm telling the magic where to go. Not the other way around." The sphere transformed into intricate patterns in the air at his command, bending to his will. "See how I'm also controlling the amount? I don't want to let everything out because then I would drain myself." The magic's brightness pulsed.

"Just try to form the sphere in your palm again."

I reached for my magic again. I pulled from the river within me. This time, instead of drawing on the entire river, I pulled on a smaller amount. It ran through my body, my arms, and down to my palm.

"Good job," Hades said proudly. I squinted one of my eyes open before fully opening them and staring at the magic in my right palm.

"You're a quick learner," Gabriel said. He glanced at Hades with a chuckle. "A much faster learner than Hades."

It was difficult to imagine Hades as anything but the powerful god I'd seen him as. "You taught Hades?"

Hades scoffed.

Gabriel smiled. "I helped him *refine* his magic."

"How old are you?" The words tumbled out of my mouth.

"Old," he responded but didn't elaborate. "Try again."

I repeated the same act of pushing my magic into a sphere in my hand over and over. Most of the time, I succeeded. Other times, I struggled, but Hades reassured me it would take practice.

"How would I use this in a fight?" I asked.

"You'd control it, but differently. I don't want to go into too much detail and overwhelm you. I want you to keep practicing this exercise. Next time, we can expand on things."

"Thank you," I said gratefully. For the first time, I felt something other than negativity toward my magic.

Gabriel bowed his head. "Don't stay here all day. Get some rest."

"I will."

He looked between us. "That goes for both of you."

43

HADES

As I stepped into the room, a fleeting familiarity came over me. It was like I could hear the echoes of our laughter over the years. I'd been in the meeting room thousands of times, but this reminded me of a period long ago when there were fewer troubles.

We used to do this a lot. The meeting room, usually reserved for our serious discussions and planning, had been transformed into an elegant dining space for the evening. Flickering candles and floral arrangements from Faerie adorned the table. I remembered when it was commonplace for me to see them every day.

Persephone studied the flowers with a sparkle in her eyes. Their petals were a vibrant shade of magenta, the tips fading to white. Persephone sat to the left of the head of the table. She was radiant. Her smile filled me with joy I'd never felt before our mating bond. My feet carried me closer to her, drawn by the invisible thread between us. I drank in the sight of Persephone, committing each detail to memory. Her dark hair cascaded over her shoulders in waves, and her dress, a deep shade of emerald, accentuated her every curve.

"You look so beautiful." I leaned in, pressing a soft kiss to her lips.

Persephone blushed, her cheeks turning to that familiar shade of pink I was addicted to seeing on her. A smile tugged at the corners of her lips. "Thank you. I had some help from the souls." Her eyes roamed my body, and I didn't mind at all. "You look handsome."

"I think you're still outshining me," I teased. Her cheeks flushed further, and I took a seat beside her.

Aurelia, Gabriel, Thanatos, Cassius, and Orion already sat at the table, their faces a mix of impatience and amusement. "Thank you for waiting for me," I said.

"It took you long enough," Orion grumbled, and right on cue, his stomach growled. "I'm starving."

"I had to catch up on sentencing souls. You know the task is never-ending," I said with a sigh. Thanatos nodded, knowing exactly what I meant. Gabriel used his magic to uncover the dishes on the table, releasing a medley of aromas. My mouth watered at the sight and smell of the faerie food.

Aurelia glanced at Persephone, her eyes full of pride. "This is food from Faerie," she said, gesturing to each dish. "These are Spring Court mushrooms sautéed in butter. Over there, are berries, blossom salad, forest soup, and these"—she wiggled her finger at the platter covered in iridescent pastries—"are pixie-touched tarts."

Persephone studied each dish as Aurelia explained each item. I placed my hands flat on the table. "Before we dig in—"

Orion groaned. Gabriel elbowed him.

"I wanted to thank all of you." My eyes flickered to each person around the table. "I appreciate your help with everything."

Gabriel smiled. "We're here for you. Always."

"Agreed," Aurelia added. She gestured to Persephone. "For both of you."

"Thank you," Persephone said, her voice choked with emotion. Persephone wasn't used to being surrounded by so many people who wanted to help her. That was something that would change for her.

"All right, let's enjoy this meal."

We each piled food on our plates. I waited for Persephone to take a bite of her food before eating mine. Her face shifted, and she released a low moan.

Her eyes snapped open, and she raised a hand to her still-full mouth. She swallowed. "I'm so sorry."

Thanatos released a loud, throaty laugh. Persephone's eyes widened, Thanatos' laughter catching her off guard. Her lips parted momentarily, and she cast a quick gaze around the room, seeking refuge from the sudden attention. I sent warmth through the mating bond.

"That's usually the reaction to Cassius' food." Aurelia giggled and nudged her brother.

Persephone set down her fork. "You made this?" Her voice climbed toward the end.

Cassius nodded.

"It's fantastic. Probably the best thing that's ever been in my mouth."

Liar. You know the best thing that's been in your mouth. I took a bite as she coughed, not breaking eye contact.

Cassius nodded. "Thank you."

"He's humble," Aurelia explained.

We continued to eat. Lively chatter and laughter filled the room, a pleasant change from the recent discussions. Persephone's laughter rang like music. I ached to hear more, even though it resulted from the group's embarrassing stories about me. It was a rare moment of peace, a chance to set aside the weight of our responsibilities and enjoy each other's company.

"I remember the day Hades stumbled into Faerie," Gabriel said. "He was a mess."

Persephone's eyes lit up.

I chuckled. "Not this story, please."

Persephone glanced at me. "Well, you have to tell me now."

Orion rubbed his hands together. "I'll tell you. I remember I was visiting Gabriel. It was Hades' first time in Faerie. For people who aren't fae, it can take some getting used to, and there are norms and rules to every realm. Clearly, Hades didn't know them. Pixies toyed with his hair, pulling it in all different directions. Willow hounds chased him through the enchanted forest of the Spring Court." Orion laughed. "It was a spectacle. Some onlookers cheered for the pixies and hounds, while others rallied for Hades. I know you've only seen him as the *boring* God of the Underworld, but this was totally different."

I scoffed. "I'm not boring."

Orion grinned at me.

The evening wore on. The candles burned lower, the plates cleared, and the conversations quieted. I couldn't help but feel a sense of warmth settle over us. Despite the teasing, each of these fae held a special place in my life, and I was grateful for the bond between us.

"Thank you all for coming," I said as the fae filtered out, Thanatos the last of the group to leave. Persephone and I lingered, savoring the quiet moment. I leaned in over the table and pressed a long kiss to Persephone's forehead. She nestled closer to me.

"Well, it seems the evening is coming to a close."

Persephone pushed her chair away from the table. "I had a good time. I'm full."

I shifted in my seat. "Hmm." I let my gaze drag down the curve of her mouth, the slope of her neck. "I have to say, I'm still craving something."

She glanced up at me.

"Something sweet."

Persephone licked her lips. "Like what?"

I didn't answer. Instead, I reached for her. One hand found her waist, fingers slipping over the curve of her fabric-covered hip. The other slid to the back of her neck. I pulled her in until our lips met. Persephone melted into me, and for a second, there was nothing but her. No missing stone. No weight. Just the soft press of her mouth and the sound of her breath catching. I pulled back only when I had to, just enough space for me to speak. "You," I whispered.

PERSEPHONE

"Show me what you've been practicing," Gabriel said as he created the dome of magic around us. Flecks of yellow danced in his green eyes.

I summoned my magic, feeling it surge and swirl within me. I guided it through my body, shaping it into a radiant sphere of pale-green light that hovered in my palm.

Hades watched from the side. He stayed silent, but his focus was unwavering. A proud smile on his face served as silent encouragement. "Very good," Gabriel remarked. "Do you feel any resistance to it?"

I paused and took inventory of the sensation. "No..." I focused on the thrum of power. "It's surprisingly easy." My magic resonated in a way that felt seamless, while before, it had been disjointed.

Gabriel nodded. "Good. That means we can move on today."

I rolled my neck and glanced at Hades. *I feel your nerves. You got this.*

What if I can't?

"Once you master the basics, it's all very easy," Hades said.

His voice soothed my unease. "Everything is about intention. You'll visualize your intention and trust your magic to follow."

I gazed at the shimmering sphere of light cradled in my palm. Gabriel positioned himself so he stood across from me, Hades off to the side between us. "Focus your mind. Visualize that same ball of energy you conjured, but this time, direct it toward me. I'm aware you've often manifested your magic in the form of vines, but just visualize it as power for now."

"You want me to hit you?"

His chest puffed. "Are you scared?"

"No." I crossed my arms. "But I don't want to hurt you."

Hades chuckled. "Don't worry about hurting him, little goddess. He's a warrior. You need to practice."

"Warrior?"

Gabriel sighed. "You're distracting her."

Hades waved a hand. "Gabriel was one of the key warriors that brought peace to Faerie."

"Faerie is split into courts, as you know," Gabriel explained. "Long ago, there was a war—a struggle for dominance. Each court sought to rule over all of Faerie, believing themselves superior to the others." Gabriel paused. "To make a long story short, many lives were lost in those turbulent times. I remember every single face of the fae I had to kill. But now, each court has a king and a queen, supported by a board of advisers. The rulers of each court work with each other to govern Faerie as a whole." He cleared his throat. "If we're finished with the history lesson, let's begin."

I nodded. There was a distant look in his eyes, and I didn't press him. My eyes fluttered closed. With a steady breath, I visualized the sphere of energy, a luminous orb of light that danced in the depths of my mind. I extended my hand, fingers trembling. It took shape in my palm. *Go,* I commanded.

I opened my eyes, and it shot from my hand at Gabriel with startling speed. Gabriel intercepted the surge of magic without so much as a flicker of effort. His stance remained unchanged. He had no reaction as he dissolved my power into nothingness mere inches from him. "Remember, channel your magic with intent. You have the control." He waved a hand. "Keep going."

I continued my relentless assault of magic. My skin was slick with sweat. The act of breathing was laborious. With each strike, I grew more attuned to the ebb and flow of power pulsing through me. I allowed myself to sink into the depths of my magic. Hades watched my every movement.

"Keep going," Gabriel would say every time I paused, thinking we were done with the same exercise. The minutes passed slowly. If I had to guess, it had been over an hour. Fatigue gnawed, and my movements grew sluggish. "Don't falter now." His voice held an urgency that was incomprehensible in my state of tiredness. "There is danger in complacency. What if I were your enemy?"

His words were a sobering reminder of the harsh universe beyond the sparring room. I took a deep breath and dug deep within myself to find the strength to continue. Sweat trailed down my face, stinging my eyes. I blinked it away, refusing to let something so minuscule distract me.

"Keep going, Persephone."

I tried.

And tried.

My knees wavered, bending before buckling. I crumpled to the ground. All I could hear was the ragged rhythm of my breathing. I closed my eyes, seeing spots. This was nothing like I'd experienced before. The fatigue when I was still tethered to my mother was different. I shoved back the unwelcome memory. This was akin to a muscle, flexed and pushed to an extreme I'd never known.

The world spun around me. Slow clapping cut through the buzzing in my ears. My eyes opened. "So now we know your limit. Now you can learn how to defend yourself," Gabriel said as if I weren't on the floor before him, exhausted.

"Now?" I groaned. "What happened to not pushing too hard in one day?"

Gabriel looked unimpressed. "I only teach defense *when* you've reached your limit." His voice lacked any sympathy. "If you can defend yourself at your limit, you'll be prepared for any situation."

One, two, three. I shifted to my hands and knees, trembling. I pushed myself off the floor. I tried to center my balance, but I was still wobbly. A ball of pale-yellow magic rushed at me. I moved in slow motion, not reacting in time before it collided with my chest. The force of the impact knocked me to the ground with a vibrating thud. It didn't hurt, but the power left me breathless and disoriented.

I glanced at Hades. The muscles in his face were taut. His hands twitched at his sides. He was restraining himself from helping me.

"Stand up," Gabriel barked. I hung my head for a second before I pushed myself up again, unsure of how I got the strength to do so. I scowled at Gabriel. I knew his intentions were good, but my frustration brewed. "That could've hurt you. But it didn't because I chose not to."

I said nothing.

"Visualize a barrier. See it forming between you and your attacker. For now, it will be visible, but as you progress and it becomes second nature, it will be invisible."

Closing my eyes, I focused on his words, willing the image of a protective shield to materialize in my mind's eye. I envisioned it taking shape, a shimmering veil of light-green power between us. I opened my eyes. Surprisingly, the barrier stood in front of me. He didn't give me any time before hurling magic at it.

It cracked and fell, but the magic didn't hit me. We repeated the routine over and over. I couldn't think. I didn't have time for it. Gabriel was relentless. "Hold the barrier up," he yelled. "Right when it cracks is when someone is going to harm you so badly, you will wish you were dead."

Another sobering reminder. "I'm trying," I ground out.

Gabriel bared his teeth. "Try harder."

I hate this.

I tried. But the next ball of magic pierced through the shield, hitting me with such an intensity, I couldn't tell if I was breathing or not. I only knew I'd fallen because I was looking at the ceiling. Every nerve in my body screamed. The edges of my vision tinged black. Gabriel stood over me. "This is how you learn."

My eyes shut.

PERSEPHONE

"I'm so proud of you," Hades whispered against my skin.

My head bowed. "I wanted to do better," I confessed, my throat tightening. I'd spent most of the day asleep, recovering from the training session with Gabriel.

Hades pulled back, his eyes blazing into mine. I felt small, like he could see every piece of me. His arms caged me onto the bed, the heat of his body everywhere. "You've made progress, Persephone. It's not realistic to expect to have everything figured out already. You're young."

My face warmed, and I cringed. "Does that bother you?"

Hades leaned in, close enough that his breath grazed my cheek. "Why would it bother me?"

I blew out a quick breath and turned my head slightly, eyes locking on a spot behind him. "Because you have to worry about me not knowing things and needing to teach me."

Warmth swelled through the bond. "Having a mate is the greatest honor of my life. I love teaching you things. I love the way your face lights up when you succeed. I love when you surprise yourself. And when you fight through something hard and win." He trailed a knuckle across my cheek. "And I love you, Persephone." His words were low.

"You—"

"Yes, I *love* you."

No one had ever used that word like that before with me romantically. He said it with such certainty, like it was a simple truth. "You shouldn't say things like that unless you mean them," I whispered.

"Do you think I would just say that to appease you? I've never meant anything more."

The bond thrummed hot in my chest. I wanted to believe him, yet fear coiled in the pit of my stomach. Loving had always been dangerous for me. Mother had made sure of that. I broke his gaze, staring at the space just past his shoulder. I forced myself to meet his eyes again. "I-I love you too." My heart swelled, the admission both terrifying and liberating. "It's just..." I paused, grappling for the right words, unsure if they even existed. "I feel like a burden. You shouldn't have to deal with stress from my mother."

"Even if you weren't my mate, I'd have to deal with your mother. She is hungry for power, always has been. She would've always wanted the stone that held Tartarus closed."

He was right. "That's true, I guess."

"It was so difficult for me to watch Gabriel hurt you, but it's important you learn how to protect yourself."

I stayed silent, too many thoughts flowing through my mind to share a coherent one.

"What are you thinking about?" he asked.

"Everything. The days are counting down, Hades. What are we going to do? There are only ten days left before I'm supposed to be returned to her..." I was finally happy. The worst part was, I knew it would end. It was inevitable. The Fates were cruel to dangle happiness in front of me only to snatch it away.

All his muscles tensed. "I won't send you back. It's not an option."

I gave him a weak smile, nodding. Words hovered on the edge of my tongue, but I held them back. I didn't say anything, afraid I'd crumble if I did. We had blissfully avoided talking about the glaring truth. In ten days, I would be ripped from my mate.

I bit the inside of my cheek. The sting helped me focus. *I have to cling to every moment until then.* I needed to tattoo them into my brain, imprinting every detail so I could hold on to them forever. To the sound of his laugh, the way he said my name, the weight of his hands on my skin. All of it. No matter what came next, she would never be able to take that away from me. "Make me forget."

Hades' eyes were on fire as he took my mouth. The kiss was passionate—desperate. Need thrummed through the bond. *I don't want this to end. I don't want this to end. I don't want this to end.* I already grieved the inevitable day I'd be ripped from Hades.

Hades pulled back. His eyes narrowed. He pressed his forehead to mine. "Listen to me, little goddess." One hand slid to my jaw, tilting it with a subtle pressure, just enough to make me meet his eyes. "You're mine, and that will not change." His head moved to the sensitive skin on my neck. "And I'm going to remind you of that over." He pressed a kiss. "And over." Another kiss. "And over." Another kiss and a little bite made me gasp.

He tugged the loose shirt I wore over my head and tossed it onto the floor somewhere. Hades cupped both of my breasts, moving his fingers over my hardened nipples. Every inch of my body was alive. My back arched at the spark of pleasure, pressing me farther into his touch.

His mouth replaced his hand.

Hades took one of my nipples into his mouth, his tongue swirling around it. His teeth grazed the tip, making me jolt. He sucked before lightly sinking his teeth into my flesh. I gasped, my fingers twisting in the soft sheets. Pleasure instantly replaced the light touch of pain. He pulled back, and I ached for his touch.

The tips of his fingers moved across the mark on my chest, his gray eyes the darkest I'd ever seen. "See this, Persephone… If you ever have any doubts, I want you to look in the mirror at this mark on your chest. As a reminder. Not only are you mine, but I am yours. I will not let you go back to your mother."

Hades didn't give me time to spiral. His hands slid to my waist, and in one quick movement, he tugged my pants down and off, removing them faster than I could've managed in my best moment.

"I don't care what I have to do," he growled. "I'll defy the Fates themselves, challenge the court if I must. None of it matters to me." Hades' eyes stayed locked on mine. "I'm never letting you go."

I lay bare on the bed, Hades still dressed. I could feel the slickness between my legs. Hades sank to his knees on the floor like a worshipper, not a god.

His hands gripped my thighs, dragging me to the edge of the bed with a roughness that made me gasp. He paused there, just breathing as his gaze pinned me to the bed like he was trying to decide how to ruin me first.

I trembled as the cool air kissed my skin. His thumbs stroked slow, deliberate circles along the insides of my thighs, setting fire to every nerve ending. His head dipped low, close, but his lips just ghosted my center.

One of his hands held tight to my thigh, anchoring me. The other slid between my legs, knuckles grazing hot skin. He dipped a finger into my wetness and dragged it up, circling my clit once, then twice, enough to make my hips buck. "Hades," I moaned.

"You like that?" he breathed against my flesh.

"Yes," I whispered, like one word was too much to focus on with all the need building within me.

Hades licked a slow, devastating line from bottom to top, sucking gently, then harder. He took his time. He smiled against my skin before giving my clit special attention.

"You taste amazing." He pulled back, slipping a finger inside of me before reaching up and holding it in front of my lips. "Taste."

My lips parted, and I took his fingers into my mouth, sucking and never leaving his eyes. His throat worked as he swallowed. A grin played on his lips.

He dropped his head again, returning to my center. Every flick, every circle sent me higher. My breath turned ragged. My legs shook. The tension built fast and hot, curling tight inside me. He pressed harder against my clit—

My eyes fluttered shut as pleasure overtook everything else. The world narrowed to just him. Just his mouth. Just the sensations. Just this blinding edge I was balancing on.

My eyes snapped open when his touch disappeared.

The loss was instant. Jarring.

Hades climbed over me, his weight shifting the mattress, his presence overwhelming in the best way. The fabric of his pants brushed my clit as he settled between my thighs, and I nearly lost it. The contact was too much *and* not enough. I couldn't stop myself from rolling my hips.

He chuckled.

"I love seeing you like this," he murmured. "So needy for me." His hand slid down to my sensitive bud again, slow enough to make my breath stutter. His fingers moved in teasing, featherlight strokes. I tried to shift my hips and press myself into his hand, but he held me down.

"Hades," I said.

He stilled, his palm pressing flat against my pelvis, anchoring me in place. "Tell me, little goddess…" His voice was a whisper against my throat. "Tell me what you want from me."

My mouth parted, but the words caught. "I want you—I need you," I corrected myself.

He pulled back, rising up off me. His absence left every inch of my skin buzzing, desperate for contact.

Hades peeled his clothes off, moving too slow.

"Could you take any longer?" I muttered.

Hades smirked. "Impatient, little mate." He stood bare, lit by soft moonlight, carved like a statue. His cock jutted forward. The sight alone made me clench. Desire poured through the bond, his need pressing into mine. He moved closer to the bed, like he had all the time in the world.

My body burned. I couldn't wait.

My fingers slipped between my thighs, finding my clit with ease. I rubbed slow, deliberate circles, trying to take the edge off. I didn't miss the way he watched me. Didn't miss the way his jaw tensed. With a flick of his wrist, his magic unfurled in thick, coiling ropes. It wrapped around my wrists and ankles, tugging my hand away from my center and stretching my arms above my head and spreading my legs wide.

Hades moved closer, the bed dipping as he climbed on. His hands started at my ankles, gliding over my calves, the backs of his knuckles brushing my skin slowly. He traced the curve of my thighs, skimmed over my center, and dragged upward. His knuckles moved past my fluttering stomach, over the swell of my breasts, until his fingers splayed across my mate mark.

It hummed under his touch, a pull that made my spine arch and my lungs forget how to work. His hand moved again, sliding up the column of my throat and settling at the base of my jaw. He brushed the hair falling into my face. "So beautiful."

His eyes stayed locked on mine as he reached between his legs and wrapped his hand around his cock, pumping a few times. I hadn't expected it to affect me this much, watching him pleasure himself. My lips parted, breath shallow, and the ache between my legs throbbed like it had its own heartbeat.

"You like watching me." Hades' voice was edged with amusement and something darker.

I swallowed and nodded, my mouth dry.

Hades stroked himself for a few more moments, watching me squirm. Watching my chest rise and fall and my legs pull uselessly at the magic holding me in place. I wanted to move. To *feel*.

He shifted forward, lining himself up at my entrance. My hips bucked. He smirked. "Needy little goddess." His hand guided the head of his cock to my clit, and he pressed, then circled it. My eyes rolled back at the contact, the sensation overwhelming. A moan slipped from my already parted lips. His hardness moved to my slit, pressing.

"Please," I moaned.

He didn't make me beg again.

With one powerful thrust, he filled me all at once. My back arched, a sound tearing from my throat that may have been a scream. Maybe not. My head was fuzzy. The magic holding my wrists and ankles disappeared.

"You take my cock so well," he said, his mouth at my ear. "Tell me you're mine."

"I'm yours, Hades." I wrapped my legs around his torso and my arms around his neck. "And you're mine."

"That's right, little goddess," he growled. "Remember that."

The pleasure inside me coiled tighter with each thrust, each drag of him against the spot that made my stomach flip. I was close—so close.

"I love the way you wrap around me." Hades cupped my jaw in his large hand, urging me to watch his length plunge into my center. "Look at how perfectly you take me. Look."

My eyes dropped just in time to see his length disappear into me again slowly. "Oh gods," I moaned.

"God," Hades corrected. "Who does this pussy belong to, Persephone?" His breath dusted across my forehead, and I shivered.

"You."

He flashed me a wicked smile. "That's right. I *keep* what's mine."

I licked my lips, his eyes tracking the subtle movement. His mouth crashed against mine. I could barely get a breath, closer to my climax. A few seconds passed. I couldn't contain myself. I shuddered as the pleasure swirled inside me, and I fell into my orgasm.

"Just like that, Persephone." His control was slipping. I could feel it in the way his rhythm faltered, in the shift in his breathing. "You feel so fucking good," he ground out. "Perfect. Made for me."

The words made my whole body flush, made the aftershocks of my orgasm roll even harder through me.

"You know what you do to me," he rasped, hips moving faster now, rougher. "You drive me out of my mind."

I bit my lip, but a soft moan still slipped from my lips.

He cursed under his breath. "Fuck, you're mine," he growled. "Every part of you." Hades came hard, his body locking above me, a low groan tearing from his throat as he pulsed inside me. His weight sank down, but he caught himself on his elbows, careful not to crush me. One arm wrapped around my back, pulling me to his chest as our breathing slowed, syncing.

We were a mess. Sweaty, shaking, spent. But wrapped in each other.

46

HADES

"We have to go to Faerie as possible. Aurelia, have you gathered enough intel?" My voice was firm, the urgency clear in each syllable.

Aurelia was usually calm and controlled. As Princess of the Winter Court, she had been groomed to assume the role of queen from the moment she could walk. If I hadn't already known that, it wouldn't have been clear to me at that moment. Her eyes darted between me and Cassius. She swallowed hard, her throat bobbing before she parted her lips to speak. Cassius cut her off. "We lost ten men trying to pinpoint the location." His tone was heavy. "We believe we know where the stone is, but we won't know for sure until we attempt to retrieve it. A drake guards it."

The room went silent at the mention of the beast. I'd first heard the legend in Faerie years ago. It came from the slurred lips of a drunken stranger in the tavern. I had dismissed his words as mere fantasy until I recounted them to Gabriel. I still remembered the way the color drained from his face.

"What's that?" Persephone asked, her voice going high.

Cassius turned to her. "The drake is a creature of ancient

legend. They say it's a serpent with poisonous blood, regenerative qualities, and razored fangs... though this is all rumor. We don't have any *living* accounts."

Orion snatched the bottle of faerie wine off the table. "Looks like we'll be needing this."

Thanatos remained silent as he rose from his seat, placing a glass in front of each person.

Persephone's face paled, and she wrapped her arms around herself. "And you're saying we have to get the stone from that *thing*?"

I sent some reassurance through the bond. "Yes."

Cassius continued, "Some believe it's a myth, a story to frighten children. But our men who returned saw... something. We have no choice. We must retrieve the stone piece."

Persephone blew out a long, wry breath. "Oh, this sounds so easy."

"And Persephone and Hades cannot use their magic." Orion let out a breathy laugh. Not because it was funny, but because of the absurdity of it all. He poured wine into each glass, ensuring they were filled right to the lip, the surface tension barely holding it back from spilling.

"Even easier," Persephone huffed.

"Yes, using our magic would alert the courts that we're there," I added. We didn't need our plans getting into the wrong hands.

Orion leaned against the table. "We can use *our* magic, though." He pointed a finger between himself and Gabriel.

"And Thanatos?" Persephone asked.

"I will be staying here and watching over the realm," Thanatos said.

I nodded. With all the recent events, it wasn't wise to leave the Underworld unattended for an extended period. I didn't know how many days it would take us to find the piece of the stone.

Cassius' eyes narrowed as he rubbed a hand under his chin. "We will send more men and have a map drawn up." The plan formed as he spoke.

Gabriel nodded. "And Persephone needs to learn how to shield her mind." He glanced at me. "It's probably best for you to teach her. You already have access to it."

"All right," Persephone said, and took a sip of her wine. Her voice was steady, but I could feel the nervous energy through the bond.

I placed a hand on her arm, giving her a reassuring squeeze. *You'll be fine.*

47

———

HADES

settled into the leather chair in my study and scanned over the papers sprawled across my desk with a sigh. *Time to issue sentences.* Thanatos had shouldered most of the workload lately, clocking in countless hours while I adjusted to the newfound rhythm of having a mate. It was a challenging shift—transitioning from a life where I moved through time on my own terms, eating when I wished, working when I wished, and doing everything on my own schedule without considering anyone else.

I closed my eyes and tugged on the thread of the Underworld. When I opened them again, I sat on my throne. Before me, a procession of souls awaited their judgment.

A small woman stepped forward. Her coarse hair was a striking shade of gray, silver-blue, cropped short around her neck. Her skin was smooth, unmarred by wrinkles, but I sensed her true age. She was a witch who died near the end of her extended lifespan. Witches, though powerful, were not immortal. They lived for centuries, their magic sustaining them until time eventually claimed its due.

She bowed her head. "King Hades," she said, her voice shaking.

I tugged on her mind. "Aithne." I paused for a moment before running through her memories. What I saw sent a chill through me. "Would you like to say anything before I decide on your sentence?"

"I hope you can forgive me. I killed myself to deliver a message to you."

I knew what she was going to say, but I needed to hear it aloud. My spine stiffened. "Speak."

"About Persephone," she added.

I waved a hand, and all the other souls behind her disappeared. She glanced over her shoulder, her face paling. Despite the trembling in her legs, Aithne managed to stay upright. "I worked for Demeter. I tried for a long time to get away—but I couldn't. Demeter is out of control—"

"This is not new information. She's *been* out of control."

The witch cringed. "Permission to continue, King Hades?"

I nodded.

"Demeter will never stop chasing Persephone."

"Why?" I barked. My voice was rough. I couldn't get the word out of my mouth fast enough.

"The power of the stone has already corrupted her. She's addicted and needs more."

I tugged on her mind again, and her face twisted in pain, but I couldn't find the answer I was looking for. "But why does she want Persephone?"

"Do you know who Persephone's father is?"

I stilled. I had never thought about it. In the pantheon, family dynamics were unlike those of most creatures. They didn't matter much. "No," I admitted.

"That's because she doesn't have one." The witch glanced down at her twitching hands, her fingers curling and uncurling in a nervous rhythm. "I'm so ashamed. I hope I can find forgiveness here. Demeter was controlling me."

"You say Demeter controlled you, but you could've left at any time."

The witch fell to her knees, a sobbing mess. She trailed on about how sorry she was, but I held a hand up and silenced her. Her face contorted with panic. She opened her mouth, but no words came out. She trembled as she glanced around the room. Tears streamed down her cheeks, leaving glistening trails on her pale skin.

Souls often had similar reactions to being sentenced, thinking I'd draw pity from their displays of emotions.

"Stop. Tell me how she doesn't have a father." I thought I knew, but I needed to hear her say it.

"The stone contains incredibly powerful energy," she choked.

I was growing impatient. My magic swirled around her, and she screamed in pain. "Out with it, witch."

"Persephone was born from a piece of the Nexus Stone."

I wanted to scoff, to tell her how impossible that was. But I couldn't, because deep down, I knew it wasn't. The Nexus Stone was unimaginably powerful. It all started to make sick, twisted sense. "Why did Demeter want a daughter?"

"Why does anyone wish for a child?" The witch's voice was soft, still trembling. "I agreed to help her find a piece of the stone so she could have a child. You know her... she doesn't exactly have suitors lined up. She was lonely. It started as something innocent but quickly twisted when she realized Persephone could be a vessel for her ambitions and powers. A daughter, molded in her image."

"Why abuse her? Not train her?"

She stayed silent.

"Witch," I commanded. My magic wrapped around her, threatening pain.

She held her hands up and shouted, "All right! As you know," she said, eyeing me, "I am a seer. That is one of my gifts. I saw a vision of Persephone here, as Queen of the Underworld, and I showed Demeter. She was controlling me! I had to kill myself to escape her."

"Enough about that."

She silenced, taking a deep breath before continuing. "The stone taints. Demeter had been growing more and more corrupt, but the vision of Persephone set her off. After that, she was never the same. Demeter forced me to create the tether that linked her and Persephone, along with the medication."

I hated that she took no real accountability, but I kept my composure. "What happened to the piece of the stone she was born from?"

"Demeter has it. The stone is powerful. It wasn't absorbed into Persephone. She was only born from it." The witch's eyes widened. "But I need to tell you something important. It will be much easier for you to find the rest of the stone with Persephone on your side. It will call to her."

It all made sense—the inexplicable pull Persephone felt toward Tartarus, her attraction to the stone.

She folded her hands together. "Will you forgive me? You know I'm not lying," the witch pleaded, her voice breaking. She was right. She couldn't lie to me here. I delved deeper into her mind, images colliding with each other—her time inside her mother's womb, her traumatic birth, her years as a young awkward girl, the years she spent with Demeter, and the desperate act of plunging a knife into her own heart.

"You will be placed in the layer meant for those who have committed suicide until you are ready to go into the general population—on the conditions that you never speak about this again unless you are asked to, and that you will tell Persephone this information yourself."

She sobbed. "I will do whatever you ask of me."

I watched her for a long, silent moment, anger curling hot beneath my skin. The thought of her being complicit in Persephone's pain twisted something deep inside me. I wanted nothing more than to give her the punishment she deserved—to make her suffer for what she had done, for what she had been a part of.

But I couldn't. Not yet.

As much as I despised her, I knew we weren't done with her usefulness. She still had more information, secrets about Demeter that we could use.

Her time would come. Aithne would pay for every sin she had committed.

PERSEPHONE

*C*an *you come to my study?* Hades spoke into my mind.

Yes, I'm in the kitchen. Be right there. I piled my plate with fruit and filed out of the room. I munched on a few pieces as I walked through the corridors. As I got closer to Hades' study, my curiosity heightened. Usually, when Hades asked me something, he gave details. His vague request left me more than a little confused.

When I reached his study, I didn't bother knocking. The door was already ajar, so I pushed it open and stepped inside. Hades stood from his seat with an impassive look on his face. My eyes fell on the soul seated across from him. My breath caught in my throat. The plate slipped from my hand, shattering on the floor with a loud clang. The porcelain scattered everywhere. Hades used his magic, and the evidence disappeared.

Aithne. Her face triggered memories I had buried deep within me. "I know you," I whispered, my voice trembling, feeling as though it came from a younger—powerless—version of myself. "I know you."

Her sullen face twisted with something between regret

and shame, but I didn't care. The memories took over; Aithne trailing after my mother, enchanting my medication, and standing by silently as my mother abused me. I froze, my breaths coming in ragged, shallow gasps.

Hades moved and placed a comforting hand on my shoulder. His touch grounded me, pulling me back to the present. My eyes burned as tears welled. And once again, I was reminded of how much influence my mother still had over my life. "Wh-why is she here?" I choked out.

"She has some answers for us. For you," Hades replied, low and calm.

"I don't want to hear anything that *witch* has to say." My voice was firm, but inside, I still trembled. I spat the word *witch* like poison in my mouth. Aithne didn't say anything. Her gaze drifted toward the floor as her shoulders hunched. "Look at me," I growled. I stepped around Hades, advancing toward her. She looked up. Her fear was palpable, and I loved it. For once, I held the power in the situation. "Tell me why you're here."

She gave me a weak smile. I wanted to rip it off her face. "Persephone," she whispered. "I'm so sorry."

"Enough."

"Would you like to sit?" She gestured to the seat next to her.

"Would I like to sit?" I repeated, irritation creeping into my voice.

"Persephone, maybe it would be best if you sat," Hades said.

I shot him a glare. "I'm going to stand right here until someone tells me what is going on."

Hades sighed. "Out with it, Aithne."

She took a shaky breath and clamped her hands around the elbow rests of the chair. "Have you ever wondered who your father is?" Her fingers twitched.

What did it matter? "No. Mother told me not to worry about it." Family relationships weren't typically something of importance in Olympus.

"Well, you don't have a father," she said. "You were born of the stone."

"How?"

"The stone is powerful. I cannot give you much more than that. If it has the power to create realms, it can easily birth a goddess," she said as if my existence was a remedial thing. "Over time, your mother became more corrupt. The stone does that to people. I don't even recognize her anymore. The night I learned of your fate, she lost it."

I inched forward. "And what fate is that?"

"Goddess of Spring. Queen of the Underworld."

Hades took my trembling hand and guided me to a chair. I didn't resist. "That's what she meant," I murmured.

"What do you mean?" Aithne's voice cracked.

I grabbed my temples, emotion overwhelming me. "The night she changed, she told me I had to listen to her, or I'd end up with the dead."

"I remember that night." Aithne continued, "When you have access to the kind of magic Demeter has, your emotions become volatile. A revelation like that did the trick."

"But what does this mean for me? Am I not a goddess?"

"Oh no, you are a goddess. You are a Divine, and you are your mother's daughter," Aithne assured me.

"Then why? Why go out of your way to tell me this? Haven't I suffered enough? Don't I deserve peace?"

"I'm telling you this because your mother is out of control. There have been whispers around Olympus that Hades has confirmed. Demeter took the Nexus Stone piece that held the Titans imprisoned." Aithne fidgeted.

"And?" I pressed.

"Since you were born from the stone, you will be able to

find the rest of the pieces easier. Your body knows it, your soul knows it, your magic knows it. It will call to you."

"If my mother has pieces of the stone, wouldn't she have the same advantage?"

"Not like you."

Hades glanced down at me. "This will help us."

"Is that all? Any other life-altering information you want to share?" I placed my hands on my knees. Hades rested a hand on my shoulder. "I want to be alone," I muttered. Questions spiraled in my mind. Who was I? A Divine? A goddess? I didn't even know who—*what*—I was born from.

Aithne shook her head. "I just want to tell you how sorry I am. I was under your mother's control."

Something in me snapped. "What do you mean, *under my mother's control?*" My throat felt raw.

She wore a pained expression. "I'm not comparing what I went through to what you endured, but you have to understand I was manipulated too."

"You are one of the reasons my life was miserable. You helped her find the first stone, didn't you?" I pointed a finger at her. "That's why she kept you around."

She stuttered, "I-I did, but I'm telling you the truth now. I cannot take back my past mistakes. If I could do it again, I would do it differently. I have to live with that for the rest of my existence. All I can do is say I'm sorry. You deserve to be angry."

Angry didn't cut it. "I'm done with this conversation." I stood up and shrugged away Hades' touch. "You know what? If you're a seer, tell us if we find the stone. Even better, tell us where it is."

"That's not how it works. I get random visions—or I used to. Now that I am dead, I will not get them."

I huffed, feeling entirely suffocated. I walked out of the room, Hades trailing me.

"Persephone."

"I just want to be alone right now, Hades."

He took another step closer to me.

"Alone," I repeated.

Hades' eyebrows knitted together. His lips pressed into a thin tense line. The corners of his mouth twitched downward. "I will check on you in a while." He turned away from me, his posture stiff.

The door to our room closed behind me with a soft click. I stood there for a moment, my breath uneven. The new information still rippled through me, each wave stripping another layer of who I thought I was. My legs moved, unsteady and weak, to the bed. It dipped as I sat and stared out the window. The last light of day filtered through, painting the room in muted hues.

My hands found the duvet, shifting it to get myself under. I gripped the edge until my knuckles turned white. The sensation was grounding—a tangible reality to cling to as my mind reeled. The pulse at my temples pounded a relentless rhythm.

Who am I? Who am I? Who am I without my mother?

The information itself was a shock, but the overwhelming weight of *her* drove me crazy. My mother. The invisible threads that bound me to her will still lingered in my life. Even in her absence, her influence remained. The freedom I ran for must've been an illusion. She would always be there. Always watching, always affecting me.

A tear slipped down my cheek, hot and unwelcome. My fingers unclenched, and I wiped it away with the back of my hand. The taste of salt lingered on my swollen lips. I fell back on the bed, my head landing on the pillow with a soft sigh.

I lay on my back, tracing invisible lines along the molding on the ceiling. It could've been an hour. Or it could've been four. I closed my eyes, letting my now-even breathing lull me into a sleep.

~

I stirred. The room was dark. I blinked, my vision adjusting to the space. "You're awake," Hades said from beside me.

I surged into a sitting position, clutching the duvet. The sudden brightness of the light beside him shocked my eyes into a squint. He reached out and pulled me close into a hug.

"You scared me," I said against his chest.

He didn't say anything but rubbed circles on my back. The fog of sleep lifted, and I was back to reality. Hades' closeness dulled the anxiety within me. "Persephone," he purred, then shifted me in his arms and took my chin into his hand. My head tilted back, meeting his eyes. There was no judgment, just understanding. I leaned into his touch. His thumb brushed across my cheek, wiping away tears I hadn't realized were falling.

"You don't have to go through this alone." He squeezed my chin lightly. "I'm here."

The knot of worry that had gripped me eased its hold, giving way ever so slightly. "I feel like I'm losing myself. She's everywhere, even now. I thought I could escape her, but I can't."

His expression softened, and he stroked my hair. "She's taken so much from you. But she can't take who you are."

I swallowed. "Tell me how many days we have left?" I *couldn't* be ripped away from my mate.

"Don't worry about it."

"How am I supposed to not worry?"

"I understand your frustration—"

"Do you?" I snarled.

"Do you think I want you to go back to your mother? You think I want you to die? Those ideas are unbearable. I love you, Persephone."

"Then what are we supposed to do?"

"I had an idea I was going to discuss with Thanatos. Besides me, he is one of the most familiar with this realm. There may be a way to get around the contract."

I stayed silent and slumped against Hades. I wished I had the same confidence he did. I hated the vagueness in his answer. But I believed it when he said he didn't want to send me back. *Why can't you just tell me?*

I can tell you, but I didn't want to tell you before discussing its validity with Thanatos. Would you like to know?

I hesitated. I didn't know if I could handle more disappointment. *Promise to tell me as soon as you know?*

Yes.

49

PERSEPHONE

*H*ades and I sat across from each other on the floor of the sparring room. We decided today I would begin learning how to shield my mind. That way, I would have some practice before our journey to Faerie. Hades reassured me encountering a Spirit Faerie was unlikely but emphasized the importance of being prepared.

It was a welcome escape from what I'd learned yesterday. I could push it all aside, at least for a little while. *Close your eyes*, he spoke into my mind.

Okay.

We have the mating bond tying us together. Picture an invisible string between us.

The bond pulsed with life. I could see it, a shimmering cord tethering our souls.

We can speak into each other's minds because of this bond. Spirit Faeries can probe your mind, creating a tether between you and them. I will be able to take similar control because of how you bound yourself to me when you came to the Underworld.

I stilled, the image of the pattern on the back of my neck and the cord between us vivid in my mind.

Now imagine a barrier between us. It can be anything as long as it works for you. I'll give you a few moments before I probe your mind.

I imagined a wall of ice cutting across the center of our invisible thread. It was smooth, impenetrable. I could almost feel the texture—cold, solid, and reassuring.

My wall splintered and collapsed under Hades' probing force. I jumped, releasing a low groan and clenching my hands into fists. *That hurts!* I yelled through the bond.

He stopped. *This is how it would feel if a Spirit Faerie attacked you. Though experienced fae can get into your mind without you even knowing. Let's try again. Make your wall stronger.*

Tremors ran through my body, my muscles tense and trembling. I added layers to the wall. Hades probed my mind again, and the wall cracked once more. I clutched my temples, letting out a silent scream.

He pulled back. *There's not much else I can teach you. When we're in Faerie, you'll have to keep that wall around your mind.*

The idea of protecting myself against one of these attacks was motivating. *Can we keep practicing?*

Of course.

We continued. Over and over, my shield fell.

I'm bad at this.

You're doing well. We just have to keep practicing. We will first be going to the Spring Court, so we shouldn't be around any Spirit Faeries yet.

I didn't like the way he said *shouldn't. When?*

Tomorrow. We need to get you adjusted to Faerie before we can think about trying to get the stone. Depending on how it goes, we might set out for it in a few days.

I didn't see how that would be possible, given that I was due to return to my mother soon, but I just nodded. *Okay. I* swallowed down a nervous lump in my throat. *Wouldn't shielding our minds with magic in Faerie alert the courts?*

Hades shook his head. *Not this. Psychic shielding doesn't register the same way as regular magic use. It's subtle. Our bond won't set anything off either.*

Before I could ask further, he added, *It's quiet. Think of our communication like a whisper between us, contained and funneled through our bond.*

We continued practicing; it took longer for the wall to crack, but it still did. The headache that had bloomed in my forehead grew unbearable. It was as if a hot iron band tightened around my temples, each pulse sending pain through my skull. My vision blurred, and nausea churned in my stomach.

Let's call it a day.

I sucked in a breath. *Have you always had access to my mind like this?*

Yes. I've had access to your mind since the moment you tied yourself to me, but I have chosen to give you privacy.

I hesitated for a few moments. *Thank you.*

50

PERSEPHONE

Gabriel's magic hummed around Hades and me. The enchantment process was necessary to disguise us as fae—we didn't want the Faerie Courts to find out about our presence. The chances of running into someone who recognized us today were low according to Hades, but not nonexistent. A tingling sensation spread across my skin. "Hold still. This will only take a moment."

The feeling wasn't painful, but I could feel my flesh shifting, reshaping under his magic. "Open your eyes," Gabriel said.

The mirror before me reflected someone I didn't recognize. My skin had taken on an ethereal glow, catching and holding the light. My hair, once a cascade of dark waves, now shimmered like spun gold. My gray eyes had turned into a vibrant shade of green. The structure of my face and body remained similar. I lifted a hand to my cheek. My skin was so smooth. I pushed my hair behind my ears and marveled at their pointed shape. "Wow."

"You're one of us—for now," Gabriel said as he admired his magic.

I looked over at Hades. His skin glowed with the same ethereal light as mine. His dark hair had transformed into a shade of silvery blond. His gray eyes were now a violet color, reminding me of a flower I liked. He was still attractive, but nothing would be able to top his usual appearance. "You look different," I murmured.

"As do you." He toyed with a strand of my golden hair. "Still beautiful." Hades pulled me into a long kiss.

Orion cleared his throat. "Are we going to Faerie or not?"

Gabriel chuckled. "Let them get it out of their systems now. I don't want to watch this the entire time we're there."

Orion groaned. Hades pulled back with a chuckle. "Oh, you two have no idea. Just wait until you two figure out who your mates are. You'll understand then."

Orion scoffed and waved. "Let's go."

Hades held my hand, and Gabriel and Orion touched Hades' jacket, whisking us away.

We stood beyond the gates, among the long procession of souls. A door appeared. He placed a flat hand on it, opening it and revealing the Realm Gateway.

"We're using the Realm Gateway?" I asked. I'd assumed we'd go right to Faerie.

"Whisking has its rules," Hades explained. "You can only whisk to realms you're are from or where you have been granted access. Anywhere else, you must use the Realm Gateway." He paused. "And fae can't whisk. I don't want to use my magic and alert the Faerie Courts."

We followed as Gabriel led the group to the Faerie opening, and the door sealed behind us. The entryway shimmered a pale green similar to the color of my magic. "Oh, right." Gabriel turned toward us. "Hades, you can be..." He paused.

"Haldor," I added. The men gave me strange looks. "What? I read it in a book."

"All right then, Haldor." Orion eyed Hades.

"And Prim," Hades said as he glanced at me. "Like Primrose, the flower."

"You only need to use those names around other fae. Just a precaution," Gabriel said before he stepped through the portal.

I nodded. Orion stepped through next. Hades grabbed my hand and pressed a quick kiss to my lips. "Let's go."

When we stepped through the portal, the world around us shimmered with vibrant life. The sun hung low in the sky, casting a golden glow through the trees. Birds with bright plumage moved between the branches. Beams of light filtered through the leaves, creating a dance of shadows that played across the forest floor. Iridescent butterflies flitted through the air, weaving in and out of the light.

The ground was a carpet of green. Flowers of every color imaginable bloomed in clusters. The air was thick with the scent of rich, fertile soil. "Welcome to the Spring Court," Gabriel said proudly.

It reminds me of when I first saw the Underworld.

Hades glanced around. *It was the inspiration for the foliage.*

I stumbled back, and Hades squeezed my hand harder. The colors of the forest blended together into a dizzying rainbow. The world spun around me. Nausea clawed at my stomach. I tried to let go of Hades' hand, but he held on as I sank to my knees. My throat burned with acid. Hades placed a hand on my back as I heaved. The cool leather of his glove was comforting against my feverish skin, even through my clothing. "Breathe. I've got you."

I could barely hear him over the sound of my own heaving breaths, the world closing in around me tighter with every second.

"I don't remember seeing anyone with such a bad reaction..." Gabriel trailed. I groaned, clutching the damp ground. Cold sweat coated my hot skin. I sucked in a gasp between another heave.

My body convulsed violently. The muscles in my abdomen tightened painfully, and I spat bile along with the contents of my stomach. The bitter, acidic taste made me retch even harder. Each spasm sent a fresh wave of pain. Tears streamed down my cheeks, mixing with the sweat on my face. I tried to speak, but I couldn't get out a word between each heave. Darkness closed in at the edges of my vision.

51

PERSEPHONE

I woke up in an unfamiliar bed. My heart raced, and my eyes darted around the room. The blanket pooled around my waist as I shot up. Cool air hit my bare arms, sending a shiver through me. The room blurred at the quick movement. Emerald-green silk sheets covered the bed beneath me. Curtains of the same color framed the window, a large arched pane. Darkness had crept into the sky, the moonlight bathing the plants outside.

The bed was crafted from the same rich mahogany covering the floor, its dark grains swirling in patterns that mirrored the floorboards. A blue canopy hung from the bed, embroidered with flowers, likely done by hand. Each was a different size and color with stray threads sticking off. As my mind raced to piece together the events that led me here, the door creaked open. Hades—still enchanted—stepped into the room.

"You're awake." Despite the change in Hades' appearance, his voice still held the same smooth timbre I was used to. "I was starting to worry about you."

"We're still in Faerie?"

Hades nodded, confirming what I thought. "We're in Gabriel's home. You had a worse reaction than we thought you would. But this is why we wanted to come before going in search of the stone."

"Yeah," I murmured, recalling the unpleasant sensations from earlier.

Gabriel and Orion walked in. The fae looked different. They were more radiant here. Everything about them was *more*, their beauty, their power. *It's their true form*, Hades spoke into my mind.

"How are you feeling?" Gabriel asked as he raised a thin glass vial with black liquid.

I nodded, feeling the weight of the gesture in my neck. I took inventory of the sensations in my body, letting my awareness move from head to toe. My stomach churned in rhythm with the pounding of my head. "I don't know."

"Take this."

I eyed the tube. "What is it?"

"You don't want to know," Hades said. "Just take it. It will help."

I took the vial from Gabriel and tipped it to my lips. It was surprisingly heavy for such a thin tube. The scent stung my nostrils. I took a deep breath and let the liquid flow. It was thick and gritty, similar to mud. The first wave on my tongue was the worst. I swallowed a mouthful and resisted the urge to heave it up. The liquid assaulted all my senses. I finished the vial and shoved it back in Gabriel's direction, my stomach roiling.

After a few moments, warmth spread through my chest, and there was already a change in how I felt. The fog filling my head cleared, and an energy I didn't have before rose to the surface. "Here." Orion handed me a glass of water.

I took the glass, swished, and gulped the water down. "I'm already feeling much better."

Something behind Gabriel caught my eye. Scattered shelves adorned the wall behind him, covered in an array of small glass bottles and trinkets. "That's quite a collection." I pointed to the shelves.

A deep furrow appeared in Gabriel's brow, casting shadows over his eyes. He cleared his throat, the sound rough. His Adam's apple bobbed. "This was my sister's room." His voice was low.

"Was?"

He nodded but said nothing. The room fell into a heavy silence. Gabriel's fingers fumbled with each other. His restless fingers found the edge of his sleeve, tugging on a loose thread and pulling it taut until it snapped. He looked down.

Maybe I shouldn't have said anything. "I'm sorry. I didn't mean to probe," I said.

He met my gaze for the first time since I'd mentioned it. "It's fine."

No one has been in this room since she died. Gabriel takes responsibility for her death, even though it wasn't his fault, Hades spoke through the bond. I shifted uncomfortably, the bed creaking beneath me.

Gabriel cleared his throat again. "Would you like to go to the tavern? It would be good for you to eat food in Faerie. We need to see how you feel."

I let out a breath, grateful not to linger on the awkward tension. "I've already had food from Faerie."

"But you didn't eat it in Faerie," Orion added.

I placed a hand on my chest. "Am I going to get sick again?"

"You shouldn't." Hades squeezed my hand. "But we have to get you accustomed to this realm so you're prepared for when we come back to find the stone."

"Let's go, then."

s we stepped outside, the cool air wrapped around us like a silken cloak. We walked along a path lined with gnarled trees whose branches intertwined overhead. Silver beams filtered through the canopy, kissing Hades' blond hair. Hades walked at my side, often glancing down at me with a smile. The stone path crunched under our boots, each step sending small pieces skittering to the side and into the darkness.

Small flying insects flickered around us, similar to the wisps. Their tiny bodies emitted a soft, golden light that danced on the leaves of the trees. We passed several homes similar to Gabriel's—small with pitched roofs, aglow with warm light. In a few, I caught a glimpse of the families inside. My smile faltered. A sharp, uncomfortable pang twisted in my chest. I understood well enough that appearances could be deceiving. The warmth of a fire and the scent of a home-cooked meal did not guarantee happiness. Yet the envy remained.

The trees thinned, their twisted forms revealing light ahead. "I haven't been here in a long time," Hades murmured beside me.

"Just like old times." Orion grinned as we grew closer. A large black sign hung above the building. It creaked as it swung in the gentle breeze, suspended by a thick chain. Its surface, weathered and faded from years of exposure to the elements, read *Willowshade Stone Tavern*.

The tavern itself blended harmoniously with the forest landscape. Moss and ivy crept up the side of the stone walls. The roof was thatched and weather-beaten. *How could somewhere like this be good?* I swallowed my judgment at the sight of Orion's excited face. Light and music spilled from the windows.

Gabriel swung the door open, holding it wide as the throb of music hit me. Hades placed a hand on the small of my back and urged me to follow Orion. The room was a hive of activity. Hades' touch didn't leave my body, making sure we didn't get separated. We weaved through the maze of dancing bodies and wooden tables where some sat. Wooden beams crisscrossed the low ceiling. Orion led us to a booth in the back corner. "Here." He spoke over the music, chatter, and other assorted noises.

We settled into the booth. I set my palms flat on the cool tabletop. My fingers twitched as they caught on a few crumbs and something sticky. I moved my hands to my lap. I'd never been anywhere like this. There were taverns in Athens, but I'd never been to one. Basile and the guards often shared their tales of drunken adventures with each other. They shooed me away whenever I ventured to ask about them. I'd never envisioned Hades in a place like this, yet he fit in. *Are you okay?* Hades asked through the bond.

I've never been anywhere like this.

Hades found my hand under the table and gave it a reas-suring squeeze. *I had a similar reaction my first time here. It was a long time ago, but as you are, I was accustomed to the Divine opulence.*

This is very different.

He chuckled.

Do places like this exist in the Underworld?

Yes, but they don't serve food and drinks.

I tried to relax, but the sense of being out of place remained. Laughter and song filled the tavern. It all seemed so foreign. A barkeep came over to us, cutting through the throng of people. Her dark-red hair was pulled back in a loose braid. A few stray tendrils framed her face, softening the angular lines of her cheekbones and jaw. Her skin shim-mered with the same ethereal glow Orion and Gabriel had in this realm. She wore a simple forest-green dress with a thin leather belt and pouches hanging from it. "What can I get for you?"

"Four ales and beef tarts," Gabriel said.

A wave of relief flooded through me. I would've never known what to order. The woman pulled a notepad from one of her pouches, scribbled the order, and wandered off. The musicians in the corner opposite us began a new song. The faeries cheered and danced around, sipping on their drinks. I'd never seen people move with such little restraint. Within a few minutes, the barkeep came back. She set the mugs of ale down, the liquid sloshing. "The beef tarts will be out shortly."

Orion slid a mug to each of us. Lifting his own to his lips, he took a long swig and let out a low moan. He raised the drink up as if it were the most beautiful thing he'd seen. "Tonight." Another sip. "We drink."

I studied the mug in front of me. It was made of a radiant, polished copper. The outside glistened with tiny droplets of condensation. Hades took a sip from his mug. "What does it taste like?" I asked.

"Try it," Gabriel urged.

I wrapped my fingers around the handle and raised the drink to my lips. I took a slow sip. Crisp bubbles danced on my tongue. A burst of ginger mixed with sweetness spread through my mouth. I took another sip, trying to get a more accurate read on the flavor.

"What do you think?" Hades asked.

"It's—" I took another sip. "It's delicious."

Orion cheered. The barkeep came back over with the tray of the beef tarts. She set them on the table, covering the wet spot of spilled ale. "I haven't had one of these in ages." Hades placed one in front of me before taking one for himself. It was a small golden pastry cradling a beef filling. Perched atop was a small purple flower.

"Just like I remember," Hades said.

I took a bite, not hesitating like I had with the faerie ale. The rich flavor of the pastry surprised me. It was the perfect combination of sweet and savory. The men watched me.

"How do you feel?" Gabriel asked, taking a bite of his own.

"I feel fine."

Orion clasped his hands together. "Thank the Fates. I hate when people vomit." He mimicked a gag.

I rolled my eyes and continued eating my pastry. The faerie ale warmed me from the inside out. It left a delightful buzz, similar to the faerie wine. We finished our round of ale. Orion flagged the barkeep. "Another round." His voice carried the easy confidence of someone entirely at home.

I can tell you missed Faerie, I said to Hades.

You're correct. It was a big part of my life.

I took another sip of my ale.

I'm glad that period of my life is over, though. The nostalgia is nice, but I wouldn't change being with you for anything. Faerie was there for me when I was grappling with the new responsibilities and weight of ruling the Underworld.

I leaned forward. *Is that when you got your death touch?* Hades didn't often talk about his past. It felt like an inappropriate place to ask, but we were already on the subject. He shifted, and I focused on the leather covering his hands.

Yes. It was difficult to come to terms with. There's a price for all things. Great power, especially.

But why would that be the price?

The Fates told me it was a reminder. Every death is personal—it's on my hands. So I needed to wield the responsibilities of ruling the Underworld wisely.

You spoke to the Fates? I didn't know you could do that.

Yes, I almost broke down their door when I learned of my death touch. Hades must've seen the confusion on my face, so he continued. *They are Divine, with their own realm. It's only one room. The three sisters—Clotho, Lachesis, Atropos—spin, measure, and cut threads, having existed in the same place their entire existence. They don't accept visitors.* Hades laughed. *They weren't happy to see me. I found it through the special connection Thanatos and I have with them.*

"Stop doing your mate thing and get up." Orion waved a hand.

Before I could protest, Hades smirked at me. He squeezed my hand and tugged me from the booth. The sudden movement sent a buzz through me, making my head spin in a good way. Orion was already moving to the beat. I had never seen him dance before. His movements were surprisingly fluid. Even Gabriel joined in.

Hades kept his hand in mine as he led me to the center of the floor, his steps confident and sure. He pulled me close, his other hand settling on my waist, the contact sending a thrill through me. "Relax," he murmured. "Have fun."

I took a deep breath, letting the ale and the rhythm of the music guide me. We moved together in a chaotic harmony. Hades twirled me, a laugh bubbling from my lips. As the song came to an end, Hades pulled me closer, our bodies still swaying to the fading beat. The night continued, the music blending from one melody to another.

52

PERSEPHONE

I swallowed my anxiety and went to the library, giving it one more chance before abandoning the search for more information altogether. I walked through the rows of towering shelves. The quiet stretched around me like a taunt. Hours melted away as I flipped through book after book, my fingers tiring from the relentless search for any mention of the trials. With each page turned without success, the weight of disappointment grew heavier.

Numbness crept up my legs, tingling and heavy from sitting on the hard floor for so long. Just as I shifted to relieve the ache, my gaze snagged on a passage. I almost missed it. My fingertip traced the lines, absorbing every word. It was vague, but it was *something*.

The text described the Titan War and the birth of the Olympian Court, forged in the aftermath of the war to prevent future conflicts. The court siphoned away half the magic from each Divine, as well as from those yet to be born. The power was withheld, only to be returned after the trials.

The trials ensured any Divine born after the court's establishment would be too weak to challenge its authority until they had completed them. Once they did, they would be bound by their blood oath, a final safeguard of loyalty that made rebellion impossible.

As I read, everything clicked into place. Hades, Thanatos, and Hermes had often spoken cryptically about being blood-bound. They had pledged their loyalty to the court. I continued reading, but the rest of the book offered no further helpful information. Despite this, I shut the book with a smile on my face and tucked the new knowledge away. It wasn't everything, but it was something.

～

HADES

I sat in my study with Thanatos across from me, the fireplace crackling nearby. "I had an idea on a way to get around the contract," I began.

Thanatos inclined his head, urging me to continue.

"When you and I completed the Rite, we finished the entire process in one go. What if Persephone only initiates the process, enough to tie herself to the magic of this realm but not enough to drain her until we retrieve the stone for Tartarus?" Although Thanatos and I had both completed the Rite, our bonds to the Underworld differed slightly. My magic was deeply intertwined with the realm, and Persephone's bond would be like mine. If not managed carefully, the realm's demands could drain her, and she would face the same strain I was experiencing in keeping Tartarus sealed.

He paused before speaking. I could almost hear the gears turning in his mind. "Do you think we can truly do that?"

"I don't see why not. She can eat six seeds of the ceremonial pomegranate initially, just enough to begin the bond. When she's ready to fully bind herself to the realm like us, she can consume the rest. That would elevate her status in this realm, making her an adult in the eyes of the Divine hierarchy." I twirled a pen in my hand. "I read the rules of the court, front to back, again and again. I think this would work."

Persephone would hold the titles of Goddess of Spring and Queen of the Underworld. A queen could not be subject to the custody or authority of another. I laced my hands together. The thought of calling Persephone *my queen* stirred something deep within me. I imagined the way it would roll off my tongue.

"What if it doesn't work?" Thanatos asked. I hated the question, but I couldn't deny its validity.

"You and I know this realm better than anyone. We understand how the magic flows, how the rituals bind us. We can guide Persephone through this process. This isn't a gamble—it's a calculated risk based on our experience." I took a sip of the faerie wine sitting on my desk. "It has to work," I whispered, and ran a hand through my hair. I cleared my throat. "I'll tell her after the gala."

Thanatos leaned back in his seat and sighed. "Gods, I forgot you told me we were going to that."

I chuckled. Sharing my idea aloud helped me solidify its worth. I couldn't risk making any mistakes—especially not with Persephone. For the first time in a while, I felt a glimmer of hope.

53

PERSEPHONE

"I had a dress made for you," Hades said as he walked into our room. I finished reading the sentence I was on and glanced up from my book. A long, black garment bag dangled, hooked over two of his fingers. I folded the edge of the page and closed the book.

"For what?"

He lowered the bag onto the bed. "The gala is tonight."

I stiffened. "You don't go to the galas," I protested. My voice came out sharper than I meant. "And neither do I." The biannual galas. I'd never been. They were glittering affairs reserved for the court and their guests. Mother never allowed me to go, not that I had any desire to.

"*They're not for you,*" she had said. It was always a relief knowing she would be occupied for hours, and when she'd return home, she would be far too drunk off faerie wine and ambrosia to bother me.

"I used to go, a long time ago." Hades unzipped the bag, revealing the dress. It was an intricate black floor-length lace gown covered in beads of the same color. "Specially made for you." His eyes focused on me instead of the dress.

"Thank you," I whispered. I still didn't want to go to the gala, but the pride evident on his face and the surge of emotion through our bond warmed my chest like a gentle golden flame.

"Don't thank me. Thank the talented souls."

Somehow, that made it more special.

"I'm sure you'll look absolutely stunning in it. You always do."

I shot him a lazy smile that fell when an uninvited thought crept into my mind. "But what if Demeter is there?"

I hated how much she affected me. I tried to push it away, but I couldn't. I clenched and unclenched my fists, my nails digging into my palms. I'd ruined another sweet moment with the thought of her, letting my past bleed into every beautiful thing Hades tried to give me. My gaze flickered around the room, narrowing in on the corners, seeking an escape route that didn't exist. There were just walls, windows, and him, and the echo of her name in my head like a bell rung by a ghost.

The bed dipped as Hades sat. He sighed and pulled me close. "I'll be right there with you the whole time. Let's show her you're not afraid." Hades' head lingered in the crook of my neck. I took comfort in the warmth flowing through our bond. "And I know we've decided to just find the pieces of the stone ourselves, but I suspect we're only one vote away from the court being able to investigate her. It can't hurt to explore all avenues."

My head jerked up. "So we have to convince one more member?"

"I believe so."

This would all be so much easier if I were a court member, I thought, making sure I didn't say it through the bond. "Are you sure we have to go?" I knew the answer, but I asked anyway. If I wanted to be taken seriously, I needed to go with him. It was my opportunity to prove I was his equal despite the self-doubt often creeping in that made me question myself. We needed to show the court members I had chosen to come to this realm on my own terms.

Hades massaged the tension out of my shoulders as he held me close. His fingers kneaded the knots away with ease. He knew my body so well. "Yes." Hades pressed a kiss onto the sensitive skin on my neck.

"Were we even invited?" My voice was low.

Hades' hands moved slowly from my shoulders down to my breasts. My breath hitched as his fingers found a peak through the fabric of my shirt. The friction sent a shiver down my spine, and a low moan escaped me before I could swallow it.

Hades chuckled. "Since when do you care about invitations?" he murmured, teasing as his thumb grazed a circle. "You didn't mind coming into the Underworld without one."

I couldn't find a response. Not when his touch moved to my other breast, just as devastating. I arched into him, all the thoughts in my mind scattering.

"Besides, I'm a member of the court. So technically, yes, we are invited, if that makes you feel better."

It didn't. Not really.

He leaned close, pulling me into a kiss. It started slow, but he deepened it. It was possessive. Demanding. Carefree, like there wasn't a long list of issues we were dealing with. I moved without thinking, slipping into his lap, needing more—of him, of this.

His hands gripped my hips, anchoring me to him as his mouth moved against mine. I moaned into his mouth, and he answered with a rough, low sound of his own. I rocked forward, chasing the friction.

Hades pulled back, leaving just a few inches between our faces. His dilated eyes locked onto mine as he smirked. "As much as I love seeing you so needy for me… you have a gala to get ready for."

I groaned.

Hades pulled me close, and the breath on the shell of my ear tickled me. Goose bumps spread across my fevered skin. "Don't worry, my love. I'll take good care of you tonight. I have an idea." His lips curved up against my ear.

I couldn't fight my shiver. I swallowed and tried to calm my ragged breathing.

I failed.

Miserably.

"Believe me, all I want to do right now is strip you down and bury my cock inside of you." His need met mine through the bond. "I bet you're so ready for me. Right? Tell me how wet you are, little goddess."

Heat coiled low in my belly. My breath shuddered.

"I knew it." His chuckle was soft.

"I-I didn't say anything," I stammered.

"You didn't need to." Hades took me off his lap and stood up. He placed a long kiss on my forehead. "I'll see you when you're ready."

My mind reeled. A shiver raced along my skin. The sensation was so jarring, I froze. Every nerve screamed with the intensity of the moment. My thoughts tumbled and collided, unable to form coherent sentences. I could not find the words, or the will, to respond.

Before the door fully closed behind him, he peeked back in. "Don't wear anything under that dress."

I closed my eyes, drawing in deep, deliberate breaths. After a few minutes, there was a soft, hesitant knock on the door. My eyes snapped open. "Come in," I called out.

The door swung open.

"Lady Persephone," Sera shrieked, and launched toward the bed. She pulled me into a tight hug. Stunned, I hesitated before wrapping my arms around her, laughing once the initial shock wore off.

"Remember, just Persephone is okay," I said as she pulled back.

She blushed. "I'm sorry."

Evangeline trailed in behind her. "Sorry about her. She hasn't stopped talking about doing your makeup since Hades told us."

"No need to apologize. I'm happy to see you two again." They set up their things, updating me on their lives in the short time that had passed, even mentioning that Sera's ex-fiancé had finally made his way to the Underworld.

"So he's completed his purgatory, if you're seeing him?" A question and a statement.

"Yes, he came looking for me." Her face twisted into a scowl. "He told me losing me was the biggest mistake of his life. I mean, I believe that, but I don't want him back."

"Are you in a relationship?"

Sera scoffed, her nose scrunching. "Gods, no. I finally have peace here."

"One day, you'll find someone," Evangeline added. She must've sensed the question I was about to ask. "I have a husband. My children aren't here yet."

"Do souls date in the Underworld?" I had heard nothing about the dynamics of the souls and love.

"Some. Sera's drama isn't uncommon. But usually, things settle down quickly. Most souls have learned their lessons and don't have a penchant for drama and theatrics."

"What did you tell him?" Her story brought me something to think about other than the impending gala. It was a welcome distraction. "Your fian—ex-fiancé."

"I told him I was over him. Then he muttered something about us being soulmates. We aren't."

Evangeline smiled as she continued to tend to my hair.

"You won't be so bitter when you find your *true* soulmate. It's wonderful."

Sera's face twisted. "I doubt it." She laughed it off, but there was hurt underneath it. I didn't press her on the issue. Sera seemed like the type to cloak her pain in humor. The souls moved silently around me, only the faint rustle of their movements breaking the quiet.

Evangeline hummed a tune I'd never heard before. She continued for a few minutes before whispering, "Done." The sisters turned me toward the mirror and stepped back. Dark, smoky-black shadow framed my gray eyes. It made them pop. My hair was gathered into a neat, low bun with a few deliberate strands sticking out to frame my face. Evangeline studied my hair, making sure everything was exactly how she wanted. She gestured to the bun. "This way, everyone will see your back."

"Wow," I muttered. The sisters had such an ability to make me look and feel beautiful.

"Agreed," Sera said quietly.

Evangeline clasped her hands together. "Let's get you into this dress."

I nodded and headed for the garment bag. I stripped off my clothing, then stood with my hands crossed over my chest. I wouldn't be able to wear a bra with this dress, the plunge was too deep.

Evangeline looked at my underwear and winced. "I'm so sorry, Persephone..." She paused and pointed her finger. "King Hades ordered us not to let you wear those."

Heat spread across my face. I was certain my cheeks were stained with crimson.

"We'll give you privacy," Sera said as she tried to hide the smile threatening to take over her face. They pooled the dress on the floor so I could easily step into it. *Why did you order Sera and Evangeline to make sure I didn't wear underwear?* I spoke to Hades through the bond.

I could sense Hades' laughter. *I told you I had an idea. I also love knowing you're bare for me under that dress.*

"Are you all right, Persephone?" Sera asked.

I pulled off my underwear before stepping into the dress and pulling it up. "Yes, I'm done." Pain throbbed through my cheeks, a relentless ache born from the grin I couldn't erase.

They turned and helped me lace up the dress, then slipped heels onto my feet. They matched perfectly. I turned to face the mirror. Sera shrieked at the completed look. "It was a pleasure serving you again, Lad—Persephone. Enjoy the gala."

The reminder triggered a weak smile. "I will," I said, just to be polite. With a quick hug and some well wishes, they left. I gazed at myself in the mirror. The black dress clung to my form, fitting me like a second skin. The intricate patterns of beads shimmered under the soft light, and I hadn't noticed before, but they mirrored the pattern on my chest. The bond pulsed, the soft glow contrasting the dark dress as Hades appeared behind me in a perfectly tailored suit, unlike any other I'd seen him in. The onyx fabric hugged his broad shoulders and lean frame. The black, buttoned shirt he wore underneath was open toward the top, revealing his chest where his bond pulsed a matching glow.

The suit, though finely crafted, seemed secondary to the bond displayed proudly on his chest. Hades quietly observed me. "Absolutely stunning," he said, low with emotion. He reached for my hand, spinning me away from the mirror, and pulled me close. "As beautiful as you look, I'm looking forward to taking this dress off you."

54

PERSEPHONE

We whisked in front of Divine Hall. A tingling sensation raced across my skin. The weight of memories pressed down on me. I sucked in a breath, not realizing how much coming back to this realm would affect me. I had changed since the last time I was here.

Divine Hall was the same.

I wasn't.

I tilted my head back and studied the stars twinkling like scattered diamonds. The moon bathed the building in a silvery sheen, illuminating all the intricate carvings.

"Are you ready?" Hades asked. His gray eyes twinkled under the moonlight.

"As ready as I'll ever be." I forced a smile. "Though I'd be happy going *home*."

Hades' eyes crinkled at the corners. "We won't stay for too long." We took the first step up the grand staircase. Hades paused, glancing over at me before continuing. Music and chatter drifted from the open doors ahead.

Hades and I stepped over the threshold and into the

building. The wave of music surged, filling my ears with a rhythmic melody. To our left was a group of musicians clad in black, playing instruments in tune with the sirens singing. The foyer dripped with opulence, a sea of marble and gold. Light glittered around the room from the large chandelier. It stretched from the ceiling to the second floor. Above us were four levels, each one lined with gold railings. Throughout my twenty-three years of living in Athens, I'd never been in Divine Hall—until now.

Nymphs held gold platters at shoulder level with small, prepared foods. The room brimmed with the Divine and their guests. This portion of the room had small standing tables, a bar, and floral arrangements leading to an open set of glass doors. Beyond them, a larger space unfolded, filled with tables adorned with gaudy decorations.

We walked farther into the room. I squeezed Hades' hand. Heads turned, necks craning to look at us. Some faces wore expressions of disbelief while others exchanged whispers and sneers. Hades released my hand, only to slide his arm around my lower back, pulling me closer to him. "Everyone is staring at us," I murmured.

"Let them." His possessive arm around my waist tightened. He leaned closer, his breath warm against the shell of my ear. "They're staring because they know they'll never be able to touch what's mine," he said, loud enough for only me to hear.

Whispers flitted through the air like butterflies. "Look at their chests," someone whispered. Hades and I stood out in our black attire, a stark contrast to the room awash in different shades of ivory, gold, and pastels. I wanted to squirm, aware of all the piercing gazes fixed on us, but I straightened my back. I couldn't let them see me weak. Hades guided us through the throng of people to a table on the side of the room next to a large floral arrangement.

A nymph with light-green hair approached us. She bowed her head, her purple eyes never meeting ours. "May I offer you some ambrosia?"

"Yes, please."

She lowered the tray, and I took one of the golden goblets.

"And you, Lord Hades?"

Hades held up his hand. "No."

I took a swig of the maroon liquid. My eyes widened as I coughed, choking on the drink. Hades patted my back as my breathing returned to normal. "Slow down, little goddess." His voice was tender and low. Hades' eyes flicked to my lips as I took another sip—much smaller this time. "I can't have you choking this early in the night. When I envision you choking on something, I don't know if I see ambrosia…"

"We're in public," I scolded, knowing exactly what he envisioned me choking on.

"A few wandering eyes aren't enough to stop me."

Desire pooled at my center. Hades' gloved fingers traced patterns on my exposed back, and I bit the inside of my cheek.

A few of the Divine and their guests came over to us. Hades introduced me every time. Though I had read about some of these people, I'd never met them. Hades moved with a measured grace that commanded respect and caution from those around him. His posture remained rigid, his movements deliberate. When he spoke, he chose his words carefully. Hades didn't engage in idle chatter.

I caught glimpses of not-so-discreetly pointed fingers and sneers from around the room. I took another sip of my ambrosia, unable to contribute much to the conversations like Hades did, even though he tried to include me. I knew little about court politics, and frankly, I didn't want to hear more reminders of what was bringing me so much stress.

"Persephone." Hermes' voice drew my attention from my almost-empty goblet. It was my first time seeing Hermes since he helped me in the courtyard. Hades nodded at Hermes but continued talking to someone whose name I'd already forgotten.

"How are you?" he asked.

I looked over at Hades and smiled. I swallowed down all the anxious rambling threatening to spill. "I'm doing well."

"You look beautiful."

"Thank you."

Another nymph carrying a tray of ambrosia passed. I stopped her, gulping down the last few sips of mine. I placed the empty goblet on the tray and took a new one. I plucked a second one off the tray and handed it to Hermes.

"I'm glad you came, Persephone." Hermes turned toward Hades. "You too, Hades." He took a swig of his ambrosia. "I've tried to get Hades to come for years. I don't know how you did it."

I chuckled and took another sip, but I didn't tell him it wasn't my idea.

"Look," Hermes exclaimed. "They're opening the dance floor. Let's go."

"We'll catch up with you in a little while," Hades said. Hermes strolled to the dance floor, and I exhaled, finally able to take a breath. My head moved on a swivel as I looked at everyone attending. "She's not here... yet," Hades answered for me.

"Do you think she'll come?" I took another sip of my drink to smother the anxiety the thought of her brought on.

"Someone has likely told her you're here by now—so yes." Hades lifted my hand to his lips and pressed a soft kiss. "I remember why I stopped coming to these."

I understood but asked anyway. "Why?"

"Because they're boring. Too many conversations." Hades

paused. "And... I didn't realize how much self-inflicted torture it would be to see you in this dress."

I smirked. "Should we dance?"

Hades tugged my hand. "I want to show you something."

I trailed behind him as he pulled me into a side room, leading me up a staircase adorned with a red velvet runner. "Where are we going?"

"You'll see," Hades said. The first flight of stairs was just the beginning; we climbed them until we reached the highest floor. "This is where I used to come when I grew tired of talking to people." Hades pulled me closer to the railing. "When I did attend the gala."

I peered over the edge of the railing. Gods, we were high. The chandelier's chain began at eye level, with the lights hanging lower. From our vantage point, we watched people talk, dance, drink, and eat. The music reverberated through the entire building, though more subdued from up here.

"Wow," I said, narrowing my eyes. I pointed a finger. "Oh look, there are Hecate and Thanatos."

Hades chuckled. "I wonder how Thanatos is holding up. We'll have to say hello later."

It was a relief to have a break from all the watchful eyes and endless chatter. Even though I'd spent time away from Demeter in the Underworld, so many people surrounding me was still alien. The years of isolation had made the simple act of conversation draining. The people below danced and conversed as if it were the most natural thing in the universe.

The billowing of elaborate gowns and the sparkling reflections of jewels and gold drew me in. I took another sip of my ambrosia, emptying the goblet. Hades moved closer, wrapped me in a hug from behind, and took the cup from my hands. His warm scent enveloped me as I leaned back into his touch.

The song shifted from an upbeat melody to a slow tune.

Hades' length pressed through his clothes into my back. I tilted my head back and swayed my hips to the beat of the music. Hades' hands slid from my shoulders, slowly trailing down my arms, his touch like fire on my skin. His fingers paused at my hips. He gripped them and tugged me closer to him. Hades groaned, and it sent sparks right to my core. "Would you rather be dancing right now?" Hades whispered in my ear.

Rebellious energy flowed through me. "Yes." My voice came out breathier than I'd intended.

"Liar."

The world tilted as Hades spun me, my back pressing against the railing, and leaned me over the edge. My heart thumped in my chest, ready to lurch out of my body. I looked down over my shoulder and swallowed the dry lump in my throat. The sheer height between me and the floor accentuated the dizziness flowing through me. Hades wouldn't hurt me. I was safe with him, but the adrenaline still flowed freely.

"Do you want me to make love to you?" Hades' voice was low.

"Yes," I whispered, my eyes coming back to his.

"And the truth finally comes out." He pulled me back so that I stood. Hades leaned down, his lips brushing across my cheek. "But you'll have to wait because you wanted to dance."

My head snapped up. "You—" I didn't get to finish my words before he pulled me into the center of the space. My chest pressed against Hades' body, one of his hands on my back and the other holding my hand. "I don't know how to dance." I looked at my feet. "Don't you remember?" My mind flashed back to dancing in the tavern. It was a rare moment for me—one of uninhibited freedom. I'd enjoyed myself, but as the memories flooded in, I couldn't shake the feeling I had looked like a complete fool.

"You know how to dance." Hades took the lead, moving slowly. "Just follow me."

I followed, the way his body moved so effortlessly entrancing me. "You dance so well."

"There are many things you'll learn about me." Hades twirled me and pulled me back in close.

I arched my neck, lifting my chin to meet his gaze. "Tell me something else. Something you like to do that no one knows."

"Hmm," he murmured. "I used to enjoy painting."

"Painting?"

He nodded.

"Why *used to?*"

"When you're immortal, you drift in and out of hobbies. But it's something I would like to get back into. I have the perfect subject in front of me to paint."

My cheeks flushed.

"You blush every time I say anything nice to you." Hades pressed a kiss to the top of my head. "It's cute," he said with a chuckle.

The music shifted back to something more upbeat, and Hades lifted me into his arms. My legs wrapped around him, and I mentally thanked him for getting a dress with a slit. Hades' hands gripped my ass and squeezed. He pressed his lips to mine, and I groaned.

Hades walked, but with my eyes closed, I couldn't see where he was taking me. I didn't care. My back pressed against the railing. Hades pulled back from the kiss, and I opened my eyes. With one of his hands, he pushed aside the fabric covering my breasts and lowered his head to my nipple. My head fell back, and I ran my fingers through Hades' hair. He swirled his tongue around my hardened nipple and exhaled against it. The sensation elicited a moan from me. He pulled himself back, setting me down so that I stood on my feet. "This dress needs to come off. Now."

I glanced behind me over the railing. "What if someone comes up here?"

"They won't. No one ever comes up here." He seemed so certain, but a nervous tremor still coursed through me. I chewed on my lip. Hades leaned into me with a smirk on his face. "Don't tell me you're scared?"

The timbre of his voice did wicked things to me. "Not scared," I said, and pressed my lips back to his. Hades held the base of my neck in one of his hands, and the other held my cheek. I pulled back from the kiss, and between a few heavy breaths, I said, "Help me get this off." I turned around with my front pressed against the railing. I fixed my gaze straight ahead, determined not to let my eyes wander. If I did, I was sure I'd lose the surge of confidence thrumming inside of me. Hades' fingers left invisible zaps on the bare skin he touched. Hades tugged at the laces, and I sucked in a breath. The fabric loosened with each gentle pull, his fingers brushing my spine as he worked. Each touch made my pulse race.

His fingers moved painfully slowly, taking time to travel over my flushed skin and draw invisible paths. I focused on every micro-movement he made. Each passing second was torture. Hades pushed the straps. The beads and lace detailing grazed my skin, leaving a tingling sensation. A shiver rippled through me. They fell off my shoulders, and the dress plummeted to the floor from the weight of the embellishments.

At some point, the dress disappeared, no longer gathered at my feet. I was too distracted to notice. He pressed open-mouthed kisses to the side of my neck, moving from behind my ear to my shoulder. The palm of his hand pressed into the center of my back. "Look at all those people down there.

They don't know all the things I'm going to do to you over their heads."

I tried to say something—anything, but I only gulped. My head grew foggy from need. Hades removed all his clothes. I reached behind me, stroking his hardness. My head still hung over the balcony, but my hand could still swirl around the crown of his cock. With my index finger, I rubbed the wet bead of pre-cum in small circles. Hades pushed me higher against the railing, using his magic to rope around me, holding me in place. I didn't pay attention to the jarring height. Hades was an excellent distraction.

I tried to fidget, but I couldn't move. Hades' tongue lapping at my center forced me back to the present. I glanced down between my legs, where Hades sat on his knees. A moan threatened to spill from my lips, but I shoved it down. Hades' hands held my legs apart. I clenched around his tongue, and his hands moved to my clit. "You're awfully quiet up there," Hades said. "Let them hear you."

"You're crazy," I whisper-yelled, but he only smiled at me. My knuckles turned white as I gripped the railing and tried not to moan too loudly. I didn't want to get caught.

Hades peppered my thighs with kisses, slipped a few fingers into me, and began pumping. He caught my skin between his teeth and bit down. I smothered my scream into my shoulder. "As crazy as I might be... you love it."

I nodded violently and bit the inside of my cheek. A flush ran through me. "I love how your pussy wraps around my fingers." Hades' fingers curled inside me and rubbed my clit. "You take my fingers so well. I can't wait to see you hug my cock."

He was trying to elicit screams from me. And I was cracking. My teeth sank into my bottom lip. His words pushed me closer to the edge.

Pressure built in my core. I clenched my hands into fists,

trying to fight the evidence of pleasure threatening to spill from my lips. Before I could tip over into my climax, Hades pulled his fingers out. I let out a series of quick breaths.

Hades replaced his fingers with his tongue. My climax washed over me, and I moaned before I could suppress it. Pure ecstasy flowed through me, and I relaxed. Hades stood up and pressed his body into mine. My head whipped back and pressed against his cheek. "I'm going to make you scream, goddess."

"There are people down there."

"I don't care." Hades groaned and waved a hand. A swirl of magic enveloped us briefly before dissipating. "Now you can scream as loud as you'd like. We have a barrier. No one will be able to hear or see you."

"Thank you," I whispered, still foggy from my orgasm.

"Next gala, I'll take you without the barrier." The threat made me gasp. I glanced over my shoulder. Hades stroked his cock. "This is what you do to me. Look how fucking hard you make me." He motioned to his hard, throbbing cock.

My eyes burned at the display. He inserted two fingers into my center and coated some of the wetness leaking from me onto his shaft. Hades ran his still-wet fingers down my back. I sucked in a breath. "Do you know how badly I want you?" His breath was hot as he kissed my skin. "I love having your ass in the air exposed for me like this. You're fucking perfect."

"I need you, Hades."

Hades took a step closer, lining himself up before pushing into my center. My back arched, and my hips pressed harder into the railing at the sudden invasion. I moaned loudly. My scalp pricked as he tugged on my styled hair. It wasn't hard enough to hurt, just enough to feel the sensation. "There you go. Take my cock and sing for me. I'll give you exactly what you need." His hands sank into my skin as he used my body to control his movements. "You're so tight."

I moaned incoherent words. My head fell forward when Hades' hold went slack on my hair.

My body trembled. Hades placed a hand on the small of my back. "More, Hades." His thrusts pushed me closer to another orgasm. "I'm so close."

Hades' fingers found my clit, rubbing in slow, deliberate circles. My body jerked at the sensation, the pleasure too much, too fast. "Let go," he whispered, his breath hot against my skin. "I want to feel you come for me." Hades growled, "Fuck."

"Hades." I moaned his name between other disjointed words as I teetered off the edge into another orgasm. A few thrusts later, Hades' warmth filled me. The binds holding me to the railing released. Before I could fall, Hades pulled me back into his arms and turned me so I faced him. I pushed away some of the hair falling into his face.

Hades blew out a breath from his parted lips. "I told you no one comes up here." He chuckled and kissed my forehead. "As much as I would love to keep filling you up, they're going to start serving dinner. Unless you want to stay up here or go home. Whatever you are most comfortable with." The word *home* from his lips was like an embrace.

I peered back over the railing, my heart pounding as my gaze swept through the crowd. It landed on a familiar face.

Demeter.

"She's here," I whispered. Tears pricked at the corners of my eyes, but I blinked them away. She stood in the doorway, an elaborate white dress cascading around her, her eyes scanning the crowd. I was certain she was searching for me. My body went taut, and that old familiar grip of control tightened around my chest. Years of bending to her will flooded back—countless moments of shrinking beneath her gaze, becoming smaller so she could loom larger. Even now, when I was supposed to be free, I felt the invisible chains slithering around me, constricting tighter with each second her eyes swept the room.

Hades pulled me away from the railing and into a hug. "She cannot control you anymore. Take your power back." His words cut through the chaos raging within me.

Take your power back. "Easier said than done."

"You're free," he murmured, his voice softer now. His chin rested on my head. "You don't belong to her. You belong to yourself." He gave me a squeeze. "And me," he added.

We stood in silence for several minutes, Hades just holding me tight. I rested my head on his chest as my mind drifted. I didn't want to think about her.

"Demeter won't be able to hurt you. I doubt she'd even try to talk to you while you're with me."

I cleared my throat. "I need to get cleaned up and go to the washroom." Hades' magic swirled around me, and the wetness leaking from my center was gone. My dress was back on, and my hair was fixed. A part of me wanted to scold him for using his magic when he was already drained, but I didn't.

Hades pressed another kiss to my forehead, this one lingering longer than the last. "Whatever you want. If you decide you want to go home, just say the word."

"Is there a washroom on this floor? I don't want to go to the main one. I just need a few minutes."

"Are you sure you don't want me to come with you? I can stand outside."

"I'll be fine," I reassured. I wanted a moment to collect myself before being in a room full of the Divine. I knew the weight of their gazes would inevitably be on me. Their scrutiny would dissect every movement, every word I said. I needed them to see I was here by choice.

"There's a washroom on the second floor. It's right next to the stairs. I'll meet you outside of it." Hades gave me a quick kiss.

"No, I'll just meet you back here."

Hades nodded.

I gripped the railing as I descended the steps. Each step was uncertain beneath my still-quivering legs.

55

PERSEPHONE

The washroom was exactly where Hades said it would be, tucked away on the second floor. I didn't notice anyone. Everyone was likely too busy, either enraptured by the music or the impressive selection of food available on the first floor.

I pushed the door open and stepped inside. A stone counter stretched along the wall, fitted with four bronze sinks etched with curling patterns. Above them, gilded frames enclosed oval mirrors that gleamed in the low light. Across from the counter, a row of stalls stood in perfect symmetry, each full-length door edged in gold crown molding. The second floor seemed deserted, but I rapped lightly on a stall anyway. When silence answered, I slipped inside and turned the lock.

A few minutes later, I emerged. The hinge gave a soft creak as I pushed the door open, the sound startling in the quiet room. I washed my hands, dried them with one of the gold-pressed towels, and studied my reflection. My fingers rose to smooth my hair, tucking back the rebellious strands that had slipped free.

"It's been a while."

I stilled. That voice.

Demeter.

She emerged from the farthest stall and stood beside me at the sinks. Turning on the tap, she let the water spill over her hands. Her movements were unhurried, almost absent, as though she were alone. Soap slid over her fingers in a thin, bubbly lather, dripping away as she ignored me.

I edged back, eyes wide. "What are you doing here?"

Her gaze lifted at last, meeting mine in the mirror with a careless shrug. "The same thing as you. I can't use the facilities?"

I was certain there were washrooms on the first floor. So why was she here? My pulse raced, and I gripped the counter to steady myself.

She chuckled, and every hair on my body rose. "You reek of sex, daughter."

I drew in a slow breath and forced my spine to straight. *She wants to see me crumble.* "Leave," I said. My voice surprisingly held firm.

Her nose wrinkled. "I should have done a better job trying to save you from a fate steeped in death. He has already corrupted you." She shook her head.

"Save me?" The words snagged on my tongue. *Save me?* "You were the one I needed saving from."

Demeter waved off my words with a flick of her hand. "Nonsense. You have already been tainted by *him*." Her lip curled. "But you are my daughter, and I will get what I want." She tapped her nails against the stone. "You have three days left to enjoy your freedom. Don't make the wrong decision. Many people will die if you do."

"I'm not your daughter anymore." My hands trembled, but I forced the words out steady. "I will keep my freedom."

Demeter scoffed.

Her strong perfume hit me as she passed me to the door. It choked the space between us. Lilies seeped into my lungs until the world tilted and spun. I stood frozen.

At the door, she glanced back over her shoulder. "Clock is ticking, my lily. I'll see you soon." The door made a soft *click* as it closed behind her.

Something inside me fissured. Her absence should have left relief. Instead, my knees buckled, and I caught myself on the counter, palms pressed flat against the cold stone. I trembled in waves, the shiver working up through bone and muscle until even my teeth ached. The nearness of her lingered like static, crawling under my skin, stripping away the armor I'd *just* put on.

I squeezed my eyes shut and forced the tether to Hades closed, sealing myself off before he could sense my unraveling. When I opened them again, my reflection glared back— eyes too wide, lips parted, chest heaving.

A stranger.

I leaned in close until I was just an inch away. "I need to do it," I whispered to the mirror. The words fogged the glass. I raised my hand, pressed my fingers flat on it. Cold bit into my skin. The mirror took my heat greedily. Three days was too soon.

I pulled away, my hand still in the air, and turned toward the door. I exited the washroom and glanced up the flights of steps leading to where Hades waited. "I'm sorry," I whispered, and rushed down to the first floor.

I hurried through the foyer and down another hall. The larger crowd had already spilled into the grand room, leaving only a few weary nymphs shepherding drunk stragglers toward the doors. My heels clicked too loudly against the marble, echoing as I followed the gold plaques marked with arrows and a single word: Courtroom.

I dared not lose my way now, not when I was risking

everything. My mind raced as fast as my feet, replaying the events that had led me here. I had always known it would come to this. It was the only way.

Persephone? Where are you? Hades asked through the bond. I sent a silent thanks to the Fates that Hades couldn't whisk in Divine Hall.

I lowered the shield, just enough. *Still in the washroom.* Then I snapped it closed and continued racing through the halls. My feet ached; I stopped only to wrench off my heels and cast them aside. They were only slowing me down. Barefoot, I ran faster.

No, you're not. His voice was dark, amused. *I'm standing here right now. Don't run from me, little goddess. I love a good chase.*

I winced, certain he wouldn't like this one. I didn't respond as I rounded a corner and saw it—the entrance to the courtroom. Large oak doors loomed before me, their gold handles gleaming under the recessed lights on the ceiling. With a shaking hand, I reached for one.

I paused. This was it. The moment that could change everything—that *would* change everything.

I pushed the heavy doors open.

The grandeur of the courtroom stretched out before me, every detail etched vividly in my memory from the day I watched through Hades' eyes from the Underworld. Now I stood inside it, half in awe, half in terror.

I'm going to find you, Hades spoke through the bond. I didn't doubt him. I had to do this before he did.

My gaze caught on a vase resting on the table beside the door. The porcelain was cool and smooth against my sweaty palms. I lifted it, hesitating just long enough to notice the delicate white-painted lilies winding around its curve.

A sob tore up my throat, raw and strangled. Of course, lilies. Always lilies. Even here, she was watching. The Fates were sending me a sign. I would never truly be free from her if I didn't do this.

With a cry, I hurled the vase to the floor.

The crash detonated through the courtroom. Fragments burst outward, skittering across the too-clean, polished floor.

I fell to my knees among them, among the ruin. My fingers closed around a long, jagged piece. Its edge bit my skin. I did not let go. I welcomed the sting, red promise pooling in my palm.

Rising, I carried the shard into the center of the room. The vaulted ceiling stared down at me. I opened my palm and held my breath as I pressed the shard into my flesh. The porcelain slid over my already-bloody palm, caught, then went deeper. The storm thrashing inside me drowned the pain.

My chest burned, my vision swam, tears spilling until the world shimmered through water. *This is the only way*, I reminded myself.

I shut my eyes and prayed the Fates would spare me his hatred. The blood spilled from my palm in slow, deliberate drops. The wall of ice I had constructed within my mind crumbled into a thousand glittering shards.

"By shedding my blood," I whispered, voice shaking but clear. "I, Persephone, Goddess of Spring, pledge to complete the Olympian Trials and prove my loyalty to the court."

"I found you," Hades said. I glanced up from the blood still spilling from my hand. Hades stood at the threshold, smile breaking, eyes hollowing.

"I'm sorry," I breathed, straightening as a powerful surge of ancient magic enveloped me, the court responding to my declaration. Guilt drove its rusted blade deeper within me, twisting. I knew—deep in my bones, in my soul—this was the only way.

Three days.
Three days.
Three days.

I would never go back to my mother again. The magic spiraled faster than my sight could follow. Hades strained through our bond, probing, demanding. Only one thought pierced through: *What have you done?*

The magic ceased. I crumbled to the marble, collapsing into the small, spreading pool of my own blood. My breath tore ragged from my chest, the taste of copper sharp on my tongue. Tremors seized my limbs, jittering them uselessly against the floor as I clawed at the stone, trying and failing to stand.

The court gathered around me. Their mouths moved, but their voices blurred into a single droning hum. I desperately tried to focus, to figure out what they were saying, but my senses were overwhelmed.

Through half-closed eyes, a single figure detached itself from the crowd.

Hades.

He kneeled beside me, his hand cradling my cheek. Hades' touch was cool against my hot skin. He picked me up into his arms, and my hearing came back with a sudden rush. I cringed as the noise hit me in waves. Curious and concerned faces loomed around us. Hades' grip on me tightened. His anger was palpable. It flowed freely through the bond.

"We need to leave—now," he hissed through his gritted teeth. He held me tight against his chest and carried me through the halls, staying silent and ignoring the court members who swarmed after us. The moment we stepped outside, he whisked us to his study.

He set me on his desk. As he straightened, I saw the strain coiled in his body—the rigid line of his shoulders, the clenched jaw, the furrow carving deeper between his brows. Hades, who had always looked at me with warmth, now met me with a gaze that was cold, unreadable. I swallowed hard. "Hades—"

He lifted his palm, still smeared with the crust of my blood. "Stop."

The word cut like a lash. I winced.

Silence stretched between us, suffocating, until he finally spoke. "Do you have any idea what you've done?" His hands —those hands usually so steady, so sure—trembled, curling into fists. "Tell me, why must you go against my wishes?"

"Had—" My voice cracked halfway through his name. I slid off the desk and took a step toward him.

His hand rose again, halting me mid-step. "No." His jaw clenched even more. "You are reckless."

"I don't understand—"

"That's the problem. You don't understand."

"But—"

"You completing the trials will not help us." He dragged a hand through his hair, eyes burning into me. "Maybe I'm selfish, but I don't give a damn. How would I ever live without you?"

"You won't have to. I'll complete the trials and—"

He closed the distance between us. His hand rose again, hesitated, then cupped my jaw. The heat of his palm seeped into my skin, gentle despite the anger radiating from him. My eyes fluttered closed, relishing the warmth of skin. His fingers traced the line of my face.

"I'm bound by blood, but—" A strangled gasp clawed its way from his lips. His hand flew to his chest, fingers curling into a fist over his heart. His shoulders sagged. "You can," he struggled to take a breath, "die. Persephone."

Hades' voice cracked, raw with the truth he was forcing out. "You'll have your magic, but the trials will strip away your immortality. If you succeed—" His voice hitched. "You'll regain it—your immortality."

Another moan escaped him as he fell to the ground, the strain of pushing against the blood bond clear. Pain flowed through our mating bond. He hadn't intentionally kept this from me. He truly was bound by blood. I dropped beside him. "But if you fail," he continued, trembling with effort, "it means you'll die in a trial." *I can't lose you when I've just found you.*

I didn't meet his eyes. A tear rolled down my cheek, and I brushed it away with the back of my hand. The cruel reality hit me, the truth hanging between us like a heavy fog. I could die. Completing these trials was a matter of life or death. If I failed, I would be a soul, trapped in a new cage—a realm I could never leave.

Why had I been so reckless? My eyes squeezed shut. How could I have been so blind, so foolish? Everyone told me not to. When would I stop letting Demeter dictate every decision, every step I took? I scrubbed my face with my hand.

"Oh, gods. When is this going to end?"

END BOOK 1

LEAVE A REVIEW

Thank you for joining me on this journey. I sincerely hope you enjoyed the story as much as I enjoyed writing it.

If you have a moment, I would greatly appreciate it if you could leave a review. Your feedback is incredibly valuable—it helps other readers discover the book.

Thank you for your time and support!

Amazon: https://www.amazon.com/author/lenajcastle

Goodreads: https://www.goodreads.com/book/show/219539596-a-goddess-of-spring-and-shadows

ACKNOWLEDGMENTS

Often, when a book is published, people tend to focus on just one person—me. But the truth is, many incredible people contributed to bringing this project to life. I can't express enough gratitude to everyone who helped make this possible. Thank you to my friends, family, and all the kind internet strangers who have provided so much support for this book.

To my father,

Thank you for always believing in me and encouraging my wild imagination. Your endless support and enthusiasm for my "Hades-and-What's-Her-Name" book mean the world to me. You inspire me to pursue what I want. Your resilience, twisted humor, and, most importantly, your love have shaped me into who I am today.

To my mother,

Thank you for believing in me and showing me what it truly means to be a strong woman.

To my alpha and beta readers,

Thank you for your kindness and for recognizing the potential in Hades' and Persephone's story. Your constructive criticism, reactions, and uplifting comments provided the support I needed on this journey.

To my editors,

Thank you for your invaluable help in refining my manuscript and taming my occasionally chaotic grammar. Your keen eyes uncovered the blind spots that appeared after I had read the book so many times that the words blurred together.

And, of course, to **you**,

Thank you so much for taking a chance on *A Goddess of Spring and Shadows*. I hope you enjoyed it! Writers dream of publishing their stories, but that's only part of the journey. You, dear reader, are the reason those dreams take flight. See you in the next one!

ABOUT THE AUTHOR

Lena J. Castle is a fantasy romance author. When she's not busy building imaginary worlds, you'll find her cozied up with a good book, spoiling her very fluffy cat, or experimenting in the kitchen.

For more about her books, visit www.lenajcastle.com and join her newsletter (https://www.lenajcastle.com/pages/newsletter) to stay up to date with new releases, deals, and giveaways.

amazon.com/author/lenajcastle
tiktok.com/@lenajcastle
instagram.com/lenajcastle
threads.com/lenajcastle